Praise for
Arnon Grunberg

"The wit and sardonic intelligence that shine through Arnon Grunberg's prose make it a continual pleasure to read."—J. M. Coetzee

"It's not light, but funny in a retch-in-the-gutter sort of way: It sours, like real literature."—*Village Voice*

"A gold mine."—*New York Times Book Review*

"A self-deprecating, desperately funny, achingly longing voice."
—*Boston Globe*

"Absurdist humor, grotesque situations, and snappy rejoinders reminiscent of Saul Bellow or, rather, Woody Allen. . . . Mr. Grunberg is without question a talent to watch."—*Economist*

"First rate. . . . Inspired."—*Philadelphia Inquirer*

"Both hilarious and tragic, but always readable. . . . It is utterly unlike anything written by British or American novelists."—*Times* (London)

"Grunberg chronicles the mistakes of a morose Dutch bourgeois and constructs a delectable psychological thriller."—*Le Figaro*

"With this novel, Grunberg advances slowly but surely toward the class of major authors who write lucidly about the incomprehensibility of human actions."—*Haarlems dagblad*

Also by Arnon Grunberg (AKA Marek van der Jagt) in English Translation

Blue Mondays
The Jewish Messiah
Phantom Pain
Silent Extras
The Story of My Baldness

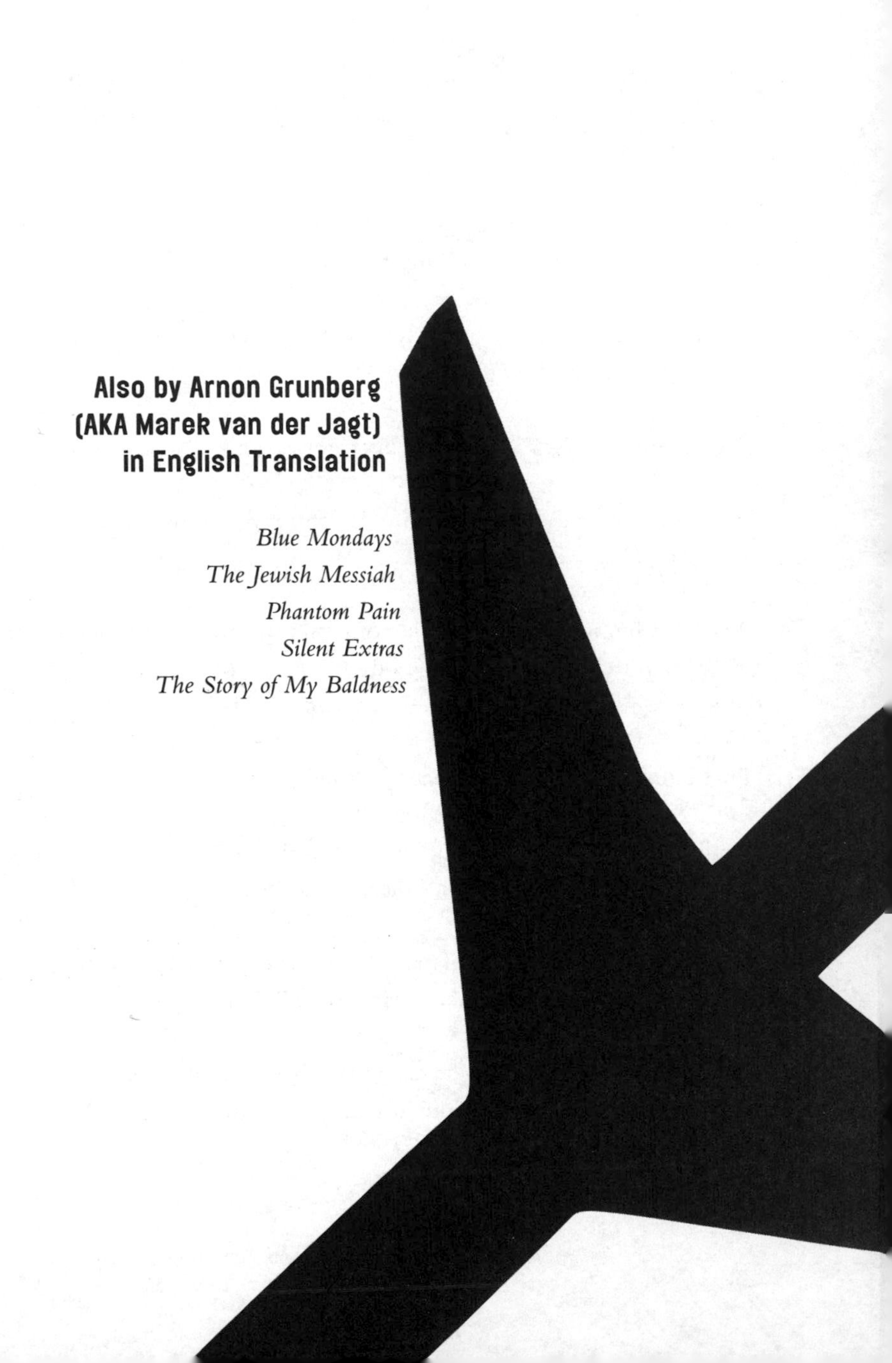

Arnon Grunberg

Tirza

Translated from the Dutch by Sam Garrett

Originally published by Nijgh & Van Ditmar,
Amsterdam, the Netherlands as *Tirza*, 2006

First edition, 2013

Library of Congress Cataloging-in-Publication Data: Available upon request.
ISBN-13: 978-1-934824-69-6 / ISBN-10: 1-934824-69-0

Printed on acid-free paper in the United States of America.

Text set in Bembo, a twentieth-century revival of a typeface originally
cut by Francesco Griffo, circa 1495.

Design by N. J. Furl

Open Letter is the University of Rochester's nonprofit, literary translation press:
Lattimore Hall 411, Box 270082, Rochester, NY 14627

www.openletterbooks.org

tirza

A couple is a conspiracy in search of a crime.
Sex is often the closest they can get.
—Adam Phillips

I

The Rent

1

Jörgen Hofmeester is in the kitchen, cutting tuna for the party. With his left hand he clutches the raw fish. He wields the knife the way he learned during the "Make your own sushi and sashimi" course he took with his wife five years ago. Don't exert too much pressure, that's the trick.

The kitchen door is ajar. The evening is sultry, the way Tirza had hoped. She's been poring over the weather reports for the last few days, as though the success of her party depended on the weather.

Before long the garden will be taken over by partygoers. Plants will be trampled. Young people will sit on the little wooden steps leading to the living room, others will drape themselves over the four garden chairs Hofmeester bought when they moved here. And yet others will find their way into the little shed where, after parties in the past, Hofmeester has found empty beer bottles and half-filled glasses of wine beside the mower, bottles with exotic labels lined up around the chainsaw he uses to prune the apple tree on Sundays in the spring and fall. A bag of chips someone forgot to open, and which he polished off himself one morning without thinking about it.

Tirza has thrown parties before, but tonight is different. Like lives, parties can be a failure or a success. Tirza hasn't said it in so many words, but Hofmeester senses that a great deal depends on this evening. Tirza, his youngest daughter, the one who turned out best. Turned out wonderfully, both inside and out.

Hofmeester's shirtsleeves are rolled up. To keep his clothes clean he is wearing an apron, which he bought once as a Mother's Day present. He looks quite masculine, especially for him. It's been six days since he's shaved. He's had no time for that. From the moment he got up in the morning he was occupied by thoughts he'd never had before, at least not to this extent: plans, memories of the children from when they could barely crawl, ideas that seemed brilliant to him in the early morning light. Later on he'll catch a quick shave. Presentable and charming, that's how he wants to come across. That is how the partygoers will see him: as a man who has not lived his life in vain.

He will make the rounds with sushi and sashimi, neatly arranged on the platter he bought at the Japanese shop just for this occasion. He will stop here and there to chat with guests, telling them offhand: "Be sure to try the squid sashimi." A self-effacing parent, that's what he'll be. That is the secret of good parenthood: efface thyself. Parental love is the sacrifice made in silence. All love is a sacrifice. Looking at him, no one will notice a thing. And what would they notice? Some of them will congratulate him on Tirza's impressive grades, one of the teachers who has been invited will ask what Tirza is planning to do next, to which he'll reply, platter in hand: "She's going to travel for a bit first. Namibia. South Africa. Botswana. Then she's coming back to study." An excellent host is what he'll be, with eyes in the back of his head. Not only will he provide his guests with food and drink, he'll also keep close watch over the lonely and neglected. Those who have no one to talk to but their own glass or their own plate of sushi, Hofmeester will entertain. The shy partygoers he will offer his company. And dancing, there will be dancing.

Hofmeester sticks his hand in a tub of tepid rice, he kneads it, and while he does he looks at the frame of the kitchen door, as though this were the first time he had ever worked at this counter. He sees the flaking paint, the dull spot on the wallpaper beside the doorframe left by a shoe Tirza once threw at his head. After she threw it, she had shouted, "Dickhead." Or was it before she threw it, he can't quite remember anymore. Pure luck that it didn't break the window.

He looks at the rice in his hand. The Japanese are always better at this kind of thing. Hofmeester's sushi is formless. The zeal with which he kneads amazes him, the same kind of amazement he feels at stupid things he's done in the past. The kind of stupid things that didn't cause too much damage.

He glances again at the flaking paint, which reminds him of his own skin. He's got a special ointment for that, but hasn't gotten around to using it for a few days. Still holding the rice in one hand, he starts thinking about selling this house, his house. At first he doesn't take it too seriously, he thinks about it the way you think about things that aren't going to happen anyway. Having yourself quick-frozen, for example, and then brought back to life a hundred years later. But slowly the conviction grows. The time is ripe. How long should he wait, and for what?

These are plans he would once have rejected out of hand. His house was his pride and joy. The apple tree, which he'd planted himself, his third child. The thought of selling house and apple tree, should things get tough, was one he'd entertained before, but how could he? It would be impossible, unnatural. Where would he go with his family? The apple tree was too big to dig up. He was fettered to this house, fettered to the whole thing. And when friends and acquaintances could no longer come up with something nice to say about Hofmeester, which happened from time to time, there was always someone who noted: "But Jörgen *does* live in style!"

To live in style. That was crucial to Hofmeester. Ambition had to manifest itself in something. Usually an address. And whenever he mentioned that address, a certain grimness came over him. As though his identity, everything he was and everything for which he stood, was balled up together in a street name, a number and a zip code. It was that zip code, more even than the name Hofmeester itself, more than his profession or the master's degree he sometimes claimed, without bending the facts too much, that spoke of who he was and who he wanted to be.

There is no longer any need for him to live in style. As he drapes a slice of tuna over the rice, that realization, the realization that it is no longer necessary, comes as a relief.

He is too old to be fired, that's what they've told him in not so many words. And when you're too old to be fired, you're also too old to live in style. When the nursing home is only a decade down the pike, that hardly matters anymore. He knows people his age who are already going senile. Admittedly, most of them had been heavy drinkers.

Away from this house, away from this neighborhood, away from this town, those are the only things that occur to him when he searches for the meaning of the word "solution." There are people who wake up each morning with the thought: There's got to be a solution for all of this, things can't go on like this. Hofmeester is one of those.

His children have left home or are getting ready to do so, his work has dwindled to a rarified activity that has nothing more to do with productivity, only with the biding of time. He could take off for Eastern Europe. Back when he was studying German, back when he held forth on the Expressionist poets as though he had known them personally, he had planned to move to Berlin and write the definitive work on Expressionist poetry. He could still do that. It was never too late for a book like that.

He could do without his zip code, without the impression his address made on some people. The air of success that clung to it. The smell of success. Now that his youngest daughter is leaving for Africa, it's time for him to shed his zip code. No more PTA meetings to attend, no more teachers to shake hands with. Who is left to impress?

The only things binding him to this place, he has to admit, are sentimentality and the fear of change. And seeing as Hofmeester has arrived at a point in his life where what he needs most is ready cash and an escape route, he vows to stop worrying so much about sentimentality and fear.

He slices the tuna hastily. That's how the sushi master does it, chop, chop, chop. The fish must welcome the knife as a friend. He puts a slice of tuna in his mouth. The shrimp are waiting on a saucer for their rice.

That morning he had driven out to the restaurant wholesaler's in Diemen. The raw tuna on his tongue is a pleasant sensation. Freshness. That's what sashimi is all about.

His wife comes into the kitchen in her bathrobe, wearing flip-flops. "Did Ibi call?" she asks.

Hofmeester still isn't used to having her back, after she ran out on him, three years ago now. The "Make your own sushi and sashimi" course hadn't helped.

But despite all expectations, she came back anyway. Six days ago. Around seven in the evening.

Hofmeester was in the kitchen at the time. After his wife ran away he'd started spending a lot of time in the kitchen, but even before that, actually. The stove was where he did his real work. The wife had never felt compelled to do much in the kitchen. Her talents were grander than lasagna, more pressing than the raising of children. There had always been something in her life that weighed more heavily than providing sustenance for her family.

Six days ago the doorbell rang, and Hofmeester had shouted: "Tirza, could you get that?"

"Daddy, I'm on the phone," she yelled back.

Tirza spent a lot of time on the phone. That was normal, other parents told him. Talking on the phone can become a hobby. He didn't talk much on the phone. When the phone rang it was always for Tirza. And the father, like a skilled employee and excellent daddy, would say: "You can reach her on her cell phone. I'll give you the number."

That evening, six days ago, Hofmeester had been fixing a casserole. The recipe was from a cookbook. As soon as the wife left, Hofmeester had begun assembling an impressive lineup of cookbooks. Improvisation was something he'd never seen as a sign of creativity, only of laziness. To him, the recipe was sacred. A teaspoon is a teaspoon. He couldn't walk away from the kitchen right then. The oven was at just the right temperature. He had already slid the casserole into it.

"Tirza, would you please get that?" he'd shouted again. "I can't go right now. It's probably the neighbor. Tell him I'll come by later in the evening. Please open the door, Tirza!"

The neighbor, a young man who isn't really all that young anymore but who is is still officially single, occupies the top floor of this house that Hofmeester got for such a bargain in the late 70s. The young man, who is studying to be a notary, regularly complains to Hofmeester about all kinds of things, and often about the same thing: the stench in the bathroom. He comes to the door at least once a week with complaints and tales of woe.

And Hofmeester always promises to see to it, even though two reliable plumbers have told him there isn't much to do about it unless he replaces all the plumbing, which would cost him a fortune.

He doesn't have a fortune, and even if he did he wouldn't dream of spending it on new plumbing.

Hofmeester, in addition to everything else, is a landlord.

He heard Tirza swear, heard her go to the front door. Then all was quiet and he turned once again to his casserole, in the conviction that the tenant was at the door with unsolicited advice and thinly veiled threats.

The rent commission, prominent lawyers, the board of housing. Is there anything he *hasn't* been threatened with? During his life as a landlord Hofmeester has received visits from all of them, but they never succeeded in backing him into a corner. Hofmeester the beast was one tough cookie.

A minute later, it couldn't have been any longer, Tirza came into the kitchen. He thought she looked pale, desperate. That, however, was something he had apparently tacked on to the story later; apparently, she always looked that way. The desperation had one day risen to the surface in her features, without him noticing, and had never gone away again.

"It's Mama," she said.

Acting on a hunch, he pulled the casserole out of the oven and turned off the gas. He stared at the oven dish. Cod and potatoes. Simple yet delicious. This, he knew, could take awhile. This was no mere stench in the tenant's bathroom. This, for a change, was not the sewer, this was the mother of his children.

Wives may not pay rent, but like the tenant, who remains by definition in a permanent state of war with the landlord, they complain. The complaint: that is what wife and tenant have in common. The accusation. The nagging. And, behind it all, dependency lingers like a disease.

Housing boards, rent inspectors, lawyers: he had shaken them all off and sent them packing, but the woman who hid behind the obsolete word "mama" had never let herself be brushed off. She was more dangerous than the board of housing, more cunning than the rent inspector.

Still holding the dishtowel he had used to pull the casserole out of the oven, he went to the door. He was surprised. To choose this night, of all nights, to come back. At dinner time.

For the first few months after she had disappeared, for that whole first year actually, hardly a day went by when he didn't expect her back. Sometimes he even called home from work to see if she would answer. She still had the keys, and he hadn't changed the locks. He couldn't believe she would never come back again. He couldn't imagine her wanting to exchange this address for an inferior one, a much more banal, inconsequential one. A houseboat, that's what she'd said.

But as time went by he had to admit that he had judged wrongly: she didn't come back. She didn't even go to the trouble of getting in touch with him or picking up the rest of her things. She was gone, and she remained gone. He learned to live with her silence, just as before that he had learned to live with her presence.

At first the wife had maintained sporadic contact with his eldest daughter, Ibi. They would meet downtown, at a café frequented by people who don't want to be seen together. But, later even that contact faded. Hofmeester never got to hear much about those meetings, and he didn't push Ibi, whose real name was Isabella, but who everyone had called Ibi from the day she was born. No, the things Ibi and her mother talked about was between the two of them. Tirza wanted nothing to do with her mother, and from the day she left the wife had not spoken a word with him, the father of her children. Not even a letter or an email. Hofmeester knew she was still alive, that after the episode in the houseboat she had gone abroad, but his knowledge reached no further than that. Between here and abroad, that was where the black hole began. And he regretted that.

The longer the silence lasted, the more regret he felt. Time does not heal all wounds, he discovered, time rips wounds open, brings on blood poisoning and infections. Death might put an end to all pain, but time did not.

Of course Hofmeester could have called her himself, or sent a postcard, but he did neither. He had his pride; he waited in silence for her to see the error of her ways. An old flame who lived on a houseboat, that had to be an error. What else could it be? A houseboat, after all, was an error in itself. And so he lived on quietly, waiting for insight to descend on his wife.

At first he had lived on with two children. But after six months the eldest did what she'd seen her mother do: she left home.

Whenever the doorbell rang in the evening, during those first few months, he would catch himself thinking: That must be her, the wife, she's come back. But as time passed the waiting became second nature, an empty habit, and hope disappeared along with the expectation. The mother of his children had gone away. That was a fact, and facts are called facts because there is usually nothing that can be done about them.

But now here she was, in all her glory, fact or no fact. Standing in the vestibule. Lugging the same suitcase she'd had when she left. A red one on wheels. She had walked out the door calmly; her departure, at least, had caused barely a ripple.

Seeing his wife affected him more than he'd thought it would, just a moment ago, as he was putting the casserole down safely on the kitchen counter. Why? Hofmeester wondered. Why tonight? What's going on? He didn't understand the reason for this visit, and Hofmeester was a person who wanted to understand things. He detested the irrational, the way other people detest vermin.

His penchant for rational motives that led to well-considered behavior was being violated here. Unwelcome thoughts rushed in on him. Admittedly though, the nerves had already struck the moment he heard his daughter speak the word that no longer existed in this household: Mama.

What God was to atheists, Mama was to the Hofmeester family.

No one spoke of the mother who had run away. No one said: "When Mama still lived with us . . ." Even at PTA meetings, which he attended with a certain grim determination, no more reference was made to the woman who was the mother of his children. People accepted him as a single father, so wholeheartedly in fact that those around him acted as though Hofmeester had been nothing else from the moment he was born. That, like a toddler, he was what he was. Designed to be a single father. And he had, there was no denying it, risen to the occasion.

There was no Mama. With that conclusion, the word's right to exist had vanished. *He* was there now, father and mother rolled into one. The one and only, and therefore the only real one as well, the king of the hill, and with him everything was just dandy.

Standing there, looking at her, Jörgen Hofmeester noticed that he was excited. Not in the sexual sense, but excited the way one becomes excited before an exam, even when you know you've done your homework well. All kinds of things could go wrong. That's what the adrenaline was telling him, that was what the concentration with which he looked at her whispered in his ear: all kinds of things can go wrong here.

He examined her, first her face, then her suitcase. For a moment he felt the inexplicable urge to take her in his arms, to hold her for a long time. But all he did was stand there, leaning with his right hand against the wall, quasi-nonchalant. The dishtowel was dangling from his left hand. Hofmeester was a man who had spent a lifetime in search of the right demeanor and who, now that that life was almost over, still hadn't found it. No demeanor perhaps, but he did have a dishtowel.

All he could think was: It always happens when you least expect it. As though that were the only reason for it to happen, because you didn't expect it.

How long had he been waiting for this to happen? To find her standing at the door. She had gone away before, before this last time, but she had always come back. After a few days, a few weeks, two months was as long as her whims had ever lasted. Then, one day, she would come home. Without embarrassment, without a word of apology, haughty, a wee bit belligerent, but she had been there, at his door. Not this last time, though, this last time had been different from all the times before. This last time had been for real.

And now, now that he no longer expected it, now that there was no longer any reason to expect it, for the children were old enough to get by without her and he was old enough to pass for a young widower, she had rung his bell as though it were the most normal thing in the world. Which perhaps it was. She was still the mother of his children. She had lived here for years, first only with him, then with him and the girls. Maybe she was only coming by to see how her pots and pans were holding up, or to admire his apple tree, which had indeed grown profusely.

He looked at the woman who had claimed that he had ruined her life, not only ruined it, but taken it away from her. He hadn't let her live. Like a conjurer he had whisked away her life, turned over the top hat three times and . . . it was gone. She wanted it back, that life of hers. That was why she left. Like the ladies and gentlemen from the housing board, she had walked out the door, calmly but not without rancor. He had even shouted after her: "Do you want me to call you a taxi?" But she had said: "No, I'll take the tram." Upon which he had shut the door, gone into the living room, and sat there with the newspaper in his lap.

"I figured: let's go by and see how he's doing," she said, brushing a few hairs out of her face. Her movements, the way she stood there, self-assured, fully confident that this was the perfect moment to come by and see how her family was doing, that she could not have chosen a better evening than this, of all evenings, the faint smile playing on her lips, the sunglasses tilted up on her head—all these things might deny it, but he could tell from her voice that she was nervous. As nervous as he was. Maybe she had walked past

No war could put a dent in it. Perhaps the hydrogen bomb, perhaps that.

But the look in the wife's eyes undermined his reservations. She was looking at him fondly, almost gently. She didn't look angry or distant, maybe she hadn't come to claim a thing. She was, undeniably, moved.

She was seeing her past, at least that's what he suspected. And she was thinking: Christ, did I really live here all those years? Is this the man with whom I spent two decades, in fits and spurts, but still? Was this my life? She saw something that was unmistakably hers, but which she still couldn't quite place.

Seeing her again like this, Hofmeester felt the urge to giggle. To laugh loud and long in order to free himself of a tension he didn't know how to deal with. Uneasiness expresses itself first in giggling, later in silence, later still in sex, and finally in silence again. The laugh that would conquer all, including the past, did not emerge. His face didn't show even the trace of a smile.

Now that the mother of his daughters was standing here in front of him again, he remembered Tirza's birth. The waiting at the hospital. There were no private rooms available. It seemed as though a dozen women had all decided to give birth that night. Early in the morning he had gone home. He couldn't take it anymore. He had run away from the blood, and at home he had prepared the crib and waited for the hospital to call.

"Did you come a long way?" he asked.

"From the station."

When she left, the neighbors had clucked in disapproval. For months on end. They couldn't stop talking about it. People here were progressive, they decried imperialism, but they were not about to be cheated out of an opportunity to cluck. Out of pride, when the gossip reached him at the butcher's, the greengrocer's or simply walking down the street, he had defended her as best he could. "It was unworkable," he would say then. "It's much better for the children this way." Hofmeester acted as though everything had gone according to plan. He had swaddled his wife's disappearance in gentle irony. And when people asked whether it wasn't awfully hard on the girls, he would say with a smile: "Most of her wardrobe is still hanging in the closet, so one of these days she's bound to show up in her children's lives again."

But, despite the wardrobe, that showing up had never happened. Until that evening, six days ago.

She still looked presentable, he thought. Less makeup. Browner, indeed, as though she had paid regular visits to the tanning booth.

"Have I come at a bad moment?" There was no audible sarcasm in the way she asked it.

He glanced at her suitcase again. The suitcase looked presentable as well. After all these years.

"I'm busy in the kitchen, but I wouldn't really call it a bad moment. I mean, what's bad?"

She stepped towards him, as though she meant to hug him. Instead she took his hand, firmly.

"I wanted to see how you were getting along," she said. "And Tirza." When that name was mentioned, a sad little smile appeared on her face. And when he heard the name of his youngest daughter, he winced briefly, as though someone had lashed him across the back.

Tirza, how might Tirza be getting along?

That was the moved look he had seen. She had gone away, but apparently she had missed something. A piece of her life was missing. On a given day she had no longer seen her daughters grow up. Her youngest daughter's adolescence was something she knew about largely from hearsay, and perhaps not even from that.

And now that she'd stood face to face with that daughter, the consequences of her life were sinking in.

She let go of his hand.

Hofmeester wiped it on his trousers as inconspicuously as possible. Other people's sweat oppressed him. The more unassailable the other person seemed, the easier it was for Hofmeester to be a predator. If there was one thing he had learned from his role as a landlord, it was that the tenant must not be allowed to become a person; people made you weak. You gave in, you said: "I'll have this fixed, I'll have that fixed. A new bed, sure, why not?" Hofmeester rented the top floor furnished. The furnished state of that apartment made it possible for him, as landlord, to get rid of the tenant without too much of a legal wrangle. For that reason alone it was important that the tenant not be allowed to become a person, for then the sentimentality could rise up like a case of hiccups and keep you from dumping your tenant at the drop of a hat. Weakness, weakness disgusted him. He detested weakness.

The wife's sweat was vulnerable sweat. That was why it had to be wiped off. He looked around, as though expecting to find Tirza standing there, but Tirza wasn't there. She was upstairs in her room, on the phone. Or she was in the kitchen, keeping quiet and listening in on the conversation. The consummate spy. Again he recalled the days, the hours before her birth. Strange that that had remained so much clearer in his mind than the birth of his eldest daughter. He remembered exactly what the gynecologist had looked like. A man to whom he had later brought a good bottle of wine, a bottle that must have cost at least thirty guilders, with Tirza on his arm. "Here she is," he'd said. And he had shown the man a wrinkly little baby with tufts of brown hair, like so many other wrinkly little babies. Tirza had come into the world wrinkled, and it took a long time for the wrinkles to be ironed out. The gynecologist had accepted the wine and wished the father a great deal of happiness. Then he said: "Difficult births often produce something beautiful, something very special." The gynecologist, when he said that, had looked as though he were disclosing a professional secret.

"We're both getting along quite well," Hofmeester said. The dishtowel was over his arm now, in his left hand he held the glossy brochure, which he folded a few times and then stuck casually into his back pocket.

"We're getting along well," he said again. "Tirza just graduated. Two nines. Eights. One seven. Nothing lower than a seven. Next week she's throwing a party."

He related this with pride, but when he was finished he realized how absurd it was to be saying this to Tirza's own mother. This was why the neighbors had clucked in disapproval of her, and probably of him too. You're not allowed to become a stranger to your children. They can become strangers to you, but not you to them.

Now that he no longer had the brochure in his hand, he was free to tug at his lower lip as much as he liked. That was what he usually did when he couldn't understand something, when he couldn't make head or tails of it.

"That's great," she said. "Those nines. But I wouldn't have expected anything else. What for?"

"What do you mean, what for?"

"What did she get the nines for?"

"For Latin. And for history. Didn't you know about that? Hasn't anyone told you? Nothing at all?"

Her ignorance amazed him, even irritated him a little. Someone who decided to come back, however temporarily, could at least inquire discretely about the latest news concerning her daughter and husband. It had to be a whim, this coming back, like so many other things in her life.

"Who was supposed to tell me? Ibi? I haven't heard from her for ages. She never calls."

He saw her looking at the hand with which he was tugging at his lower lip. He knew she hated that old, familiar tic of his, and stopped.

She never calls. The wife was apparently of the opinion that her children should call her. Not the other way around. It all centered around her.

"If it's not too much trouble," she said, "could we go in?"

It was indeed becoming increasingly uncomfortable, standing there like that in the hallway.

"Yes, come in," he said. "I just put something in the oven. I mean . . . it's not in the oven anymore, but it was."

She looked at him. She was holding the handle of her suitcase, ready to roll it into the room, but she let go of it then and said: "I know what you mean. I know exactly what you mean. You're, well, you're just the way you always were. You haven't changed a bit."

That was something the Christians and other believers had never counted on: that being reunited in Paradise could turn out be very uncomfortable indeed. Chit-chat in heaven. A handshake that should have been a hug.

Without a word he helped her out of her coat, a light-blue raincoat he'd never seen before. It was not an inexpensive coat, he noticed that right away. She had never gone in for cheap things. He hung the coat up carefully.

Slowly, he regained his composure. Hofmeester was in control again. This was how life went. People disappeared. And sometimes those people came back again, of an evening, in early summer. Just when you had a casserole in the oven, but they couldn't possibly know that. When you looked back on it all, the careful planning vanished, the whims emerged, coincidences bobbed to the surface, everywhere you looked the confluence of events came pouring in.

Now that he was the very picture of peace and calm, she seemed to be hesitating.

"Or is there someone else here?" she asked. "Do you have someone else?"

Hofmeester heard his youngest daughter approaching from the kitchen. Just as he'd figured, she'd been eavesdropping. Curiosity is a sign of intelligence, but an intelligent child also forces parents to stay on their toes. With an intelligent child, you never know who's fooling whom. Tirza tossed her father a withering glance and went up the stairs. Past her mother, past her mother's blue raincoat hanging so demonstratively on its hook.

"Do I have someone else?" Hofmeester asked once his daughter had slammed the bedroom door. He couldn't help but laugh. "Someone else? Not really. No. I live here with Tirza. She's someone else, of course, but not in the way you mean." Hofmeester kept laughing. He couldn't stop, it embarrassed him now. "Come in, come in," he said once the laughter had faded. He led her into the living room. They paused in front of the couch, but she didn't sit down. She turned on her heel, as though trying to take it all in. As though there really were someone else, a stranger, in this room where she had lived so long, where she had spent entire evenings, with him, alone and with guests, where they had thrown parties, where they had set up cradles and cribs, where their daughters had crawled across the floor, where she had occasionally painted still-lifes.

"It hasn't changed much," she said. "Neither have you. Like I said. Unchanged, really. Have you had the painters in?"

"The bookcase is new. As you can see. That chair over there too. Tirza picked it out. Some things have changed." He ignored her question on purpose. If you pretend not to hear questions, you can't put your foot in your mouth. In his role as landlord, he failed to hear most questions as well. Absentmindedness was an excuse that could serve for years to come.

She didn't look at the chair Tirza had picked out, or at the bookcase. She came and stood right in front of him, she looked at Hofmeester. Like a painting that you know only from postcards or catalogues, but now that you're standing in the museum, right in front of the original, you stop and try to figure out what it is that makes it just a wee bit disappointing. Not a lot, just a bit.

"So you didn't have the painters in," she said after a few seconds.

"I can see that now, it's all going yellow. You haven't taken very good care of it, the interior. You have to take good care of a house on the inside too, Jörgen. But you *have* taken good care of yourself."

She sounded pleased. But at the same time surprised. What had she expected? A drunken shambles? An invalid? Shaky hands, rattling dentures? A mental wreck plagued by moments of lucidity? Who, in those lucid moments, had nothing better to do than to have the painters in, to have the parquet lacquered and the sewer pipes replaced?

He had gotten by without her and that seemed to defy all her expectations, but it disappointed her as well. The same way the lack of new paint on the walls disappointed her.

The tenant and the wife: the comparison was not entirely gratuitous. Both were capable at all times of finding a ceiling in need of paint, neither ever failed to stumble upon something in the house that was in need of replacement. They had no idea of the value of money. They hadn't the faintest idea what workmen charged these days. There was always some complaint; in the case of the wife, a complaint that happened to disguise itself as loving care.

She took a step back. "Are you glad to see me?" she asked.

The question took him by surprise. The question seized him by the throat.

"Glad," Hofmeester said. He looked at his watch. "Yes, I'm glad, but I'm also busy in the kitchen. If I'd known you were coming I would have made more. You could have called. The number hasn't changed. But . . ." He had to stop for a moment, not due to emotion, but in order to figure out what he really wanted to say. "It's good to see you. I suppose you were curious to find out, I know I was."

It amazed Hofmeester to find that the words he had planned to speak when he saw his wife again wouldn't cross his lips, that they hadn't even come up in him. Now that he finally had the chance to speak them, he had forgotten them. He wanted to appear charming. Strong. The reed was not only unbroken, it was unbruised.

"Curious about what?

"About you," he said. "How you're doing. What you're doing. How your life is coming along. How things went."

"How my life is coming along? But then why didn't you ever call? For three whole years. I would have told you. In detail. I wouldn't have kept it a secret. Not if you'd taken the trouble to call."

That was typical of her. She disappeared and then expected people to go running after her, to keep track of her ups and downs and ask whether there was anything she needed.

"It didn't seem the right thing to do," Hofmeester said, "to call you. I didn't want to impose. If you're really hungry, I could always fry an egg. Besides, I didn't have your new number."

"I didn't come here to eat," she said, settling down on the couch where she had sat for years. Hofmeester had had it reupholstered. Tirza had picked out the leather. He and Tirza picked out lots of things together.

"Maybe something else, instead of an egg?"

"Jörgen, I'm not hungry." She didn't so much say it as state it emphatically.

"You don't have to be hungry to eat an egg. I'm fixing my casserole. It's famous. Tirza's girlfriends are wild about it. Besides, we don't eat because we're hungry, we eat because it's time for dinner." He said it like a teacher doing his best to recommend a book he knows his students will detest anyway.

That tone of his must have sounded familiar to her, the tone of the copyeditor, the tone of someone who has built his life around catching other people's mistakes. "*I* don't," she said. "I've stopped eating simply because it's time to eat. I don't live by those stupid rules anymore. I eat because I feel like it. And I didn't come here for your casserole."

She lit a cigarette. Her handbag was new. A bit too hip and youthful for someone her age. With all kinds of ornaments on it. Hofmeester thought about the handbags Tirza's girlfriends carried. Early in the morning, after parties, they stood around the kitchen with their handbags, with beads on them, pieces of glass, anything could serve as an ornament these days. Whenever he came into the kitchen in his pajamas and found Tirza and her friends in a state of exuberance, stinking of smoke and sometimes of food gone bad, Hofmeester would apologize. He would quickly pour himself a glass of milk or take an apple from the fruit bowl and hurry back to his room, or, if the weather was fine, to the shed, where he sat down beside the rake and the chainsaw and waited until the girls had gone home or off to bed. Tirza was popular. A few times he had come across unfamiliar boys in the bathroom, boys he didn't know and who had never been introduced to him, but who had spent the night. Boys Hofmeester felt compelled to ask: "Would you like a clean towel?" Because Tirza was a sound sleeper. Once she fell asleep, she could sleep through anything. The boys always woke up before his daughter did. They didn't smell particularly inviting, those characters he had run into in the bathroom from time to time. What Tirza's boys had in common was how they stank. But she had a serious boyfriend now; Hofmeester had not yet been able to ascertain whether he stank. But he feared the worst.

"You've started smoking again," he said, his eyes fixed on her handbag.

He sounded worried. Which irritated him. What he'd said was too personal. As though her cigarettes made any difference to him. Her lungs were her own business. Her whole body, for that matter. Her body was no longer his concern.

"Does it bother you?"

"Not really," he said. "Not me. I'll ask Tirza to get an ashtray. I've put away all the ashtrays."

He turned to face the hallway and called out: "Tirza, would you please bring an ashtray for Mama?"

Hofmeester stood there waiting, but Tirza didn't answer. She was probably on the phone in her room. A true hobby never wears thin. She talked to her girlfriends about everything, right down to the smallest detail. She'd told him that before, at the dinner table. "About me, too?" he had asked. "Do you talk about me, too?" "Of course," she'd said. "You're my father, aren't you? Why wouldn't I talk about you?"

The wife smoked on, oblivious.

"Tirza," Hofmeester called out again, a little louder now, "an ashtray for your mother. Please."

He looked at the cone of ash that was growing longer, that would soon fall, he couldn't take his eyes off it, he seemed mesmerized, he said: "She's always very helpful. Not like she used to be. Even while she was studying for her finals, she insisted on helping out around the house."

Hofmeester spoke as though in a dream, he babbled on as though talking more to himself than to her, as though there were no one else in the room, only him. As though he were rehearsing what he would say when the others finally showed up.

When Tirza didn't come down, he went to the kitchen himself in search of an ashtray. Where were they? No one in this house smoked anymore. And Hofmeester seldom had visitors. Even the cleaning lady didn't smoke. She had a little drink now and then, but smoking, no. When Tirza had girlfriends or boys who smoked, which they rarely did, they always went to the garden. Or leaned out the window. Tirza didn't like smoke, but she did like boys.

He couldn't find an ashtray. Hofmeester had put the ashtrays in a safe place, assuming he would never need them again. He took a saucer instead. It wasn't really dignified, but it would do for the moment. Dignity, that was the crux of all morality for Hofmeester. If there were anything he might say in his own defense, it was that he had acted with dignity.

When he came back into the room he saw the ash cradled in the wife's left hand. He gave her the saucer and asked if she wanted a damp rag. "My hands are fireproof," she said and laughed. Just like she used to. People don't change much. They find new surroundings for their obsessions. Wrinkles are added, teeth fall out, bones break, vital organs are replaced by machines, but they themselves don't change.

When she was finished laughing, she said: "If it pleases you, if you really want me to, and I know that you really want me to, I'll have a bite to eat. But don't go to any great lengths. Just give me the leftovers. Don't go out of your way."

Hofmeester stepped over to the dinner table and slid aside the vase of roses. The flowers had been a gift for Tirza, a few days ago. He was making room for the wife, who was going to eat with them. He wondered whether, before making her sudden appearance with suitcase and all, the wife had first taken liquid courage at one of the local cafés.

"Cooking isn't going out of my way," he said quietly. "It's one of those things you do. I have a family. I cook. That's my responsibility."

The table was already set for two. He always set the table long before dinnertime. Sometimes he started on it as soon as he got home from work. Because he couldn't wait for the moment when he and Tirza would sit down at the table together, because that moment restored the balance that always seemed about to disappear. Tirza and he, at the table, eating. The semblance of a family, and more than that, of an alliance. A holy alliance.

He took a plate from the cupboard. He had not forgotten his responsibility. The casserole, the oven, there was cooking to be done. He stood there uneasily, plate in hand, as though unsure of whether it was polite to leave the visitor behind. Whether he should invite the guest into the kitchen. To talk about this and that, things from long ago. How did one go about inviting someone like that? "Would you like to come into the kitchen?" He put the plate down on the table. Now it was set for a third person. The wife. Tirza's mother.

A bite to eat, that was how it had all started. A lamb chop had been the start of the Hofmeester family. Jörgen had cooked for the woman who later turned into the wife. She had liked the man more than the lamb chop. He thought about the suitcase standing in the hall. The first time she had come to eat dinner with him she had brought a homemade pie.

"She's changed," the wife said, her gaze resting on a painting on the wall. She had hung it there herself, painted it herself as well, and Hofmeester had never gone to the trouble of taking it down, even though Tirza had asked a few times: "Are we going to spend the rest of our lives staring at that bowl of fruit? Is that absolutely necessary?"

"Who? Tirza?"

The dishtowel was still draped over his arm.

"Yes, Tirza. She's become pretty."

"She's a woman now," Hofmeester said. But as soon as he said it he was sorry. A woman? What is a woman, anyway? Okay, she had grown breasts and something like hips. But when did one actually become a woman? What made him a man? Was it that thing dangling between his legs?

He didn't know what else to say about Tirza, what he wanted to say about her. So all he said was: "She always *was* pretty. When she was a baby she was wrinkled, but then all babies are. Ibi was less wrinkled, she had other things wrong with her. Would you like something to drink?"

She shook her head. "I'll help myself if I do. For the moment I'm completely satisfied."

He stared at her. The satisfied wife, who had never been that way in the past, no matter how many still-lifes she'd painted. But who was satisfied now. The happy ending was tucked away somewhere in the story, he just hadn't been around to see it.

Hofmeester went into the kitchen by himself. She should be able to entertain herself in the living room. He slid the casserole back into the oven, uncorked a bottle of white wine and set the egg timer to thirty minutes. Hofmeester couldn't cook without an egg timer. He put the cookbook back on a pile of other cookbooks.

He remained standing by the oven. His hands slid over the counter like a blind man reading Braille. Once dinner was on the table, he'd be sure to come up with something to say to the guest. "Have you done a lot of traveling?" Or: "Is your mother still alive?" Her mother had been seriously ill when she left him.

He thought about his job, about Tirza and the trip she was going to take. Botswana was malaria country, he'd read somewhere.

The egg timer rang, and he carried the oven dish into the living room with unmistakable pride. The wife was lying on the couch. She had taken off her shoes. Her eyes were closed and the room was foul with smoke.

"I'll get you a knife and fork," he said, putting the casserole on the table.

She didn't budge. She lay there, flat out and content, as though she'd never left. As though she had only popped out to buy some raisin buns and been delayed along the way. A traffic jam, that was all it had been, her three-year absence, a traffic jam of human flesh.

In the hallway he shouted: "Tirza, dinner!" He went into the kitchen to get some silverware and a glass for the guest, and the bottle of wine.

"Where shall I sit?" the wife asked once he had poured the wine. All three glasses equally full. Every detail counted. He reveled in his role. The waiter, the houseman.

She struggled up off the couch. Walked over to the table, barefooted.

"Here, at the head of the table," Hofmeester said. "That's where our guests always sit. Those are nice shoes. Are they Italian?"

"French."

They sat down. Hofmeester dished up the food. He shouted again, louder this time: "Tirza! Dinner!"

Dinner was served. But no one was eating yet. They were waiting for the child.

"A present," the wife said, fork in hand already. On her left hand she was wearing a ring he'd never seen before.

"What?"

"The shoes. They were a present."

"That's nice. You still have about ten pairs here too. Did you know that? I meant to send them to you, but I didn't have the address."

He took a piece of bread from the basket. It had already been on the table for a few hours.

"I thought you'd probably given them away."

The bread was stale.

"Give them away, to whom? You mean your shoes?"

"My shoes, yes. I thought you'd get rid of them. That you'd get rid of all my things. That's what I thought. Not so unlikely, was it? I bought all new things."

"But who else wears your size? I don't know anyone who wears your size. You have a difficult size. Tirza, dinner! It's all still there in the closet, just the way you left it. You could have moved right back in."

She looked at him questioningly, as though trying to see whether he was joking.

"My feet are a pair of matching jewels, or so I've been told," the wife said after a brief pause. She smiled cheerfully. She was doing her best, that was clear. But so was he. That's what they had become: two people doing their best. Who knows, maybe that's what they'd always been.

"Have you looked at them? I've taken good care of my jewels."

She shifted in her chair a little and stretched her legs out beside the table. Her toenails were painted pink. The tips of her toes touched Hofmeester's thigh.

He froze.

Holding the dry bread, he glanced at the wife's bare feet and calves. The toes that were touching his trousers. Then he stuck the bread in his mouth and started chewing.

"Don't you have anything to say, after all these years?"

"Anything to say?"

"Anything pleasant. Are you glad to see me?"

"About your feet, you mean? Anything pleasant?" The bread was awfully dry, but he didn't feel like getting up and putting it in the oven.

"You know how important certain things are to me. You might say something affectionate, after all this time. You do have feelings, I suppose." She wiggled her toes a little and Hofmeester glanced at her feet again.

Affection, so that's what was expected of you when your wife showed up at the door after three years.

"Your feet haven't changed a bit."

"Is that all?"

"I believe so."

"They're a pair of matching jewels, Jörgen. My feet. Admired by many. I've often been told that."

She slid her legs back under the table.

Hofmeester stared at the roses. It had been an expensive bouquet. Maybe thirty euros. Who had given them to Tirza? She hadn't mentioned a name. She rarely mentioned boys' names. At the dinner table she tended to talk about everyday things. The news, the food, the weather, her girlfriends, her exams, a few times she had mentioned her plans to travel around the world. But political topics were avoided. They held different opinions on Africa.

"I think . . ." Hofmeester started to say. But because he didn't really know what he thought, he paused. Then he heard Tirza coming down the stairs and decided that there was no reason to finish his sentence. That it was up to Tirza to come up with something pleasant and affectionate to say, if anything affectionate really needed to be said, which he doubted, but if it did then it was up to Tirza.

"Jesus, it stinks in here," Tirza cried. She was wearing a white blouse, she had changed her clothes. Normally, she never dressed for dinner. Not unless there were visitors. And when there had been visitors during the last few years, they had always been Tirza's visitors. The cleaning lady from Ghana was the only one who came for Hofmeester, but you could hardly call her a visitor, not in the strict sense.

She sat down. Hofmeester raised his glass and said: "Let's drink, Tirza, to your mother's unexpected visit. Let's drink to the fact that all of us, or almost all of us, are here together again as a . . . well, as a family. And that we are in good health."

The daughter had already raised her glass, but now she put it back down and said: "I'm not going to drink to that. And it stinks in here, Daddy, don't you smell it? She's been sitting here puffing away. No one's allowed to smoke in here." Tirza, when she felt like it, could be rather overbearing as well. Her guidance counselor had once told him: "She's a born leader, she takes the initiative. She leads and the others follow."

No one spoke. Hofmeester was nervous enough to stick another piece of dry bread in his mouth.

"A toast to . . ." Hofmeester began.

"No," Tirza said. "I'm not going along with this . . . with this nonsense."

She jabbed her fork into her father's famous casserole.

"All right," Hofmeester said. "Then let's drink to life. To your grades, okay, Tirza? To your finals. To your future. To you." Before anyone could butt in, Hofmeester raised his glass to his lips. The wine wasn't quite cold enough, but it would do in a pinch. On an evening like this, lots of things would do in a pinch.

Hofmeester's casserole had been better before, but as long as it was being eaten everything was going well. It was under control: the evening, the gathering, the family.

After a few bites the wife took the sunglasses off her head and asked: "So, Tirza, how are you? I was just telling your father how pretty I thought you'd become."

Tirza picked up her knife and used it to fish out a string of melted cheese. It was a casserole with cheese, a recipe from a French cookbook. "Like you really care," Tirza mumbled.

"Yes, I do care," the wife said. "I care a great deal. I've thought about you often. You have really become very pretty."

"Become?"

"Even prettier than you already were. You always were pretty, but now you're really . . . how shall I put it, in full bloom."

And Tirza replied: "Oh, that's funny." She was picking at her food. Eating like a child. Making a display of her lack of interest. She was playing with her food.

"Funny?" the wife asked. "What's funny about it?"

"Funny that you even remember how pretty I was. Funny that you care how I'm doing. Because I didn't notice much of that in the last few years. Nothing at all, to be exact."

After this little incident, the three of them ate in silence. But the nerves had a hold of Hofmeester now, even more than when he'd been standing in the vestibule staring at his wife's suitcase. He stuffed a few more pieces of dry bread into his mouth. He ate everything in the breadbasket. It had to be finished. It would be a pity to throw it away.

When her plate was almost empty, the wife asked: "What kind of wine is this?"

"South African," Hofmeester said. "Tirza and I have discovered the South African wines."

"Discovered?" She grinned. "What do you mean, discovered? What exactly have the two of you discovered?"

"Every Saturday afternoon the wine shop around the corner organizes tastings. Tirza and I go there sometimes. Don't we, Tirza?"

Tirza's mother examined the label and said: "Oh, you two turtledoves. Wine-tasting on Saturday afternoon. How romantic. Who would ever have thought? That the two of you would get along together so well?"

"Daddy," Tirza said.

But the father pretended he hadn't heard. He said: "Tirza is deeply interested in South Africa, in that whole region. In fact, Tirza is interested in Africa as a whole. Am I right when I say that, Tirza? In Africa as a whole? What Tirza would really like to do is travel by public transport from South Africa to Morocco, but I've told her I won't allow it. Besides, there is almost no public transport there. Public transport in Cameroon, what are we to imagine by that? Sudden death. I saw somewhere that they don't even have hearses there, that they take their dead to the cemetery on the bus. They tote the body under their arms."

He laughed. The idea of toting dead family members to the cemetery on the bus made death seem much less threatening. If you acted as though it wasn't such a big deal, then it wasn't such a big deal. He felt a foot hit his shin, painfully, under the table. That was the sign for him to gather the crumbs from the breadbasket and stuff them in his mouth. To eat was to obtain mercy.

"So you want to travel through Africa by public transport?" Tirza's mother was doing her best, but it wasn't working. Her intentions were excellent, they always had been, but she was too wrapped up in herself.

Tirza didn't answer. She kicked her father in the shin again, hard. Perhaps one could see that as an answer.

"I told her," Hofmeester said, "that public transport in Africa . . ." Another kick to the shin.

"Tirza," Hofmeester said when his mouth was empty, "I can't do anything about it. This is something I really can do nothing about. For a change."

All Tirza did was shake her head. She kept shaking her head, like a little child who should have been put to bed long ago and has started whimpering from exhaustion.

"It's not whether you can do anything about it, Daddy," she said.

"It's that I can't stand this. I can't stand it. Would you please stop it? Please do me a favor and stop it."

She was stressing each syllable.

Hofmeester looked at her. Half of her dinner was still lying untouched on her plate. The other half had only been toyed with. He didn't understand people well. Sometimes even his own children were beyond him. Familiar, but strange. Like the boys Hofmeester came across in the bathroom from time to time, strange as well, but familiar somehow. As though they'd been waiting for him in the bathroom all night. For him and for a towel. His daughter's boyfriends, to whom he was nothing but a glorified bit player, even though—he had no intention of kidding himself anymore—he desperately wanted to be more than that.

"What is it you want me to stop doing?"

"To stop acting like this. Stop this conversation. Stop this ridiculous conversation. I want you to stop acting differently towards me than you usually do. You've got to stop this play-acting, Daddy. Just because this woman is here at the table."

When she said "this woman," her voice grew louder, she was almost shouting.

"Am I acting differently?" Hofmeester asked. He was trying to keep an eye on his wife and his daughter at the same time. As though they would fly at each other if he lost sight of them for a instant. "Am I talking differently? Eating differently? Have I suddenly stopped smacking my lips?" He laughed at his joke, but he was the only one.

"You're not smacking your lips, but you're not talking the way you usually do either. That's right, Daddy. Normally I'm the one who talks and you nod or ask: 'What kind of work does her father do?' And then we do the dishes. Then you don't say much either. You listen to what I say. And that's okay. Sometimes I ask you: 'What did you do today?' And you say: 'Not a whole lot.' That's fine with me. That's who you are. That's all you can do. And that's still a lot more than *she* can. But this chit-chat, this ridiculous chit-chat, that's what I can't stand."

Hofmeester reached out and felt the side of the casserole dish. It was still warm.

"I talk to you sometimes, Tirza. You know that. You know that very well. And I often read to you from the newspaper. The funny parts. You know that, too."

"It doesn't matter, Daddy. You're sweet in your own way. In your own way you're really sweet. And when you read the funny bits from the newspaper while we're eating, I like that too. I don't always think they're all that funny, but okay. You think they're funny. That's the important thing. But could I ask you something, now that we're talking, now that we're not reading the funny bits from the newspaper, could I ask you something?"

"Yes, of course," Hofmeester said. "Anything, Tirza. Ask me whatever you like."

"Why didn't you kick that woman out the door the moment she showed up?"

For a moment he felt the urge to tug at his lower lip, but he restrained himself. Hofmeester poured a little more wine, first for Tirza, then for his wife and then for himself. He tried to toss his wife a knowing glance, but she smiled faintly without really taking notice. Then he said: "You don't kick women out the door, Tirza, especially not a woman who has given you two children. That woman is your mother. That's why I let her in instead of kicking her out the door. That seems like a good reason to me. She's your mother. That's what she was. That's what she'll always be."

Tirza's mother adopted an expression that looked as though someone else's mother were being discussed here. Another mother of another child.

"With difficulty," she said then, toying with her sunglasses. "It was not without difficulty, Jörgen, that you sired two children. Oh, you were good at talking, talking, talking. Sometimes it sounded like an erotic radio play going on in our bed. But in order to make children you have to do something, Jörgen. Not do something, do *it*. You have to place your instrument in the proper receptacle."

Hofmeester's thoughts had come to a halt at the bit about the erotic radio play. He had always seen himself as a quiet, discreet individual, but other people seemed to see that differently.

"She ran out on us," Tirza said, pointing her fork at the woman who had been showing Hofmeester her feet only minutes before. There was still a piece of casserole on the fork, it fell onto the tablecloth. "She may have had reason to run out on you, Daddy, she probably had all kinds of good reasons to do that, but she had no reason at all, absolutely no reason, to run out on me." Her voice cracked. Hofmeester felt panic rising up inside. A horrible sense of panic.

"Don't point with your fork, Tirza," the father said. "Don't do that. It can be dangerous."

He reached up and smoothed his hair back, as though that would help, as though that would divert the conversation into a different, less perilous channel. The summers, which used to be so much sunnier. School. Africa, if need be. Public transport, anywhere in the world.

Tirza's voice was growing louder. Hofmeester knew what that meant. The weeping was about to start. Tears, that was one thing he couldn't stand. His own weakness made him nauseous. His children's weakness made him furious.

He glanced over at his wife; she was drinking her wine calmly, as though none of this had anything to do with her. He had to salvage the situation, and quickly, because no one else would. No one else could.

"You shouldn't say that," Hofmeester said. "She didn't run out on us. She went looking for self-fulfillment."

The wife sighed. She put down her knife and fork. "There's no reason not to say that I couldn't stand being around you any longer,

Jörgen. Tirza knows that as well as I do, the whole neighborhood knows that. You don't have to call it self-fulfillment. I couldn't stand it here anymore. No one could have stood it. No normal person."

"Fine," Hofmeester said, "self-fulfillment. Let's leave it at that for the time being. Isn't that a fair compromise? Sometimes self-fulfillment is the same as not being able to stand it anymore. There's not that much difference."

"Daddy," Tirza shouted, "don't be so stupid. Don't let her treat you like this."

"I want to eat in peace," Hofmeester shouted, "that's all I want, Tirza. To eat in peace. I made this casserole in peace, and now I want to eat it in peace. Which is exactly what I'm going to do. The way I've been doing for the last three years."

The daughter slammed her left hand down on the table. A fork fell to the floor. "I don't want to sit at the table with that woman," she shouted. "I don't want to see that woman ever again. Never, ever."

Tirza stood up. "I hate you," she screamed. "I wish you'd never come here. It would have been better if you'd never come back. I wish you were dead."

Then she ran up the stairs.

Hofmeester wiped his lips a couple of times, slid the wine bottle a few inches to one side and asked: "Would you like dessert?"

The wife stared at her glass, then removed the crumb of cork that was floating in it. "She always *was* like this," she said calmly.

"There's some left over from yesterday," he said. "I made tiramisu. I always do that on Wednesdays. Could I offer you some of that? Or would you rather have fruit?"

"She's incapable of forgiveness."

"I could make some fruit salad."

"She can't forgive herself, either. Can you forgive yourself, Jörgen, are you actually able to forgive yourself?" She put her sunglasses back on, as a kind of headband.

"Fruit salad then? Shall I make some for you? It's no problem."

The wife sighed.

"All right, let's change the subject. If that's what you really want. How is the window washer doing?"

"What window washer?"

"The man who did the windows here every month, the old man. How is he doing?"

"Oh, him," Hofmeester said. "He died."

He sat there, tugging at his lower lip.

"You *have* learned to cook," the wife said. "One must admit."

"Thank you," Hofmeester said.

He got up and climbed the stairs to his youngest daughter's room. But halfway up he reconsidered, stood there for a moment, then went back to the living room. He sat down at the table again.

The wife was still sitting there. Not like a guest, but like someone who felt at home. Which, in the strictest sense, she was. She had never officially changed her address. The wife's voter registration cards still came to this address, and Hofmeester remained faithful to tradition by placing them atop the little cupboard in the hallway, until the elections had passed and he noted with a certain melancholy that the wife had once again failed to exercise her right to vote.

"Does she have a boyfriend?"

"Tirza?"

"Yes, Tirza. Who else?"

"Sometimes I run into a boy in the bathroom."

"In the bathroom?"

"In the bathroom, they seem to find their way in there quite often."

"What do they do in there?"

"The things people do in bathrooms. Take showers. I assume. Use the toilet. I don't ask them: 'What are you doing in here?' I'm not that inhospitable. This is her house. This is Tirza's house, too."

The wife sighed deeply and emptied her glass. "So what *do* you say to them?"

"It may come as a surprise to you," Hofmeester said, "but I ask them: 'Would you like a clean towel?' But maybe you have another suggestion, perhaps you have a better idea, perhaps I should ask them: 'Feel like a glass of champagne, young man? Did you have a nice fuck? Hopefully you used a condom, but if not, well, it's not really the end of the world.' You'd do it differently, I'm well aware of that, you always were jealous of your daughters' boyfriends. But all I ask is: 'Would you like a clean towel?' And that's it."

"Stop it!" she shouted.

It was quiet for a moment, then Hofmeester said: "We're shouting at each other."

"Yes," she said. "It's stupid. We've started again, and we don't have any reason to shout at each other anymore. We really have absolutely no reason to do that anymore."

She went over to the couch, took the pack of cigarettes out of her handbag, lit one, and came back to the table.

"Are those French as well?" Hofmeester asked, pointing at the sunglasses with the ridiculously large lenses which she insisted on wearing as a sort of headband.

"Italian. The shoes are from France, the glasses are from Italy."

The smoke bothered him too now, but he didn't say anything.

"Did you turn her against me?" she asked. "Or did it happen by itself?"

"It happened all by itself," Hofmeester said. "I didn't have to do a thing."

2

"Jörgen, I asked you something. Did Ibi call?"

A few grains of rice are sticking to Hofmeester's hands. He wipes them on his apron.

"Ibi," he says, staring at the mother of his children, who is standing there in her bathrobe. "Ibi. Yes, she called. But I didn't speak to her. Tirza had her on the line. She's on her way over."

The wife smiles, not a particularly happy smile though, she wipes his cheek with the back of her hand. She removes something that must have been hanging from his nostril. He can't see what it was. A little piece of shrimp, a flake of skin, something green and indefinable, wasabi perhaps.

"You need to shave," she says. "You look like a tramp."

"I'm going to. But first I have to finish this." He points to the raw fish.

She starts to walk away. Hofmeester stops her, grabs the back of her bathrobe. "Leave this party to Tirza, all right? Just leave the whole thing to Tirza. Stay in the background as much as possible."

She looks at him, grinning as though he had just told a joke. One of his old, oh so timeworn jokes. Then she walks away slowly. He turns back to the sushi with a devotion that no longer surprises him. This is his life, and this is his rice. It's enough for him, in spite of everything. It's been enough for him for the last three years.

That evening, the first evening of the wife's return, six days ago now, Tirza went to her room and did not come out again. After a while he had gone upstairs again and knocked on her door, but she didn't answer. He had stood there for five minutes or so, with no idea what to do. Hesitantly, anxiously, weighing the possibilities. That's how he stood at her door.

When it came to Tirza, fear was what he had always felt, even before she became ill, from the moment she was born, actually. A fear he'd never felt with his eldest daughter, at least not to that extent, a fear that never left him from the first moment he held her in his arms: the fear of loss.

"Tirza," he called out quietly, but she didn't answer this time either. Then he went downstairs and opened a second bottle of white wine, South African too. By eleven o'clock the second bottle was empty as the first.

He and the wife drank in silence. There wasn't an awful lot to say. Her return took place silently, calmly, poignantly. Precisely because it was so completely unremarkable. One moment the wife was there, just as she had not been there a moment earlier.

She sniffed. "Did you have something else going in there?" she asked.

"In where?"

"In the oven. I smell something."

"There's nothing else in there, you're smelling things again," he said caustically.

Hofmeester waited a few minutes, then looked at his watch and said: "It's getting late. I don't know where you're planning to sleep, whether you've arranged something. Are you staying with friends?"

"With friends?" She shook her head. Laughingly again, as always. She wore her hair a bit longer these days, he saw. He hadn't noticed at first. There had been so many things to look at. Her shoes, her suitcase, her raincoat, her ring, her sunglasses, her lips. Her hair was longer than when she'd left, it didn't look bad on her.

"Which friends would those be?"

He didn't know what to say to that. Which friends she might still have and which ones she'd disposed of, he had no idea.

"No, I haven't arranged anything," she said then of her own accord.

She sounded proud, as though she had walked up to fate and spit in its eye. That was something she had always enjoyed doing. She was constantly busy reminding fate that she was still a force to be reckoned with. As though fate could ever have forgotten.

He took the plates, the cutlery, and the two empty bottles to the kitchen. When he came back to the living room, he said: "If you want, you can sleep here."

He hadn't had to think about it much. It wasn't really a decision, more like the opposite: a lack of alternatives.

"That's sweet of you," she said. "I'm really quite tired. It was a long trip."

His wine glass was still half-full. He sat down again. "Yes, well," he said.

Hofmeester played with the two corks on the table, spun them around, kept doing that, and then, when one of them fell to the floor, said: "Okay, then that's arranged."

It was too late now to go looking for a hotel for her, or a pension. Besides, that would be discourteous, and cold, that too. A hotel for the mother of your children, that went against the grain of everything Hofmeester believed in. He didn't want to be cold, he preferred being warm. Glowing.

Perhaps the word love meant less than it used to—almost all words did—but half a century of living bore certain consequences, and Hofmeester had lived for half a century now. There were people you let in, you gave them food and a bed. A sense of responsibility, a deep and permeating sense of responsibility—life had left him with that.

He was accustomed to living with Tirza. Accustomed to the big, empty house where you could putter about quietly without running into too many other people. The absence of a partner had turned out not to be a curse, but a liberty—a grinding, defective sort of liberty, but still: liberty. He was together with his child. And it was as though that was how things were supposed to be, as though this had always been in the cards. Inseparable they were, the girl and he. Sometimes she knew what he was going to say before he even said it. The boys he had run into in the bathroom from time to time were only passersby.

Having a guest was going to take some getting used to. Even if the guest was the wife. He emptied his glass, picked up the cork, and went upstairs. He walked past the red suitcase on wheels, still waiting demonstratively in the hallway. What could be in there? he wondered. Past the blue raincoat, and then past Tirza's room, he saw that she had turned off the lights. Only when he reached his own bedroom did he notice that the wife had been following him at a polite distance.

She sat down on the bed. On her side. The side where she used to lie. Where books and newspapers were piled high now. She put the books and newspapers on the floor. The dust that had accumulated beneath the books and newspapers she swept onto the floor as well. And so the twin bed became a twin bed once more.

She rested her head in her hands, then looked up. Her hair was not only longer, it was also a different color. The color it had once been. Long ago. She laid her sunglasses on the nightstand.

Hofmeester took off his tie and hung it over a chair.

"The mattress," she said. "Is it still the same one?" She leaned on it with her hands and bounced it up and down, and he looked at the necktie, one of the presents he'd received for two decades of faithful service. A very nice necktie indeed. Tasteful. The secretary had picked it out herself, downtown, at the Bijenkorf department store. It was so much easier to be faithful to employers than to private individuals.

"It's the same mattress, as far as I know."

"It's worn out," she said. "It was already worn out when I left. You can't sleep on the same mattress forever."

He viewed the scene before him. The wife, sitting on the bed, commenting on the mattress. As though she were at home, as though she had never gone away. It was almost laughable.

"So you're going to sleep here?" he asked, glancing at the books and newspapers that had been lying beside him for months, no, for years, like a wife. The flesh, in his life, had become word.

"Well, you invited me."

"But here?" He waggled his finger at the bed, the mirror, the nightstands.

"Where else? In Ibi's old room?"

"But doesn't it feel a little strange?"

"Strange? What's strange about it? Does someone else sleep here?" she asked. "Will I be lying on the spot intended for someone else? Will I be occupying a part of the bed that isn't meant for me?"

"Not really," Hofmeester said after a moment's hesitation. "No one sleeps here. I mean, I sleep here. With my newspapers."

"Okay, well then?"

He took off his shirt. Sitting on the bed, she examined her bare feet.

"Still, it's strange," he said, more to himself than to her. "Everything about you is strange."

She turned around so that she could see him, standing at the window with his shirt in hand. She said: "You're so white, even whiter than you used to be. It looks like you're getting whiter all the time. Don't you ever get any sun? Women don't like pale skin."

He hung his shirt neatly over the back of the chair, then sat down and took off his shoes and socks. He tucked the socks into his shoes. The socks had been a present from his employer as well, after twenty years of service. Two decades then—now that was already more than three. At his place of employment, they liked to give people useful presents. Things you could put on. And take off. "Since you left," he said, "I haven't had any complaints. Not about my pale skin. Not about a lack of sun. Not about anything. The complaints just went away. The tenant still comes by once in a while, though."

When he was no longer expecting it, after he had almost forgotten she was still there, she whispered: "So pale, it's almost scary. Your skin."

Her voice hadn't changed either. There was something about that voice that had started to annoy him long ago. Ever since the moment when what was special, unique about her stopped being unique and became just plain irritating.

Her dress was colorful. A summer dress. In the old days she had almost always worn black. Jeans, lots of jeans, that too. Until one evening he'd felt compelled to tell her: "You're not a teenager anymore. Isn't it about time you tried a different uniform?"

"As though you're ill," she said. "As though you're about to die. Are you dying? Is that what it is, Jörgen, are you dying?"

He went into the bathroom and turned on the light. She followed him. Barefooted. Her shoes were still downstairs, beside the couch. She looked at him in the mirror above the sink. She *had* changed, after all. Wrinkles where no wrinkles had been, her face had grown fatter too, or was it thinner? Now, in the bright light of the bathroom, he saw it. Three years were tucked away in those minimal changes. Little is so frightening, and therefore elicits so much hatred, as the ageing woman. She sums up all decay, she arrives on the scene to avenge herself on all lust.

Hofmeester cleared his throat, slid aside a jar of hand cream.

"My overnight bag is downstairs, in my suitcase," she said. "I don't feel like getting it. I don't have the energy. I'm so tired. Do you have a toothbrush for me?"

There were two toothbrushes beside the sink. She looked at them.

"The green one is Tirza's," Hofmeester said.

She picked up the blue one, squeezed some toothpaste onto it, and began brushing her teeth in the mirror.

Hofmeester watched in dismay as his toothbrush slipped into her mouth. Watched it move around and around. There was something about it that angered him, disgusted him, the thought of his toothbrush being in her mouth was unbearable. He felt like shouting: "Stop it, you dirty pig, stop it right now!" and yanking the toothbrush out of her mouth, but instead he said: "I can get a new one for you, from downstairs. Maybe that would be more pleasant."

"Don't bother," she replied, her mouth filled with foam. "This is fine."

"What did you say?"

"Don't bother," she repeated. "That's what I said. This is pleasant enough."

He waited until she was finished. She took so long. Then he rinsed the toothbrush carefully. She remained standing beside the sink, in thought, but seeming comfortable. As though she had stood there yesterday and the week before too, last month even. And he went on rinsing. He scrubbed the toothbrush as though it might infect him with something. An idea. A belief. A disease.

Her legs had grown thicker, Hofmeester noticed now. A bit swollen, less refined than they used to be, less imposing. But he had changed too. He'd had dental surgery, twice. You could tell, he could tell, she must be able to tell, but she hadn't said anything about it. She didn't say much about anything. And he hadn't volunteered much either. Why should he?

Then he thought about Tirza. She would be here at home for a few more weeks. A few weeks, that was all. Then she would leave on her trip, a sort of trip around the world with her boyfriend, whom he hadn't met yet, but whom he was going to meet, at her party, her big party. He had already asked her: "Is he one of the boys I ran into in the bathroom, early in the morning?"

Looking at him in amusement, she had said: "No, come on, Daddy, those were one-night stands."

He had smiled and mumbled "Oh, I see." He had never directly associated his daughter with the world of one-night stands, and her mentioning it so offhandedly threw him off guard. He wasn't really shocked, perhaps a little perturbed at most. To him there was something uncomfortable about the juxtaposition of those words: "daughter" and "one-night stand." Uncomfortable, that was all. "I offered them a clean towel," he told her, but that couldn't disguise his discomfort. Tirza must have noticed, because she said: "Don't worry, Daddy. I know what I'm doing, I'm not crazy."

"No, no," he had said, "of course not," and turned back to what he was doing, even though he had long forgotten exactly what that was.

Brushing his teeth now, standing beside the wife, he thought back to that conversation with Tirza, about the boys who had been in this bathroom, often in semidarkness, apprehensive as they were about turning on the light. As though they realized that they were trespassing in his bathroom, Jörgen Hofmeester's bathroom.

"There's no need for you to be afraid," she said. He turned to see her better, took the toothbrush out of his mouth. What on earth was she talking about? Turning back to the sink, he leaned over to spit out the foam, then rinsed his mouth. August was coming and

Tirza would be gone. He would be alone, aroused from his musings at most by the tenant coming to report a new defect. A new phase in his life would begin, the Tirza-less phase.

"There's no need for you to be afraid," she said again.

He wiped his mouth on a towel. There was a sore spot on his lip, he'd probably bitten himself.

"Afraid of what?"

"Of me lying beside you."

He folded the towel. A white one. Which hadn't come out of the wash completely clean. There were still little bloodstains on it.

"Why would I be afraid? Of what?"

"Of me."

"Of you?" He couldn't help grinning.

"Where's the soap?" she asked. "I want to wash my hands."

"We only have liquid soap. Tirza uses only liquid soap, if she uses soap at all. She says it isn't good for your skin, it's much better to use only water, only lukewarm water." He opened the cabinet and handed her the liquid soap.

She took off her ring. He looked at it, wondered what she had done with her wedding ring. She washed her hands.

"Later, when I'm lying beside you," she said, holding her hands under the tap, "there's no need for you to feel uncomfortable."

He looked in the mirror at his chest, his shoulders, his upper arms. White skin, indeed. Rough. Even rougher than it used to be. A little dehydrated, that too. The doctor had given him an ointment to use against the flaking. Old flesh. Old men, he had noticed at work, often thought they were still attractive to young women, but the only thing those women were attracted to was the men's position, their power, their money. A tragic misunderstanding was maintained between them, a misunderstanding he had often observed. A hormonal misunderstanding.

"I mean," she said, "that you shouldn't make anything of it. I mean . . . I'm sorry, what I'm trying to say is that it doesn't mean anything."

Hofmeester washed his hands now too.

"That *what* doesn't mean anything?"

"Me, here. My being here."

"I never thought it did mean anything," he said. "You're here, you need a bed. A person has to sleep. Even a child knows that. I didn't attach any special significance to it, I took it as came. I take everything as it comes."

"Yes, I know all that, a person has to sleep. I was only trying to say that you exercise no sexual attraction on me. That you don't have to be afraid of that. That you don't have to do anything you don't feel like. God, why do you make me explain like this? Why don't you help me out a little?"

Hofmeester scrubbed his hands thoroughly. As though he'd spent all day grubbing in the dirt. As though he'd been working in the garden. He mustn't forget, tomorrow morning, to get a new toothbrush from the cupboard where he kept them, under the kitchen sink, and put it in the bathroom. To each his own toothbrush. The rightful distribution of property was the beginning of all happiness.

"In principle, I do very little that I don't feel like doing. But what one feels like is not always what matters. Let me put it this way: You don't do things because you feel like doing them, you do them because you must." He scratched his right arm. An insect had bitten him there. Yesterday evening perhaps, while was standing in the garden bare-chested, looking at his apple tree, at his tomatoes and pumpkin plants. Pumpkins were like weeds. If you treated them right, they spread like wildfire. It had been a lovely evening, the first nice evening of the year. Not quite hot yet, but still nice. The promise of heat.

"I'm not talking about work," she said. "I'm not talking about keeping house or about senile parents you have to care for. I'm talking about sex. That's not a matter of *must*, that's a matter of feeling-like. I said: 'You don't have to do anything you don't feel like,' to keep you from thinking that I'm here because I hope we'll start something again, that we'll have something together again, because that's not what I'm hoping for and that's not what I want. I don't feel like it. I don't want it anymore. I just wanted to see how you were getting along. You and Tirza."

"I don't follow. I have no idea what you're talking about. You're raving. And it's late. Let's go to sleep."

"What I mean is that we shouldn't have sex, we're not going to start that again." She spoke as though explaining it to a child who's a little slow, a child with a learning disability.

"That's fine," he said, drying his hands. "It would only make things unnecessarily complicated."

"Things?"

"This household. Everything is running smoothly here. Everything is well-arranged. We've got a housekeeper. A new one. She's from Ghana. There is a Daddy. He's not from Ghana. There is a child. There's money, food, there's love, I realize that may come as a surprise to you, but there is love. And in the last few weeks that Tirza's here I don't want any complications, any fuss, any tension that keeps growing and growing until it becomes unbearable. After you left, Tirza's grades skyrocketed. I'm not saying there's a causal relation, but it is striking. Don't you think? That it's striking?"

He put the blue toothbrush down carefully beside the green one, the way he did each evening.

"I won't get in your way, the two of you," she said. "I'll be on my best behavior."

He leaned on the sink with both hands. Although it wasn't particularly warm in the bathroom, he could feel the sweat under his arms.

"Why did you come?" he asked, not looking at her. "What do you want? What else is there to talk about?"

"That's what I just said. I don't want anything. To see how you two are getting along. That's all I wanted. And I definitely don't want to talk about anything."

She reached out and grabbed his earlobe, his left ear, and pinched it. He stared at the washing machine. It used to be in the kitchen, but it got in the way there so they'd moved it to the bathroom. It had been one of the last things the wife had organized around the house, before she left.

"Does it bother you having me here?" she asked. "Am I bothering you? Shall I go away?"

He rubbed his hands to feel if the skin was still rough and dry, and wondered whether you could tell how old he was by looking at his hands. He had read that somewhere. The struggle against age had shifted from the face to the hands.

"I don't know," he said, "if it bothers me. To be honest, I don't know. Maybe it would have been better if you hadn't come, but you're here now. That's okay. And you want to sleep here. That's okay too."

She was still holding his earlobe between her fingers. "Oh, Jörgen," she said. "My Jörgen." She let go of his ear. "You know? I never have felt attracted to you. Never. Not even at first. Do you know what that is, attraction? Does the word mean anything to you? Other than theoretically?"

He ran his hand over his cheeks. He felt the stubble and moved his face closer to the mirror, not much closer, only a few centimeters.

"Attraction, what kind of attraction? What are you talking about?"

"The beast," she said, "that's attraction. The beast. It's something you can't think about, because it's just there. There's nothing to reason away. Nothing to smooth out. Something more powerful than yourself. That's attraction. That what happens to people sometimes when they see someone else. It can die too, it usually does, you still see the other person but you no longer perceive him as a creature with a sex organ. As a creature with a functional sex organ."

He examined himself in the mirror, then her, in the mirror too.

"I don't feel any attraction to you," he said, quietly now, because suddenly he was afraid of waking Tirza. Still looking at himself, he whispered: "If that's what you want to know, if that's what you mean. I don't find you exciting. Never did, either. Maybe you were to other men, but not to me. I found you, above all, presentable. I could take you along when I went to meet other people, without feeling embarrassed, generally speaking, with a few exceptions, that's why I chose you. A wife went with my career and my house. And I thought you would be the one. The woman who would complement my career."

He moved his face up a little closer to the mirror. No, his skin was not as taut as it used to be, not as smooth. There was something puffy about it. He was developing a double chin. Used to be, that phrase contained more than just his own life story, and therefore hers as well, and Ibi's, and Tirza's, lest he forget. That phrase contained all of life.

"But Jörgen," she said, "do you think I never realized that? Do you think I never saw that? And never felt it? Do you think I never noticed how you looked at me, when you happened to look at me at all? The disgust in your eyes? The panic?"

He didn't reply. He was no longer concentrating on his reflection in the mirror. His gaze slid across the bathroom, the marble, the bathtub, the sink, the towel rack that was a heater as well, so that you had warm towels in the morning. All of it orderly, clean. All of it the way it should be.

"But you," she said, "you didn't see anything. Nothing. All those years. You were blind. I didn't want you any more than you wanted me. But you didn't see that. I thought you were too old. But you didn't feel that. You were preoccupied. I don't know with what, but you were preoccupied."

"Old?"

"Too old."

"Too old? What do you mean? When is someone too old?"

"Old, Jörgen. Just plain old. Too old for me. My girlfriends asked me: 'What are you doing with that old fool?' I thought you were dull, not only in bed, also out of bed. So horribly dull, almost to the point of being pathetic, as though your sluggishness somehow made you special, that's how you acted. And when you weren't being dull, on the rare occasions when you weren't dull, then you were . . . then you were . . . oh, well. But do you know why I stuck around? Because the men I fell for, the men I did find exciting, stimulating, the ones I fell in love with, sometimes for weeks, months—they all had something nasty about them. They wouldn't have been good to my children, if they had wanted children at all, but that wasn't even the biggest problem. The problem was that they would never have cared for them, I thought, the way you would."

Hofmeester tore off a sheet of toilet paper, blew his nose in it, and dropped it in the toilet. He looked at it, how it floated in the water. Then he flushed. The sound of rushing water came as a relief, it seemed to break the tension that he felt, for a second there, was becoming unbearable.

"We're not that far apart in age, are we?" he said, staring at the pot. "Too old? What are you blathering about anyway? How many years' difference is there between us? Is that why you came by? Because you forgot to tell me something, back then?" He chuckled. The thought was absurd, too absurd, like some of the tenant's complaints. As absurd as being told you were too old to be fired.

"There's enough of a difference. And the gap widens all the time. The age difference increases all the time. Haven't you noticed that? The point isn't our exact ages. It's something mental. It doesn't have to do with years, with the date of birth in your passport. You're just *old*, and you have been for ages. You've stopped being exciting. To the extent that you ever were. Exciting, does that word mean anything to you?"

He tore himself free of the toilet bowl's sway. He turned to his wife. "You're right," he said. "There was never any lust between us. But lust is not the greatest, the loveliest, the most important, the only thing. I, for example, was disgusted by the smell you gave off.

But I never said anything about it, because smell isn't what matters. If smell is what matters, after having two children, then something's wrong. Don't you agree? Are smells anything to whine about then?"

"What smell?" she asked, stepping closer to him. "What kind of smell are you talking about?"

He held up his index finger, tapped it against her breastbone. An offhand gesture.

"You know. You know perfectly well. Your smell. The smell you give off. All the time, twenty-four hours a day." He stepped away from her, towards the washing machine. He stood leaning against the washer, pensive and casual, his arms folded across his chest. It was a pose. He was not as calm as he seemed. He was tense. All rejection, anything in which he detected rejection, rattled him. In life he had detected rejection. That's why life rattled him too.

"What are you talking about? The way I smell? Do you think you can get away with this? Just because you survived without me for a couple of years? Do you think you're suddenly a different person? Better than me? Stronger?"

The heated towel rack had been a present. He'd had it put in around the same time they had taken that "Make your own sushi and sashimi" course. That had been the marriage counselor's idea. Do something together. Make something together. Give each other a present now and then. Be special for each other.

"You may be younger than me," he said, "which is factually correct. You may find me, and always have, old and sluggish, almost to the point of being pathetic, which, by the way, is a rather subjective observation . . ."

"An old workhorse."

"Let me finish. You may believe all that and announce it too, but the smell you gave off was god-awful, unbearable."

He began massaging his right hand, the way he often did after a day of writing letters and emails.

"Could you describe that smell?" she asked. "Could you be a little more precise? Do you mean stench? Is that what you're trying to say, that I stink? Are we talking about a stench here?"

She was standing in front of him. He couldn't back off, the washing machine was behind him. He could make out the individual pores in her face, the black of her mascara. Maybe she was right, maybe he had been disgusted by her. But disgust was no grounds for divorce, disgust was the zenith of intimacy. The conclusion of intimacy. Its logical conclusion. The familiarity of disgust, the immutability of it, the wistfulness it elicited. The desire to be disgusted by the other person, just one last time. And, with that, to always be a little disgusted by yourself as well.

"Not stench, not per se. Stench. A sewer gives off a stench. Stench is what the tenant complains about. Not every unpleasant odor is worthy of the name stench. Try to exercise a little discernment."

"So I stink, is that what you're saying? Is that what you're trying to say?"

"No, not at all," he said. "You're not listening, but then you never did. Smelling unpleasant is not stinking; smelling unpleasant is smelling unpleasant, and I'm sure I'm not the first to have told you this, so don't be coy. Don't try to act innocent."

"And where did that stench come from? If I may ask?"

He looked her straight in the eye, only for a moment, but that was enough. Strange things had a way of taking place inside her head, things short-circuited there. Lightning struck there from time to time. He had forgotten about that, he had done his best to forget it.

"What is it you want to know? Didn't I just say that it doesn't matter? I don't want to talk about it anymore."

She grabbed his arm, the arm that itched because something had bitten him there.

"I want to know," she said. "I have the right to know." The word "right" sounded hard and resolute. As though she did indeed have a right to something she had now come to claim. Her share of the spoils.

"Your breath," he said. "Especially when you'd been drinking wine. But then you drank wine every day, so that didn't make much difference. That smell became so overpowering that it seemed to come from the tips of your toes, from your hair, from your whole body. Unbearable, that's what it was. And appalling. If there was anything unusual about the way I looked at you, it was probably because of that."

She pinched him gently, almost tenderly, on the arm. "Do you smell it now? That smell? Can you smell it? Is it there now?"

He shook his head, confused and irritated. Rattled was how he felt, by her presence, by her questions, by her being so close. A few hours ago he had just started in on his casserole, happy in fact, but without being aware of it. Happiness you recognize only in hindsight. Oh, I was so happy then, stupid of me not to have paid more attention.

"I have a cold," he said, "and besides, you just brushed your teeth. All I can smell is my own toothpaste. That's no great thrill either."

"Come on," she said, "Take a good whiff." She brought her mouth up close to his nostrils. She blew. He could feel her warm breath on his face. She blew again. She was very close now. Everything was in full view. But he had stopped looking.

Hofmeester raised his left hand and took her by the throat. He squeezed her throat. She blew again. He squeezed her windpipe, he looked away. He bore down. "Keep doing that," she whispered, "just keep doing that. Do you want me to call the police again? Like before, Jörgen? Do you want me to call them again?"

Then he pushed her away. She fell against the wall beside the bathtub. But it didn't take her long to recover. She slid aside the shower curtain and spit into the tub a few times.

"Now I know," Hofmeester said slowly, opening and closing the hand with which he had squeezed her throat. As though he was at the physiotherapist's, obediently performing the exercises assigned him.

"Now you know what?"

"Now I know why you came. Because you couldn't stand it. You couldn't stand me being happy. The thought of me building a life here with Tirza. Getting along without you. You've always found happiness unbearable. If you don't have a reason to moan and groan, you feel like you're not alive. If you can't hide your face behind a veil of tears, you think you're missing out on all the good things in life. Without tragedy, life means nothing to you. Nothing. And . . ."

"Do you call this living?" She pointed at him. She pointed to the washing machine and the towel rack.

He didn't reply. Instead, he opened the medicine cabinet and looked for something to rub on the insect bite. There had to be some ointment left over from last summer, the mosquitoes had been terrible and Tirza had been bitten all the time. He had bought her a mosquito net, but somehow, miraculously, they had even gotten through that.

He couldn't find anything. Iodine, adhesive bandages, aspirin. No mosquito cream. At wit's end, he jabbed his thumbnail into the bite.

"Jörgen," the wife said.

"Yes?" he said, still holding his nail against the bump.

"Who *do* you actually find attractive? Not me, I know that. I've known that for a long time. But I'm glad you've finally said it in so many words. Better to say everything. Better to get it off your chest. What I'm curious about, though, is who you actually *do* find attractive. There must be people you're attracted to. I was wondering whether maybe it was men. I never dared to ask you that, I was afraid it might come as too much of a shock and that nothing would be left of you, nothing at all, even less than now. I was afraid you would feel unmasked, helpless, that you would shrivel up and turn to dust. But now, now that we're friends, just good friends, no more than that—who knows, maybe even best friends—I figured: Well,

I can just ask, can't I? Is it men you long for? Boys? Young boys? Blond, wearing tight jeans? Or maybe more the Oriental type?"

She approached him again. He didn't move a muscle. His left hand moved mechanically over the insect bite. It hadn't really helped, sticking his nail into it. The itch had, at best, become a little less intense.

When she was two steps away from him, she stopped.

"Is that why you're happy now?" she asked. "Because you can finally be yourself? Undisturbed. Still on the sly of course, imagine if it should get out, but still, undisturbed. Do they come over late at night, when Tirza is asleep, or during the weekend when she's staying at a friend's house? Alone, or two a time? Wearing leather? Sporting a moustache? With slicked-back hair, still wet and glistening with gel?"

On her face, for a moment, he saw the same emotion he had noticed about five hours ago, when she was standing in the vestibule with her suitcase on wheels. It was an emotion he'd never seen in her before. By turns, amid all the arrogance, amid all her ironclad sarcasm, there appeared on her face something that reminded him strongly of desperation. A glance, a tugging at the corners of her mouth. The way she looked past him. The sound of her voice. The desperation was new, and made her unexpectedly fragile. And made him that way too. There where she broke, he broke as well.

"Go away," he said. "You're insane."

"Insane? I've heard that from you before. Insane? Just because I know about it? Just because I refuse to play along with your ridiculous charade anymore? I kept my mouth shut all those years in order to make you feel better, to let you believe in your own deception and rest calmly in the illusion that everyone, including me, had fallen for it. I was insane *then*, because I left you and your self-deception in peace, because I never said: 'Jörgen, it would be better for all concerned if you just came out and admitted it, just admit it, this isn't the nineteenth century anymore. There are worse things.' But now that I ask in a friendly fashion about how things are going, suddenly now I'm insane? Now that I ask, out of interest, purely out of interest, out of friendship, who it is that you find attractive, then it's suddenly me who's losing my mind?"

"You're insane," he repeated. "More insane than ever. Why does everything have to be dragged out in the open, why can't you leave well enough alone, why don't you have any respect for silence? Why is that so threatening to you, so unbearable?"

She pulled her dress up over her head, then tossed it down beside her hurriedly. Not the hurriedness of desire, but the hurriedness of habit. The haste of the sleepy. Sleep now. Quickly. The way you long for sleep after a wakeful night on a long flight that was delayed to start with. She wasn't wearing a bra. He lowered his eyes.

"Jörgen," she said quietly, "is this what you're afraid of? Is this what you hate about me? That I'm a woman? Is this the stench you were talking about? The stench of a woman? The stench you can smell from ten feet away, because the more afraid you are of something the better you can smell it; that's the law of the animal kingdom, isn't it? Is that what disgusts you so? You can tell me honestly now, I really want to know. It won't hurt my feelings. The truth can't hurt me. The silence hurts. The lies. The sneaking around."

"Go away," he said, his head bowed. "Please go away. Go to a hotel. Right now. I'll give you the money."

"For what?"

"For a hotel."

She took her breasts in her hands and lifted them slightly. She was tanned all over, she still couldn't resist the urge to sunbathe without a top.

"Do you see them," she asked, "or are you afraid to look at them? These are the breasts that fed your children. Do you see them? They haven't started to sag or shrivel like other women's. Nothing is worse for the skin than shrinking and expanding, shrinking and expanding, but my breasts have never shriveled. They've stayed just the way they were. Have you ever actually taken a good look at them? Did you miss them? The disgust they may have summoned up in you? You can miss that too, can't you? Thank God though, there's still one thing more powerful than your disgust, if I'm not mistaken, and that's your desire to abide by social convention."

He ignored her breasts. He looked her in the eye, and when he couldn't do that anymore he looked past her.

"I'm sorry," he said at last. Because he didn't know what else to say. Because she was standing in front of him, touchable and unreal at the same time, but above all naked.

A naked wife. Getting on in years.

He raised his hand and felt his hair, his scalp, that itched too.

"What are you sorry about?"

He hesitated, he wasn't exactly sure what he was sorry about, all he knew was that he was sorry.

"That it wasn't me," he said at last.

"That what wasn't you?"

"The man you longed for."

"No, you weren't that."

She let go of her breasts.

"But I wasn't the one either," she said after a few seconds. "I wasn't the one you longed for either."

"No." He could feel the sore spot on his lip again. "I suppose you could put it that way. If you had to. Then we're even, I suppose." His lip felt like it was bleeding.

"We're even, yes. That's one way of looking at it. Even-steven. Still, there *have* been a few hunks in my life. Don't start feeling guilty, don't let it make you uncomfortable." The way she said it was dreamy and businesslike at the same time. She was summing up the facts, now that she was here anyway. He was being presented with the profit-and-loss account.

"Hunks?"

"Hunks. One of them had dreadlocks."

"Is that what they are? What you call them? Is that what you say?" The term sounded more like something his daughters would use. Hunks. If he had been able to laugh, he would have. Heartily and elatedly. For a long time, slapping his thighs. Mother and daughter in search of hunks.

"The man I long for is a hunk, that's right. My girlfriends always said: 'He's not a hunk, but he'll take good care of your children.' They said: 'He's dull, but he'll cook for you and do the shopping, don't forget that.' My girlfriends said: 'He's old, but once he's dead you'll still have your whole life in front of you.' Look at me and tell me: What do I still have in front of me? A few days ago I went to a fortune teller. 'A lot of things are going to change this year,' she said. 'Everything is going to be different. Wait and see. Everything is going to be different.' Look at me, Jörgen. What is going to be different?"

He ran his hand through his hair, which had lost its original color. It was white now. For the first time he felt something like pity for her, for the first time in years she was not the woman who had left him and his children in the lurch in order to search for some smutty brand of happiness aboard a houseboat.

"You and I made two children together," he said.

"Yeah, so? Is that supposed to be my comfort and my salvation? What's a woman without a child? A whore. Not even that. A whore can have children too. And like I said: You seemed absolutely suited to make children with. I couldn't find anyone better, Jörgen. At least no one who was willing. But the children didn't save me. The helpless desire in a man's eyes has done more for me than my daughters' imploring looks ever have. Other mothers think that's love, but it's hunger, Jörgen: normal, everyday hunger. And then all that shrieking, sometimes the whole night through, that's right, you used to wear earplugs, and later on you didn't mind the shrieking at all, you loved it, it gave you something to do, but I had other ideas of what life was about, more than listening to the shrieking of my thirsty little girls."

He did his best not to see her. Again he ran his hand through his hair. He could always dye it, if it made him look old. In fact, he thought it looked good on him, that white. That it had a distinguished air about it, he thought it suited him. He felt that the color of his hair lent him a certain authority. But maybe he was mistaken.

"I don't know what it is you want from me," he said quietly. "I don't know what it is and it's really none of my concern, but I am not a homo. And I never have been."

He realized then that he had dreamed about this, that he had been through it all before in a dream, that he had stood with her in the bathroom and that she was naked. She was often naked. When the children were younger, she used to organize parties for them at which she then appeared in a state of partial or even complete nudity. Until the other parents complained about her behavior, and Hofmeester had to promise that she would no longer mingle in the nude with the children as they were playing cowboys and Indians beneath his apple tree, not even on stifling hot afternoons. Not even partially nude, he had conceded of his own accord. He knew the wife well enough for that. But in the dream in which he had been through this already, the conversation had gone differently. It had not been about homos.

"What are you then?"

"What am I when?"

"If you're not a homo. What are you then? What are you, for God's sake?"

"Is that what you really want to know?"

"Yes. Maybe it is. Now that you mention it. I think I can come to terms with what has happened, with everything that's happened, if I finally know what you are. Who are you, Jörgen? Who are you?"

Hofmeester took a deep breath, his hand was no longer resting on the top of his head. There was a bruise on her thigh, he saw. She had bumped into something. Or been kicked.

"I'm no one," he said. "My ego was large, but I cut it in half and you ground the rest of it to a pulp. I am the father of Tirza and Ibi. Especially that. That's what I am, that's right, not a great deal more than that, but also no less. The father of Ibi and Tirza. I'm a father."

"You know," she said slowly, as though searching for the right words, as though speaking a foreign language, "what it is I wonder about? Haven't you ever thought: Wow, isn't it weird?"

"What are you talking about? Wow? What I was I supposed to find weird?"

"What I'm talking about? Come on, Jörgen, now don't you be coy."

"I don't know. I have no idea what you're talking about. I haven't known what you're talking about for a while now."

"Haven't you ever thought: How peculiar that I was never able to give my wife an orgasm? How strange? Maybe it's time I tried something, or found out how to do that. Whole books have been written on the subject, you can buy instructional videos at almost any health food store. Haven't you ever thought: I should do something about it, even if only once? Haven't you ever thought: What a pity. For her? What must she think of me? Maybe I should read up on it. Maybe I should practice. Until I'm finally able to do it."

He stared at her, as though she were a mouse he found in the same mousetrap that had been in the same kitchen cupboard for the last twenty years, a trap no one had ever found a mouse in. And then, one morning, suddenly, there it is: a mouse. It's unbelievable. You think you must be hallucinating. That it's some kind of mistake.

No, in the dream everything had gone differently. Not that it had been a pleasant dream, fairly unpleasant in fact, but this was even less pleasant.

"Shall we put an end to this conversation?" he suggested. "Put something on. Let's go to sleep. Put on some pajamas. Or a T-shirt. And let's just go to sleep. As though nothing has happened. You have plenty of T-shirts here. Your pajamas are here too. Everything's still here. Everything has been lying in readiness for you."

Again his gaze travelled to the bruise on her thigh. She was careless, and clumsy. She bumped into things often. Her panties were pink, a pleasant pink, salmon pink. Not that glaring, hot pink that hurts your eyes but that has something special about it too. Something exciting, precisely because it does hurt your eyes.

"I really would like to know," she said. "There are a couple of things I'd really like to know, now that I'm here anyway. This is one of them."

He nodded.

"You want to know," he said. "You want to know. Well, as far as I can recall, but then maybe my memory fails me, maybe I'm descending into premature senility, but as I recall I sometimes gave you an orgasm, not regularly, but from time to time it did happen. Not every month, not every three months, but from time to time. But whatever the case, I find it ridiculous to be talking about this now, at this moment. I find it absurd. I find it unseemly."

"Never," she said. "Not you, Jörgen. Others, yes. The man with the dreadlocks, almost every day. But you, never. Never, do you hear me? Never."

He took a step in her direction, for a moment he felt the urge to grab her by the throat again, he was already raising his arm, but he held himself in check.

"I gave you," he hissed, "two children. Isn't that better than an orgasm, isn't that a thousand times better? What are you whinging about? Two children, two healthy children, doesn't that outweigh all the orgasms in the world?"

He stepped back.

"So you deluded yourself," she said, "you labored under the illusion—it's a scream. Have you ever bothered to figure out who you were living with all those years? Have you ever really looked at me? Where were you, anyway? What planet were you on all those years?"

He massaged his wrist. Since he'd sprained his wrist playing tennis, he often massaged it at odd moments. Sometimes in the middle of the night, when he couldn't sleep, or in the garden between bouts of weeding and sawing. And there was a lot of weeding to be done in his garden. And sawing. And then there was the little house in the country that belonged to his parents, with a garden, and what a garden!

"What do you want? I was wrong. Is that what you want to hear? I'm delighted to say it. I was wrong, I never stopped to think about it. I thought I had given you an orgasm, but I was wrong, as it turns out. Okay, congratulations. And it's too late, thank God it's too late to start rehashing that. Your orgasms are no longer my affair, and vice versa. Others will have to see to your needs, others *have* seen to your needs. Why come to me with your complaints? For three years you've been having the time of your life, for three years you've been fluttering from one orgasm to the next, if I understand correctly, so why are you getting worked up about the couple of years before that, when life included more than orgasms?"

"Couple of years? Couple of decades, you mean."

"You could have done it yourself," he shouted. "If it was really all that important, if it was really such a matter of life and death, you could have done it yourself."

"I *did* do it myself," she shouted back. "I could hardly wait around for you to do it."

"Then I really don't understand what you're complaining about, or why you've come here, raking up the past. Forget about it. Clear out the attic of your memory. Make room for the future. Stop picking away at your resentment and hard feelings. You're still young. You said so yourself. Start something new. You already started something new. That it didn't turn out the way you'd hoped, I'm sorry to hear that, but leave me alone, leave Tirza alone. It's been hard enough for her as it is."

"Too late?" she said. "But Jörgen, it's never too late. None of it is actually over. You took my life away. That's still the way things stand. I can't make room for the future. I can't get into the future. My life must still be around here somewhere, because this is where I left it. And I've come to get it back."

Looking around her, she waved her arms and pointed at the bedroom walls.

She's off her rocker, he thought. Nuts. Worse than ever. Crazier than ever.

"I gave it back to you. Three years ago. When you left for your houseboat. If . . . that is . . . I ever took it away from you at all. Opinions differ on that score too. I never forced you into anything, not into having children, not into marriage, not into sex. It was all your idea."

"Exactly," she shouted. "Now you admit it yourself. It was all my idea. Everything we did was always my idea."

They both thought they heard something, and were quiet for a moment. They thought they had woken her. The child.

When it turned out they were mistaken, she went on, less loudly now: "That's why I came, Jörgen. That's why I'm here, because I want it back."

She looked around, slightly distraught but no longer insane, in a strange way less insane than ever. Sober and resolute.

He was sweating, like on a summer day in the tropics. He wiped his forehead.

She looked at him, her dress still lying there beside her, as though she had only tossed it on the floor for a moment before putting it in the washing machine. He would pick it up, he would wash it, he would iron it—if the label called for ironing, that is.

'Which part of a woman's body do you actually find most disgusting, Jörgen?" she asked. Her tone had a kind of deadly charm now. "Is it the breasts? Or the buttocks? When you look at me, what disgusts you most?"

He felt his jaw. Sometimes, when he exerted himself, the pain came back. It wasn't actually pain, more like the awareness of having something like a jaw.

"I already told you, I'm not gay. I like women."

She laughed. It was a loud, unpleasant laugh.

"But which ones then? What kind of women? Do they have to come from Uranus or from some other galaxy? Dwarves maybe, female dwarves?"

Hofmeester gulped. He regretted having told her she could sleep here.

But how else could he have dealt with the situation? She had shown up, with a suitcase, she ate dinner, she drank some wine, and after eating and drinking it was time to sleep. But he hadn't expected this. This was something he hadn't counted on.

"Tirza is asleep. Let's be a little quiet."

"I asked you something. What kind of women do you like? What sort?"

His face felt sticky, his hands were sticky, and he could feel his jaw, grinding like the gears of a machine that is slightly out of whack.

"I've never divided them into sorts. I'm not your type. You're not mine. Isn't that enough? Don't we know enough now, in so far as we didn't know that already? We've never awoken the beast in each other, at least not often, maybe never, *tant pis*. But we did have two children. That's more important. The beast in us is dead."

He walked to the sink, held his mouth under the tap and drank. The water was lukewarm, but he didn't mind, he drank thirstily.

"Not in me, Jörgen," she said, "the beast isn't dead in me. You did your utmost, but it's still alive. It is alive."

He closed the faucet and turned to her. "Good," he said, "but in me it's dead, dead as a doornail, I've vanquished it. I've got it under control. I am stronger than the beast. That's why I'm free and you're not. Put something on. You'll catch a cold."

"Your beast," she said, "is not one I would ever have said was alive. Alive the way a beast should be. Your beast was mortally wounded, right from the start. You tricked me into thinking it was alive and kicking, but that was only in order to seduce me, to drag me in here, I barely even had time to settle in before the beast died like a plant you forget to water. Oh, once in a while it would wake up, but that was only a game. The things I had to do to get your beast out of hibernation! That's the past, you're right. But now, now that I'm here, and I'm not here that often, then please tell me, Jörgen. Before I go away thinking that I lived with a homo all those years, that the father of my children is a homo. Not that there's anything wrong with that, not that I have anything against homos. But just tell me: What kind of women excite you?"

He pressed his hands to his temples, as though trying to dispel a sudden headache.

"Come on, just tell me," she said in her sweetest voice. "Are they masculine girls, girls with mustaches, without breasts, women with short hair or maybe no hair at all? Quasi-infantile? Invalids? Women with wooden legs? The kind they can screw loose before climbing into bed?"

He shook his head.

"Or is it really men after all? You can tell me now. I'm your friend, your very best friend. Someone who knows everything about you but still doesn't hold it against you, because it's all behind me now. The marriage. The affair."

"I like," he said, he gulped and gulped again, trying to get rid of the unpleasant feeling in his jaw, "I like vulgar women."

For a moment it was still. Then she started laughing. She howled and tossed her head back.

"How vulgar?"

"Vulgar. I don't know how vulgar. I think that's what you'd call it. Vulgar. Isn't that enough information for you? Can we go to sleep now? Is it over?"

She kept laughing. She didn't stop.

"Wasn't I vulgar enough? How vulgar does a woman need to be? Before she lives up to your standards?"

"I don't know," he whispered. "I don't know, and you're tipsy."

"Come on, Jörgen, tell me. Tipsy, from that little bit of wine? Please. You can tell me everything. At last you can tell me everything. Don't be afraid of making me angry. I'll never be angry again. I have no stake in this anymore. It is, as you said, none of my business. When you encounter a vulgar woman, does the beast in you wake up again? Or is it really dead, like you said, dead as a doornail?"

She came one step closer. He saw her breasts, not wrinkled, that's right, almost intact. He looked over at the sink, where a green toothbrush lay beside a blue one, ready for the next morning.

"Cashiers," he said. "Women who work at the bakery. Women in shops and cafeterias. What does it matter? Salesgirls, in all shapes and sizes."

A hissing sound came from her mouth. Exaggeratedly long and exaggeratedly hissing. "Sex," she said, "is nothing to you but class conflict."

"Colored girls."

She grabbed him by the chin the way an elementary school teacher might grab a naughty pupil. Grave and ironic at the same time. The punishment was just part of the game. "Racist," she said. "Colored girls."

She didn't let go of his chin. She came a little closer. She was going to try to kiss him. He could feel it, see it in her eyes. She pressed her lips against his. And he would respond to her kiss, he had to respond to her kiss, he could do nothing else, even if only to keep from putting her to shame, the mother of his children, Tirza's mother. He couldn't refuse her kiss, not even if he wanted to, he had to respond.

From the position he was in, it wasn't easy, but he smacked her against the side of the head anyway.

She staggered. Fell back. She doubled up.

For a moment it looked like her eyes were crossed. Maybe it was the bad lighting, or his own fatigue.

"See?" she said, still doubled over as though he had punched her in the stomach. "See what I mean? You're wrong. The beast in you isn't dead, it's awake again. I woke it up."

Taking a piece of toilet paper, he dabbed at his lip. It was bleeding. He had bitten it. The agitation, the stress, that happened sometimes. He wiped his mouth with the piece of paper.

"I'd like to offer my apologies," he said.

She was squatting down. Beside the washing machine. She was looking at him.

"I apologize," he said. "I tried to answer your question, because you were so persistent. Because you wanted to know so badly. I tried to answer your question as honestly as I could. I shouldn't have done that."

She stood up. She hoisted herself to her feet. The red blotch on her cheek made him furious. But it wasn't an active fury, it was passive, a calm and silent fury that would result in the combing of his hair, the ironing of sheets, the preparation of a casserole dinner.

"You see," she said again, "the beast is there, the beast will be there as long as you live, Jörgen. I'm the only one who can wake it with a kiss, admit it."

He looked at his partially nude wife with her glowing cheek, and for a moment he seemed to remember something, for a moment it seemed as though the past had come to life, but then it was over. Like when you're about to say something, something important, but can't remember what it was.

"What does it matter?" he whispered, mostly to himself. "What does it matter?" And then, louder: "I've already said that lust is not the greatest good. I've already said that this household is a household built on love."

"That's right," she said, "you did all you could. Every shop you go into is a new fantasy, shops must be heaven to you. But do you ever actually succeed? Or does it just remain a fantasy? All of life, nothing but a fantasy that reality can't hold a candle to, a place where nothing ever happens because the little fantasies would be too threatening if they came true? God, when I think about the way I had to stuff that half-erect thing of yours into me, it's a miracle we ever had children at all. A miracle. And God knows all the other maneuvers I had to perform. It was all so pitiful and clumsy. And the whole time there I was thinking that it was because you were a furtive homo. But you simply didn't think I was vulgar enough. And now? Don't you find me vulgar now?"

He took the toilet paper from his lip. He looked at his feet. Then he looked at the piece of toilet paper. There was a little, dark red drop on it.

"You are vulgar," he said quietly.

The wife's left cheek was still a dark red, as though she were blushing deeply on only one side.

He was sweating more all the time now, more profusely and more intensely.

"So why did you stay," he asked, "if it was all so pitiful and clumsy?"

"For the children."

"But then why start in on having children?"

"I told you already. Are you listening? Do you even listen to what I say?"

She was standing in front of him, right in front of him. With one quick move she reached out and grabbed him by the crotch. She grabbed him there and held onto him.

She's insane, he thought. But he didn't do anything. He stood there with the piece of toilet paper in his hand.

"Has there been even one woman," she asked, "who didn't burst out laughing? Or are they so dull that they don't even laugh anymore when they see you mucking about? Has any woman ever shown the kind of patience I did? How long does it take you, anyway, to finally get a hard-on? The greatest part of an evening, sometimes longer? Or do you take pills for that these days? Vulgar women. It would be a scream, if it wasn't so sad. Do you just run into them sometimes, or do you actually have to go out looking for them? Do you have to go downtown? Or out to the colored neighborhoods?"

He seized her by the throat again. There was nothing else he could do. She had hold of him and she wasn't letting go. He couldn't just let that happen.

"Do it," she said. "Show me that the beast isn't dead yet. Admit that I woke it up, the way I was always able to awaken it in you. Come on, Jörgen. Box my ear again. But not so gently this time. Like you used to. After all, that's the only way you can do it, isn't it? You can't do it otherwise. Only when you're punching people do you say 'I love you.' So say it!"

As sure as he was that Tirza was his daughter, as sure as he was that they had told him at work that he was too old to fire, that's how sure he was right then that he hated her. He hit her with the back of his hand. Across the other cheek. So hard that she let go of him and fell to the floor.

For a moment it was silent. Deathly silent. It was like being in the mountains. As though they were high in the mountains, with no other people around, just snow and rocks.

Only then did he notice. Standing in the doorway was Tirza, holding her cuddly toy. She still slept with a cuddly toy. A blue donkey, or at least a donkey that used to be blue.

She was staring at her parents. The wife, wearing only her panties, crawled across the floor to the sink and hoisted herself up on it. Her one cheek was red, the other an even darker red, almost blue.

"It's okay, Tirza," Hofmeester said. He took a step towards her. She looked at him impassively, stolidly you might almost say, with the donkey in her arms.

"Don't be afraid, Tirza. Don't ever be afraid. Mama and I are playing."

3

He shaves quickly but carefully. With his fingertips, he occasionally he feels a spot he has missed. In this light, you can feel it better than you can see it.

The sushi and sashimi are ready. He did a lot of shopping beforehand; Hofmeester is prepared for hungry guests. As always on such occasions, he has let himself be guided by the fear of there not being enough, of people going home hungry and saying: "When it comes right down to it, after all, the Hofmeesters *are* a bit stingy." He bought sardines as well. He plans to fry them with a bit of garlic, later in the evening, when spirits are high. Simple but tasty. He's tried that before on summer evenings, and it's always been a success.

In the mirror he can see the wife shuffling down the hall, still in her bathrobe.

The first guest will be arriving in an hour. The ones who come early because they're planning not to go home too late, and who, despite the best intentions, end up hanging around and finally only climb on their bikes at four in the morning, shirt-fronts covered in grease spots. It's comforting, to watch young people grow more and more tipsy. Their frenetic attempts to imitate the grownups, the way they go to all that trouble to simulate some state that hasn't yet arrived and which—as he knows by now—never will. Their attempts are a comfort to Hofmeester.

He washes his face, makes sure to wipe the foam from his ears and nostrils, then goes looking for a shirt and matching tie. For a few seconds he stands before the closet in the bedroom, shirt and tie in hand, looking at the wife as she rummages through her side of the closet, where her dresses are still hanging. Then he makes a decision: no tie. This is Tirza's party, this is what they used to call a "do." One attends such things without a tie, even if one *is* the father of the one throwing the party, even if teachers will be attending as well. Not all her teachers, of course. He left the invitations up to Tirza. It's her evening. Her farewell to secondary school, to puberty, who knows, perhaps even to Amsterdam and to him, Jörgen Hofmeester, the father who has now apparently acquitted himself of his paternal duties. The parenting is over, he'll have time all to himself again, although he has no idea what he'll do with it. The remains of his life stretch out before him like a desert.

He holds the shirt up against his trousers, to check the colors. Do they clash? Colors have never been his forte. Perhaps it would be better to say: clothes have never been his forte.

Hofmeester has his favorite teachers. He never missed a parent-teachers' evening. He almost always arrived too early, because duty called, and with the passage of time he had befriended that duty. He would have liked to befriend Tirza's teachers too, but friends have never really been his forte either. When Tirza was still in elementary school, he had invited a teacher over for dinner once. It was enjoyable. At the end of the evening they'd played a board game. "We need to show Tirza's teacher," he had explained to the wife, "how special our daughter is, and the best way to do that is invite her over to dinner. That way she can see Tirza in her natural surroundings."

Having children was the wife's idea, to start with. One morning at breakfast, a breakfast which now seems to him as though it was consumed in another lifetime, she had said: "We're going to have a baby."

"How can that be?" he'd asked.

And she had replied: "I stopped taking the pill."

"A baby," he said. "My God, aren't there enough of them in the world? And how can you be sure the child will be healthy?"

But all she had said was: "If I'd left it up to you, it would never have happened."

All morning long the idea had flustered him, but by the time lunch was over he had decided to shoulder his responsibility. He waited till work was over at five, then bicycled to the bank and took out a life-insurance policy, without telling the wife about it. It was to be a surprise, the money the policy would pay out if anything unexpected happened to him.

That, then, was how Jörgen Hofmeester became a father; as a man who knew nothing more about fatherhood and wanted to know nothing more about it than that it was wise to take out life insurance before the child entered the world.

When at last Ibi was born, the responsibility took on a different form. For the first few months Ibi lay between her father and mother, even though her room contained a perfectly fine cradle. But the fact was that she slept more soundly in the big bed, safely between her parents.

And when she turned two, she was sleeping there still, *die Dritte im Bunde*. Sometimes he would wake up the wife to show her Ibi. "Look," he would say, "look how peacefully she's sleeping."

Then came Tirza. The wife told him: "If we already have one, then we might as well have two." Hofmeester had nodded and, a few months later, went back to the bank to raise the coverage.

He takes another shirt out of the closet and holds it up to the light to check for spots, but the color doesn't appeal to him. He wants to look neat and distinguished. For the teachers who will be coming, for Tirza's friends, for Tirza herself. Yellow is anything but distinguished.

In the wake of the fiasco of the runaway wife, three of Tirza's teachers had called him: her math, German, and Dutch teachers. They had heard about it—there was no way you could cover up something like that—and they spoke words of encouragement, words based sometimes on personal experience, and said they were impressed by how well Tirza was holding up under such difficult circumstance, that's right, there was no need for him to worry about Tirza. Mrs. van Delven, the Dutch teacher who was also Tirza's home-room teacher, asked him: "Would you like to come by some time to talk about it, in as far as it concerns Tirza too? Would that be useful?"

"Oh no," he had said, "there's no need for that. Kind of you to offer, but it wouldn't really help either."

He was pleased that she had called, but a truant wife wasn't something you felt like discussing in public for too long. So he continued to insist that the wife's running away was all part of a greater plan. That he actually approved of it. "You can't really call it running away," he had told the math teacher, "it's more like we've decided to take a holiday from each other. I told her: 'Go on, go ahead, you'll come back.'"

If his favorite teachers don't show up tonight, he'll talk to them some other time, or send them a letter. Their absence this evening will do nothing to change his feelings for them. From time to time he will think about them. Once a week, at least, perhaps more often.

Feelings. The word gives him pause, if only for a moment, the way you might pause at a point of interest along the road. He hangs the shirts and necktie back in the closet. A polo shirt would be better.

"I should have bought something new," the wife says. "What am I supposed to wear? I took all my best things with me. I lost most of them. And the rest don't fit me anymore. Or don't look good on me."

Hofmeester points to what she's holding, a dress he apparently didn't know existed. An airy dress, but then she likes to go dressed airily. And this kind of weather calls for it as well.

"You really don't give a shit, do you?" she says. "Can't you see how hopelessly out of fashion this is? How horribly dated it is? Besides, there's no way. The fat . . ." She looks at him, helplessly really. Affronted by the changes her body has made.

"Fat?" he asks. "What fat?"

She acts as though she's come back to her master, he thinks. To dream of freedom, you must first have known the leash. For some people, the leash is hope.

He starts towards Tirza's room, but she stops him.

"Jörgen," she says. "They won't think it's weird that I'm here, will they?"

"Who?"

"The guests."

"The guests? They don't even know you."

"That's what I mean. Won't they wonder: Who is this? Who is this woman?"

"I don't think so. There are going to be a lot of people. One more won't make much difference. Besides, you're Tirza's mother. However you look at it. If people ask: 'What are you doing here?', you can just say: 'I'm Tirza's mother.' That seems to me like a plausible enough reason to be at the party."

She looks at him doubtfully, she's not convinced. And the clothes she's holding in her hand are out of fashion. Which makes it all that much worse. "But I left."

"No one's denying that. But people don't know that anymore. Or they've forgotten it. People have short memories. So many people go away. At Tirza's school they've always been very understanding about the situation. They've always shown me a great deal of consideration."

He smiles at the memory. The teachers who called him when the wife ran off with an old flame. He'll never forget that, how kind they were, without being pushy. For the rest, no one ever called, at least not for him.

They had sent Ibi to prep school at Barlaeus, but after some less-than-favorable experiences there, they had decided to send Tirza to Vossius. It was Hofmeester, mostly, who had decided that. He felt that Tirza was gifted. He had felt that way even back when she was only eleven months old and taking her first steps. Five steps, no more than that, but still, it was what one might call walking. He talked about it to anyone who would listen. "She's already walking, she's quite precocious." He was particularly keen to announce that to parents with children of about the same age, and he never noticed—in his own enthusiasm—how it irritated them. The word 'precocious' was always on the tip of his tongue. In the evening, when she was only a few months old, he would stand over her crib for minutes at a time, sometimes for almost half an hour, simply watching her sleep. Her arms spread-eagled. Sometimes she would smile in her sleep. Not even Tirza's mother was exactly sure what he was looking at. What he saw there. What he saw in the baby.

Ibi had moved to her own bed, it was Tirza who slept between them now. And when the wife wasn't there or when she came home late, Tirza slept next to her father. Sometimes the wife would find him curled up in one corner of the bed, because Tirza had a way of taking up a lot of space. He didn't mind. The bed was hers.

Gently, almost tenderly, he bumps the wife to one side.

Tirza, he notices, has closed her bedroom door. He doesn't want to disturb her, so he goes downstairs and checks on the kitchen.

Everything is in readiness. Everything is ready to be served and eaten. The color composition of the sushi and sashimi has a professional air to it, a look that transcends the domestic. As though it had been prepared by a catering service. That's how it looks.

Hofmeester leaves nothing to chance. One must always be on guard for what can go wrong. If you find yourself needing an excuse, you simply haven't prepared yourself thoroughly for a potentially fatal error.

In the garden he has set out torches, four in total. Later, when darkness falls, he will light them.

Jörgen Hofmeester walks to the shed, moves the lawnmower, the shovel, the chainsaw, and some smaller tools to one side. That way there's enough room for partygoers who want to step inside for a moment, to kiss discreetly. He steps out of the shed and looks at the trees. In his parents' garden in the Betuwe there are lots of trees too; now that his parents aren't around anymore, he, as the only child, is responsible for the garden. Fruit trees require pruning.

He saunters across the lawn, back to the house. He takes a deep breath, he is content. It's going to be a lovely party. Just the way Tirza hoped. "This is going to be my last party in this house," she'd said, "so I want it to be a big one. Is that okay, Daddy? A really big party."

"Yes, of course," he'd said. "But how big, exactly? What do you mean by 'big'? And do you want me to go away, would you prefer that? Shall I go out to the Betuwe for the weekend?"

"No," she said, "stay here. You always think my parties are fun, don't you?"

And he had nodded. "Yes," he said, "lots of fun."

Back in the kitchen, he hears the doorbell. He waits for a moment to see whether Tirza or the wife will open it. When they don't, he goes to the door himself. The ladies are too busy prettying themselves up.

It's Ibi. She's carrying a little weekend bag, which disappoints Hofmeester a bit, because it means she won't be staying long. She lives in France these days, about sixty kilometers northwest of Geneva.

He hugs her, forcedly, a bit clumsily, he steps on her toes, apologizes, mumbling. And that apology has something clumsy about it as well.

He had expected a great deal from his children, more from Tirza than from Ibi. From Ibi he had expected a great deal, from Tirza the world. That's how it was. That's how you'd have to put it. The world.

"You're squeezing me to death, Daddy," Ibi says. "Take it easy."

Sometimes his hugs are too curt, at others too enthusiastic. It's hard to find the right balance.

He takes her by the shoulders, steps back, but doesn't let go of her.

"You look good," he says, without knowing whether he means it, without really having looked at her at all.

"It's been frantic. The season has started."

Ibi, almost four years Tirza's elder, broke off her study of physics in order to start a bed and breakfast in France. When he thinks about it, when he actually stops to think about it, when he really lets it sink it, it makes Hofmeester sick. How can you give up physics for a bed and breakfast? Ibi met a Frenchman, she started the bed and breakfast with him. It was his idea, of course. What normal person would ever come up with something like that?

If you ask Hofmeester, he's not a real Frenchman at all, even though he has a French passport. He's just a colored man who, in accordance with the rules of the game, is after her money. He's already taken her honor, so what else is there? Hofmeester doesn't feel like talking about it anymore. It's a battle he's already lost.

When she told them she had decided to drop out of school and, as though that were not enough, informed her father and sister of her imminent plans to move to France, Hofmeester had decided to contact a social worker, who had then referred him to a psychologist.

"How can you trade in physics for a bed & breakfast, how can you abandon science in favor of making beds?" he had asked the man a few times during the session.

"Could it be, perhaps, that it makes your daughter happy?" the psychologist suggested at last. Hofmeester had looked in amazement at this man, this traitor to science, this charlatan. Happy? That both his daughters would take their degrees was something he assumed obvious, as the very least, the very least of the least. He wasn't about to abandon that assumption, and for the sake of what? For fleeting happiness. He spat on that. He clung tightly to the assumption of success, the image he'd devised of his childrens' lives. A beautiful, wonderful image it was, a classic vision, grand and impractical, but above all grand. He had raised them to serve science, not to be an innkeeper, folding sheets with a man of dubious origin. Ideals were not to be traded in for filthy happiness. He had stood up, shaken the psychologist's hand, left without a word, and never went back.

Ibi walks to the kitchen. She looks around. "Jesus, you've gone whole hog again. How many people are you expecting, anyway? Where's Tirza?"

"Upstairs. I suppose you've already heard?"

"What?"

"From Tirza."

"Heard what? What was I supposed to hear?"

"That Mama's here again. That she's come back. I don't know for how long, but she's back."

"Oh."

Ibi doesn't seem to consider it particularly big news. Perhaps it isn't big news. "Could I get something to drink?" she asks.

"Of course." Hofmeester is a bad host, he thinks, and a bad host is a bad father. He opens the fridge. "What would you like: beer, wine, lemonade? I've got homemade lemonade. Lemon, mineral water. and a little sugar. Natural as can be. Just the way you like it."

"A glass of milk."

He pours her a glass. She drinks it in one gulp. Then she wipes her mouth with the back of her hand.

"So, had you already heard or not?"

"About what?" She looks at him as though he's lost his marbles.

"About Mama."

"Yes, I'd already heard. Am I supposed to have an opinion on the subject?"

"Well . . ." He hesitates. Is she supposed to have an opinion on the subject? It's a good question. Is *he* supposed to have an opinion about it?

"I don't know whether you're supposed to have an opinion about it, but maybe you have something to say about it and, yes, maybe even an opinion."

"They're your lives." That look again. Maybe she's tired after the long trip. She had to leave home very early this morning. Change trains at Paris. With the metro from one station to the next. He's said it so often before: "If you've got baggage, take a taxi, I'll give you the money for it afterwards." But Ibi thinks taxis are a waste of money, and she jealously guards her independence.

Now that he's grown a bit used to Ibi's presence, he looks at what she's wearing. A pair of camouflage trousers and a T-shirt in colors he's not too wild about.

"So how are things?" she asks, putting the glass down on the counter. "I mean: otherwise. How are things otherwise?"

"Otherwise? Busy." He rinses the milk glass.

"Doing what?"

He feels her anger, no, more than just anger, her hatred. The inability to forgive, the hatred that smolders on long after others have forgotten.

"Work at the publishing house."

He doesn't ask her how things are going at her B&B. Her inn he buries under a mountain of silence. There is no greater service he can render. The fact that finally, when he saw that he'd lost anyway, he had given her money to open the bed & breakfast is something he has not been able to bury successfully. There are no blank spots in his past. No things he doesn't know about anymore, things he's removed from his memory. That has never worked for him. He remembers everything. He thinks. The historian's task is to select those details of importance for future generations; in doing so he consigns other details to oblivion. He who cannot forget has no life. In the forgetting lies the future. Hofmeester had stopped his own study of history after only six months, he had switched to German and criminology. He was unable to forget a thing. For that very reason, he groped around in his own past like a blind man.

All one needs in order to sabotage the truth is a defective memory. *Terra incognita.* One could go out exploring one's past like an unknown country. Like the jungle. Pygmies, a cauldron on a campfire. The cannibals wish you welcome and, while the water is slowly heating up, you see all the blank spots, no longer as blank spots, but as exactly the way things are. Like in a film, in a way. You finally realize who you are and then the water comes to a boil. Everything has its price.

She points to his cheek.

"You're bleeding."

"I just shaved."

She tears a little scrap off a paper towel and presses it against his cheek. There they stand, father and daughter, awkward but intimate. There is no denying it, this is what intimacy is, this is what remains of it after the perfunctory hugs in the hallway, at the airport, in a parking garage.

In her eyes he sees a remarkable coolness that he knows well, but which he's never gotten used to and has never wanted to figure out. He counts on the other to be forgiving, because he himself is prepared to forgive, once he has already withdrawn his talons. The talons of a predator, the talons of the real Hofmeester.

"Are you happy?" he asks as she dabs at his cheek with the piece of paper. Some of it sticks.

She looks at him in astonishment, but it's astonishment that is laid on thick, it's not real astonishment. It's the final, stubborn remainder of rage.

"Since when are you interested in my happiness, Daddy?"

He takes a step back. "I'm interested in your well-being. You're my daughter. I have only two daughters."

"Well-being isn't the same as happiness. Don't move, let me get the rest of the paper off your cheek."

He stands still as Ibi scratches at his cheek, he can feel her fingernail against his skin, he holds his breath and tries to remember his life back when he had no daughters, when he had no function; when he, as he has had to admit to himself afterwards, moved through space like an unguided missile, a missile which was, in addition to an editor at a publishing house, nothing more than a landlord.

The day Hofmeester went to the notary public to sign the deed for this house was the same day he decided to rent out the top floor. Otherwise it could be too much of a squeeze, the money, his meager wages. Whichever way you looked at it, the house was too big for him, even with a family.

At first he rented the floor only to travelling businessmen, for two or three months at a time. Men who worked all day and came home at night exhausted and collapsed on the bed, then left hurriedly in the morning in their neatly pressed suits.

The top floor was equipped with inexpensive but practical furnishings. The view, above all, was glorious. It looked out on Vondelpark. Whenever Hofmeester showed someone the apartment, he always made a point of showing them the park, in a way that made it seem as though it belonged to him. His park, his front yard.

And if the businessman said: "Fine, I'll take it," he would quickly produce a handwritten contract that could, if desired, be automatically prolonged each month.

"And if you pay in cash," Hofmeester said at the signing, in a tone that made it sound like a special, highly exclusive offer, "on the first of the month, if you pay in cash then, I'll give you a five-percent discount."

A five-percent discount. The tenants were keen on that.

And so, on the first of each month, Hofmeester would climb the stairs to collect his rent, which was usually waiting for him on the table in a little envelope. If it wasn't, he would hang around for a while, engaging in small talk, a meteorological dissertation, because he spoke about the weather with pleasure and apparent enthusiasm. And he waited. He was patient. Until the tenant finally reached for his wallet and counted out the agreed upon amount.

When it was time for the travelling salesmen to leave, Hofmeester always found a reason not to return the security deposit in its entirety, or actually: not at all. A rip in the wallpaper, a doorknob that had fallen off, a crack in the marble washbasin. "I'm sorry," he said, "but it wasn't like that when you moved in three months ago. I'll have to have it repaired. It's a shame, but this is going to cost me."

Not that Hofmeester acted in bad faith; he just needed the money, he was short on cash. His future depended on it. His daughters' future as well, later on. What was freedom if you had no money to finance it? Only the rich were free, and sometimes not even them.

He fibbed a bit from time to time, he didn't enjoy it, but he could fib along with the best of them. He pointed out dents in the ceiling that had been there for a long time, spots on the wallpaper that weren't new either, or he counted the knives and forks in the kitchen—the cutlery was part of the furnishings as well—and pretended to come up short. And along with these little white lies, shame entered his life.

He hated the tenant for not saying: "Well then, shall we agree to half the security deposit?"

So why not the entire security deposit? He hated the tenants for making him lie, because they were stingy, because they wanted to have their cake and eat it too. So that he, who had successfully studied German—all right, he hadn't completed his master's, but those were details, there was a perfectly good reason for that—was forced to nose around on the top floor of his own house, in search of new damage. He who had better things to do was forced to haggle about how much it would cost to have a dividing wall repainted. There were tenants who said: "You know what, I'll buy a bucket of paint tomorrow and do it myself. That will save you a lot of trouble and save me money." But that wasn't the point. It wasn't about the wall or the paint, it was about the deposit he couldn't pay back. The deposit that wasn't there anymore.

Skillfully, Hofmeester talked in circles, he exaggerated, he sighed, he moaned, he elicited pity and then, apparently for no good reason, he became aggressive. "If we can't agree on this before you leave, then you'll have to come down and get the deposit yourself, but I won't give it to you, because you have no right to it, you don't have a leg to stand on, you've made a mess of this place." He shook his fist and meant it, he lost himself in the negotiations the way another person might lose themselves in a film, a book, a play. There were moments when he was beside himself, when he had to get a grip on himself, to take a deep breath. After he had done that, he was all right again. A person has to be able to control himself, otherwise other people will do it for him.

The same way that went with his parents, who had grown increasingly eccentric in the '90s or, in hindsight, maybe even as early as the '80s. It wasn't senility, it was something else, an illness with no name. Hofmeester hadn't known how to deal with it, so he'd had his parents ruled incompetent. Once he'd done that it was all up to him—he had to see to everything, their finances, the house, the garden. He had their money transferred to his own account. He needed it. You couldn't actually call it immoral; his parents, after all, were not competent to handle their own affairs. The lawyer had assured him of that. The term said it all. Incompetent to handle their own affairs.

Hofmeester's father used to run a hardware store in Geldermalsen, his mother had sung in a choir, but she hadn't earned any money with that. Singing was her hobby.

And he, the only son, had moved up the ladder of success, that was what one had to do, that was what was expected of you. To move up. Because the richest of the rich were the only ones who didn't get browbeaten.

Hofmeester's parents had been browbeaten, you could tell by looking at them, you could smell it on them.

Once he had regained his composure, he would point out archly that the tenant had been allowed to stay in the house five days longer than was agreed, at no extra charge. And finally he would say: "You know what? I won't charge you for any of the extras, but we'll forget about the security deposit. We'll forget about that. The security deposit. Deal?"

Then he would go back downstairs as quickly as possible, able only to shake off the nagging self-repulsion by reminding himself for the umpteenth time that he was doing this for his family. First of all for himself and his wife, later and above all for his daughters. For their future. Saints, he had once heard in church, require a past; sinners a future. His daughters were the exceptions to that rule: they required a future, but they were no sinners.

Gradually the tenants began staying longer. It saved him the trouble of looking for a new one every three months. Or calling in an agency that would only charge absurd rates for abominable service; he'd always sworn never to do that.

Hofmeester preferred to see to things himself. He sought out tenants as though they were a bridegroom for his daughters, that's how carefully he went to work. To find the right one, he pored over want ads in almost every newspaper he could lay his hands on.

The quietest, the neatest, the most reliable, the cleanest. Preferably one who had another address elsewhere, who only needed a pied-a-terre, who officially resided somewhere else. And Hofmeester went to considerable lengths to keep this supplementary income out of the hands of the tax service. Liberty and hunger, after all, were foes. And although he had never known hunger, he had been raised with a fear of it that had never left him.

What remained was the climbing of the stairs on the first of each month, if the tenant failed to drop the envelope with the agreed sum through Hofmeester's mail slot first. That was the recurring ritual in his life. His high mass. Thus, and only thus, did he serve the godhead. On the first of the month he retrieved that which was his.

When he came back down again, always with the feeling of having sullied himself, he would sit in the living room and count the money. Then he would tuck it away in a safe place, until he had accumulated enough to deposit discreetly on a foreign account. First Luxembourg, later Switzerland. And as he counted and recounted, he was regularly overcome by thoughts of financial independence. Overcome, that was the word for it, the thoughts came over him, wouldn't let go of him. At such moments he was held hostage by his own visions. He calculated how many years stood between him and that independence. He counted the months. If only sickness and death didn't get to him before financial independence did. Then it was a matter of decades. Maybe less. If the financial markets helped out a bit.

But the joy concerning the capital now gradually accruing abroad, the money which would see to it that Ibi and Tirza would never know anything like poverty, which would open to them doors that were opened only to the rich, which would allow them to study at the best universities anywhere in the world, was decimated by the humiliating climb Hofmeester was forced to make on the first day of the month. He could never figure out why the tenant didn't just come by with the rent himself, especially after he had insisted on that a few times. But at eight o'clock in the evening on the first of the month, if the tenant still hadn't shown up, he would go outside and ring the bell of the door next to his. The door that opened onto the dwelling Hofmeester rented out. He couldn't put it off any longer, he was too afraid that the tenant might forget him altogether.

He would ring the bell, even on Sundays. The first of the month was the first of the month. Hofmeester knew no Sundays, for he had a dream. And he forgave his debtors just as they forgave him. The money was the forgiveness. Ultimately, when push came to shove, forgiveness was always money.

But even this forgiveness couldn't keep him from sleeping fitfully, starting on the twenty-seventh or twenty-eighth of each month. He dreamed about the tenant, about the envelope, about breakage in his apartment. He dreamed that he climbed the stairs to the tenant's and found everything gone; the furniture, the cutlery, the tenant himself, the clothes, the cupboards, everything; the only thing he found there was water running over the floor and the corpse of a cat, in an advanced state of decomposition, in the kitchen sink. Even though he had clearly informed the tenant that pets were not allowed. Not even goldfish.

The gentle but distressing sound of water drip-dripping onto a carpet, that's how his dream always ended. With the cat's corpse in the sink, and with Hofmeester wailing and searching the apartment for an unfindable envelope containing the rent. His nightmares were soggy with leaks, moist with mold, fuzzy with cat hair. In his sleep he was haunted by the ghosts of property management.

One day, desperate as he was, tense from a lack of sleep, he suddenly had a brilliant idea. "Ibi," he said. She was twelve at the time, she played the violin, she played tennis and was generally seen as intelligent and good-looking. "Ibi," he said again, "how would you like to earn five guilders and an ice cream cone?"

She nodded dreamily. She was a dreamy-eyed child. Others called her hazy. He didn't, he stuck to dreamy-eyed.

"I want you to go upstairs in a minute, to the tenant, and I want you to say: 'I've come for the rent.' He'll give you an envelope. And you bring it to me. Don't dawdle and don't take anything else. But don't forget your manners either."

He walked her to the door, opened it, then stood there and watched as she rang the tenant's bell.

There she went. His daughter. One of the two apples of his eye. A wonderful child. There was no denying it. That was how he often put it: "She's a wonderful child. There's no denying it." As though that were a foregone conclusion, not open to discussion. Sort of like the force of gravity.

When he heard her climbing the stairs he would shut the door and wait impatiently in his own vestibule for her to return, his eyes fixed on the doormat, his arms crossed.

Two minutes later she was back and Hofmeester pounced on the envelope like a hungry beast. He counted it once, he counted it twice. The banknotes flashed through his fingers as though he were shuffling a deck of cards. Then he tucked the money away in the chest of drawers, in his secret hiding place, and, after running his hand fondly over Ibi's dark blonde hair, handed her five guilders and a little more for ice cream.

"Can I go and buy it now?" she asked.

"What?"

"The ice cream."

"Yes," the father said, "that's fine. Go on. But hurry. We're going to eat dinner in a few minutes."

And she ran out the door. Happy and relieved. Unhampered by any shame or filth that might be clinging to her. Filth meant nothing to her.

From that day on it became a family tradition: Ibi collected the rent.

Ibi did what the father could no longer do. On the first of each month she went upstairs to retrieve that to which the Hofmeester family had a right.

After a time she grew so used to it that she herself was often the one who said: "Papa, today's the first. I'm going upstairs."

And he had come to rely on her talents, her charm, her insight into the human psyche, which boiled down to insight into the tenant's psyche. She actually seemed to develop a peculiar—in Hofmeester's eyes, almost perverse—pleasure in performing this task, which he had always somehow felt too good for, he felt that it besmirched him, besmirched him more with each passing month, made him more impure with each step he climbed. But there was one major difference between Ibi and her father: Hofmeester collected the rent for real. She only had to play that she was doing it. As she climbed the stairs, she was imitating her father. She parodied him, one might say. She was not an adult, but she pretended to be, and with a vengeance. She did so with verve. And that imitation was an act of deliverance; by mimicking him she expelled her father's demons. In her imitation of him, in her sometimes grotesque hyperbole, lay her freedom.

After a time, Hofmeester no longer even needed to warn her. "Don't dawdle and don't accept anything else from him. Come back right away." She knew the rules, she was aware of the protocols that accompanied the ritual, and she was actually proud to have completed the monthly mission with flying colors. To her, the rent was booty to be taken, and she was allowed to share in the spoils.

On occasion she would come back from her visit to the tenant and tell her father: "He asked if it's okay to pay you in a couple of days."

Then Hofmeester would say: "Of course that's okay, but not with a five percent discount. I only offer the discount if they pay in cash on the first of the month, not if they pay in cash on the third or the fourth. Then it's the full sum. Don't forget that. The first of the month is over at midnight, and after that it's payment in full."

And when she would show up on the third or fourth of the month with the full sum, he would sit down at his desk and count, adding machine within reach. The money in the foreign account grew, for after all, money is supposed to grow. With fertile ground, and in the right hands, it proliferates like weeds. She stood there and watched. Ibi stared at her father as he counted the money, with a knowing look and something you could call tenderness. As though she were already a step ahead of him. It was no longer the father looking tenderly at the daughter, but the daughter gazing tenderly at the father.

And once he had scraped enough cash together, he would take two days off from work and travel to Switzerland to deposit the rent money at a reliable bank, where experts invested on his behalf, in order to bring financial independence just that much closer. Slowly, but closer. Day by day. Hour by hour. Minute by minute.

Ibi grew older, she started high school, started wearing makeup, in as far as she hadn't already done so in elementary school, she started wearing more makeup, she became moody and swore at her parents, she lost interest in the violin; oh, the bitter disappointments of raising children, but what never changed, what remained, was the ritual: on the first of the month, she went upstairs to collect the rent.

And when she came back down with the envelope, she would look at her father conspiratorially, as though she knew what she had just done, as though she understood her complicity, as though she realized it was wrong. As though she could see through his shame. And that insight made her less free, it made her an accomplice to the man she had to call "Daddy."

When he was finished counting he would hug her, he pressed her against him and held her like that for a moment. This ordinary mission had taken on substance, meaning. It was what bound father and daughter together, it was their secret, even though it wasn't really a secret, it was their covenant. It was in fact the only moment when they became father and daughter again, not strangers who just happened to live in the same house, use the same bathroom and occasionally scarf down dinner at the same table.

He no longer gave her money for an ice cream cone, but for a skirt or a movie. He no longer said what it was for, he simply gave it. Silently, with a wink. Sometimes, when he saw financial independence approaching faster than expected, for the stock market in those days was doing its utmost, he would give his daughter a raise.

Often she came downstairs with messages from the tenant as well; that he wanted to give notice, or perhaps even that he wanted to prolong the contract. She shielded her father from that which he detested so badly. And after a few years it was as though it had never been any other way. As though this was meant to be. The Hofmeesters had a family business.

Tenants came and tenants went, but on the first of the month Hofmeester's eldest daughter climbed the stairs to the top floor. Admittedly, for her it was a piece of cake: people enjoyed paying her. Paying her was a pleasure. That she came in person to receive the envelope was a favor done to the tenant.

Once Ibi began collecting the rent there were fewer complaints about moisture on the wallpaper, radiators that were on the blink, a window that didn't close completely. Her smile took away the complaints, her legs caused the sneaking suspicion that one was paying way too much to vanish into thin air. Her eyes compensated for the leaky faucet. Ibi was more important than any defects in the furnished apartment.

And then, one autumn evening, on the first of the month—always the first of the month, when Hofmeester looked back on his life he saw an endless series of paydays—she stayed away for a long time. Hofmeester was reading the evening paper and listening to one of Elgar's cello concertos. But when he got to the op-ed page, for he read the newspaper from cover to cover like a book, he began to worry. She had been gone for more than half an hour. He read on, but the readers' opinions no longer sank in. After each sentence he became bogged down, and his thoughts gravitated to Ibi.

Of course you couldn't just grab the money and run, sometimes you had to stop and chat a little. He remembered that from when the unwelcome task had been his to fulfill. But half an hour was no chat anymore. That was a conversation, that was half an evening meal.

He had already walked to the door twice to see if she was coming, the way one looks for streetcars that somehow refuse to arrive. In the ridiculous assumption that looking will make any difference. That a cursory glance could summon that which it seems will never show up.

She couldn't have been mugged; she didn't even have to leave the house.

It puzzled him, and it continued to puzzle him. His wife had gone to pick up Tirza, who was playing at a friend's house. Hofmeester had no one with whom to share his anxiety. He switched off the Elgar, went into the garden to look at his apple tree, then peered up through the branches at the windows behind which no tenant could be seen, but he detected nothing unusual. The curtains that had always hung there (in fact, they needed washing). But no movement. It was a lovely evening, for early October. Nothing rustled in the bushes. No screams. Silence. Eternal silence.

He went back to the living room—what else could he do?—and took the newspaper off the couch.

A few days earlier, Ibi had turned fifteen. Some of her birthday presents were still on display on the buffet. They always did that when it was one of the children's birthdays. The "gift table," they called it. Even now, even though Ibi had already turned fifteen. The paper streamers, too. Hofmeester hung them from the ceiling the way he had once collected the rent: systematically and diligently.

He stared at the presents, including the watch he had given Ibi, the watch she had asked him for. And he had picked out a good one for her, he had shopped around for days. It was an expensive watch, but why not, when your daughter has just turned fifteen?

He wanted to buy her something she would like, a watch she really wanted to have, one she could show proudly to her friends.

There was a pair of slacks on the gift table as well, and a game he couldn't figure out. A bathing suit. Two books. A drawing Tirza had made, of a boat. The rest had already been put away, eaten, or were already in use.

Then he decided to ring the bell. This was taking too long. The tenant, he was almost sure of it, must be bothering her with all kinds of ridiculous complaints with which he—Andreas was his name, a young German architect—had already harassed Hofmeester the last time they met on the street. On the street! Tenants these days had no manners. No sense of propriety. He could sense it, he could see it and he had read about it. People had grown reckless, that recklessness hung in the air like a greasy pall. That was what Hofmeester smelled in the evening when he went out for a walk in the park. A combination of lethargy and recklessness had taken hold of the city's inhabitants, and it was a combination that frightened Hofmeester, that excluded him, that he couldn't take part in because he had realized early on that recklessness was the natural enemy of achieving his deep-rooted objective: making sure the children were better off.

The opposite of recklessness was: counting on everything that can go wrong to in fact go wrong.

He shook his head, even though there was no one there to see him. Downright rude, that's what it was, confronting a fifteen-year-old girl with the defects of a furnished apartment!

Hofmeester rang the bell of the door beside his own. Firmly, but not too persistently. A landlord had to remain polite. The wooden doorframe could stand a lick of paint, he saw; next spring, perhaps. Not now. Now he had to save money, otherwise he could kiss financial independence farewell.

Maybe Ibi had gone off shopping. But she knew she always had to give him the rent first. She'd always been reliable. She understood the importance of the ritual. She knew what it meant to her father.

No one answered the door. The bell had been rung, but the door did not open. Apparently the architect was not at home, or else he was sleeping.

Hofmeester's unrest grew. He took his key ring from his pocket and searched for the key to the tenant's door.

On weekdays, when he happened to be at home during the day, he would sometimes sneak into the upstairs apartment. Not really to spy on his tenants, only to see what was really going on, who he was actually dealing with here. Just to know one's bird, as they say. He opened cupboards and drawers, but rarely found anything damning. Never anything more than a little pornography, a notice from the debt-collection agency, love letters. He always leafed through them. You couldn't be too careful. Yet it had made one thing clear to him: When people have secrets, they don't hide them away in their pied-à-terre.

Again he rang the bell. Just to be sure. A little more persistently this time, but not overmuch. That would be impolite.

No reaction this time either.

Cautiously he opened the door, with a vague sense of guilt, a little like an intruder actually, and climbed the steep stairs. Slowly. He was, he noticed, a bit short of breath.

That evening was the first time he realized he was getting old. Physical shortcomings brought with them the inevitable end to the last illusions of youth. And shortness of breath was a physical shortcoming, there was no denying that.

He panted. He heard music, something modern, but with violins. So there was someone home after all, or else the architect had forgotten to turn off the stereo. Leaving lamps on all day. Turning on the heater in winter with the windows open. They became more decadent and impertinent with each passing year. It wasn't even decadence, really; it was a perverse indifference that Hofmeester took as a personal affront, because it was something he couldn't permit himself. Because it was something he refused to permit himself.

The shortness of breath grew worse. Halfway up the stairs he paused. He wasn't developing heart problems, was he? Maybe he should go in for a checkup, have them do a cardiogram or whatever those things were called. In any case, a total and radical checkup. Once, long ago, he had smoked cigars, but while the wife was carrying Ibi he had given them up. It couldn't be the cigars, it had to be something else. Another, unknown ailment was to blame for his shortness of breath.

The higher up the stairs he came, the louder the music became. He could make out every word of the lyrics, but he wasn't paying attention. Never before had it cost him so much effort to climb a little flight of stairs. So this was how death began, with a shortness of breath on the stairs. A joke, that's what it was. Life.

Hofmeester entered the space that served as the living room. The door was open. There was no occasion to knock.

The tenant was standing behind Ibi. His pants around his ankles.

Hofmeester's daughter was lying bare-chested on the dining room table he had once picked out himself, and which had seemed to him extremely well-suited for an apartment that was to be rented out fully-furnished. Her denim skirt was hiked up around her waist. Hiked up, that was the expression that stuck in Hofmeester's mind. Hiked up. Hiked up.

The scene reminded him of certain movies broadcast after midnight by those unsavory cable channels. And then that music.

All worries about his shortness of breath had disappeared. His thoughts of an early demise, there on the stairs a few moments earlier, were forgotten.

For a second he stood and looked at Ibi. Then he took a step forward. Still panting a bit, he reached out with his left hand and picked up a little floor lamp the wife had bought for their own home, but which they had ultimately found less that suitable. Castoffs found their way upstairs.

His daughter was being fucked like an animal. A sight one expected on a farm, in a stable. Not on the most exclusive stretch of Van Eeghenstraat.

Hofmeester's lungs peeped.

He tightened his hold on the floor lamp. He was nailed to the spot. It felt as though he himself were being fucked, hard and deep. As though the thrusts were directed not at his daughter, but at him. As though he were being debased, the landlord, the owner of this house, humiliated in his own home. His whole body hurt. His body was gasping for breath.

He had the peculiar sensation of being ripped open. The longer he watched, the more convinced he became that he was the one the tenant was fucking, hard and indifferently. With disdain.

At last they heard him.

That is, at least the tenant heard him. The man turned, saw his landlord, let go of Ibi, his hands slipped from her waist.

Then the architect did something Hofmeester couldn't stand: he grinned. With his pants, with a pair of gray trousers, down around his knees. He grinned as though it were all a joke, an unfortunate yet comical encounter. The grin of hilarity was glued to the architect's face. This may all be a bit distressing for you, old man, but what a laugh! That was what he exuded. Hilarity, nothing but hilarity.

No shame, no fear. A grin.

Hofmeester tightened his grip on the floor lamp. He took a few steps towards the tenant, looked him in the eye, and then, while Ibi was clambering off the dinner table as though it had occurred to her only now that an untimely end had come to their copulation, he brought the lamp down hard on the tenant's head. Hofmeester heard the sound of breaking glass, then saw spots, as though he had stood up too quickly. He felt dizzy, but he did not fall to the floor. The tenant did.

Without much at all in the way of noise, the tenant fell.

Perhaps it was the music, which was playing so loudly that everything else was drowned out. How could people play music so loudly? Didn't they have any respect for their neighbors? Didn't the noise of city traffic punish one's ears badly enough as it was?

The architect had fallen. Hofmeester stood there with the floor lamp in his hand and heard his daughter wail: "Daddy."

On the floor around him lay glass. The little spherical lampshade had shattered. And there he stood, the remains of the floor lamp in his hand. A stick, that's all that was left. For a split second he had no idea where he was anymore. Or why he was there, what he had come there to do. He had to get a grip on himself, he had to stop and think.

She was wailing. Ibi was wailing like a baby. Like a hysterical woman.

She ran to one corner of the room and then back again. She covered her breasts. She pulled her denim skirt down around her hips. She didn't forget to do that. She wasn't *that* hysterical. She kept tugging at it, she clutched at it, she clamped onto her denim skirt as though it were a life-buoy.

If you only heard her wailing you might think: A mental case, a fugitive from the psychiatric clinic down the street. You might say: She's in the grip of madness, her madness has got the best of her.

Her face looked older than her body. It was probably the makeup that did it. By pretending to be grown-up so often and with such verve, she had actually grown up a little. You could see it in her expression. In her eyes. In the way she looked.

But her body told a different story.

Her upper arms were thin as could be. Thin as a child's. There was no flesh on her backside. That was all still to come. The story her body told was childlike.

No reason to wail like that, no reason to act so hysterical.

In combination with her denim skirt, her tennis shoes, a popular brand whose name Hofmeester could never recall, had something touching about them.

Everything, he was seeing everything, he took it all in as his daughter ran back and forth across the tenant's living room, as though unable to figure out what had happened to her, which was probably exactly the case. An animal, driven to panic by a thunderstorm of a summer's evening.

But the father couldn't utter a word. He stood there with the remains of the floor lamp in his hand.

He saw an envelope on the table. The rent.

That was why Ibi had come here. It had been lying there, waiting for her, the envelope. But something had happened and the envelope was still lying there. Innocent and untouched.

The money brought him back to his senses. Money was like a bucket of cold water in the face. The thought of the rent freed him from his overpowering sense of paralysis.

Slowly, the tenant's body was beginning to show signs of life as well. He moved. He struggled to his feet. He stood up. He pulled himself up on the edge of the table. Blood was dripping from a cut high on the left side of his forehead.

His trousers had fallen down around his ankles again.

The grin, fortunately, had been wiped from his face.

Then Hofmeester realized precisely where he was. It registered. He looked for Ibi. His Ibi. That's why he was here. Ibi had not come home.

He had been listening to Elgar and reading the paper, until it started taking too long, until he became suspicious.

He put down the floor lamp, or what was left of it, and cleared his throat.

The tenant looked at him, confused, as though he too had no idea what had happened, as though no one here understood exactly what was going on.

But Hofmeester remembered the humiliation, the tenant standing behind Ibi, triumphant and hungry, that's how he'd stood there. The triumph of the beast, he wouldn't be forgetting that soon. The triumph of the man. Because that's what sex is for a man, a conquest. I have her, I take her, I use her, I put her to use.

And because of that memory, Hofmeester also remembered what it was he was planning to say. What he had to say, what he had been meaning to say for a while now.

"Turn off that music," he shouted.

He remembers that too, now that he thinks back on it; he didn't speak, he shouted. He was able to shout louder than the music, he could shout and drown out everything and everyone.

The young architect stepped back, and only then, as he tried to walk, did he notice his predicament. How uncomfortable it was to face one's landlord with one's trousers and underpants around one's ankles.

He pulled up his trousers, quickly and clumsily. On his forehead was a big, bloody spot. The blood hadn't clotted yet, it was still fresh and it dripped. But the nakedness seemed to bother him more, the nakedness was more urgent.

The architect wore boxer shorts, Hofmeester noticed. He despised boxer shorts.

And he noticed something else: the man was not wearing a condom.

Hofmeester was disgusted by the architect. He had disliked him from the very start. Too chummy, too ingratiating, too unctuous and, when it came right down to it, too demanding. If his daughter hadn't been there he would have wrapped his hands around the architect's throat and throttled the life out of him, the way you might squeeze the life out of a kitten. Just bear down a little, don't let up, just stay focused and the life is gone.

Once the architect had more or less arranged himself—his shirt was still unbuttoned to his navel—and moved out of Hofmeester's reach, he stumbled over to the CD player and turned it off.

"Well, well," Hofmeester said, "it was about time. Christ."

He ran his tongue over his lips and gestured to the tenant, but the tenant didn't understand.

"Button it," Hofmeester said, "your shirt. I can see everything. I don't want to see everything. I've seen too much as it is."

Ibi was standing at the door, her upper body swaying rhythmically back and forth. She was crying soundlessly.

The tenant buttoned his shirt, all the way to the top.

Then Hofmeester brought his right fist down on the table so hard that it hurt, and the tenant took two steps back. "You pay for this apartment," Hofmeester shouted. Because he remembered that he needed to shout, that he had resolved to roar wildly, like a wounded animal. "You pay for the furnishings, for the gas and electricity, for the view of the park, for the privilege of living on the best part of Van Eeghenstraat, in the best part of Amsterdam, and that at a reasonable price, extremely reasonable I might add, but you don't pay for my daughter. Do you read me? *Not* for my daughter."

He pressed his right palm against his forehead, as though trying to think of what else he wanted to say, but he had nothing else to say. This was what he had wanted to say. He had said it. Now he could leave. Yes, he had said everything there was to say. He could go now. He had denounced an abuse.

But, contrary to what he had expected, the architect did not simply stand there crestfallen, in guilty silence. The architect said hoarsely: "You're going to regret this. You haven't heard the last of this." He dabbed at his forehead and saw the blood sticking to his hand. He looked at it dazedly, more dazed than shocked really. Being confronted with his own blood, it seemed, brought on the pain. For now he moaned. No, he whimpered. A namby-pamby, on top of all the rest. Namby-pambies were the worst.

And Hofmeester heard his daughter whisper: "Andreas."

That was what infuriated him. Ibi's whisper. His daughter calling the tenant "Andreas." To him, the tenant had no name. A tenant who had a name was in the process of becoming family, which made it impossible to kick him out. The tenant's name was tenant. Nothing more.

Where had he gone wrong? Why hadn't he paid more attention? How could he ever have let this man into his house?

"I'm going to file a complaint," the architect said, his accent more pronounced than ever. "You can count on that. I'm going to report this, Mr. Hofmeester. This is going to have consequences." He kept staring at the blood on his hand. It wasn't that much blood. A few drops. Like he'd cut himself while working in the garden.

As though by reflex, Hofmeester picked up the floor lamp again. But only to have something to hold on to, really, more to lean on than to have a weapon in his hand. What kind of weapon, after all, was a broken floor lamp?

As a boy, Hofmeester had found himself covered in blood often enough. Had he ever made a big fuss about that?

"So will I," was all he said. "You can count on that as well. I'm going to file a complaint. My daughter is not for rent. She is not included in the price."

He was shouting again.

Then he snatched the envelope from the table and strode over to Ibi, who had stopped crying. She was standing against the wall, shivering.

How thin she was. Still only a child. Now that the diddling was over, that was clear to see. No one could deny it.

"Come with me," he said.

She shook her head.

"Come," he said again.

"I'm staying here," she shouted.

Hofmeester looked at his daughter. Her hands covering her little breasts. On the couch lay her blouse, a birthday present as well. From her mother. And from Tirza. They had gone together to buy it for her. He picked it up, handed it to his daughter, and said: "Put this on, Ibi, and let's go."

The architect was still standing beside the CD player, the back of his hand pressed against his forehead. Afraid of bleeding to death, probably.

The man was too dazed or too timid to go to the bathroom and look for something in the medicine cabinet. A Band-Aid. That would have been enough.

Ibi turned to face the wall and put on her blouse. Like in the locker room at school. She barely went to the trouble of buttoning it. She wasn't wearing a bra. She didn't think that was necessary. "I'm almost completely flat anyway," she had said one evening. "Why should I have to wear a bra?"

It was a rhetorical question, and Hofmeester had left it unanswered. His wife was not at home that evening. His wife was rarely at home. "You run around like a bitch in heat," he'd told her once. "What are your daughters supposed to think?"

"I'm staying here," Ibi said, once her blouse was buttoned and she no longer needed to face the wall. "I'm staying with Andreas." She had grown calm. Along with the calm came the stubbornness.

Andreas. That name again. Hofmeester felt like he'd been hit with a poker. He didn't know any Andreas. He didn't want to know any Andreas.

Idi looked pale. A few tears were still running down her cheeks. That was part of being an adolescent. Screaming, wailing, weeping. Nothing to worry about. Other adolescents did the same.

She looked at the tenant, the way she had probably looked at him the first time they'd met, when she came here to collect the rent, strict but yearning, straightforward but enticing. Confident,

"What floor lamp?"

"The tenant's. The one you bought for us, originally."

"Is that what the problem is?"

He sighed. He switched the envelope from one hand to the other.

"The problem?" He tried to remember what the problem was and how it could best be formulated in a few words. "No, that's not the problem."

Then the wife looked at her daughter. "Ibi," she said, "what's going on here? What's the problem?"

Ibi said nothing. She stared at her father. Contempt, pity, and rage, that was what he saw. His eldest daughter held him in contempt. Then he turned back to the wife.

"The problem," Hofmeester said, "is the tenant. The tenant has to go. He's destroying us."

Ibi stepped forward. Not towards her mother, towards her father. "No," she said, "Andreas isn't the problem. You're the problem, Daddy. And you have been for a long time."

Instinctively, he raised his hand.

He didn't hit his children. He hit, but not his children. Except for this one time. A minute or so ago. An exception. A little faux pas.

He lowered his hand. This time he held himself in check, he had everything under control again. He had to keep himself under control. The rest would then follow. Dealing with day-to-day concerns, watering the lawn during dry spells, pruning the trees, collecting the rent, life itself. Keeping yourself under control, that was the main thing.

"Go ahead, hit me again," Ibi said. "You can't beat my love for Andreas out of me anyway."

Again that name, that horrible damned name.

He looked at his wife, but saw no sign of understanding there. No sympathy.

Love for Andreas. At some other moment he would have laughed, laughed loud and hard, but with just a touch of concern. What did his daughter know about love? "Such grand words," he would have liked to say, "do be careful when you use them."

"Could someone please tell me what's going on?"the wife asked. She sounded annoyed. As though he were a stranger to her, a boy who had accosted her daughter on the street, and she wanted to hear exactly what had happened before passing judgment.

Without answering he went into the kitchen, stuck the envelope in his pocket, and washed his hands. Once, then a second time, and then a third time he washed his face, in the hope that it would dispel the smoldering headache. He dried his face with a dishcloth. He couldn't find a towel.

When he came back into the room the wife and his daughters were sitting on the couch, the three of them, looking at him. They didn't say a word. The only sound was the smacking Tirza made as she sucked on her lolly. It was deafening.

The newspaper had slid to the floor. He folded it and laid it on the coffee table.

Why weren't they saying anything? What did they expect from him? What else could he have done? Nothing? Look and then go sneaking off?

He loosened the top button of his shirt, as though that was what was making it hard to breathe, constrictive clothing.

"Tirza," he said, "throw away that lollipop. Lollies are bad for your teeth."

There was no reaction. The mother wasn't backing him. All the mother said was: "Leave the child alone. You've done enough damage as it is."

The shortness of breath was gone. What arrived in its stead was a feeling of stiffness, all over his body. Maybe he should make an appointment with a physical therapist. Or play more tennis. Pain, that's what it was, his body was in pain.

"Damage?" Hofmeester said. "What damage? What are you talking about? Damage? Do you have any idea what was going on up there? Do you have any idea at all what goes on in your own home?"

"It was your idea," the wife said quietly, "to rent out that floor of the house. You didn't have to do it for my sake."

The muscles around Hofmeester's mouth seemed paralyzed. As though a dentist had deadened his gums and he still couldn't speak properly.

"Didn't have to do it? But how could we have stayed here otherwise? Didn't have to do it. It was for you," he shouted, "for all of you, that's why I did it. For your future. And Tirza, take that lollipop out of your mouth."

He looked at his wife and daughters, but they didn't seem to understand. "Didn't have to," he mumbled. "Didn't have to." All he could do was shake his head at such obtuseness.

"Jörgen," the wife said, "Ibi is a big girl. Ibi is a woman. This is no way to act towards her friends."

"But it's not her friend," Hofmeester shouted. "It's the tenant. Don't you people understand that? Don't you understand anything? And she isn't a woman yet. She's a child, a child. It's my fault. I should never have sent her upstairs for the rent."

He looked at his own family, in search of something like sympathy, but saw nothing of the sort. He was speaking a different language. He was from a different country. He was foreign to his wife and children, a *Fremdkörper* in the body of the family. A vestige, but of what? Of the impregnation. Of the fact that he had impregnated his wife on two occasions. That's what he was the vestige of. A vestigial organ, like an appendix. And only one thing stood between him and total obsolescence: the money.

"You're so out of it," Ibi said. "Do you really think I'm the only one in my class with an older boyfriend?"

He looked at the wife, but she seemed to think this was normal. One of those everyday statements that go floating past like clouds in the sky. Everything that amazed him, she found normal. Everything he repudiated, she approved of and considered no problem at all. Old-fashioned was what he was, a stick in the mud. Indeed, a vestige from some other epoch.

"But," Hofmeester said, and he heard the desperation in his own voice, "that's not your boyfriend. That's the tenant. That can't be your boyfriend. That's the tenant."

"Daddy," Tirza said.

He looked at her. She was small for her age. She was one of the smallest children in the class, but the pediatrician had said her growth spurt would come in good time. That there was nothing to worry about.

"Daddy," Tirza said again.

"Yes?" he said, and he realized that he was standing before his own family as though before a tribunal. "Please get rid of that lolly. You don't even like it. It's pure chemical garbage. And there's other candy you like better."

"I have a boyfriend too. He's in Miss Stine's class."

Hofmeester wiped his forehead. Sweat on his hands, sweat on the back of his neck, sweat everywhere. Maybe it had something to do with his shortness of breath, and to the stiffness in his chest, arms, and legs. This body of his had become a liability. An instrument that no longer served its purpose and which he should actually dispose of, if replacements weren't impossible to get. This was old age, it had started today, on the stairs.

"That's very nice," he said. "You can tell us all about it this evening, at dinner, about Miss Stine."

"Not about Miss Stine. About my boyfriend."

"Of course, that's what I meant, Tirza, of course that's what I meant. About your boyfriend."

Then they all fell silent. Hofmeester's mind began to wander and he felt that everything had now been set aright. That this evening they would all talk about Miss Stine and about the boyfriend. They would sit at the table the way they did every evening. Perhaps a bit uncommunicatively; Ibi was often brusque these days, but that was part of being an adolescent. They would sit at the table, he would sit at the table. This was his family, these were the members of his family. He belonged with these people, that would sink in later, at the table, once Tirza started talking about Miss Stine, or about her boyfriend.

Just when he had almost convinced himself that everything was back to normal, that everything was going the way it always had, he heard the wife ask: "So how are you going to make up for this?"

He straightened his shoulders. Whenever he was thinking hard or lost in daydreams, he had a tendency to slouch a little.

"Make up for it? What are you talking about?"

And Tirza, in her high, sweet little voice, said: "Yeah, Daddy, how are you going to make up for this?"

He tugged at his lower lip. He had the feeling there was nowhere for him to run, and that in his own home.

"But Tirza," he said, as though she were the only one who had posed the question. "There's nothing for me to make up for. The tenant has something to make up for. Because he's a dirty man. He's a dirty architect. He's a dirty tenant. He's so dirty that he can't even make up for it anymore. I'm going to throw him out of the house."

"Then I'm leaving too," Ibi shouted. "Then I'm leaving right now. I'm packing my bags. I'm leaving tonight."

She got up, walked over to the gift table.

"Don't you see what you're doing?" the wife asked. She spoke neither quietly nor calmly now. "Don't you see what you're doing? Do you understand anything about your own daughter?"

"I understand a great deal about my daughter," he said. "I understand that she has been molested. No: that she has been raped, and that she's confused. That we need to see a doctor. To go to the police. That's what I understand. That she may be pregnant."

"No," Ibi screamed. "Make him stop. Make him stop."

She picked up the watch he had given her for her birthday. She held it in her hand.

"Stop what? What am I supposed to stop, Ibi? Are you telling me what to do in my own home? Are you trying to tell me what I'm allowed to do?"

"I'm not pregnant," Ibi screamed. "I'm on the pill, dickhead." She threw the watch down on the floor in front of her and stamped on it with her right foot, as though trying to squash a big spider. She kept stamping until the creature was dead. "And I don't want that either," she shouted. "I don't want anything you have to give. I don't want anything from you ever again."

Hofmeester wiped his nose, although nothing needed wiping. Too old, he had been too old to become a father, and against his will in fact. Back when he was young, there had been Expressionist poets who had served as both the child and the pet in his life.

"Why don't I ever hear about anything?" he asked quietly. "Why doesn't anyone tell me anything? Why am I always the last to know?"

"Because you never ask," the wife said. "You never ask anything. Do you actually exist? Do you really live here with us?"

So that's it, he thought, I never ask anything. But how does one go about asking certain things? And when? During dessert? Or on a rainy Sunday afternoon?

"That's fine for you to say," he said, calmly at first, "you who go running off almost every night like a bitch in heat. I do everything, I'm pleased to do everything, by the way, I go to the parent-teachers' meetings, I stay home to watch the kids, but you're not there, you don't have to be there, because you're an artist. Yes, dear children, your mother is an artist. No one will buy her work, and strictly between us: it's a horror to look at. But that doesn't matter to her, she just keeps on painting." Now he raised his voice. "And then she blames me for not knowing that my eldest daughter is on the pill. How was I supposed to know? Am I supposed to turn the bathroom upside down once a month to see whether I can find my daughter's pill at the back of the medicine cabinet? Or ask my

and looked at him from the hallway. As though he had snuck into a peepshow. Not to look at a naked woman, but at an injured tenant.

The man still hadn't bandaged his forehead. The blood had clotted. But the shards from the floor lamp had been cleaned up. He was just sitting there. Not doing a thing. With the door open.

When Hofmeester entered the room, the man didn't move. He glanced over at his landlord and then went back to staring at the table on which a few sheets of paper were lying, a magazine about architecture, a couple of pencils.

Hofmeester searched his pockets, panicked for a moment when he thought he had lost it, then found the envelope in his back pocket. He put it on the table. He wiped his face, his throat. He felt like he was going to sneeze.

He stood there like that, waiting, as though he only wanted to see whether the tenant would take the money, but the envelope remained on the table.

He waited and he waited and finally he remembered what he had come for. He remembered everything. Hofmeester said: "I've come to bring back the rent."

There was no reaction. The architect looked at Hofmeester, then back at the tabletop.

"I've come to bring back the rent," Hofmeester said again, "because you are no longer welcome here. You have five days. I'm giving you five days' notice."

The architect looked at him. Expressionlessly, completely bland, as though Hofmeester had said: "Nice weather we're having, but they say it will start raining in another four or five days."

Once Hofmeester had stopped expecting him to say anything at all, the architect said: "I don't know what your daughter has told you, I take it she told you the truth, Mr. Hofmeester, but it's not what you think, not what you seem to think. What took place between your daughter and me, that was mutual."

Hofmeester placed his warm hand on the table, in the other he was still holding the empty plastic bag, he leaned towards the man, he recalled the dream about the cat in the sink. This man sickened him. Sickened him more than all the previous tenants put together.

"Mutual," he said, after he had shaken off the old memory of the dream, "how can something be mutual between a man your age and a girl of fifteen, barely fifteen? Do you have any idea what you're saying? How can that be mutual? How old are you anyway? You have no idea what mutual consent means. Between you and me, that could be mutual. Between you and me. Mutual. A girl of fifteen. Don't you have any sense of honor? Are you an animal? Is that what you're trying to tell me, that you're an animal disguised as an architect, that there is an animal living above me and my family? That I have rented out the best location in Amsterdam to an animal?"

Hofmeester was almost weeping. It wasn't sorrow, it was impotence. He wanted to go on, but realized there was no use. He placed his left hand on the back of his neck. His neck was hot and moist. As though he were running a fever.

"Your daughter," said the tenant, looking blissful, as though he were thinking about angels, about someone who had picked him up and lifted him from the mire, "is an intelligent and precocious girl. Not a child."

The word "precocious" struck Hofmeester like a blow to the face.

"Precocious," he said, "what do you mean, precocious?"

"As in: early-ripe."

Hofmeester shook his head, slowly at first, then faster. "You're a pervert," he said. "That's it. That's all I can figure. A lying pervert. I'm going to deduct the price of the floor lamp from your deposit, I assume you realize that. That's only fair. It was a rather expensive floor lamp." He was panting with effort, from the pain in his chest, from the tension caused by the man's words.

Then, at last, the tenant's expression changed. The money had awakened him, money always awakens the tenant. The landlord saw rage in the architect's eyes.

"There is nothing fair about that, Mr. Hofmeester."

He started to his feet, but Hofmeester said: "Don't get up. Unless you want an accident to happen, don't get up. I can't guarantee what I'll do. You know what that's like? The feeling that you can't guarantee what you'll do, that you no longer have yourself completely under control? That someone else is controlling your body?"

He showed the man his big, warm hands. He showed them to the tenant as though the mere sight of them should be enough. The hands with which he worked in the garden, his own garden and the garden that had belonged to his parents.

Perhaps it was the cut on his forehead, or maybe it was something in Hofmeester's voice, but the tenant didn't get up. He remained seated and didn't move.

Hofmeester paced around the room, his eyes fixed on the floor. He slid aside a chair, looked under the table. Finally, in a corner, beside the couch, he found what he was looking for. A pair of underpants, black. He picked them up and put them in the plastic bag.

For a moment, he stood there.

He looked at the man who now no longer, in any way, resembled the person who had been fucking his daughter like an animal. The architect sat there like a schoolboy who has been caught cheating. He looked younger now. More a boy, in fact, than a man. Then Hofmeester said: "In six days' time I'm coming back here, then your things will be gone, then you'll be gone. And then you will leave me and family alone, forever. My daughter is not included in the rent. Remember that. Children are not included in the rent."

"Mr. Hofmeester," the architect said, staring at the table top. "There's something you don't realize. Something you don't want to realize. This has nothing to do with the rent, this has to do with love."

Hofmeester tightened his grip on the plastic bag containing the underpants, as though he were afraid someone would snatch it from him. The architect looked at it. He had raised his head.

It was a clear plastic bag. It was easy to see what was in it.

"What you did to my daughter," the father said, "has nothing to do with love. It's a punishable offense. That's all it is. That's all there is to say about it. Love is never punishable."

He was about to turn away, but the architect stood up. He didn't move towards Hofmeester, he just stood up.

The architect was a tall man. Tall and thin. Not unattractive, but not handsome either. Seeing him on the street, the only thing you might notice about him was his height.

"Do you think I was the first?" the architect asked. "Is that what you think? Is that what's bothering you? Well then, let me set your mind at ease. I was perhaps the fourth or fifth. I didn't even dare to ask which one I was. There was nothing I had to teach her. More like the other way around." He snickered. At first it had been a smile, but it became snickering, louder and louder. The memory of Hofmeester's eldest daughter made the architect snicker.

Hofmeester stood there with the plastic bag in his left hand, looking at the tall man, at that ridiculous cut on his forehead. The cockiness the man displayed, that so many people these days displayed, the recklessness, the lack of adversities suffered, the obviousness with which they laid claim to all kinds of things, the idea that everything was for sale or rent, even his daughter, he despised that. When he was still at secondary school a nun had taught him that being human was a matter of recognizing one's own puniness. The more clearly one saw one's own puniness, the more human one became. These people no longer recognized their puniness, they had forgotten all about their own puniness. They had risen up in arms against it, but there would be a price to pay. Without puniness, it was all over.

"It's not about whether you were the first," Hofmeester said, "or the eighth. You were the oldest. That's what it's about."

The plastic bag crackled in his hand.

"She took the initiative," the architect said. "I told her: 'Is this really a good idea? I have nothing to offer you.' But she didn't want to listen. They start early these days, Mr. Hofmeester. Earlier all the time. Everything starts earlier and ends later. Your daughter doesn't belong to you. Not like you think. Not like you hope. That's not the way it is. Someday you'll find out. She was looking for a willing ear. She was looking for someone she could tell everything. Her own family, apparently, was too busy with other things. All right, that's the way things go. One thing leads to another. She was looking for—I'm sorry I have to say this straight to your face—she was looking for warmth."

The man sat down again. As though he had said everything he wanted to say. As though he were at a conference and had only stood up in order to correct the speaker on a few points, amiably but decidedly.

Hofmeester took a deep breath. Breathing deeply always calmed him. But the deeper he breathed, the more clearly he felt the pain in his chest.

"How long has this been going on?" he asked at last, once he had regained his composure.

"A few weeks, a couple of months, no more than that. God, I haven't really kept track. I have other things on my mind beside your daughter, Mr. Hofmeester."

Hofmeester snorted like a wounded beast.

Then he nodded. He had no more questions. He knew everything. The architect had other things on his mind.

He remained standing there, more for form's sake really. He wanted to see the man take the money. He wanted to be there when the tenant took the money, which was no longer wanted around here, and put it in his pocket.

When he saw that nothing was happening, he said: "Take the money."

The tenant glanced at the envelope, then slid it towards him and put it in his pocket with a faint smile.

With that, an end had been put to this incident. It was over. Hofmeester had done what he had to do.

"I feel sorry for you," the architect said.

"What do you mean?" Hofmeester was already on his way out the door, but he turned.

"What do you mean?" he asked again.

"I pity you. I feel like putting an arm around your shoulders. Because I feel for you. I'd like to put an arm around your shoulders and tell you that it's not all that bad, that she'll turn out fine. Ibi. She's young, pretty, intelligent, hot, I'm sorry to have to use that word, but that's important for a woman these days, and that's what she is, more than anything else. And she knows it, she knows it all too well. She's a sly one, too. No, she's going to be fine. I guess you've noticed it as well? How hot she is, how she uses that to drive men nuts?"

Hofmeester listened to the summary of his eldest daughter's favorable traits. And he laughed a little, deep inside himself, because he had the distinct impression he was going insane.

"Me?" Hofmeester said when the summary had come to an end. "You feel sorry for *me*?"

"I'm not the only one. It was other people who opened my eyes to it. Through other people, I started seeing you differently. Not just as an insufferable landlord, but as a person, a person with foibles, with a story, a history, someone you can understand. Oh, you tell yourself, so *that's* why he acts that way. That's it. And then you can learn to live with it."

The bag with Ibi's underpants in it seemed to grow heavier all the time. As though it contained iron, or two pounds of steak. Hofmeester took a step back, away from the door, a step towards the table. The word "hot" was still bothering him. He had never looked at his children that way.

"What do you mean?" he asked. "You're not the only one?"

"Like I said."

"So what are you saying?"

"That other people pity you too."

"Who? Who are these others? Am I supposed to know them?"

"Your daughter, for example. Ibi. She pities you too. She's not only ashamed of you, she pities you. She told me so herself. She didn't come here just for sex. She also wanted to talk."

If there had been another floor lamp, Hofmeester would have hit the architect over the head with it again. Hard and long.

There wasn't another floor lamp. And he knew what he was doing. He kept himself under control.

"You try to protect them," Hofmeester said, without knowing who he was talking to, "as best you can, because you can't really protect them, but you try, and then one day they meet someone like you. That's how it goes. Apparently. And then you go back, you go back in time, and you think: Where did I go wrong, what did I miss, what did I do that I shouldn't have done? Hasn't that ever entered your mind, hasn't it ever come up, that thought? That she's a child? Didn't you ever think: She's a child? My landlord's child?"

The architect shook his head. "But she's not a child," he said. "She stopped being a child a long time ago. She's less of a child than the two of us put together. Do you know what she said to me? 'Sex with boys my age is always so clumsy. And clumsy sex is bad sex.' Yeah, I could barely believe my ears. Clumsy sex is bad sex. Well, she didn't think I was too clumsy." The architect giggled.

Hofmeester stared at the man the way one might stare at a figure in a haunted house that suddenly turns out to be real, not just a dummy hanging there to frighten people, no, in the face of all expectations, a real corpse. Something that was alive once, but hadn't been for a long time now.

"She's saving up," the architect said, "and I helped her out now and then. Because it's her dream. Well, her dream, it's more like one of her dreams, I think. She's willing to make sacrifices to get there, the way people her age often are."

"Saving up? For what?" Hofmeester posed the question automatically, without thinking about it. His body was still under control, but not his voice, not any more.

"For a breast enlargement. She says: 'I'm completely flat up there.' And she's right. On top she's like a boy. She's given up all hope that nature will come to the rescue, but she's saving up, like I said. Sometimes I give her a little money. Fifty, or a hundred. You could laugh about it, but for her it's a matter of life and death. The tits. Yeah, she's a special girl, an energetic young woman who knows what she wants. You may be proud of her. You are proud of her, I know that. Just like I am. We're proud of her."

Hofmeester walked out the door without a word, he went down the stairs, entered his house, and walked straight through to the kitchen. He was, what was he? He no longer knew what he was. Or rather, he did know; miserable, that's what he was. A lump of misery, misery made of bones, flesh and some brains.

Tirza was in the kitchen, standing on a stool, busily opening cupboards.

"What are you looking for?" he asked.

"Something to eat."

"We're going to have dinner in a few minutes."

He put the plastic bag on the counter, took out the panties and returned the plastic bag to its place beneath the sink, where all the plastic bags were kept.

"Why are you angry, Daddy?" Tirza asked, climbing down off the stool.

"I'm not angry."

"But then why did you hit Ibi?"

"I didn't hit Ibi." He searched for words, but the only word that kept coming back, that wouldn't let go of him, that would never let go of him again, was the word "pity." Can daughters feel pity for their father? Fifteen-year-old girls? Girls of barely fifteen? And why would they? There was no reason to pity him. He lived with his family on the best stretch of Van Eeghenstraat, he had a respectable job as editor with a literary publishing house, two beautiful daughters, one of them already attending prep school, the other heading in that same direction. He had a wife and a cleaning lady, he was not without means, thanks to perceptive financial planning intended to benefit both him and his family. He was not a man to pity. All right, his eldest daughter was saving up for a breast enlargement. Adolescents did the strangest things. There were probably tens of thousands of fifteen-year-old girls saving up for breast enlargements. It went with being young. Nothing to worry about. He was, perhaps, too old to be a father, but he was not a man deserving of pity.

"I was helping her to calm down," he said collectedly.

"She says you hit her."

He rubbed the back of his neck again, it was still moist.

"Ibi's a little confused. How was your day at school?"

"Ibi says she's not allowed to have a boyfriend anymore."

"Of course she's allowed to have a boyfriend."

"Am I allowed to have a boyfriend?"

"You can have a boyfriend too." He picked Tirza up and put her back on the stool. "Of course you can," he said, "I love you, don't I, Tirza? You're allowed to do anything."

She looked at him earnestly, searchingly, and he dabbed the sweat from his face. Only when he went to put the cloth back in his pocket did he see that it was Ibi's panties.

He put the underpants back on the counter, looked at them for a second. A pair of black ones, with an insignia he couldn't place. An insect. A butterfly? A bee? A bumblebee?

He saw Tirza looking. He picked her up. It was difficult. It had been a long time since he'd picked her up. And so he stood there, in his kitchen, with his youngest daughter on his arm.

"Papa," she said, "are those Ibi's?" She pointed at what was lying on the counter.

"Yes," he said. "Those are Ibi's underpants. She forgot them."

The two of them looked at the underpants, Tirza and her father.

"When I grow up," Tirza asked, "am I not going to have tits either?"

He took a deep breath.

"You'll have them. All women get breasts. You too. And Ibi too. But we have to be patient. You have to learn to be patient. Everyone has to be patient."

Then he pressed Tirza to his chest and he remembered how he had held Tirza when she was a year old. He had lifted her high in the air, above his head. "Tirza," he had said, "my prettiest of pretties, my sweet of sweets. Do you know what you are? You're our sun queen. That's what you are. And later, when you grow up, maybe you'll learn to dance, or discover a new star, or become a writer and win the Nobel Prize. You can do anything, dear Tirza, anything you want, because you're the sun queen. And now I'm going to hug you to pieces."

Actually, he had wanted to name her Mala, he had read about a Mala, until a few days before the birth his wife said to him: "Mala means 'bad woman' in Spanish. You can't name someone that."

So they'd decided to name her Tirza, first with an "h," later without, in order to avoid associations with the Hebrew.

He didn't want his youngest daughter to be called "bad woman."

"Upsy-daisy, there you go, Tirza," he said. "You're too heavy. I'm putting you back down."

II

The Sacrifice

1

Hofmeester has been expecting them for ages, but the guests still haven't arrived. It's seven-thirty, and still there's no one. So he eats the first batch of fried sardines himself. He meant to fry them later in the evening, but he couldn't resist. He's already eaten three sardines. Bones and all. You barely notice the bones, they're such small fish.

He goes to Tirza's room to offer her a freshly-fried sardine. He finds her wearing a black dress that's been hanging in her closet for years, not the dress he went with her to buy for this party. A three-hundred-euro dress, with matching shoes that cost almost the same.

He must look crestfallen, because she puts an arm around him and says: "I'll wear it sometime, Daddy, but it doesn't look right on me tonight. Really, not tonight. I'm not in the mood for it. It's just not the dress for this evening."

He smiles magnanimously, the plate of sardines in his hand. "But we bought it for this evening, Tirza, especially for your party," he feels like saying. He says nothing. His disappointments are his own concern. They should remain invisible to the outside world. "Everything looks good on you," he says, and leaves her alone.

Hofmeester opens the bathroom door. Ibi is taking a bath, reading *Elle*, the kind of magazine she used to despise. "Dad," she shouts, "can't you knock?"

He lets his gaze glide absently over her body, he stares at her stomach for a few seconds. "Oh, sorry," he says then. "But you're not pregnant, are you?"

"Daddy," she shouts, "don't ask such weird questions, and leave me alone!"

He closes the door and goes into his bedroom. The wife still doesn't know what to put on. In order to postpone such a difficult decision—perhaps it will come to her later—she has decided to blow-dry her hair first. She is sitting, naked from the waist up, before the bedroom mirror, the blow-drier held loosely in one hand. A cigarette butt is smoldering in an ashtray. She seems to have found the ashtrays somewhere.

For a moment Hofmeester looks at her in silence, he feels like saying something, something reassuring and friendly, something you might say to an old friend who has stopped by after you haven't seen them for years. Nothing comes to him. Then he goes back downstairs. He wonders whether she will ever go away. He dreads her leaving, but the thought that she will never leave again is every bit as disturbing.

Now he's back in the kitchen, sitting on a stool and eating yet another sardine, but without really savoring it. He forgot all about treating his youngest daughter to a sardine. "Tirza," he calls out, his mouth half-full, "come and taste this. They're so fresh, even fresher than the ones you get in Portugal." No reply comes. He wishes he could carefully lower a fried sardine into her mouth and stand there, watching her enjoy it. Then he would like to wipe her lips with a paper napkin, but he doesn't want to be obtrusive. He sits there, his mouth full, and hears someone close the front door behind them loudly. Could that be Tirza going out, so soon before her party, now that the guests will arriving any moment? He doesn't understand why she doesn't take the time to come in and see him for a moment, to enjoy the sardines with him. Slowly, Hofmeester resumes chewing. There are so many things he doesn't understand. More and more all the time.

He has already strolled into the garden twice with the platter full of sushi and sashimi. To practice for when the young people start arriving. He bought the platter at the Japanese shop on Beethovenstraat, just for Tirza's party. He's proud of it. They know him by name in that shop.

The torches have been lit. A few weeks ago Hofmeester pruned his apple tree, to make sure no one would run into a low-hanging branch while tipsy.

And he has spruced himself up as well, he feels he's looking neat yet inconspicuous. The way fathers should look, at least if they don't want their child to be ashamed of them. To see how natural it is to assimilate, all you have to do is look at a child. A child wants nothing more than to take on the color of its surroundings.

Jörgen Hofmeester is like a rocket ready for launching.

He gets up off the stool and pours himself a glass of kir. He has set up a makeshift bar on the counter. He is ready to make five different kinds of cocktails.

To be honest, he doesn't really like kir, but it's Tirza's favorite drink. They've agreed that all the guests will first be offered a glass of kir, unless they explicitly ask for something else. Because of the color, too. It will look good. All that light-red.

His kir is too sweet for his taste, he adds a little more white wine and empties the glass quickly. Then he looks at his watch. A quarter to eight and still not a soul in sight. They *will* show up, won't they? It's not his party, he hasn't thrown a party for years, for decades, but still it worries him. He has visions of them dropping Tirza like a hot brick and leaving the Hofmeesters to eat all the sushi. Those visions make him sad, standing there with the glass of kir in his hand, as though he were already certain that they would be borne out. As though he had no doubt that his fearful dreams were going to come true. He fixes himself another glass of kir and drums his fingers lightly on the counter. This is the way he used to feel at book launches sometimes, the fear that he would be left standing there alone with the author, the shame that would overpower him when forced to turn to the author with the words: "Well, it looks like we'll have to make do with just the two of us, but that should be no problem." The panic that sometimes overcame him just before giving a little speech in which, earnestly but with the right dosage of irony, he was supposed to sing the praises of author and book, or translator and book. In front of the press, which rarely showed up. But that's all behind him now.

He knocks back his second glass of kir. "Tirza," he shouts. "Tirza." There is no reply.

He picks up the platter of sushi and sashimi and carries it into the garden for the third time. He imagines that the garden is full of guests. He will tell young people he has never met that he is Tirza's father, and he will listen to their stories with interest. Who knows, perhaps he will poke a young man jovially in the stomach and whisper: "Didn't I run into you in my bathroom one night?" Nothing will throw him off balance. He will be the perfect host. They, the children, will go home and think: Doesn't Tirza have a wonderful father?

After circling the garden once he brings the platter back to the kitchen, covers it with foil, and puts it in the fridge. He remains standing at the sink, panting. Toting raw fish around has exhausted him. He pours himself another glass of kir.

No, book launches are one thing he no longer has to fear. There's been a reshuffle at the publishing house. At first they were planning to fire him, until they found out that his age made that impossible.

The law would not allow it, the law stood between him and dismissal, and in such cases the law was unrelenting. In early April he was called into the office of the managing editor, who usually dealt only with financial matters and directives from the holding company. A fierce and fickle god, the holding company was.

At first they had chatted pleasantly about everyday matters, the managing editor and Hofmeester. The children. The climate, both financial and social, but also in the more meteorological sense. Global warming merited a subordinate clause. And then on to less pleasant matters. The terminal illness of the head of the marketing department. Moroccan young people who caused trouble, the congestion on the roads. That latter point, above all, was a thorn in the managing editor's flesh. He lived fifteen miles away from Amsterdam, in the town of Naarden.

After they had dealt with the burgeoning traffic jams, the managing editor slouched down in his chair, as though the conversation were in fact already over, and then asked: "Jörgen, which important author have you discovered for us, actually, in all the years you've worked here? Have you ever, in fact, actually discovered an author at all?"

The question came as a surprise to Hofmeester, after their talk of Moroccans and traffic jams.

He looked out the window, then at the managing editor, then at the desk and then back out the window. There was a tree outside the window. The tree was just beginning to bud.

"I mostly did translated fiction," Hofmeester said. "I mostly do translated fiction," he corrected himself. "Germany, Eastern Europe, the Caucasus, there are lots of interesting things going on there these days. And I worked on sports books for a while, but to be honest that wasn't my cup of tea."

"No," the managing editor said. "Sports books aren't your cup of tea. But you could also have discovered an author in Germany, or in Eastern Europe? Am I right? The problem with the authors you've brought in is that they've only cost us money, never generated it." He slouched down even further. "You know, Jörgen," he said, "you're won't believe what I'm going to say to you now. We wanted to fire you, but our legal department found out that that would be impossible at your age. So do you know what we're going to do? We're just going to pay your salary for the full two-and-a-half years, or what is it, the full two years and eight months, that you still have to go. We're going to pay that, including everything: medical coverage, holiday allowance, the whole kit and caboodle. But you don't have to come in anymore. You never have to come into the office again. You are free to go."

The managing editor stood up and held out his hand to Hofmeester with a grin, so that Hofmeester felt obliged to stand up as well. The look on the managing editor's face was like that of a TV quizmaster about to hand a contestant first prize, but Hofmeester couldn't believe that the editor really thought this was the first prize. No one would think this was the first prize.

"So what do you think of that?" the managing editor asked. "What do you say to that, Jörgen?"

Hofmeester did his best to look affable. For the first time in a long time he thought about his parents, and about his days at secondary school. It didn't seem to matter how old you were, fifty-four, fifty-eight, sixty-two; once a beaten schoolboy had taken up residence inside you and you hadn't chased him away quickly enough, he stayed on. The humiliation, that was the constant factor, that was what bound him to the person he had been at thirteen. The sensed humiliation, perhaps even worse than the real one.

"I don't know what to say," Hofmeester said, withdrawing his hand carefully from the managing editor's grip. His always warm and moist hands, his eternal fear of getting caught, but at what he had no idea. There was, in fact, nothing for them to catch him at. He had never so much as taken a thumbtack home from work with him.

"I would have liked to go on, but of course this is fine too," he said. He asked himself why he was unable to say that, as far as he was concerned, this was not fine at all, he wondered why those words wouldn't come out of his mouth. Why he was so bent on making people think that everything was going well. That everything always went the way he'd hoped.

This time, for a change, he did not try to create that impression with any great conviction. He felt desperate and he didn't doubt that, entirely against his will, that despair was written all over his face. And perhaps even more than despair: mortal fear.

To dispel that fear, Hofmeester suspected, to give the whole thing the semblance of a pleasant conversation, the managing editor slapped his officially unfired employee twice on the shoulder and said: "Isn't this what we all dream of? To keep pulling our paychecks without ever having to work again? Enjoy it. Go travelling. Or go rowing. You've always enjoyed rowing, haven't you? Empty out your desk and take it easy. I envy you. I kid you not, I envy you, but I can't, I can't leave here yet, Jörgen." The managing editor seized Hofmeester's hand again, and Hofmeester felt like a puppet under someone else's control. It wasn't he himself, but someone completely different who was controlling his movements, his expressions, even his thoughts. Something stronger than his own will. The fear, the shame, the estimation that it was better not to rock the boat.

There is a sort of pride secreted away in the man who lets everything roll over him, who doesn't stick up for himself. The pride of someone who simply dusts himself off and presses on as though nothing has happened.

"We haven't forgotten what you've done for this company," the managing editor said. "It was a lot and it wasn't always easy, we know that. Of course there will be an official farewell too. Let us know how you'd like that to go, when the time comes of course, something intimate perhaps. Dinner? Or a gift certificate? But right now, all I want to say is: It was a pleasure working with you. I wish you well, Jörgen. Enjoy yourself! You know . . ."

He moved his face up closer to Hofmeester's, as though about to pronounce a secret that had been fighting to get out the whole time. "It may sound strange coming from someone who has worked on books all his life. But books aren't the greatest thing in this world; the greatest thing in this world are the children. Go visit your daughter in France. Before long you'll have grandchildren. That's wonderful. Take them rowing, go sailing with them, take them pedal-boating. Children love the water."

Hofmeester felt a tiny seed in his mouth, from a grape perhaps. At lunch he had eaten a bowl of fruit salad. He swallowed the seed.

The managing editor was finished talking.

Hofmeester walked to the door, deep in thought. There he turned and asked: "The unfinished business, is there someone I should turn that over to?"

The managing editor waved his hand dismissively. A jovial gesture, boyish. He sat down on the edge his desk. "Forget it," he said, "forget it. Fiction from the East, that only costs us money. We're going to start doing things differently around here. The days when you could only buy a book at the bookshop are over. The gas station, the supermarket, the bank, that's right, the bank, the pharmacy, the doctor's waiting room, the coffee shop, we're going to push our books everywhere, we'll flog our books on every corner of every street. We're not going to let ourselves be marginalized. That's a real threat to any society, when the leading edge withdraws from the fray, when the elite lets itself be sidelined. True culture, real culture, is the power of numbers and nothing else, Jörgen. The power of numbers." The managing editor was drooling a little, Hofmeester noticed, a sign that he was enthusiastic. He rarely waxed enthusiastic, but when he did he always drooled a little as he spoke. Hofmeester had no choice, he had to remain standing at the door, because there was still something coming, an encore to this dismissal that could not be called a dismissal, a swan song for his vanishing, an improvised song of farewell for the editor of translated fiction.

"The groups, Jörgen, about whom they say 'Oh, those people never read,'" the managing editor went on, "we will introduce to reading. Men without much of an education. You'll see: in five years' time those people will have discovered books; maybe not through the bookshop, but then through the gas station, or the video shop, or the liquor store . . . or the peepshow, as far as I'm concerned. But discover books they will. 'Muslims? Forget it,' everyone says. 'They don't read. Illiterates is what they are.' Nonsense, I say, you just have to know how to reach them, you just have to find out what it is they need. Orthodox Jews, same story. Jehovah's Witnesses, those people watch TV too sometimes, on the sly, and if they watch TV on the sly, why can't they read a book on the sly as well? Selling is all about demographics. And we're going to approach the customer demographically, we're going to investigate him, examine him, and then we're going to custom-service him. Consumer-friendly. And custom-tailored. Including the long-term unemployed, the hooligans. What goes for the mass media goes for publishing as well. We can only survive if we treat the customer like an equal partner. If we stop haggling over the customer's head about what's good and what's not. Everyone can do anything these days. Let the customer and the writer collaborate. And people have no time anymore. No time for the newspaper, no time for books or for TV. We have to take that into account. We have to make books for people who have no time to read. That's right, Jörgen, what's on its way now is nothing less than a revolution. Digital by nature, without ideology. Or rather, with the only ideology that will outlive us all: the realization that the customer is always right, Jörgen. We've forgotten about that, because we've isolated ourselves, because we've let ourselves be marginalized with our eyes open. You'll see it all happen, I suppose, from a distance. Clear out your desk and immerse yourself in freedom. You've been a brave soldier. Others will take over from you now. With new weapons."

"I've never gone rowing," Hofmeester said in parting. Then

he closed the door behind him and walked quickly, as quickly as though he had to go to the toilet very badly, to his own office. He could still hear the managing editor laughing about the revolution that would roll over everything and everyone, digital or otherwise.

He sat down at his desk. Beside the computer was a cold cup of tea. He drank it slowly. He answered a few emails, in none of them did he mention his forthcoming departure or the revolution that was on its way, and then he waited.

He waited until everyone had left the building. He waited motionlessly, sitting in the chair in which he had sat for thirty-three years. Little had changed about this place. Now the changes would come. Without him.

Hofmeester didn't think about a thing, not about his future, not about the time he had spent here, not about his wife or his children. The only thing he did think about for a moment was Tirza. That she must never know about this, that no one should find out about this. This was a disgrace. And it seemed to him that his whole life had been leading up to this disgrace. Again he heard the managing editor ask: "Which important author have you discovered for us, actually, in all the years you've worked here?" He hadn't known how to answer that question. He had nurtured talents that had withered before they could reach fruition, but was that his fault?

When he was sure everyone had left the building, that only the cleaners were still around, he got up and went to the window. He looked at the garden, where in the summer he and a small group of old-timers ate their sandwiches and fruit salad and where a few employees went to have their cigarettes, the smoking ban having finally reached this organization as well. He stared at the garden unmoved, there was nothing sentimental in his gaze, at most only amazement at the thought that he would never see this garden again. That the parting had come so quickly and so casually, especially so casually. The parting had turned out to be a rush job.

For a moment he thought about how his wife had left, which had been just as unexpected. Not the leaving itself, he had taken that into account, but the fact that she had not come back, that was what had surprised him. After Ibi and Tirza went to bed back then, he used to wait for minutes, sometimes hours, beside the phone, waiting and hesitating at the same time, thinking about what he would say if she called. The realization that she could have contacted him if she'd wanted to, that was the affront. That had stuck with him, it was still fresh in his mind, that was what he would never forget.

After standing there like that for a few minutes, he looked at his watch and said quietly to himself: "I need to get my things together, I need to get moving."

He had never brought many personal effects to work with him. Unlike those colleagues who did their best to furnish their office as though it were a living room, he had kept his—spacious by today's standards—as sober and plain as possible.

Most of what he had hung up were pictures of his children, at all ages. Toddler, pre-schooler, adolescent. Some of those photos were taped to the side of his computer screen. He removed them carefully, in order not to damage them. Then he tucked them into his pocket diary to keep them from getting wrinkled. On the wall was a postcard Tirza had sent him from Rome, during last year's school excursion. Even though the trip to Rome had taken place eighteen months ago, he had left it there, because the words on the back he found touching. About once a week he would turn over the card carefully and read the short text that began with the words: "Dear Daddy."

Beside the keyboard was a little wooden camel that Ibi had brought back for him from Egypt. He went to the restroom, tore off some toilet paper, and wrapped the camel in that, so that it wouldn't break in the bag on his bicycle on the way home.

On the wall there was also a drawing Tirza had made, a self-portrait. He took that down too, careful to damage neither wall nor drawing.

other people was one in which he had never put credence. In fact, he had always found it strange that it was precisely that quote from Sartre that had become so famous. There were better, more interesting quotes from Sartre to be found, less cynical, less black, less lonely.

What he did discover was: the less the other person exists, the easier that is to take.

He waited in the arrival hall, like dozens, sometimes hundreds of others, but unlike the people around him he was waiting for someone who didn't exist, he had come to meet someone who would never show up, he raised his hand without believing or even entertaining the hope that his gesture would be seen by someone on the far side of the glass wall. At most, he waved so that a random passerby would think: there is just another person.

There were advantages to picking up passengers who never arrived. It saved him the trouble of hearing stories that could turn out to be boring, disappointments, accusations: "You're not listening!" Tensions.

One time a man came up to him holding a sign with a passenger's name written on it. "You've been here for a while, I see," the man said. A chauffeur probably. "How long, if you don't mind my asking? What flight are you waiting for?"

"I've been here for about six weeks," Hofmeester should have answered, but instead he said: "A couple of hours." And he held on tight to his briefcase, as though it contained his life.

"But what flight are you waiting for?" insisted the chauffeur, a sweaty, thickset man.

What flight was he waiting for? He had never looked at it that way before.

"I'm not waiting for any flight in particular," Hofmeester said.

Then he opened his briefcase as though he were looking for something. He found an apple and took a bite of it. The chauffeur stood there watching Hofmeester eat his apple. As though hoping that something else was coming, a word, a glance, a sign of mutual understanding. Two men in the arrival hall who are getting on in years, who know what it means to wait. Hofmeester didn't speak another word. He ate his apple and stared at luggage carousel number twelve.

Even though Schiphol had now become his work, he never left home without his briefcase. It had been a present from his wife, long before she disappeared for the first time, long before Ibi, soon after they had started living together on Van Eeghenstraat.

The less people existed, the easier they were to take. He discovered that at the airport. But that still didn't mean there was anything wrong with people who did exist.

Editor of literature in translation, that is what he had been. All his life he had involved himself with the non-existent, with the possible at best, with the probable perhaps. Now the difference between what existed and what did not had grown fuzzy, the line separating them had become vague. Misty as the airport on an autumn morning. You had to lay the lash of fantasy across the haunches of reality, or reality would throw you from the saddle like a bucking horse, that much Hofmeester knew for sure these days.

He raised his right hand on high. Sometimes he went to passport control and waved to those who were waved farewell by no one else.

After eating the first batch of sardines all by himself, he goes upstairs. The bathroom door is open, Ibi is no longer in the tub. In the bedroom, the wife is still sitting in front of the mirror. Her hair has been blow-dried. Her torso is still bare. She is wearing a denim skirt, she has a lit cigarette in her mouth.

"What's that supposed to be?" Hofmeester asks. He points at the skirt. His arm extended. His lips still greasy from the fish.

"This? This is one of Ibi's skirts." She speaks without taking the cigarette out of her mouth, and looks at herself in the mirror.

"Yes, I see that, that it's Ibi's. But why are you wearing it?"

Only now does she remove the cigarette from her mouth. The

movie-star pose is fading. She has become the wife again. The wife who has returned out of the blue.

"Because I don't have anything else to wear, and because it fits. I'm just about as thin as Ibi was when she was fifteen. Do you remember what a fatty she was when she was eleven? She had just started menstruating, and we called her The Garbage Can. Because she ate all the leftovers. She was hungry all day long."

Hofmeester shakes his head. He doesn't want to talk about the past right now. This is not the right moment to evaluate the past. The question remains, of course, which moment if any would be the right one. "That's ridiculous," he says. "That's taking things too far. And I don't want you to smoke in the bedroom."

The wife looks at herself in the mirror. There is a brush on the table in front of her, the blow-dryer, lipstick, a comb, hairpins. She inhales and blows out the smoke, like a child practicing for later, a child who doesn't yet know how to smoke.

"What do you mean, ridiculous? Don't you think it looks good on me?"

"It's . . ." Hofmeester says. He pinches his nose, as though he's caught a cold, and starts all over again. "It's not about looking good or not looking good. It's too short. A miniskirt. That doesn't cover anything. You can't do that."

"You think it's too short? Don't you think my legs are pretty?"

She slides around in her chair and, with a little effort, holds out both legs for him to see.

"Don't you like them? I actually thought you thought my legs were pretty. I waxed them. Especially for tonight."

"That skirt," Hofmeester says, pinching his right arm, "is slatternly."

"Slatternly?" She stares at him.

"Yes, slatternly. I don't know any other word for it and, I'm sorry to have to say this, but I think you're too old for it. It seems more like something for an eighteen-year-old, something for Tirza and her friends. But even they don't wear clothes like that anymore. And no matter how desperately you wish you were, you are *not* one of her girlfriends. You are her mother."

She turns around in her chair again. Her legs are now almost hidden from Hofmeester's view.

"But I thought," she says, "you appreciated a little sluttishness in women, that men in general appreciate that. That that's what they want, even if they don't dare to say so, men like you. Not that responsible, prudent stuff. That primness. I've got to flaunt it, Jörgen. If I don't do it now, there's no point anymore."

He takes off his polo shirt, a regular dress shirt would be better after all. He's sweating too much anyway, it's too warm. Lovely for the guests, a balmy evening, but he has to do the serving. To observe people's hands. An empty hand means an empty stomach.

He will feed the hungry and not be superfluous. He will never be superfluous again.

The polo shirt is soaking wet. He tosses it on the bed.

While he is looking for another shirt, he says: "It's Tirza's party, so if anyone is going to flaunt it, it should be Tirza. But she won't do that, she's too discreet for that. Too unassuming."

"Jörgen, what would she flaunt anyway?"

"What do you mean?" He takes a shirt out of the closet and walks towards the wife. "What do you mean?" he asks again, taking the shirt off the hanger.

The cigarette is extinguished. Finally.

"What do I mean? You know that better than I do. She's got nothing on top. She's as flat up front as she is at the back. I don't know why neither of our daughters have actually grown tits, they don't get that from me. Look at me. I'm voluptuous. Do you find it surprising that men refer to me as 'voluptuous?'"

Hofmeester drops the shirt. The hanger is the only thing he's holding. He stares at the wife. Madness, he thinks. Total madness. This family is driving me mad. No, not this family, this woman.

My wife. How could I ever have waited for her, how could I have spent evenings by the phone, thinking that I would call her and then deciding not to, how can she have shown up in my life? Because I hate her. If only she had never come back. If only she had just stayed away. That would have been better. How can you be jealous of your own daughter? You can be jealous of anyone, of your neighbors, your colleagues, your family, your husband, your wife. And Hofmeester has, at some point, been jealous of almost everyone, but never of his children.

Tense as he is, he doesn't notice that he has started slapping the wooden hangar against his thigh.

"How dare you say that about your own daughter?" he says at last. "And what's more, it's not true. That's the worst of it. Tirza is a lovely woman, a lovely young woman. Everyone's crazy about her, all the boys are crazy about her. Everyone loves her, all her teachers tell me that. I don't know of a prettier girl. And she's not flat. That she doesn't have those big, blubbery, coarse, droopy tits like you do, the kind only Moroccans and Turks go for, well, that's a blessing."

She turns around. Away from the mirror.

"Droopy tits?" she asks.

He slaps the hanger, once requisitioned from a Swiss hotel, rhythmically against his thigh.

"Take a good look, Jörgen. Are they droopy? Do you call this droopy? Are you so old that you've become nearsighted? Do you need glasses? Can't you tell the difference anymore between voluptuous tits and droopy tits?"

She grabs her right breast, she caresses it, no, it's not a caress, she rubs it absentmindedly and Hofmeester stops slapping his thigh. Somewhere in the house a door slams.

"They're not really droopy, at least not yet," he says, sorry about having started an argument right before the party. He is going to need all his powers of concentration for doing the serving, for the sardines, the cocktails, the wine. But now that he has begun to speak the truth, he can't go back. "I'm no expert in this area, I don't know where the droopy tit starts and the normal tit begins, but I know that they're starting to droop, you can see that. If you look carefully you can see them starting to droop, if you look carefully you can see that it's all over with your tits, just like it's all over with you. That's why you came back. Because you have nowhere else to go. Because you know it's over, your little adventures, your flirting, your décolletés, your little paintings, it's over and done with. Period. That's why you're here. Because there's nowhere else you could go. But that's no reason to talk about your daughter like that, your daughter who is throwing her big party tonight. That kind of thing nauseates me. That kind of thing makes me sick. The way you used to make me sick, and still do."

He regrets the words already, even as he speaks. And again he thinks: madness. There's a curse on this family. It doesn't matter who's been cursed, my wife, the children, me; in the end the curse is on all of us. We share the curse.

She doesn't say a word, she holds her right nipple between her fingers, it looks like she's pinching it.

He picks up his shirt, lays the hanger on the bed. They went on vacation to Curaçao once, with the whole family, but he's never felt this warm before. It's the excitement, the heat from frying the sardines. The hot oil. His polo shirt reeks of it. Fish. Grease.

"Jörgen," she asks, "shall we fuck?"

She looks at him, in the mirror. The blow-dryer is lying in front of her. One of Hofmeester's last gifts to her. She is naked, except for Ibi's denim skirt. It is five minutes past eight.

"Now?" he asks.

"Yes. Now."

He looks at his watch.

"But why? If you don't mind my asking."

"Why not?"

"Because the guests will be arriving any minute."

She shakes her head. "They're not coming yet. You're always so panicky when it comes to guests, so over the top. You have no idea when parties start. You're out of it. You've always been out of it."

"The children . . ." He starts to say something else, but decides to leave it at that. The children, that says enough. The children, that explains everything.

"They can take care of themselves. They're grownups. Have you forgotten that? Your daughters are adults. They're not children anymore."

"I thought," he says, after staring at the ashtray in front of the mirror for a few seconds, "I mean: why now, all of a sudden?"

"All of a sudden? It's not so sudden, Jörgen. We've done it before."

"But it was always a fiasco."

"Yeah, God, if you want to call it that."

She is still looking at him in the mirror, and while he looks back it occurs to him that he has spent a major part of his life with this woman. The best part of his life. The lion's share.

"I didn't think that was supposed to happen. You didn't feel attracted to me. I don't mind, but that's what you said. That couldn't have changed so quickly, could it?" He takes a deep breath. Deep and expansive, as though he were at the doctor's. "I thought you came by because you wanted to see how we were doing, the children and I."

"I did."

He closes the door. Quietly, like a burglar.

"You're here as a guest. We agreed. We're not going to start all over again, are we? We'd agreed on that, that we weren't going to start all over again. We've started over again so often. It gets worse every time. We used to tell each other: 'It will be better for the children.' But you said it yourself, the children have grown up. We don't have to do it for the children anymore." He talks as though he's pleading a case in court.

His torso is bare, but the sweat is still running down his back.

"We're not starting all over again. And starting over again with what, for Christ's sake? With what?"

He gulps a few times, he wipes his mouth, the back of his neck, he removes as much moisture from his body as he can.

"With the fiasco."

She laughs. Their fiasco is a laughing matter. The echo of tragic failure: shrill laughter.

"Why do you say things like that about your own daughter? I find that unacceptable."

"What did I say?"

"That she's flat."

"But she *is* flat. Like two peas on a plate." She sighs. "You can't protect your children, Jörgen. Not all their lives. The more you protect them, the weaker they become. You have to get them ready for the world. It's what other people will say about her. That she's as flat up front as she is on the back. If I don't say it, other people will. She's better off hearing it from me, because I say it with love."

"She has a lovely face."

"Oh sure, she has a lovely face, beautiful hair, and a nice little figure. But no tits, Jörgen. No tits."

"Tirza is your daughter. Your daughter. She was inside you. Tirza is . . ." What else is Tirza? He doesn't know.

"Well, so what? I know she's my daughter. Does that mean I have to see things that aren't there? She has no tits, period. And to tell you the truth, I can't stand her. I know a mother isn't supposed to say that, that it's terrible, and bad, and maybe it is, but it's the truth. I can't stand her. She's turned out to be a little witch, she already was one, as a toddler. She's evil. And she's never liked me, Jörgen. Never. Not even as a baby."

He hears the words, but they don't sink in anymore. Hofmeester remembers Tirza's illness, her puberty, her presence in his life when there weren't very many others present in it. Her school. He decides that the wife is confused. She must be going through menopause. When does menopause start? Earlier these days. Everything starts earlier all the time. But the more he thinks about it, the more he has the feeling that she was always like this.

"She doesn't have to like you. She's your daughter."

"Well she could still be nice to me. She ignores me."

"She blames you for going away. She needed you." He despises his own words, he finds them so ineffectual.

"Was I supposed to give up my life for her?"

Yes, Hofmeester wants to say. Yes, for your children you give up your life. Maybe that's all parenthood is about. The rest is just details. But he says: "No one asked you to do that."

"She does, Jörgen. She does." Another cigarette is lit.

"I find smoking in the bedroom unpleasant. You know that. And tits aren't everything. Besides, she has . . . She has little bumps."

"Bumps aren't breasts, Jörgen. What are you waiting for?"

He unbuttons the shirt he plans to put on later. He has to concentrate on the role he will be playing in a few minutes, in half an hour. The bell could ring any minute. The first guest at a party is always the most difficult. Everything is so untouched, so fresh and new. The conversations aren't running smoothly yet.

His wife used to throw parties all the time. He never felt at home at them. Whenever he could he withdrew to the bedroom, but sometimes partygoers had gathered there as well, those were wild times. In the end, he would go out on the balcony and look at what was happening in the garden. At such moments the sense of being completely isolated, which never bothered him otherwise, was painful. The isolation felt like an illness. Like a painful illness that wouldn't respond to medication.

Their friends were *her* friends. Polite chit-chat bored him, because he had to chitchat politely so often with translators, authors, and colleagues. Until he discovered that it helped when he made the rounds with the hors d'oeuvres. No one bothered to talk to a man who carried the hors d'oeuvres around. And so he transformed himself into a servant in his own home. An outsider might have thought he was the waiter. Gallant, but silent. Always discreet. A man who is one with his unobtrusive but obliging deeds. Sometimes the partygoers were surprised to discover that this servant, this amiable slave, was the owner of the house.

"What do you want?" he asks. "What do you want, anyway?"

She stands up. Ibi's denim skirt is tight around her buttocks. She can't move freely. The sight of it moves him. Unexpectedly, and more than he would have imagined. This is his wife in her younger years, wearing the skirt that belongs to her eldest daughter. It is perhaps not ludicrous, but something very close to it indeed.

"What do you want, for God's sake?" he asks. "The guests will be here any minute."

"To fuck."

"But why? It never worked for us, it was, what did you call it, a fiasco. Not just the fucking, let's be honest. Our marriage." He smiles, because the truth compacted in a couple of words sounds so innocuous. So unavoidable. Something no one could do anything about. A traffic accident. It was a foggy night. An oncoming car.

"Because we don't have anyone else."

He moves away from her, towards the balcony doors, like an animal on its way to the killing floor that goes on resisting, if only for the sake of principle.

The expression on her face has changed. She is looking at him closely. "Or is there someone else? Someone I don't know about? Do you have someone else? Are you covering it up? What have you been up to, anyway, all the time I was gone?"

He shakes his head. "No, no, no one. Nothing steady, nothing worth mentioning. Why didn't you stay with your old flame? On that houseboat?" He closes the balcony doors, afraid the children might hear.

"Things went wrong."

She takes a few steps towards him. The denim skirt cracks as though it is going to rip at the seams.

"Don't you want to hear what that was?"

He nods. "Of course I do. What went wrong? Tell me, but keep it short."

"He wanted a child."

She laughs at the memory of it. She grins. There she is, standing in front of him, half-naked. She looks like Ibi. Or rather, Ibi looks like her. Tirza doesn't. Tirza doesn't look like anyone.

"So why didn't the two of you make one? You still could have when you left here. You were fertile when you left me. There's no reason why you couldn't have."

"Because *he* couldn't. He wasn't able. He was sterile, as it turned out. And then he went crazy. He said it was my fault. He went bonkers. That's the way it is, Jörgen. That surprises you, doesn't it?" Again, that grin.

He lays the shirt, which he has been holding in his hand all this time, on the bed. He glances at his watch. What does he want from this woman, with whom he shares little else but two daughters and about half his life? Perhaps not even that much. When she showed up at the door six days ago, why didn't he say, after the casserole was finished: "I'll arrange a hotel for you. Shall we meet up somewhere tomorrow? A cup of coffee somewhere?" Why can't he let go of her? It's about time he did.

"His sperm was dead and he said it was my fault." She grins, as though she's telling a joke only she herself can appreciate.

Then he bends down and takes off his shoes.

He looks at her, and the wife nods approvingly.

Hofmeester takes off his socks, and it occurs to him that the sushi and the sashimi are in the fridge downstairs, ready for the guests. He is proud of that. Proud of what he himself made in the kitchen that afternoon, attentively and lovingly.

The socks are stuffed into the shoes. "Dead sperm," he says, "is no laughing matter."

He removes his trousers quickly.

He hangs them neatly over a chair, they are his best trousers, he will have to play host all evening in them.

And so he stands there in his bedroom, in his underpants. He's got a bit of a paunch, but for a man his age, it's hardly worth mentioning.

"Why did you come back?" he asks.

She clears her throat. "You said it yourself already," she says. "You know everything, you've always known everything."

"What did I say?"

"That I had nowhere else to go."

He sees the denim skirt, he sees the flesh that bulges a bit above the waistline, it's not really ugly. It's almost charming, and this woman, whom he hates and whom he detests—if not all the time, then certainly on a regular basis, more often than he'd like—moves him. More than he would have imagined, more than he would have admitted to himself. What is left of her makes his knees go weak. Because there's so little of it. He sees it clearly, there's no denying it. So little. He is the curator of her past, the guardian of her seductive power, he remembers everything, he can still see who she was, right through everything. In him, her infidelities live on, each day anew.

"Then we went to France," she said. "But it didn't help. Dead sperm doesn't come alive in France."

He looks at his feet.

Then he turns his gaze on the wife.

She says: "I've made myself as cheap as possible for you, do you see that? I've never looked cheaper."

"Yes, yes," he says. He sees it.

"She can't be cheap enough for you, can she? The woman you lust after?"

He nods, his breaths are short and shallow. Not from excitement.

From misery. The memory of happiness is misery. The memory. Having to admit that you were mistaken. And that that mistake produced two people. Two mistakes, if you viewed it clearly. That too, he has on his conscience.

"Oh yeah," he says. "I see it. You've never been this cheap before. And you're that way for me. Just for me."

His socks are a dark blue, with light blue stripes, they stick out of his shoes like little leprechauns.

"We have to be quick about it," he says, "the guests will be here any minute. They should have been here already, in fact."

"Fast," she says. "Real fast. How do you want it?"

"How do *you* want it?"

She shakes her head. "You see?" she says. "The beast in you isn't dead. See that it's still there?"

Hofmeester takes a few steps towards her. He reaches out, he touches the nipple she was pinching gently a few minutes earlier.

"Why are we doing this? Aren't we too old for this? Shouldn't we know better?"

She pushes his hand away gently. "You really can't see it?" she asks. "Has it really not sunk in yet? Are you blind? We don't have anyone else." She stresses each word, every syllable, as though reading aloud a dictation exercise.

He moves his face up closer.

"Is that it?" he asks. "Is that all?"

"Why do you think I came back to you? Because I knew you wouldn't send me away. Because I knew you didn't have anyone else. Who would still want you? Take a good look, Jörgen, we're the remains. We're what's left over. Of us, of the beast inside us."

"How did you know I wouldn't send you away?"

"You never have, so why should you start now? You were always too afraid. The leaving itself, you couldn't care less. But that people would speak poorly of you, the way they do about bad husbands, you couldn't live with the idea."

He gulps back a bit of saliva.

"Now you're the only one, Jörgen, the others . . ." She laughs. "The others are dead, sick, or crazy. Or they've found something better, something younger, and they don't want me anymore, not even for a kind word and a cup of coffee. Their new life mustn't be put at risk. You're the only one, you're the survivor. In the end, you're the winner. You have me all to yourself."

The curse, he thinks, the curse. It never lets go of you, it floats over your head like a cloud, and when you die it passes itself along to your children. That's why he'd never wanted to have children, intuitively, he didn't want to pass along the curse. Until they actually arrived. Then he was lost, he lost himself, first in Ibi, later in Tirza. He forgot about the curse.

"Do you find me cheap as all get-out?"

He looks at her and nods deliberately. "Yes," he says slowly. "Cheap as all get-out."

"How do you want to do it, Jörgen? It's up to you. It's your evening. It's also your party, in a way. You took care of Tirza all these years."

Tirza, the name seems to awaken him rudely, to bring him back to his senses. Tirza. It's true, he has taken care of her all these years. And lived for her, lived through her, lived beside her, lived under her. He feels the urge to scream, to scream for help, but no one would hear.

"I want to take you over my knee," he says.

She smiles and for a moment he can imagine how she stood in front of the others, in better days. In front of her old flame, for example, on the houseboat, proud and unreachable. The rocking of the houseboat, pleasure craft passing by, the shouting and singing of the passengers. Summer. And then the dead seed.

Hofmeester sits down on the bed, on his side of the bed. He looks at the balcony doors. The sound of children's voices is coming from the neighbor's garden.

"This is what's left of us," she says, walking over to him. "It's not much, is it? But my beast is lithe, my beast sometimes drives me mad, it's so insatiable, and your beast is still there too, Jörgen. It's there and it's been waiting for me all this time. You don't have to say it. I know it. It's been waiting for me all this time."

She lies down on her stomach, across his knees. He can still hear children's voices, but they're crying now as well. Someone has fallen down. They fall a lot, the neighbor's children, they're young and impetuous.

His left hand is resting on the denim skirt that belongs to his eldest daughter, on the buttocks of the wife who went to a houseboat. That is the story, the myth of his life.

"So cheap," she whispers. "So terribly cheap, you should really be ashamed of yourself."

Hofmeester caresses her buttocks absently, the way you pet a cat that has come to lie on your lap.

"I'm naughty," she whispers. "That's all I've ever really been, naughty. I'm your fantasy. Nothing else but that. I'm the fantasy you can touch, Jörgen. That's why I came back. Because I'm your fantasy. Say it. Say that I'm your fantasy."

"Yes," he says, "you're my fantasy, you're the fantasy I can touch."

He pulls the skirt, which does not belong to his wife, up a little higher. With the strength of someone who fears for his life, he brings his right hand down on her buttocks and, almost at the same moment, he says: "They made me redundant."

But she doesn't understand what he's saying.

He slaps her again on the buttocks, with the same mortal fear, and cries: "I've been made redundant. And now I'm going to make you redundant."

She still doesn't understand him. She crawls off his lap. She pulls her daughter's skirt down a bit. As though propriety suddenly somehow mattered.

"What are you shouting?" she says. "I can't understand you. What are you saying?"

"Nothing."

"Sorry," she says, and runs a hand over his hair.

"What is it?"

He's sitting on the bed, the same way he was a minute ago. She could crawl right back onto his lap. The game could go on as though it had never stopped. As though it had been going on all these years.

"I'm sorry," she says.

"What are you sorry about? You didn't do anything."

"It's not working."

"What?"

"This."

"What do you mean? What's not working?"

"The fucking."

He gets up off the bed, he straightens the sheet. Even though it's still as neat as it was before he sat down.

"It was a mistake," she says. "I was mistaken. I'm sorry. We're friends. Aren't we? I wish it could be different, I wish I could, but I can't. I can't fuck you. Not anymore. I'm sorry."

She kisses him on the side of the neck. "I can't do anything about it," she says, "but I find you disgusting. I forgot about that, I forgot all about it, but suddenly I knew. Suddenly I remembered everything. When you touched me. Right here." She shows him where he touched her.

"It doesn't matter," he says. "I warned you beforehand."

"I'm sorry," she whispers, "that I wasn't able to help you. I would have liked to help you."

They are facing each other. She runs her fingers through her hair. Then she opens the doors to the balcony. The air outside is still warm.

"No one has to help me," Hofmeester says. "I don't need help."

She looks out over the gardens of Amsterdam-South and he stands there in his bedroom in his underpants and wonders what he is doing, who is steering him, what demons it is he obeys.

"Come on," she says. "give me a little kiss, just so I know you're not angry."

She walks over to him quickly. Just as quickly, she seizes his head and they kiss. For ten, twenty seconds. They kiss they way they used to. No, more than they used to. They kiss as though death is already taking possession of them. And for a bit, for as long as the kiss lasts, the past comes back. Somewhere in the past, life is hidden, and suddenly it's there again, as though trying to remind Hofmeester that it was once there, as though to make sure Hofmeester never forgets what he's missing.

Then he pushes her away gently. "Enough," Hofmeester says. "I have to start getting ready for the party."

For a brief moment she looks at him fondly, the way she used to, in the beginning, the cursed beginning. Then she asks: "Do you have a nail file I could use? I need to do my nails."

At that moment, the doorbell rings.

He stares at his wife, listening to the sounds in his own house, a door that is opened and another one that slams shut in the draft—the garden doors are open downstairs—but otherwise nothing. Silence. No one is opening the front door for the first guest.

Panic overtakes him.

That is why he pulls on his trousers and runs as fast as he can down the stairs.

"Jörgen," the wife calls out. But he has no time for her now. He has other things on his mind. The party has begun. At last.

With a yank—the haste and the nerves cause him to slip and cut his index finger—he opens the front door. And there she is. The first guest. He recognizes her face, recognizes it very well in fact, that's not the problem. He just can't quite remember her name.

He shakes his index finger. He points it at her. "Geography," he says. "Geography, isn't it?"

The woman standing before him, quite a young woman actually, no more than in her late thirties, shakes her head.

"Veldkamp," she says. "Veldkamp is the name. Biology."

Only then does Hofmeester see himself, the way he's standing there. Pointing at a strange woman, one of his youngest daughter's teachers, with a bleeding index finger. He drops his hand to his side.

"Of course. Please excuse me." He claps his hands. "Biology. How could I forget? Miss Veldkamp, of course. We've met often enough. The last time was . . ."

She looks down, and he follows her gaze. Only at that moment does he notice his bare feet and, almost at the same time, his bare stomach.

"Oh, God," he says. "I must excuse myself."

"For what?" Miss Veldkamp asks.

"For this." He points to his stomach. His bare chest.

"Oh, that's no problem."

"I was taking a shower and I heard the bell and my daughters are . . ." He coughs. "My daughters are nowhere to be found."

"Shall I go for a walk around the block first? I don't mind at all. It's such lovely weather. And I have this bad habit of showing up too early all the time. Am I much too early?'

"No, not at all. You're right on time."

Taking her right hand, he drags Miss Veldkamp into the house. He closes the front door with his foot.

Only after a few meters does he realize that it is rude to drag your children's teachers into your house. At the door to the living room he lets go of her abruptly and says: "I'm afraid I owe you another apology."

"For what?" Miss Veldkamp wants to know.

"For treating you so heavy-handedly."

"Oh, but that's all right." She laughs curtly and a bit ironically. "In fact, I rather like it when people deal with me a bit heavy-handedly now and then."

He looks at her in doubt. Not only is he half-naked, as though that weren't unpleasant enough already, now he also has the feeling he's being laughed at.

"I'm afraid I'm not myself," he says. "It's the heat, the party, the leave-taking. Tirza, as you know, is going to Africa."

"We're all not ourselves from time to time. It would be very boring if we were ourselves all the time, Mr. Hofmeester."

He examines her face to see whether she is serious, to rid himself of the nasty feeling that he's being laughed at. Then he begins to realize that a half-naked man is no disaster. Half the world runs around naked. There's nothing to get upset about.

"Please, do make yourself comfortable. I'll be right with you."

He hurries up the stairs. In the bedroom, his wife is busy doing her nails. She holds out her hand. "What do you think of this color?"

He pulls on his socks and shoes, then goes for the polo shirt anyway, even though it smells of sardines. The whole house will smell of sardines soon enough. He stops in front of the mirror for a moment and realizes, to his surprise, that he feels sad. A sadness that wins out over all those other feelings that sometimes well up in him. The shame, the fear, the realization that he is an embarrassment.

"Is this a nice pink, or is it too bright?" she asks.

"You're right," he says. "All we have is each other. We can't get anyone else. That's it."

"Is it too pink?"

She holds her hand out closer to him. The smell of nail polish prickles his nostrils, mingles with the odor of fried sardines.

"So you can't get anyone else either. Relegated to the scrapheap. That's why you came." He is talking more to himself than to her.

"Is it too pink? Be honest."

"No," he says. "It's exactly right. Miss Veldkamp is downstairs. She saw me half-naked."

"Who is Miss Veldkamp? I don't have any idea who's who anymore. Later on, you'll have to sort of introduce me to all these people. I'm sure I won't be able to link up faces to names."

She talks as though nothing has happened. The way she's always talked. As though nothing has happened.

In the bathroom he splashes on a lot of aftershave, to mask the sardines.

Ibi is in there, brushing her teeth. "Where's Tirza?" he asks from behind a cloud of aftershave.

"She's picking up her boyfriend," Ibi says, and goes on brushing.

With a bounce in his step and smelling sweet, Hofmeester descends the stairs. He walks straight on through to the kitchen, takes the platter out of the fridge, removes the plastic foil and parades into the living room, where Miss Veldkamp is sitting on the couch, all alone.

"Sushi," Hofmeester says, "and sashimi. And there's wasabi mayonnaise in the kitchen."

"How lovely," she says.

"I made it myself."

"The sushi?"

"That too. But I was referring to the wasabi mayonnaise. I make it myself. It's not easy, but I've dabbled in it a little."

"Oh."

They look at each other for a moment, the biology teacher and Tirza's father.

"Wait, I'll put on some music."

He walks over to the CD player.

Tirza has burned a few mix CDs especially for this evening. They are lying in wait, a little stack of them.

He puts on the first CD and waits to hear which music will

follow. She has not only put her own music on them, but also a few songs he likes particularly well.

"The Andrews Sisters," he says delightedly, "this is one of Tirza's favorite songs."

That's because of him. It is, in fact, one of *his* favorite songs. Even when Tirza was still in the crib, he used to play The Andrews Sisters for her. He would dance around the room with her in his arms, and he forgot about the curse. For a moment there was no curse, no history, only the baby in his arms, her look, the smell of somewhat sourish milk, her warm head, and The Andrews Sisters.

Now there's no Tirza, there is only a platter of sushi and sashimi and a man getting on in years who, despite the aftershave, still reeks vaguely of fried sardines.

And he sings along quietly with the music, in front of Miss Veldkamp, who sits motionless on the couch.

"I'll try to explain. *Bei mir bist du schön.* So kiss me and say you understand."

Miss Veldkamp smiles. She has probably seen plenty in her day, and when Hofmeester is finished singing, she says: "A little wasabi mayonnaise would be very nice."

He goes to the kitchen, comes back with the wasabi and a saucer, and lets Miss Veldkamp serve herself with a little wooden spoon. From the Japanese shop on Beethovenstraat as well.

He watches proudly as she eats his sushi.

Of happiness, of the intense, unrelenting, rapacious happiness of youth he remembers only a rumor. A fairy tale he never read himself.

What is left of his youth, or what passes for it, is a worn-out song.

He walks over to the CD player and pushes restart.

And while Miss Veldkamp, sushi in hand, looks at him a bit surprised and rather anxiously, he sings for her.

"Ridi," Hofmeester sings. "Ridi ridi, ridi ridi ridi."

2

By nine o'clock the room is filled with more than a dozen young people—as well as Miss Veldkamp and an economics teacher who Hofmeester is supposed to call "Hans"—but there is still no sign of Tirza. The wife keeps to herself in the upstairs bedroom, smoking probably, smiling occasionally at the thought of the old flame with his dead sperm, the way one smiles furtively at someone else's failure. Someone else's colossal failure.

And Hofmeester himself walks around the house with raw fish. He hands out glasses of kir, talks about subjects he has never spoken of before, he has already mixed two cocktails, a caipirinha and a screwdriver. Both mixed to a T. He has outdone himself, this evening he has outdone himself again and again.

Without much in the way of effort, tonight he towers head and shoulders above the Jörgen Hofmeester who, at his wife's parties all those years ago, would sit silently in a corner, pass out hors d'oeuvres or get up halfway through a conversation to water the plants. Riotous parties those were, attended by men many years younger than

Hofmeester, men to whom his wife had awarded the status of "friend of the family."

Jörgen Hofmeester is making progress. He has become more sociable. Milder and more accessible. More than anything else, though, he is now Tirza's father, and in that role he is jovial to the point of exuberance. If the party is a flop, it won't be because of him.

Halfway through a round of edamame he thinks he recognizes a boy he once ran into in his bathroom, one early Sunday morning last winter. The boy had been sitting on the edge of the tub, sick and pale, with red-rimmed eyes. But when he asks the boy about it, politely but directly, while offering him some edamame, the boy denies it. "I've never been here before," he says. Hofmeester is sure he saw him the bathroom, even smelled him, but he doesn't press on. Young people, too, have a right to little white lies.

Ibi has come downstairs and is sitting the couch, beside the biology teacher. At least one of his daughters has come to the party.

After a long initial silence, Ibi and the teacher start up a conversation. That comes as a relief to Hofmeester. Ibi can be so grumpy. Ibi used to be against everything. There are days when she still is.

The doorbell rings again and again, and when it does Tirza's father races to the door to do what his youngest daughter should be doing. Shaking hands, pecking people on the cheeks, being admired, receiving compliments. Hofmeester limits himself mostly to a firm handshake, accompanied in a few cases by the words that should explain everything: "I'm Tirza's father." When he speaks those words, there appears on his face what he himself assumes to be a winning smile.

"She'll be here any minute," he says again and again, "she's just gone to pick up her boyfriend." It sounds as though he knows exactly what that boyfriend is like, as though the Hofmeester family has already been on vacation with the boy at least three times.

Some of the guests hand him a present meant for Tirza. They mumble: "Here, this is for Tirza," and hand him something, without looking him in the eye. Shy boys, who Hofmeester suspects must once have been in love with Tirza. Who wrote her letters, sent desperate text messages in the middle of the night of which they were later so ashamed that they didn't dare to go to school the next day. He tries to buck them up a little. He doesn't want them to lose hope. Shyness can be a curse. Never lose hope, that's what it's all about. Whatever happens. Don't abandon hope. Stick with it.

"I'm sure she'll love it," he says, without knowing what is hidden beneath the wrapping paper. And he places the presents on the buffet table, amid other packages large and small, the usual bottles of alcoholic beverage, a few bouquets. The tradition of the gift table continues to be held in honor. A family is a construct of traditions. Hofmeester dearly wants them to be a family, a small family, half a family perhaps. That is why he safeguards the traditions, that is why he honors them, all alone if need be.

As he is walking through the hall with a tray holding three beers, two glasses of red wine, and a vodka-ice, he sees the wife coming down the stairs. She's wearing Ibi's old denim skirt and a blouse that is too tight. Much too tight. Everything is bulging out of it, the way a woman's body can bulge.

She is wearing high heels. Shoes, blouse, skirt, it looks like she found it all in a box the children use for playing dress-up in the attic.

He remains standing in the hallway until she reaches the bottom step. The tray in his hands, the light odor of sweat, aftershave, and fried sardines surrounding him. The smell of the party.

"Jesus," he says quietly.

None of the guests have yet worked up the courage to go to the garden. The torches there are burning unseen. The guests cluster together in the living room. They're waiting for the others, they are waiting for Tirza.

The wife stops in front of him and turns full circle. In high heels, her legs still compare favorably with the way they used to be. When they first met, during the first days, the first weeks. The days when you are still an unknown factor to the other, the freedom that that brings, the happiness. Somewhere in her legs is the freedom Hofmeester lost, and found again at Schiphol. But the taste of freedom no longer appeals to him, or rather, he now knows what freedom really tastes like: gall.

Somewhere in her legs is the memory of happiness. They had always been pretty, those legs; long, slim but muscular. When she was set to impress, she would wear a short skirt. He remembers the looks other men gave her, he remembers realizing for the first time that he had had children with a woman who was actually too young for him, who went along with neither his age nor his status. Her still-lifes had never amounted to much, but as still-life herself she was unsurpassed. In the 1970s, Hofmeester had been seen as a coming man, an editor who would ultimately work his way up to publisher. Someone to watch out for. But he stayed put in his office on Herengracht, with his view of the tree, concentrating on translated fiction and sometimes on the tree, until one day he woke up and had to admit that no one needed to watch out for him anymore. Only he himself, that was all. Hell was not other people. It was him. Hell was deep inside him. Tethered, hidden and invisible, but still alive, still warm. Glowing hot.

"Isn't that a bit too much?" he asked.

"What? This?" She pointed at herself. She shook her head. "Am I too much? I don't think so. Do you think it's too much, Jörgen? And I did so do my very best for Tirza's party."

"Yes, that's precisely it. Precisely because this is her party, her big party, you could have . . ." He gropes for words, for diplomatic solutions. He looks at what is bulging out of her blouse. She looks desperate, but still not unattractive. The word "slut" comes to mind. Now that youth has abandoned his wife, he sees in her the slut she probably always was. "You could have contained yourself."

"Contain myself? What do you mean? Don't you like it?"

The tray rattles in Hofmeester's hands. The doorbell rings.

"Go upstairs and put something else on," he says. "I beg of you. This is inappropriate. You're not sixteen anymore. We are not sixteen anymore."

"But Jörgen, you're only as old as you feel. Didn't anyone ever tell you that? I am the flower of eternal youth."

She pushes the tray a little to one side and kisses him quickly on the lips. "Can you taste it?" she whispers. "The flower of eternal youth?"

He twists away, he doesn't want to kiss her, he never wants to kiss her again. Never again. Two words like a charm. The world's shortest prayer. Jörgen Hofmeester's Prayer. Never again.

The bell rings again. "It's a disgrace," he says. "You're a disgrace, the way you look now. And I'm sorry, but you are not the flower of eternal youth."

She tries to press her mouth against his again, but he steps back. The rattling of the tray becomes worse.

"Then I really do belong with you," she says. "If I'm a disgrace, then we must be identical twins. Then we were made for each other." She laughs. She laughs as though nothing has ever happened between them. Good-naturedly. To underscore the bond that no longer exists, that's how she laughs.

Then she walks into the living room, and Hofmeester hears the conversations falter. He remains standing in the hallway, he wishes he could scream, the way people do when they're trapped in an elevator, but the only thing that comes out of his mouth is the sound of his own labored breathing.

He goes back to the kitchen, sets the tray on the counter, and pours himself a glass of white wine. "The flower of eternal youth," he mumbles. Other memories force themselves upon him, pleasant ones as well. In the swamp of his memory, nice recollections are also hidden. If you can remember happiness, then it did exist.

A colleague once said to him: "You can't live off of memories." What it was that prompted him to say that, Hofmeester can no longer recall. The point of the conversation has slipped away from him. All he knows is that the colleague told him: "You can't keep poking around with a knife in your past, like it's some garden you need to cultivate, Jörgen, because someday you'll poke that knife into yourself."

Not long afterwards, that colleague died of a heart attack.

You're a slave to your memories. That's just the way it is, Hofmeester thinks. Some people remember things that never happened. You get that too. They're slaves to fiction. Carrier pigeons of their own myth.

He drinks the rest of his wine, not noticing much more than the cold, slightly sourish taste. Only when the bell rings for the third time does he suddenly realize that there is someone at the door.

He runs to get it, angry at himself, angry at his wife, angry at the person who now, of all moments, has to show up at the door. Hofmeester strives—there's nothing he can do about it—for perfection. This is the party that has to be perfect, that has to prove that the rumors going around about him are not true. How well it has all turned out, that's what he wants to say, that's what he wants to get across, how well his life has turned out, how well the children have turned out.

That's the hidden message behind the kir, that is what the sashimi is meant to say, that is the story behind the caipirinha: the story of Tirza's father, the story with the happy ending. He had to raise his youngest daughter all alone, but everything turned out well. Yes, let his message for this one evening, for God's sake, be one of good cheer.

There is a girl at the door. One of Tirza's many girlfriends, one he's never seen before.

"Hey," the girl says.

"Hey," says Hofmeester, thinking at the same time about the wife, who has turned out to be a disgrace, and wondering exactly what's going on in the living room right now. Just like he wondered after she left, in the evening when Tirza was upstairs doing her homework or on the phone with her friends: where is she now? What is she doing? In whose arms is she lying? What is she wearing? Does she feel regret? The silence sometimes forced him to turn on the TV. There was no one left to argue with. He had become his own enemy. If he wanted to get annoyed, he had to watch a talk show. His shouting was aimed then at the TV. Until he started feeling sorry for the TV, and sat across from it in silence.

"Are you Tirza's father?"

He nods, almost delighted at this distraction from what are, of course, needless worries. They're not a couple anymore, they have no relationship. If his wife wants to make a fool of herself, that's her business.

"I'm Ester," she says, "without the 'h'."

"Ester without the 'h'," he repeats. "I'm Jörgen, with an umlaut above the 'o'." He suspects that his snappy answer is funny, and that suspicion, amplified by the white wine, brings on a brief moment of euphoria. For a moment Hofmeester is liberated, for a few seconds he strides down his own hallway like a conqueror.

At the closet he stops to take her things, a jacket, a present, a bag, but there is nothing to take. Ester without the 'h' is wearing a pair of grubby jeans, and she has two phone numbers written on the back of her hand, he sees. On her feet are a pair of flip-flops. She has arrived without a present. She has, one might almost say, come undressed. Hofmeester doesn't like people who won't try to be accepted.

"Could I offer you a glass of kir?" he asks.

The question with which he has greeted almost every guest this evening. A question that covers all the bases. After that, experience tells him, the conversation flows.

"What?"

"A glass of kir. Could I offer you one?"

She shakes her head. "Do you have tomato juice?"

"Yes, of course. I also have tomato juice."

"Without ice."

"Without ice," Hofmeester repeats, as though he has spent his whole life doing nothing but this: taking orders, hanging up jackets, introducing people whose name he has barely been able to make out to other people.

"And could I use the toilet?"

He shows her the way. The toilet is next to the kitchen. He opens the door, turns on the light, and quickly checks whether the toilet still looks respectable. Better than he'd expected. For a party.

In the kitchen he searches for the tomato juice. He'd had three packs of it. But where are they? From the living room, he can hear his wife's voice above the music. She's talking as though she were on stage at the national theater and had to be heard all the way in the back row.

He bought them, yesterday, he's sure, three packs.

Once again he opens the fridge, the tomato juice must be in there somewhere. He squats down, he kneels, maybe in the vegetable drawer? He pushes aside a few packs of orange juice and, in doing so, knocks the milk onto the floor.

Now Hofmeester is kneeling in a puddle of milk, in front of the open refrigerator door, and staring at a plate of the sushi he prepared so lovingly earlier in the day.

I mustn't lose my senses, he thinks. This is no time for that.

He stands up quickly and closes the refrigerator door. He pours himself a glass of wine and says quietly: "This is a lovely evening. This is Tirza's evening."

Then he takes a roll of paper towels and carefully wipes up the milk.

For at least thirty seconds he stands there motionless, the wet clump of paper towels still in his hand. The toilet flushes. He squeezes the paper towels gently above the sink. As a charming host, that's the way he wants to be remembered. That should be a realistic enough ambition.

That realization forces him into action. He throws away the paper towels and has the feeling of having narrowly escaped from something. Of having averted danger. There are still two wet spots on his knees, but who will look at his knees at a party like this?

He straightens his hair; picks up the tray with the beer, red wine, and vodka-ice; and walks with into the living room, wearing the smile he has been practicing for decades. The smile of fiction in translation.

"I'm her mother, can't you tell?" he hears the wife say. She is standing with a little group of Tirza's classmates. The children, in so far as one can still call them children, are standing around her as though she were a big fish they had just barely landed.

Hofmeester takes a few more orders and turns up the music a little louder, to keep all too many people from having to listen to the wife's words. Despite the higher volume, he hears the wife say, loud and clear: "I was traveling. Tirza got along wonderfully with my husband. She's a very independent child, always has been. She didn't need anyone."

Hofmeester carries the empty tray back to the kitchen. He makes two new rolls of sushi, one with salmon, the other with tuna, drinks a glass of white wine, then calls Tirza on her cell phone, but she doesn't answer. He is growing nervous. A father is someone who is called upon at all times to worry. Especially when the mother refuses to do so.

He hears her voice. "Hi, this is Tirza. I can't answer the phone right now. But be sure to leave a nice message."

That part about the nice message is something he's never understood. There are times when you can't leave a nice message, aren't there? "Does your phone only receive nice messages?" he asked her once.

"Yes, Daddy," Tirza had told him. "My phone is for the nice messages. If the messages aren't nice, they have to call you."

"Where are you?" he says to the voicemail recording. "Tirza, please come home as quickly as possible. Your party started a long time ago. We're all waiting for you."

Then he sits down on the stool. He presses his hands to his temples and remains sitting there like that, until he sees the economics teacher come strolling into the kitchen.

After walking around the kitchen twice, the economics teacher stops, he leans against the counter and stares at Hofmeester a bit rudely, the way people do at parties. The way guests wander off to look around the house. In the living room they stand before the bookcase for a few minutes, then say to themselves: I wonder what the kitchen looks like? Kitchens say a lot.

Hofmeester is not about to be intimidated, he just stares back, without being able to move a muscle. The man's good humor seems hostile to Hofmeester. Other people's cheerfulness is threatening.

The man has a bottle of beer in his hand, his linen sports jacket hangs loosely over his back and shoulders. He could just as easily be a student, but he is a teacher, and he is grinning. The economics teacher, it seems, is a man who grins all the time.

"How's it going, Mr. Hofmeester?" he asks.

Hofmeester gets up from the stool. He feels as though he's been caught red-handed, as though he were a stranger in his own home, as though he were doing things in his own kitchen that cannot stand the light of day. There are still spots on the knees of his black trousers. Otherwise there's nothing more to be seen of the milk. That's the good thing about black. It doesn't show much. But he can still feel it, the moistness. He feels it right through his pants legs. Wet is what he is, a wet man getting on in years. They mustn't see it, he won't let them see it.

"Excellent, thank you. But call me Jörgen. I'm Jörgen. And you? Are you managing to have a good time?"

Hofmeester speaks quietly and civilly, like someone who is holding himself in, but without that costing him any great effort.

Are you managing to have a good time? Is that a question you would ask an economics teacher? He has his doubts, but it's too late to do anything about it now. He remembers that the economics teacher's name is Hans. Wasn't there a fairy-tale about someone named Hans?

Hofmeester is feeling dizzy. He doesn't want to sit down on the stool again. He concentrates on the economics teacher's shoes, black shoes with a buckle. A fairy-tale character named Hans, he can't put his finger on it. He used to read aloud to the children all the time, even from books they weren't yet old enough to understand. To instill children with a love for art and culture, you have to make them stand on tippy toe. At the age of ten, Tirza heard the adventures of Don Quixote, at twelve she was spoon-fed Madame Bovary and her adultery, at fourteen, when she didn't want to be read aloud to anymore, Hofmeester would still climb the stairs to her room with a volume from the Russian Library under his arm. "Go away," she would shriek when he came into her room. "I don't want any notes from under the ground, I don't want to hear them. Go away, Daddy. Go away, just go away." She fretted and fumed, but he would sit down on the foot end of her bed and caress her until she grew calm. Then he would open the book and read to her for fifteen minutes from *Notes from Underground*. You can't start too early with an introduction to the great Russians. Catch onto nihilism as an adolescent and you won't have to go through it yourself later on.

"The party is wonderful," Hans says. He looks around, he makes no move to leave. The kitchen seems to appeal to him, it's cozy and comfortable. Leaning against the counter, you can let the hours slip away. Another evening accounted for.

Weekends in the comfort of one's own home, the sound of the juicer in the morning, the TV in the evening, a party once every three months. Going shopping together. Buying a CD together.

Working on a crossword puzzle together. That must be the way the economics teacher leads his life.

It seems familiar to Hofmeester, the family life, but also not. He smoothes his hair and offers the economics teacher some sushi, while trying to imagine the man's existence: a well-ordered and happy one.

Long ago, before silence entered this house, he had sometimes regretted not being able to play the piano. Then he could have sat down at his piano in the evening or on Sunday afternoons, a group of three or four enthusiasts around him, the way other people sit in a café with a group of friends.

He had no talent for friendship, just as others have no talent for drawing or for foreign languages. It was precisely for that reason that he wished he could play an instrument. Rather than talk to people, he would have preferred to make music for them. One talks in order to express thoughts. Hofmeester's thoughts were mostly ones that should not be expressed, that are private and should remain so, in the interests of both parties.

Tirza used to play the cello. She was very talented, but she had put the cello aside. Only occasionally, after the wife left, when the silence in the evening was about to drive him mad, when he could no longer endure it, no matter how he tried—after walking around the garden twenty times, reading to himself aloud from Dostoyevsky's *A Writer's Diary*—at such moments he would climb the stairs and knock on Tirza's door.

"Have you finished your homework?" he would ask. If she said "Yes," he would ask: "Would you like to come downstairs and play the cello for me?" But he only asked that when she was done with her homework. School took precedence, school took precedence even over the cello.

"A special girl, your daughter. Sensitive, gifted, quick on her feet." The economics teacher stands there pensively, beer in hand, as if he regretted all of that. Having to say farewell, the fact that

Tirza had passed her exams, his own career. The man wipes his lips. "Sushi is one thing you shouldn't eat too much of," he says.

Hofmeester nods. He opens his mouth. He has decided to say something. It has to happen now. He's going to talk.

"She is indeed very sensitive," he says. "And very gifted, even as a toddler. When she was only eighteen months old, she understood everything you said. There was nothing she didn't understand."

"She's also very pretty."

"Pretty, too," Hofmeester agrees.

"And grown-up."

Hofmeester nods again.

"She's going to take a trip around the world, I hear."

"Not really around the world. She's going to travel for awhile. Africa. Botswana, South Africa, Namibia. Perhaps Zaire. That continent has always interested her. Would you like another beer?" Hofmeester is leaning against the counter now as well. From the living room, voices filter through vaguely to the kitchen. Whatever the wife is saying, Hofmeester doesn't want to hear. He relaxes and thinks about Schiphol, the departure hall where he lingers five days a week. In the same way a plane is built to fly, he is built for loneliness. Only occasionally does he touch someone else, like a plane touching the runway. Only to take off again quickly, engines sputtering. A plane that stays on the ground too long will never come free of it again. Every day a crash landing. Every hour a crash landing. His life, one long crash landing.

"Yes, that would be nice," the economics teacher says. He puts his empty bottle in the sink.

"A glass?"

The man shakes his head. "Do make sure she takes her own needles with her if she goes to Botswana and Zaire." He takes the beer bottle from Hofmeester and raises it to his lips immediately.

Hofmeester watches. Again, he feels himself growing dizzy.

"Her own needles?"

"Hypodermic needles. When you go to Africa, you need to take your own hypodermic needles. You never know when you'll end up in a hospital."

Tirza's father can imagine that students, secretly or less secretly, have fallen in love with the economics teacher. He radiates that something that everyone needs. Confidence, not only in the future, but in everything. In life itself. In the goodness of all that is alive. An intense confidence, that's what he radiates.

"So you've been there yourself?"

"Africa?" the man says. "Never. Well, Egypt, Hurghada, the Canary Islands. But you can't really call that Africa, can you? I know people who have been to the real Africa, and they took their own hypodermic needles with them. If you go to Cape Town you don't need them, but is Cape Town still really Africa?"

A silence settles in. With Cape Town, the conversation seems to have drawn to an end.

"Could I ask you something?" Hofmeester lets go of the counter. He crosses his arms. "A strange question, perhaps."

"Of course," the man says. "Of course you may. Anything. Even strange questions. I've heard plenty of them." He laughs and takes a big slug of beer.

Again Hofmeester feels the dizziness. Worse now. The dizziness is the symptom of an unwelcome thought. Thoughts that shouldn't be there, but that won't be blotted out, that's what hell is.

"What is a 'hedge fund,' exactly?"

A moment ago the economics teacher had been laughing jovially and invitingly. You could ask him anything. That's what he was there for. To give answers, even to unanswerable questions. But this apparently was something he hadn't expected.

"A hedge fund?"

"A hedge fund," Hofmeester repeats. Had he asked: "What's that like, I mean, the sex life of the crocodile?" the silence could not have been more oppressive.

"Well, how can I explain?" the economics teacher says after a few seconds. "It's sort of an investment fund. An investment fund that makes a profit, or could potentially make a profit, even when markets are depressed. Hedge funds usually aren't open to the general public." He is about to say something else, but seems to have forgotten what that was. He smiles, for the first time now a bit helplessly as well. Lost in a conversation he would rather have avoided on his night off.

About five years ago, when Hofmeester had gone abroad again with seven months' rent in his briefcase, the consultant at the bank had talked to him about hedge funds. No, he had talked to *her* about hedge funds. Hedge funds were all the rage then.

He had read about them, he had heard about them. The hedge fund was making a big buzz, like a deep but extremely seductive secret.

The bank consultant's explanation of hedge funds hadn't really seemed clear to him at the time, but in cases like this one had to rely on one's intuition. His intuition had never betrayed him before, at least not when it came to banking matters.

"A hedge fund requires a minimum investment of one million euros," she said.

One million, that was pretty much all Hofmeester had in the bank. He had saved conscientiously, oh, he had transferred more than the rent alone to his account here. The occasional minor inheritance, the proceeds from the sale of a boat, often enough his vacation allowance as well. Everything went to the investment fund that was going to give his daughters access to worlds Hofmeester himself had never entered. "But are you sure you don't want to diversify a little?" the consultant had asked. She was a young woman, with blonde hair, wearing a tight black pants suit. Luxuriant hair. She was new. Before that he had always talked to a man. A man had advised him on investment matters. A man with brown hair. At least, what was left of it had been brown. The man had bald spots all over his scalp. Hofmeester saw a lot, and the more he saw the less he dared to say. The more he saw, the more thoughts came bubbling up in him that should not be shared with the world at large. Blindness, for that reason alone, would have been extremely convenient for him.

"You have to be willing to go out on a limb," Hofmeester had said. "Taking risks is all part of the game." The thought of looming financial independence, which would keep his children from having to kowtow to anyone, as well as the consultant's tight black pants suit, made Hofmeester hopeful. Hopeful to the point of recklessness. Oh, there was hope, you only had to keep your eyes peeled for it. The results the hedge fund had achieved in the past were spectacular. There was no other word for it. That much, at least, had registered with him. Spectacular. A word solid as a rock. A word that reminded him vaguely of sex, covert sex in an elevator or a restroom.

"I must warn you, though, the administration costs are quite high."

"But the results *are* spectacular."

"The results *are* spectacular," the woman from the bank concurred. She pronounced the word "spectacular" as though it were a rare delicacy. "And it's an extremely popular hedge fund."

The look she gave him, he thought, was radiant.

"I want it," Hofmeester said, his mouth dry. "Give me the hedge fund."

And he stared at her as though she were the hedge fund. The way she sat there across from him, like a fashion model, left no room for even a smidgen of doubt: the young lady from the bank was a hedge fund of human flesh.

"Shall we do it then?"she asked. She made it sound like a question, but it was clearly a question posed for the sake of form. "Everything?"

"Everything," Hofmeester said.

The fund to which he was now going to transfer his holdings had a name that was exotic but also reliable, as though it had always been there, as though it had been leading a secret life for decades. And this beguiling phenomenon had revealed itself to him only now, like a god who had nevertheless chosen him, out of the blue, to proclaim its existence.

The young lady wrote something on a slip of paper that Hofmeester signed cheerfully, almost magnanimously, with his own fountain pen, then she asked: "More coffee?"

"Yes, please."

"A cookie to go with it?"

"Lovely," Hofmeester said.

When the cookies arrived, Hofmeester took one from the plate so eagerly that it crumbled in his hand. He looked at the crumbs, he looked at the young lady.

But the lady from the bank didn't notice, and he remained who he was, the man who came to bring the rent. Not for him, for his daughters. For their future. For a better future. Happiness at a price.

In March of the following year he went to the bank with the last few months' rent. The hedge fund was doing extremely well. Spectacularly, that was the word for it. Yes, financial independence was now within reach.

One year later, at the end of March, he made the trip to the bank again. Nothing had changed, everything was the same, the same train trip, the same office, the same computer, the same female consultant, although this time she wasn't wearing a tight black pants suit but a gray skirt with a white blouse. It was all there, including her blonde, luxuriant hair and the coffee lady and the cookies, they were all there. The only thing that wasn't there anymore was the hedge fund. It had gone up in smoke. Vanished. Vaporized.

"How can that be?" Hofmeester asked.

What followed was a long and technical story that made no sense to him, because he was unable to listen to it. He couldn't concentrate. Sticking to the moist palm of his right hand were countless crumbs from a shortbread cookie.

All he could think was: I've been beaten. But he didn't know who or what had beaten him. Not the young lady across the table, with her red lips and her white blouse, a woman he would have enjoyed kissing sometime. But he had his lust under control. His lust was a trained sheep that performed tricks for a small-but-faithful audience. It was not the tenants who had beaten him, they had paid as they should, and it was not the bank, the bank couldn't do anything about it, at least that's what he gathered from the words of the woman with the friendly smile. She truly regretted it, and he almost believed her too. She regretted it as much as he did, and the term "international economy" came up again and again. It sounded like "international Jewry," but then more innocuous, and therefore more grisly.

He, Jörgen Hofmeester, who had outfoxed the taxman and the tenants, who had saved in order to provide his daughters with an enviable degree of financial independence, who had worked because he lived in the conviction that work was the panacea for sorrow and misery, had been beaten by the international economy. That's what it came down to. The international economy had forced him to his knees. In the international economy he had met the foe who was too strong for him, too strong for the predator. A worthy enemy at last. But it was an enemy without a face or a name. An enemy from whom one could claim no damages. The international economy was an enemy that would not break the silence. This was not an enemy that could make his blood run hot. He could not seize the international economy in his arms and quietly bite it to death. The international economy had no face.

"We've been having a difficult time," said the young lady, wearing a sad expression, but still he could see that she wasn't really sad, more like cheerful. "First the dot-com bubble, then September 11th. There have been some hard blows dealt out, and some market players just didn't recover."

"What does September 11th have to do with this?"

He remembered that day itself as clearly as the one when the Wall came down. How he'd said to his daughter: "Pay attention, remember this, this is history." And that is how he had viewed it as well. As history.

"Oh, Mr. Hofmeester," she said, "these days everything has to do with everything else. You know what they say: When a butterfly flaps its wings in Brazil, it causes a tornado in Texas. But how are your daughters? You have two daughters, don't you?"

History was now on the point of getting personal. The anonymous international economy was taking on a face, a body, a name. Mohammed Atta, he was the one who had taken away Hofmeester's money, his financial independence, his children's freedom, which had been so close, so horribly close. Mohammed Atta was behind all this, Atta had beheaded Hofmeester's hedge fund.

"I'm sorry, what did you say?"

"How are your daughters doing?"

"Very well, thank you," he said. "But why didn't you call me?"

"We couldn't reach you."

The end of the conversation was slowly approaching. There was still a bit of money on his account, something like two months' rent, and he also deposited the eight months he had with him.

The lady from the bank asked: "Do you want to invest this?"

"No, just put it in a savings account."

They shook hands. "Well, see you next year," she said.

Then he was out on the street. Early spring. Sunshine. People walking down the sidewalk for the first time without a coat on. The cheerfulness that went with that. So this is how financial independence ends, he thought. The way everything ends. Done and gone in an hour. They give you an extra cookie. And a pitying look. The sympathy mustn't take more than ten minutes though, because the cost of labor is going up.

He walked down a shopping street, looked at the faces of the other people and wondered whether they, too, had been beaten by the international economy. Or by Mohammed Atta. Or by both, simultaneously. Was there some way they could recognize each other, the ones who had been beaten? Or would they remain anonymous forever? The winners and the losers shoulder to shoulder like brothers, strolling together down an exclusive shopping street. Promenading for all eternity. No one could tell where the wheat ended and the chaff began.

He stopped in front of a shoe store. He looked closely at the men's shoes. Brown seemed to be the fashion this spring. He didn't like brown shoes. Not brown suits either.

He asked himself why it was that he had nothing anymore. Why everything had been taken away from him. He couldn't come up with a good reason. What purpose did this serve? What game was being played here, anyway? And who was playing it with him?

He went into the store and tried on a pair of black boots, then realized that he could no longer afford them. From now on, there would be very little he could afford. For a moment, for a fraction of a second, he struggled with the urge to rip off the saleswoman's clothes and penetrate her there, on the spot, if only because self-control no longer had anything to offer him. Lust is the highest form of indifference. He looked at her. "Would you like to see some other boots?" she asked. "Or perhaps some dress shoes? That might be nicer, with summer coming up."

He who commits an offence is never alone anymore. Wherever he goes, the offence goes with him. But he didn't have the nerve, the security man at the door was already keeping an eye on him, and he hurried out of the shop. So hurriedly that he left his briefcase behind. The saleswoman came running after him.

He looked in it. In addition to two manuscripts, four pencils and a banana, the briefcase contained folders about hedge funds and other varieties of investment fund. Colorful folders, printed on glossy paper, and he knew what printed material cost. Standing in the middle of the busy shopping street, he flipped through the folders, the briefcase clenched under his arm. People bumped into him. He was standing in the way, but he remained standing. He saw the charts, the figures, the language with which the future was described, a rosy, carefree future.

Then he put everything back in the case. Defeat was no longer a fearful dream, a vision for muggy summer evenings. It was here. The defeat had arrived unannounced.

How do you go on living after you have been defeated? Do you look people in the eye, or is that precisely what you don't do? Perhaps it's better to keep your eyes averted, in the hope that they won't see you as long as you don't see them.

At a McDonald's he bought a vanilla ice cream cone, which he ate sitting on the curb outside, beside a group of young people. For a few seconds they looked at him, amazed and laughing, their packs full of schoolbooks on the ground beside them, then they decided to ignore him. The old man with his ice cream cone. They let him be. They left him alone.

He still had Tirza. Not everything had been taken from him. They had left him something. Tirza. They had left him the loveliest, the best, the dearest. They had left him the sun queen.

He stood up and, though beaten still, walked to the station without averting his eyes. Because Tirza was still there, waiting for him somewhere, in another world where there were no hedge funds, in another country, another life.

In the train on the way home, however, the thought of the sun queen could not keep him from feeling ashamed at having been beaten by the international economy. He was overcome by a powerful sense of shame, an all-embracing shame, which ended in a single thought: I can't face people anymore.

So he became a man who averted his eyes as he walked down the street, a man who stared at his shoes as he pushed his cart around the supermarket, a man who avoided the gaze of others as though afraid that the history of his life was written across his forehead. History as a scrofulous rash. A brand.

At home he hid the hedge-fund folders in a bottom drawer. It felt as though he were burying not only the folders, but his entire life.

"They're very popular these days," says the economics teacher. "But you have to be careful with them, that's for sure. The institutional investors have to put their money into something, every day. So when the market stagnates, they go looking for alternatives. That's where the hedge fund comes from. In fact, though, the whole thing is already past its prime. But why do you want to know, if you don't mind my asking?"

Hofmeester reaches out and fingers the lapel of the economics teacher's linen sports jacket, almost in passing. As though he has just noticed a spot on his guest's jacket which he, as a good host, wants to brush away.

This evening it's different. This evening he looks people in the eye. This evening all is forgotten. This evening he is who he used to be, but then better, an improved version of the old Hofmeester, because this party is for the sun queen.

"You have to be careful with them, indeed," Hofmeester says. "Like with a loaded gun."

"I never thought about it that way before, but yes, that's one way of looking at it."

A chuckle, a slug of beer. Another chuckle. The economics teacher really is charming, almost disarmingly so.

Hofmeester lets go of his lapel, he picks up the cocktail shaker from the improvised bar and begins shaking vehemently. Tirza's friends should really try a few more of his mixes. When your youngest daughter throws a party, you should be exuberant. Vibrant. Full of good cheer. Hopeful. At your youngest daughter's party, you're sort of the birthday boy yourself. He puts the shaker back down on the counter and pours himself half a glass of wine. He ticks his glass against the economics teacher's beer bottle. "She's something very special," he says. "She's . . ." For a moment, he's at a loss for words.

The thought of his daughter overwhelms him, leaves him with nothing left, reduces him to an appendage of that daughter. An insignificant and superfluous appendage.

"Tirza? Oh, she sure is. I have a special bond with her. I have that with a few students in her class, it's a rather unique class, but particularly with Tirza. So cheerful, so open. And who know what next year is going to bring."

The economics teacher moves towards the door. He's had enough of the kitchen. He doesn't feel much like sushi at the moment either. And he's never been much of one for cocktails. He's going back to where the real party is happening, to its epicenter, the living room.

"They vanish sometimes, hedge funds, don't they?" Hofmeester shouts after him. "They cease to be. As though they never existed." Hofmeester is hoarse. He remembers his agitation after the conversation at the bank. Decades of rental income and capital gains vanished. What happened to his money, that's what he'd like to know? He doesn't need to have it back, for he has come to terms with that loss as well. As far as he's concerned it's no longer there, but he'd like to know who has his money now. Capital is never really annihilated, is it? It only disappears from one pocket and reappears in another. He'd simply like to have a face to go along with that. A photo of the man who has his money now, a photo of the house where all that carefully saved rental income lives now. Just as he is still curious about the wife's old flame. A perhaps pathological curiosity about the one who has beaten him.

"Yes, sometimes hedge funds vanish," Hans says, already standing in the hall. "Just like in the natural world."

Then he walks off, the same way he came in. Carefree, beer bottle in hand. A lucky devil. Hofmeester watches him go.

He washes his face, dries it with a paper towel, calls Tirza again, but only gets her voicemail, then goes to the living room to take orders, to chat a little.

While he's mixing a couple of cocktails, he quickly drinks a glass of wine. He needs to be relaxed, like Hans. To let it roll over him. He can handle it. He's reached the age where nothing can throw him off balance.

That is how he goes back to the party, feeling as though he's doing much better than he was earlier in the evening. The white wine has relaxed him, made him almost light-hearted. On the borderline with frivolity.

People are dancing in the living room. The lights above the dining room table have been turned off and a few chairs have been lined up against the wall.

Three girls, a boy, and the wife are dancing.

The wife is dancing with the boy. He knows the boy, the boy has been here at the house a few times, but Hofmeester can't remember his name. All he knows is that it's a one-syllable name. Sometimes he has that when he's reading too: the contents don't sink in, but he sees the syllables. He counts them, one, two, three, four. The syllables bounce up and down before his eyes, the way the wife is now bouncing up and down with the boy before his eyes. Dancing, they call that. Full of abandon, not ungraceful, not when you realize that her body has been squeezed into a piece of textile into which, by all human standards, it should never have been squeezed into at all.

Dancing was something she'd always been good at, and she loved it. She's still not bad. Only when you look at the pictures of her from five or six years ago do you see how old she's become. Only when you see the pictures are you startled.

That, more than the mother of his children, is what Hofmeester sees: a woman just before the wilting sets in, dancing with an eighteen-year-old boy as though there were no such thing as wilting. As though her youth will go on forever.

And he regrets that. He catches himself feeling regretful, the exasperation has almost disappeared, the irritation has subsided. It's so much easier to see the enemy as the stronger one. And then it turns out that the enemy is just as weak, maybe even weaker, than you. Beaten too. A wilted enemy is no longer an enemy.

The story, the myth in which you swaddled your identity all those years, turns out to be untrue. The mother of my children who ran away with her old flame. The mother of my children who thought she was a painter. The story no longer applies. Because the old flame is no longer around. And, suddenly, the mother of your children is. In slightly absurd clothing, but that detracts in no way from the fact that she is there.

That's what he sees when he looks at the dance floor. His own life story disguised as self-deception. The flower of eternal youth. The flower makes him think of a hedge fund. Promises, glossy paper, spectacular results. A dream of a hedge fund. A dream of a woman. Frail happiness within reach.

The wife rests her hands on the boy's shoulders. God, what's his name again? He had dinner here, twice in fact. A polite boy, a bit quiet, that's true, but otherwise there wasn't much wrong with him. He even tried to help clear the table.

Hofmeester thinks the boy had something going with Tirza for a while, but he's not exactly sure. When it came to love, until about six months ago, she had been rather fickle. From the age of fifteen she had been bound and determined to go to Africa after her exams, but when it came to boys she changed her mind every week. "All I have are good friends," she said, "and some of those friends happen to be boys, but that doesn't mean anything. If only it did mean something." And then she laughed, as though she thought it was all a big joke, and Hofmeester laughed with her.

Three years ago, only a few weeks after the wife disappeared on her way to the houseboat, Tirza had asked at dinner one night: "Papa, when am I going to lose my virginity?"

Hofmeester was busy spooning up dessert, panna cotta from the delicatessen a few streets down. He heard what she asked, and stopped spooning. Then he glanced at his watch. "Everyone loses their virginity," he said. "Sooner or later it happens to everyone, Tirza."

"In my class almost everyone's lost their virginity already. When's it going to happen to me, for God's sake? You're the one who knows everything, aren't you?"

"Not everything. In fact, not much." He licked his spoon and put it down. He didn't feel much like panna cotta anymore.

"But you have an opinion on everything, right? You've got an opinion about the weirdest things. What's your opinion of the fact that I haven't lost my virginity yet? That everyone in my class has already lost their virginity, except for the idiots, the nerds, and the pimple-faces, everyone else except for me. What do you have to say about that?"

Ibi wasn't around. In those days Ibi was busy disappearing as well, busy dissolving, busy distancing herself from the world that had brought her forth.

Hofmeester looked at his silverware. He was alone with his youngest daughter, and he was going to stay alone with her.

"Things happen for a reason, and if they don't happen, there's a reason for that too. The fact that you still haven't lost your virginity is because you haven't met the right person yet."

She sighed, Tirza did, and said: "Pppfff." And then she said "Pppfff" again. She still had half a serving of panna cotta on her plate, she cut it into three pieces with her spoon. "That's such complete bullshit, Daddy," she said. "That's so passé. It's not whether you lose your virginity to the right person. It's whether or not it happens. That's the important thing. That's the only thing that matters. I want you to help me. I want you to tell me who I should lose my virginity to."

Hofmeester pressed his hands against his cheeks, as though he had just come down with a gigantic toothache.

He looked at Tirza, his gifted youngest daughter who should not lose her virginity to just anyone. When she was younger she'd done a lot of swimming. She had competed. Three times a week, after work, he had brought her on the back of the bike to the Zuiderbad pool. He had been almost as fanatical about it as she was. No, more so. He wanted his daughters to do what he hadn't done, what he had failed to do, what his situation had caused him to neglect doing: excel. Because if there was one thing you couldn't say about Hofmeester, it was that he'd overlooked the fact that this world had room only for those who excelled. The others were slaughtered, or simply shoved aside, tossed into a corner with a bored flick of the wrist. And even the ones who excelled didn't always avoid that.

Until Tirza fell ill. Then the swimming was over.

"I'll name the names of all the suitable boys, and at a certain point you just say 'Stop!' Okay, can we do it that way? Because I can't choose. I really don't know."

She had stood up from her chair, she was standing behind him now with her arms around him.

And there he sat, staring at his panna cotta, listening to her voice, his face in his hands, and suddenly it occurred to him that the wife might call at this very moment, to tell them where she'd been all these weeks.

"You have to help me," Tirza said. "Fathers are supposed to help their daughters, that's what fathers are for, isn't it? So help me out here, Dad."

"Tirza," he said, "stop acting crazy. Please stop acting so crazy. Knock off the nonsense and finish your panna cotta."

She squeezed his chair even tighter.

"I'm going to name the boys' names, accompanied by a brief description. Are you ready? David, slicked-back brown hair, about five-foot-eight."

"No," Hofmeester shouted. "No, Tirza. Sit down. Stop this. Sit down." He slammed his hand down on the table.

She let go of him, went back to her own place.

She stood there for a moment, and standing she ate a bite of panna cotta.

"Don't be sad," she said. "Don't be sad, Daddy. It's just that I want to lose my virginity so badly. I'm not ugly, am I? So why doesn't it happen?"

He choked back a piece of his dessert as well. She sat down. He wiped his hands, even though there was nothing sticking to them, and pressed them to his cheeks again.

"You are *very* pretty, Tirza," he said. "Incredibly pretty, it's not that. But boys can be shy, they only become less shy later on, and even then not all the time. You have to make the boys feel at ease."

"How do I do that?"

He put his hands over his eyes, he remembered how he had driven her to the clinic in Germany, and for the first time in his life he began to pray. Not with words, it was a kind of singing, a buzzing. Inside he was buzzing like a giant insect.

"So how do I do that?" she repeated. "How am I supposed to make boys feel at ease? They act so weird."

He pressed his hands more tightly to his eyes. The buzzing stopped. "You mustn't forget," he said quietly, "that they're a little afraid of you. They're afraid of everything, but especially of you. That's why you should take the boy you've chosen to a place where no one can see you, it has to be a secret place. And there you have to touch him, gently. It will scare him at first. But don't let that scare *you*. You just have to touch him again. And then you have to say it: 'I'm Tirza, and I love you.'"

He pushed his hands even more tightly against his eyes, if that was possible, only hoping that his hands would catch the tears, that they wouldn't trickle down through his fingers, that they would be blocked from the eyes of the world by the hands with which he liked so much to do a bit of gardening.

"And then, once I've said that?"

"Then . . ." He gulped. "Then—is he wearing a T-shirt or a shirt or a jacket? The boy you chose?"

"A shirt."

"Well, then," Hofmeester said, "then you have to open his shirt slowly, first the top buttons, then the lower ones. He'll try to stop you, he may even try to run away, but you have to grab his arm and say: 'Don't run, because I'm Tirza and I love you.'"

"And then what? Tell me."

Hofmeester was almost unable to go on. His head sank further and further. His eyes felt red and swollen, his hands clammy and old.

"Then . . ." He took a deep breath. And another. The way he had walked up the stairs that time, looking for Ibi who hadn't come back from the tenant's. The same sensation of breathlessness, of suffocation. "Then you have to hold him tight and forget how scared he is, that he's more afraid of you than he is of dying, because you're a woman, Tirza. And then you have to feel him, you have to feel him, how he is and how he's standing there, you have to smell him, you have to kiss him, you have to press him against you, you have to hold onto him as though he wanted to get away, and he does too, but you can't let go. Because he wants to be held, too, he wants to get away and he wants to be held, but you have to be stronger, that's the only way. And then you have to say: 'Who are you, anyway? I'm Tirza and I love you, but who are you?'"

At that moment a cry escaped Hofmeester's lips, a cry like a foghorn. Short but loud, one that could have been heard miles away.

Tirza was standing up. Hofmeester, startled by his own cry, stood up as well.

"What is it, Daddy?" she asked. "What's wrong?"

Afraid as he was that she would see his tears, he pressed her against him. He held her tight and he kissed her, her hair, her cheeks, her nose, her lips, her ears. "Nothing, Tirza," he said, "it's nothing. I had a daydream, I had a terrible thought. It's nothing. Everything will be fine. Everything is fine."

He opened the door to the garden, he took her out into the darkness of the garden, even though it was really too cold to go out without a coat, but he hoped that out there she wouldn't see his red eyes.

"So that's how I have to do it," she said, once they were finally standing on the grass. The wet grass.

"That's how you have to do it," he replied, his head turned away a little, staring at the shed, the trees, the houses along Willemsparkweg.

"But why are boys afraid of me?"

Somewhere across the street the lights went out in a room, probably a child's room. The time for bedtime stories was over.

And, still with his back half-turned to her, he said: "Because they think you're unapproachable. Once they've broken you, they won't be afraid of you anymore."

She stood on tiptoes. She whispered in her father's ear: "I'm Tirza, and I love you."

3

Hofmeester is standing beside the couch, next to Miss Veldkamp, who hasn't moved from her spot all evening, and for the umpteenth time he wonders where Tirza has gone, why she hasn't called. She's sensible, not a child anymore of course, grown up. More grown up than many of her contemporaries, so there must a good reason for her to be so late. Maybe it's become passé, showing up on time for your own party. He's no longer sure what is passé and what isn't; in fact, he never really has been.

He looks at Miss Veldkamp. She seems to be enjoying the kir, this is her fifth glass. She smiles at him, he smiles back, and then he surveys the partygoers like a general viewing the field of battle. No one is lacking in anything. Their orders have been taken. Just to be sure, he told them: "There's beer and wine in the kitchen, you can help yourself." No one will have to stand around with an empty glass. No one will be left unsatisfied this evening.

Ibi is still sitting on the couch beside Miss Veldkamp. But she's not talking anymore. She just sits there, the way she often used to sit there, withdrawn, closed, already gone in fact, maybe without really ever having been there, maybe as a child she had already decided she didn't want to belong to this family. That she didn't fit in. She's probably thinking about her bed and breakfast, her husband, her boyfriend, or whatever you might want to call him, the man Hofmeester, in any case, doesn't want to talk about. There are things you don't talk about. You resign yourself to them, but talk about them, no.

Briefly, almost by accident, Miss Veldkamp touches Hofmeester's hand, just to get his attention. "Lovely, isn't it?" she says.

"What?"

"The people dancing. The children."

"Yes," Hofmeester says. "Very lovely." But he would rather not have seen the wife dancing. And especially not tonight. With all those children crowding around her so hungrily.

Then Ibi gets up abruptly and starts dancing too, wildly and exuberantly, as though she were in the jungle, at a spot where no one can see her, where she is all alone and shame has no function. Shame needs other people. You are ashamed because you think the other person is looking, because you know that the other person is looking.

It's already past ten. Hofmeester stands staring at Ibi for a few seconds, the way fathers do, wistful and proud, although in his case there's also an ungrounded fear that goes along with it. In his children he rediscovers his own fear, in the encounters with his progeny that fear comes to life, in them he recognizes all the things that have wrested themselves from his grasp. He feels that he has prepared his daughters for life too poorly and too haphazardly. They blame him wordlessly, his children make him who he is, and who he is—he has to be honest about that—is unbearable.

Someone turns up the music, as she dances the wife throws her arms around the boy, the boy who has eaten here occasionally. Hofmeester still can't remember his name. He goes back to the kitchen and pours himself a glass of wine.

When the glass is empty, he calls Tirza. Her voicemail again. "Hi, this is Tirza. I can't answer the phone right now. But be sure to leave a nice message."

"Sweetheart," he says, "your party is in full swing. Everyone is here already. You really need to come home now. The party is wonderful."

The doorbell rings. Once again, it isn't Tirza. It's Mrs. Van Delven, her former home-room teacher. He chats with her a little about things in general, about politics, about a novel by a Belgian author he's never heard of.

Then Hofmeester walks out into the yard.

The torches are still lit. Yes, he did that well, they're still burning away.

He goes into the shed. Between the power saw and the rake, he leans against the wooden wall. He says something out loud, something even he can't quite make out. Only after a couple of beats does he realize that he is repeating the order he took about ten minutes ago, and when he is finished, when he has convinced himself that he has not forgotten anything, that his memory works, it dawns on him that he still doesn't know what a hedge fund is. The economics teacher couldn't explain it to him, no one has been able to make it clear to him. The hedge fund remains an enigma. More than three years after the disappearance of his hedge fund, he still does not know exactly what it is that disappeared.

With both hands he rubs his freshly shaven cheeks. He remembers his wife saying to him, "To fuck," when he had asked her, "What do you want, for God's sake? The guests will be here any minute." He thinks about the balcony doors in the bedroom, he remembers the night she showed up again on the doorstep, with her suitcase, not even all that long ago, but it seems like another lifetime. He just stands there like that, hands pressed against his cheeks, his memory filled with something that can only be a misunderstanding.

After a couple of minutes he pulls himself together. There's a party. There's a host. There is no pain. Pain is a fiction, most pain is anyway. He who experiences pain must concentrate until he no longer feels anything. Hard to do with a broken leg, true. But he doesn't have a broken leg. He hasn't broken anything.

Someone opens the door of the shed, but he can't see who it is.

He peers into the semidarkness, then recognizes the girl who ordered the tomato juice.

"The party's inside," he says, sounding less friendly than he means to. "This is the shed."

She seems startled. She probably wasn't expecting to find anyone in here, just old junk, silence. But she pulls herself together quickly. Maybe she was even following him. Perhaps she wasn't startled at all. Maybe he was the only one who felt an ungrounded fear.

"But then what are *you* doing out here?"

"Me? I'm taking a breather. Getting a little fresh air." He sniffs like a bad actor who needs to underscore his words with sounds. "I couldn't find the tomato juice. It must be somewhere. But I couldn't find it."

Coming from him, in this shed, on this night, it sounds like the explanation for an entire life, for the absence of a lot of things, for the absence of happiness. The tomato juice could not be found.

"That's okay. I'll drink something else."

She has left the door of the shed open. He looks at her flip-flops, at her jeans, which have been rolled up a couple of times at the bottom. It's probably the fashion, but he finds it odd. Then he remembers her name: Ester. Without the "h."

It reminds him of Tirza. No "h" either.

"Are you a good friend of Tirza's?"

"Not really."

He moves away from the wall, where he was leaning so comfortably. He has to get back to the party. They need him. His daughter has probably arrived by now.

"I'm not a friend of hers at all, actually."

The father eyes the girl suspiciously. Then what is she doing at this party? What has she come here for? This evening is for Tirza's friends, not for stray animals. Not for people who want to drink for free because it tastes better to them when they don't have to pay for it.

He rests his hand on the lawnmower. He'd wanted to be a different kind of father, which is to say: a better father. When it became clear that there was nothing else for him to excel at, he chose fatherhood. So that his children might look at the world contemplatively and critically. What is intelligence, after all, but the critical distance with which you view yourself and the things around you? His children were not to take anything for granted, everything was to be questioned. Trust nothing but your own intelligence, that's what he'd taught them. He had elevated intelligence to the status of a god. The god who would make everything all right. And now he has the urgent sense that he has overlooked something, that the critical gaze with which he compelled his daughters to look at the world provides no answers to fundamental questions. Personal intelligence as god leaves a lot of bases uncovered. There are a lot of blank spots. The god cannot get to them, the god has no answer for them.

"So then why did she invite you?"

He brushes some imaginary dust from his shoulders and steps towards the door.

The girl doesn't reply. She is standing in the doorway, toying with one of her flip-flops. She looks at his tools, the lawn chairs, an empty crate that once contained mandarin oranges and that, for some reason, he has never thrown away. He waits. Still no reaction.

"So do you know what you're going to do, now that you're finished with school?" he asks, just to put an end to the conversation. Friend or no friend, a conversation has to be ended neatly.

"I'm not finished with school. I flunked."

"I'm sorry to hear that." Hofmeester finds a handkerchief in his pants pocket and wipes his forehead. His forehead isn't wet, he just thought it was.

"I'm no good at school. They say I'm smart, but it's not true."

This confession leaves him at a loss. This entire conversation leaves him at a loss. He wipes his forehead again. More forcefully this time, as through there were scabs on his forehead that he needed to scrape off.

"Have you tried my sushi yet?"

"I'm no good at relationships either."

"Have you tried my sushi yet? There's sashimi, too, you know." He's insistent. Answers are what he wants. He can't stand it when people ignore his questions.

"I don't eat fish. They never last long. A month or so. Two or three weeks. Sorry to be telling you all this."

"Never mind. Are you a vegetarian?" Hofmeester puts away his handkerchief. He needs to get back to the party, but he can't. The longer he stays in the shed, the harder it is for him to go back, to resume his duties.

"Well, I don't eat fish. Especially not raw fish."

A difficult girl. Difficult eaters are difficult people. Hofmeester likes people who eat everything, especially everything he makes. Eating is important. People who don't know how to talk have to be able to eat. Even people who don't know how to live have to be able to eat.

"So are you a vegetarian?"

"I don't eat fish. But I do eat meat. I don't know what that makes you. What does that make you?"

Hofmeester thinks about it for a bit. Is there a word for that? If there is, he doesn't know it. "That makes you someone who doesn't eat fish," he says after a few seconds.

She stands there, and doesn't look like she's planning to step aside, she doesn't realize that he has to get through.

"I guess that's what I am then. Someone who doesn't eat fish." She laughs, but it's not a real laugh, more like a parody of laughter.

"I'm sorry," he says again. He's standing right in front of her now, he should really elbow her aside, he needs to get back. "About the relationships and about school, about the fish too, I'm sorry, but I'm sure you'll find someone who loves you. There are vegetarian snacks as well. Olives."

"Come on," she says. "'Love' is so old-fashioned."

"What do you mean?"

"We don't go in for that anymore." It comes out almost aggressively. Like a reprimand. And that's exactly what it feels like to Hofmeester—he feels he's being reprimanded. He has committed a faux pas, and this girl is letting him know, albeit subtly.

His hand is already resting on her shoulder to push her aside, friendly yet firmly. The image of his wife dancing in the living room with Tirza's friends percolates up inside and upsets him, it makes him nervous. Sick, one should say. Sick.

"What do you do, then?" he asks, his hand still on her shoulder.

She stands there, tough but fragile, and her toughness emphasizes the fragility, or rather: it emphasizes the things that have already been broken.

"We enjoy each other," she says. "Or at least we try."

He runs his right hand through his hair. His left hand is still on her shoulder, as though that hand were paralyzed.

He doesn't like her answers, he doesn't want to hear them anymore. A so-called rebel, that's probably what she is. A person who never does a thing, someone who's never realized that what it comes down to is looking at the world critically, that you have to work, work, work, and work some more, who believes that everything is about pleasure. Such overweening pride. Such heartless, overweening pride.

"We," he says. "We? I'm not sure there even is a 'we'. You and I, for example, are we a 'we' now? I wouldn't say that. Who is 'we'? Who do you speak for?"

What's gotten into him? What kind of discussion is he getting into? What is he trying to prove to this child, who apparently likes neither fish nor school? He should leave her alone, let her stew in her own juices. He shouldn't stoop to her level, whatever that may be. He should stand above it, he's a man of almost sixty. Men who are almost sixty stand above things. But what he finds out, time and again, every hour, every fifteen minutes, as if someone out there never tired of rubbing it under his nose, is that he does not stand above it. He is not above anything.

"I think there is a 'we.' I think I can say, '*We* don't go in for that, we don't go in for "love." We don't. Maybe you do. But we don't. We sure as hell don't.' I don't mean to be rude, but I think you're talking nonsense. I think a lot of people talk nonsense, and that they think they can get away with it, that it's no problem at all, because they're older. Or because they have money. I'm not smart. Not as smart as they think I am, but I know nonsense when I hear it."

"I have to get back to the party," Hofmeester whispers. "We'll talk about it. Later. Some other time. You can't do away with love, Ester. I tried, when I was your age. I wanted to do away with love. There's a lot I can tell you about that. Come by for dinner sometime. Tirza would like that. Before she leaves. She's going to Africa, you know."

"We. Now you said it yourself. *We*'ll talk about it. We—you see, it does exist. The two of us, we are a 'we.' Whether you like it or not. We are a 'we.'"

He looks at her face. His hand is still on her shoulder. He realizes for the first time that life causes him pain—not life as such, *his* life: he realizes that, as he looks at the face of Ester without the "h." He has to think about what that means. What does pain mean? "I have to get past you," he says, and he hears how plaintive it sounds, how lacking in authority, how hopeless. "Let me through."

"Do you mind if I stay here?"

"Here?"

His hand slides from her shoulder. It's a warm evening, but suddenly he feels cold. He fights back the urge to chatter his teeth.

"Yes, here." She points at his garden tools. He sees a bag of manure, a bag of potting soil, the chainsaw, a rake, a lawnmower, a bucket, the crate that used to contain mandarin oranges.

"In the shed? But this isn't where the party is. There's nothing here, girl. There's nothing here at all."

"But I like being alone. I just have to . . ."

She picks up the bucket, upends it and sits down on it.

"Look," she says, "I'm fine here. I'm not bothering anyone."

He hesitates. Is he supposed to approve of this? It doesn't seem exactly normal to him. Withdrawing to the shed while the party in the living room is in full swing. Fine, when his wife used to throw parties he would sometimes withdraw to the bedroom, but he's a man, and by the time he did that he was already a man getting on in years. A man who couldn't make friends, but who'd decided that having two daughters was good enough for him.

"Fine," he says. "As far as I'm concerned. If that's what you want. If this is your idea of a party. I'll get you something to drink. What would you like? You can turn on the light if you like. It's over there." He points at the light switch. "Do you want me to get you something to read? Today's newspaper?"

"Thanks. I don't need anything to read. I'm just going to caress myself gently."

He leans forward, as if he were hard of hearing. He thinks he must have misunderstood. "You're going to do what?"

"I'm going to caress myself gently. Like this." She raises her right hand and begins stroking her left arm softly. She does it slowly, as if touching something scary and strange. A reptile. Her arm is a reptile.

He watches for a couple of seconds, with a vague feeling of discomfort. With a discomfort that becomes increasingly urgent: he does not want to see this. Not now. Not ever, in fact. He hears the music from the party in the distance. Voices.

She rubs the hand with the phone numbers written on it and then her bare arm again. Back and forth. Not any faster, but also without stopping.

"Ester," he says, putting into his voice all the conviction he can muster, "there are plenty of people inside who would be happy to caress you gently. Come with me to the living room, I'll introduce you to all kinds of nice people, but I suppose you already know them. Come with me. Don't stay here. This is no shed for you."

"I'd rather do it myself. The caressing. I'm better at it myself."

He stands frozen in place for a few moments. He feels torn. He needs to persuade her, but he doesn't know how. It doesn't seem responsible to leave her here all alone. Totally irresponsible, in fact. When you get old you can lock yourself in the shed while the party in the living room is in full swing, but not while you're still young. Otherwise you'll fall prey to unwelcome thoughts.

"Mr. Hofmeester," she says, still rubbing her arm, "do you ever get caressed gently?"

He leaves the shed without a word. He has no desire to let this conversation run on any longer. Enough is enough. He feels the urge to scream: "Where do you get the bloody nerve? You've got some nerve!"

But instead, when he gets outside, all he shouts is: "What would you like to drink, then? Shall I get you a glass of orange juice, seeing as there's no tomato juice?"

"Orange juice would be fine," she shouts back. "But no ice."

He steps briskly to the kitchen.

Ibi's generation was different. She's not that much older than Tirza, but still, he can't remember Ibi's friends coming up with things like this. Not eating fish, caressing yourself gently in a shed, thinking you're not smart. So much inertia drives him crazy.

After he has poured the orange juice into a wine glass—he can't find any other glasses—he feels a hand on his shoulder.

He turns around.

"Tirza," he says. "Where were you? Where have you been?"

She is perspiring. Her eye shadow is smudged.

"I biked hard to get here," she says. "I heard your messages. So then I biked really hard. Has it been fun, are the people having a good time? Do they like your sushi, Daddy?"

She is perspiring, but she is glowing. Her eyes are glowing.

He presses her against him and he understands—never before has he understood so clearly, so overwhelmingly, so undeniably—that he wants to have no reason to live without Tirza. Without her, life is no longer conceivable, and what is inconceivable is undesired. She is his right to exist. What he is pressing against him now provides him with both the privilege and the obligation to live. Without her there is no more obligation, but also no more right. He can barely remember how he lived before she was around. Waiting, that's what it was. That's how he lived all those years, waiting for Tirza. Of course, he didn't know then that it was Tirza he was waiting for.

"Daddy," she says, "stop crushing me. There's time for that later. At the airport. You're always so rough. There's someone I want to introduce you to."

She points to a person who, Hofmeester realizes now, has been standing in the kitchen doorway all this time.

A boy, maybe even a man. Hofmeester figures he must be about twenty-three, twenty-four. Older than Tirza, in any case. Fairly dark skin, a broad jaw, thick eyebrows that make him seem surly. Or maybe he really is surly. Who's to say?

"Daddy," Tirza says, "this is Choukri, my boyfriend."

Hofmeester takes a few slow steps towards the doorway.

In the time it takes him to move from the counter to the doorway, he thinks about the devastating power of old age. He is almost dead. And what is the difference between almost dead and completely dead? What kind of fine distinction are you making then, how many square millimeters of ground still separate you from the enemy? Hofmeester holds out his hand.

"What was your name again?" he asks. But before the man can respond, Tirza says, "Choukri, Daddy. His name is Choukri. I already said that, didn't I?"

"Chou-kri," Hofmeester repeats slowly, and he shakes the man's hand. "I'm Jörgen Hofmeester. Tirza's father."

The man looks familiar to him. The longer he looks, the more Hofmeester has the sneaking suspicion that he has seen him before.

"So you are . . ." Hofmeester says, but since he doesn't know what else to say, he pauses, and Tirza avails herself of the silence to say, "That's right, he's my boyfriend. He's going with me."

Hofmeester is still clasping the man's hand, the hand of his youngest daughter's boyfriend. It's a big hand, a cold hand. No elegant, soft fingers. No piano fingers.

"With you? Where to?"

"To Africa. I told you he was going along, didn't I?" Tirza says. She's almost hanging on her father's arm, but he still doesn't let go of Choukri's hand. "He's my boyfriend and he's coming along to Africa, Daddy."

"Yes, of course, to Africa. And what do you do?" he asks.

"I make music."

"Music. What kind of music?"

"I write songs. And I play the guitar. Among other things."

"The guitar. Among other things." He turns the man's hand over and studies the fingernails.

"I can tell," Hofmeester says. "You have long fingernails. People who take the guitar seriously often have long fingernails. I don't have long fingernails. But then I don't play the guitar. I work in the garden." He shows the man his hands. He holds them out for him to see. He wiggles his fingers as if he were playing an invisible piano. "Look," he says, "gardener's hands. The hands of a gardener."

"Daddy," Tirza says, "this isn't a cattle market. You don't have to compare hands. He just got here."

Hofmeester laughs, and at the same time he is almost sure that he has seen the man before, on TV. But he can't remember which program it was, not even what it was about. Was it a sitcom, was it the news, a talk show?

"You're right, Tirza, you just got here. I shouldn't ask so many questions." He turns to the man. "I guess I'm just inquisitive. An inquisitive father. And Tirza is an inquisitive daughter. Aren't you, Tirza?"

He fixes two glasses of kir royal and pours himself a glass of white wine. Without asking whether he feels like a kir royal, he thrusts a champagne glass into the man's hands, the other one he hands to Tirza. He puts his arm around her, he presses her close—his life, his right to exist, his youngest daughter. "Cheers," he says, "to this evening. I've heard a lot about you, Choukri, and I'm pleased to meet you at last Do you do anything else, besides make music?"

"Social work."

"A social worker?"

"That's right."

"Nice. Useful, too." Hofmeester takes a swig. And another. His glass is already empty. It's going quickly. He still has a tight hold on Tirza. As though to keep her from running away. "You don't need to go to university for that, do you? To become a social worker, I mean? You can do that without going to university, can't you? What kind of training do you need for that, exactly?"

"Training," the man says, "but not university, no."

"Anyway, not everyone is cut out for university," Hofmeester declares. "Some people have no interest in science, some people have no aptitude for science. Which means they have no business going to university."

"Daddy," Tirza says. She laughs as only Tirza can, friendly but severe, put-on yet sincere, polite but mischievous. She caresses her father's cheek. "Not now. Don't start in about science now."

"No," he says, "Not now. Another time. When you come for dinner. Then we'll talk about science." He looks at his daughter's boyfriend and he no longer has any doubt: he has seen him before. He knows him. He just doesn't know where from.

"Is it possible," Hofmeester asks, "that I've seen you on TV? Are you ever on TV?"

The man shakes his head. "I make music, but I'm not famous. I've never been on TV."

"But we've met before, haven't we? We know each other."

The man shakes his head. "No, really. I've never seen you before."

"Daddy, don't act so weird. You've never met Choukri. You couldn't have seen him before."

"Maybe here in the neighborhood?"

"Choukri never comes here. Choukri lives on the other side of town."

"Which part?"

"Close to Central Station," the man says. "On one of the islands."

Hofmeester nods. On one of the islands. He fixes two more glasses of kir royal, for the man and for his youngest daughter; he sticks to white wine himself.

"This," he says, when all the glasses are full again, "this, where we are now, is the best part of Van Eeghenstraat. Further up, past Jacob Obrechtstraat, it's not quite as nice. Oh, it's still nice enough, but I wouldn't want to live there. In fact, this spot, these few square meters, constitute the best spot in Amsterdam and, therefore, in the Netherlands."

He clinks his glass against the man's glass, then gently against Tirza's. "To this evening," he says. "To the party. To your happiness and that of all people. Spinoza once said that no man can be happy if his own happiness detracts from that of others. You know who Spinoza was, I assume?"

"Daddy, no Spinoza, not tonight. No Dostoevsky, no Tolstoy either. Not right now, okay? Please?"

He empties his glass and refills it right away.

"You can tell," he says. "You can tell, Choukri, that my daughter's got me under her thumb. My daughter is my boss. She has been ever since she was born. From the very first moment. And do you know why?" He starts to whisper, as if a secret is coming, something no one else should hear. "Because she's the sun queen. Tirza is the sun queen. Be careful, she'll have you under her thumb, too, before you know it."

Hofmeester takes a swig, puts his glass on the counter, takes Tirza's champagne glass, empties it, puts it on the counter as well, and lifts her up.

He lifts his daughter high in the air. As high as he can. And with difficulty, in a stifled voice, for it is hard to keep breathing regularly, he says, "See? I can still lift her, my sun queen. If need be, I'll carry her halfway across Amsterdam. Isn't that right, Tirza?"

Then he spins around with her in his arms, and again, and again. He spins her around in the kitchen, like a trophy, like an idol. He keeps spinning until he can't spin anymore.

He sets her back on the floor. He is dizzy, he has to hold on to the counter. The kitchen is spinning before his eyes. His daughter is spinning before his eyes.

A silence falls. No one knows what to say. Tirza takes Choukri's hand.

The three of them stand there like that in the kitchen.

Hofmeester clears his throat. Gradually the kitchen starts spinning more slowly. He gets a grip on himself.

But still no one knows what to say.

The silence continues. The silence becomes painful.

"Come on, let's go in," Tirza says to her boyfriend at last. "Let's join the party. My mother's here, too. Just so you know. But I'm not going to introduce you to her."

"It was nice meeting you, Mr. Hofmeester," the man says. "But we'll see each other later, I suppose?"

"Oh sure, we'll see each other," the father says. "Later in the evening. Or some other time."

His daughter leads and the man follows, his hand in hers. Tirza gives Jörgen a quick wave, she winks at him. Then he is alone in his kitchen.

And right away he realizes what it is he forgot. The sushi. He didn't offer them any sushi.

He looks at his watch. It's almost a quarter to eleven.

Hofmeester holds his head under the cold tap, and again he detects a buzzing in that head of his, the buzzing of an insect, but now he knows what that buzzing is. It is a prayer.

He doesn't dry his face, he stands there dripping in the middle of the kitchen. He is back in charge again, he is refreshed. Tirza has arrived. The party can begin.

He takes a plate of sashimi from the refrigerator, removes the foil, and arranges the fish on the special platter. "At eleven," he says to himself, "I'll fry some more sardines."

The wife has the boy, whose name Hofmeester still can't remember, pressed up against the wall, she's talking at him, the table has been pushed to one side, the lights have been dimmed even further, but the sashimi is a hit. People are drinking and eating with gusto. Hunger and thirst go hand in hand.

Tirza and her boyfriend are talking to Miss Veldkamp. A girl, he's forgotten her name too, says to him, "Come on, Mr. Hofmeester, come on, let's dance." He shakes his head resolutely. "I'm here tonight for the catering," he says with the friendliest of smiles.

She barely hears his reply. The girl has already forgotten about him. She grabs the economics teacher by the hand and drags him along. And Hans readily lets himself be dragged.

Hofmeester is standing in the middle of the room with the platter in his hand. He feels invisible. Not an unpleasant feeling. He's there without being there. The man no one notices, that's what you might call him. And, oddly enough, he is proud of that. It hadn't made him proud before. A colleague would say, "I was at that book presentation and do you know what happened?" And a couple of minutes later, when the conversation lulled, Hofmeester would remark: "I know, I was there, too."

He had been there, he had been present, but no one had seen him.

He looks around the party. Tirza and her boyfriend are still talking to Miss Veldkamp. Who would have thought that Miss Veldkamp could carry on such a lively conversation, she's loosened up. Mrs. Van Delven seems to be having fun as well. Yes, this is the point at which people loosen up, and when people loosen up, that is when Hofmeester likes to pass around his sashimi. You need something in your stomach before you contact your deepest, most secret urges. He looks at his youngest daughter's boyfriend, he keeps his eye on him.

Someone bumps into him and asks: "Is there still some tuna?"

As in a trance, he points to a piece of fish, then goes back to staring at his youngest daughter's boyfriend.

He keeps staring.

Hofmeester knows now why that face looked so familiar to him, now he knows who the boy reminds him of. It's all clear to him now. Mohammed Atta. Like two peas in a pod. The same chin, the same eyes, the same haircut. Mohammed Atta's brother. His doppelgänger. Mohammed Atta himself, he'd almost bet on it, if he wasn't pretty sure the man was already dead.

He walks back to the kitchen, the plate of hors d'oeuvres still half-full. He knocks back a glass of wine, leans with both hands against the refrigerator and thinks: Mohammed Atta is in my house. Atta has arrived. Atta has arisen.

He puts a pan on the stove, the oil, the garlic, the salt, the pepper and sardines within easy reach. The pan has to be good and hot first. He ticks his index finger against the edge. Patience. It's not quite ready yet.

Hofmeester isn't sure what to do, he doesn't know how to call a halt to this disaster, so he concentrates on the sardines. But that it *is* a disaster, he has no doubt about that. Mohammed Atta is a disaster. What else could you call it?

He opens another bottle of wine. Italian Gewürztraminer. He and Tirza bought the wine together. He always goes with Tirza to buy his wine. They've been doing that for months, for years. She tastes, she decides, he buys.

"Jörgen."

He turns around.

His wife.

Her body seems to be bulging out of the textile even more than at the start of the evening.

He has no time for her now. He's about to fry sardines.

"Jörgen."

The pan is getting hot. It goes slowly when you watch it. Very slowly. But it's ready now. It's time to add the oil.

"Jörgen, I'm talking to you."

"I'm cooking. Can't you see that? I'm frying sardines."

She comes a few steps closer.

"I'm not going to interrupt you, I just wanted to know if there's any rum left."

The sardines can go in the pan now. He puts them in, one by one. These are the moments he enjoys. He loves cooking. Even more than the eating itself, he loves the cooking. "Do you know who's in our living room right now?"

"Who, Jörgen? Who's in our living room? The love of my life? Did you see him out there?" She giggles, as though she's just told a good joke. The love of her life in the living room. She's reached the age at which that has become a joke. What was it that girl said in the shed? We don't go in for that. Love. Hell if we do.

"Mohammed Atta."

There are five sardines in the pan now. There's room for one more. The sixth. All lying beside each other like old chums. This is nice. This is what Hofmeester thinks is nice. The sardines have never let him down. For as long as he's been doing the housekeeping, for as long as he's been cooking for Tirza, this has been his specialty.

"Who's Mohammed Atta, Jörgen? Have I met him? Is he the love of my life? Should I paint his portrait? Would he make a suitable model?"

"Mohammed Atta, don't you know who Mohammed Atta is? Holy hell."

She shakes her head. She touches him. The father of her children. She sniffs his shirt.

"No idea," she says. "Should I know him?"

"Where have you been living for the last few years? In a cave? Did that houseboat drift out to sea or something?"

The oil is crackling gleefully.

Hofmeester grabs an apron and ties it on.

"I have no idea who Mohammed Atta is, please excuse me. Apparently he's not the love of my life, but that's okay. I was just wondering whether there was any rum left, I started out with a rum and coke and I'd like to stick with that. Is there any left?"

"Mohammed Atta!" Hofmeester shouts. "Mo-ham-med At-ta!"

"Don't shout like that, Jörgen."

She puts her arms around him from the back. She presses herself against him. She squeezes his upper arm. The man she traded in for her old flame. Traded in and taken over. And taken back. Or halfway taken back. A love life is an endless series of takeovers.

She disgusts him, and the more she disgusts him the more he hopes she will keep pressing against him like that. Not for long, just a few seconds. Longer than that is not necessary.

"I have no idea what you're talking about. But it doesn't matter. I only came by for the rum. These boys are so nice, Jörgen. Tirza's boys. Such nice, sensible boys."

"Didn't that old flame of yours ever read the papers? Couldn't he afford a subscription? Was he poor? Or just stupid? Or poor *and* stupid? Did you ever turn on the TV in that houseboat? Did you even have a TV? Where were you? What planet were you living on? And besides: when all that happened, you were still living here. At least officially."

"I was in love, Jörgen, I was in love. Then you miss things sometimes, and I think you're sweet, in fact I find you sweeter than I ever have before, but now please tell me where the rum is. And after that please do tell me who Mohammed hitchymajigger is. About all the things I missed. There on that houseboat. I promise, I'll listen carefully. Haven't I always listened carefully to you when you're handing out nuggets of wisdom?"

He stares into the pan. A few more seconds and then he has to turn the little fish over. Sweat is running down his neck, but he has no time to pull out his handkerchief. This is a very tricky operation. Frying sardines is harder than people think.

"Four years ago," he says, taking the pan from the fire to spread the oil around better, "four years ago, the Third World War started."

"Oh, well yes, I guess I missed that one. The Third World War. Was there widespread starvation as well?"

"Knock it off," he shouts, "knock it off! The widespread starvation is still to come. And I hope you're the first to be affected. You've deserved it. People like you deserve widespread starvation, not just once, no, four times over."

She presses against him even more closely.

"What kind of person am I then?" she whispers. "What category do I fall under? The category 'deserving of widespread starvation'?"

"The category that considers itself so happy and unassailable that it doesn't bother to read the newspaper. That's the category I'm talking about."

He picks up a spatula, moves the sardines around to keep them from sticking to the pan.

"I missed the entire Third World War. Forgive me, Jörgen, forgive me for taking a world war so lightly, but where is the rum? Don't keep stringing me along."

He pushes her aside with his elbow.

She comes back. She presses her pelvis against his buttocks.

"Go away," he shouts, still holding the spatula. "Go away! Filthy woman, go away!"

"Is the Third World War over yet?" she whispers in his ear. "Or is it still raging? Inform me. Enlighten me."

He turns the fishes over. Cooking calms him.

"I'm not in the mood for inanity. There should be a bottle of rum in the fridge. And you embarrass me. Uncultivated. Barbaric. That's what you are. When I first met you I thought you would be cultivated. A painter. A woman like that would have to be cultivated. Or so I thought. Art academy. She probably knows a thing or two. Ha! Forget it. Finding your own butt, but only if you use both hands. That's as much as you're capable of."

"I'm not in the mood for inanity, either. I'm not inane. I want some rum. I want you. I want someone. Are you someone, Jörgen? Are you someone?"

Hofmeester pokes her again with his elbow. And keeps his eyes on the pan. The way the boiling oil spatters doesn't bother him, he stares at it, mesmerized. Sardine skin is so lovely, lovelier than human skin, but then he has to admit that he's never seen what human skin looks like when you fry it in a pan.

The wife opens the fridge. She bends over. She searches around, the way he searched around for the tomato juice about an hour ago.

"Mohammed Atta," he says, "was one of the hijackers, he was the ringleader of the hijackers. And Tirza's boyfriend is his brother, or a half-brother, or a cousin. Or an uncle. Or an uncle by marriage. Whatever the case, a kind of Mohammed Atta. The same flesh, the same look, the same jaw line. The same ideas, of course. The same hatred. Hatred towards us. Hatred towards what we are, who we are, and why we're like that."

"But who *are* we, anyway, Jörgen?"

She take a couple of bottles out of the fridge. She sighs. "You've packed too much stuff in here," she mumbles. "How can you expect to find anything this way?" And while he's wiping his hands on his apron, he realizes that, just now, he was talking about "we." We, without thinking about it. It popped out, carelessly and naturally. He hates "we."

"I think I know now," she says. She has found the rum. "Mohammed Atta, from the eleventh. The eleventh, right? Wasn't that it? The eleventh?"

She opens the bottle. Then she takes the cola out of the fridge.

She mixes the rum with cola. She takes a drink. "The eleventh of September, wasn't it? Jesus, that seems like ages ago. I was so happy back then. In love. I felt young, I don't know, I felt like . . ."

The sardines are ready. He puts them on a plate. He hasn't glanced at her even once.

"Twenty. Eighteen. Sometimes even sixteen," she whispers.

He sprinkles them with parsley. Looking at his sardines, he can barely suppress a grin.

"Do you know," he says as he takes off his apron, "why they hate you and me and the neighbors? Because we believe in happiness. Not in God, but in happiness. Because we're individuals with an individual identity. Not part of the herd."

She drinks her rum and cola like a child, both hands wrapped around the glass. She looks at him, her face bears the signs of the dancing, the crowdedness, the heat in the living room. Her makeup hasn't started running, it's more like it's faded and dried-up. Her wrinkles have become visible.

"Jörgen, don't try to tell me you believe in happiness. Your god has always been the god of unhappiness. You never wanted much from life except to be unhappy. And you've served him well, that god, you've never been unfaithful to him, not even when you could rightfully have felt betrayed by him, you kept serving the god of unhappiness. You were his most devoted servant. You deserve applause. Why do you think I left you? I wanted to be in the limelight myself sometimes. I wanted, on occasion, to lie next to someone who didn't worship unhappiness. I couldn't stand it anymore. Couldn't stand you. Or at least the things you worshipped."

She comes towards him. She's going to try to kiss him, he can sense it. He knows it.

He pushes her away. "Get out of here," he shouts. "Don't touch me, you bag."

She picks up her glass. She fills it up. "So who are we?" she asks. "Now that we're on the subject, who are we that they hate us so much? Who are we, Jörgen? What are we, anyway?"

She comes toward him, glass in hand.

"You have to put ice in it," he says. "Rum and coke without ice is terrible. Don't you have any style?"

She throws her arms around him. He doesn't push her away. He doesn't have the strength.

"You know who we are?" she whispers in his ear. And for a brief moment she sticks her tongue in his ear. "You know what we are, just the two of us? We're ruined." She pronounces the word as though it were something sexy and nice, as though it were unbelievably exciting to be ruined. The greatest, sweetest thing on earth. Something usually reserved only for fashion models and movie stars. Ruined.

"But don't tell anyone. It's our little secret, okay? No one else must know. Only the two of us." She won't stop whispering. Even though there's no one else in the kitchen. Then, at last, she lets him go.

Hofmeester pulls out his handkerchief and dries his ear.

He picks up the plate of sardines. "They have to be eaten while they're still warm," he says, more to himself than to the wife.

In the living room he calls out, like a bad imitation of a street vendor: "Sardines, even in Portugal they're no fresher than this."

The guests are leery of the sardines, or else they're already too full. He has trouble getting rid of his fish.

The young man with the one-syllable name takes one. "This is happiness," Hofmeester says, pointing to the little fish, "this is pure happiness."

He watches the boy eat.

And when the boy puts another sardine in his mouth, Hofmeester says: "I hope you'll excuse me, but I've forgotten your name."

"Bas." He speaks with his mouth full. But "Bas" is a name you can pronounce well even with your mouth full.

"Bas," Hofmeester repeats. "Are you enjoying the party, Bas?"

"Yeah," the boy says. "Especially with all the nice snacks."

Hofmeester nods. "I bought the fish this morning at the wholesaler's, at VEN, out in Diemen. You can taste it."

For a moment they stare at each other, the old man and the young man, they look at each other, wondering what to say next. The old man is thinking about VEN in Diemen.

Then, to finish off the conversation, Hofmeester says: "VEN, that's the place for fish, Bas. Remember that. Put that information to good use."

Without waiting for a reply, he walks over to Tirza. She's still talking to Miss Veldkamp, as though Miss Veldkamp were her best friend. In fact, the Veldkamp woman shouldn't really be called "miss." She's more like a missus. He doesn't understand why she didn't say that to him right away: "I'm not Miss Veldkamp, I'm Mrs. Veldkamp."

"The last one's for you, Tirza." He holds the plate under her nose, so she can smell how fresh they are.

"No, Papa," she says, "I'm not hungry yet."

Mohammed Atta is standing behind Tirza. He has not joined in the conversation. As she talks, he toys with the fingers of his right hand. Hofmeester watches him for a few seconds. He finds it abhorrent.

In the kitchen he eats the last sardine himself.

The wife is still standing at the counter, just as he left her.

"Did they like them?" she wants to know.

He says nothing. He holds the plate under the tap.

"So what are we going to do about it?" he asks.

"About what?"

"About what? About what? Do you even listen when I talk to you?"

"I always listen. I'm a better listener now that I used to be. You also say more interesting things than you used to. About us?"

He dries his hands.

"About us. No, not about us. I'm finished with us. What are we going to do about Mohammed Atta? No matter how much you dislike her, she is your child. It's my Tirza. But she's also your child."

She mixes a little more rum and cola.

"Don't get so worked up," she says. "It's just a whim. Tirza isn't nearly ripe for a real boyfriend. She's much too preoccupied with herself. We just have to be real sweet to Mohammed Atta. The sweeter we are, the sooner he'll go away."

He shakes his head. Being sweet to Mohammed Atta, only the wife could come up with something like that.

The buzzing in his head is getting louder. He goes upstairs. He has to concentrate now, on the rest of the party, on the snacks, on Mohammed Atta, on the guests.

In the bedroom, he opens the balcony doors.

Hofmeester takes a deep breath. It is, he sees by his watch, twenty past eleven. The party is approaching its destination. Parties reach their climax somewhere between eleven-thirty and one-thirty, that's what he remembers from the parties the wife used to give. Even when Tirza was only a few months old. The parties took precedence, her parties took precedence.

He looks at the garden, the houses, the neighbors' lawn. He thinks about Tirza's trip, the one she's going to make with Atta. Atta, so that's her boyfriend. Atta, so that's the man she thinks she'll be better off with than with him. He tries to imagine what the coming months will be like in the big, empty house. Who's he going to buy wine for, who's he going to shop for? Who is he going to work in the kitchen for? He remembers her illness, like it was a person who had lodged with the Hofmeesters for a while. An uninvited guest. At first he hadn't noticed a thing. Neither had the wife, of course. He took Tirza to cello lessons, her teacher was an older, visually impaired lady, he took her to the pool. She was a good swimmer, she took part in swimming meets, she could have been a champion if she had kept it up. He picked her up from the pool, and in the evening he read to her from the classics, particularly the Russians. Tolstoy who denounces his own art because he sees it as insignificant, as entertainment that adds nothing to people's happiness, Hofmeester thought that was lovely. So lovely that he never tired of reading aloud from Tolstoy. Fantastic, he thought, this man who makes his own family unhappy, who drives his own wife crazy, who abandons his own talent to pursue the happiness of mankind.

And all that time, Hofmeester hadn't noticed a thing. Maybe he hadn't wanted to notice anything. Until he got a call from Mrs. Van Delven, Tirza's homeroom teacher.

The wife was at her studio, she still had a studio back then, God knows what she got up to there. What did she actually do in those days, except sleep in? He had once met a woman who said: "I sleep in all the time now, because soon I'll have children and then that will all be over." The wife had taken a different approach; she had started sleeping in *after* the children came.

"Perhaps," Mrs. Van Delven said on the phone, "you and your wife could come by to talk about Tirza?"

"I'll come, but I'll come alone," he said. "My wife's too busy."

He made an appointment for four-thirty on Friday afternoon. It meant he had to leave the publishing house a little early, but pretty much the only thing people did in those days on Friday afternoons was get together for drinks.

At ten past four on Friday afternoon, he put the manuscripts he was planning to read that weekend into his briefcase and cycled to the south side of town.

In front of the Vossius Gymnasium he locked his bike to a lamppost and wondered what it was they wanted to talk to him about, what Tirza could have done.

He walked through the school corridors with the briefcase clenched to his side. Almost everyone had gone home. He felt uneasy, the way he always did when he had to play the role of father in public. He preferred to play that role where no one could see him.

Three boys were standing at the coffee dispenser. "Excuse me, I'm looking for Mrs. Van Delven's room," Hofmeester said. A short, rather grubby-looking boy with an earring showed him the way, and as he climbed the stairs to the second floor, the briefcase still under his arm, he realized he was being watched and that he was ridiculous. Not ridiculous as a man, that would be something he could live with. No, ridiculous as a father. A ridiculous father, that's what he was. A father who had also felt deeply uneasy standing on the playground, back when his children still attended the Amsterdam Montessori School, amid other fathers and mothers, waiting to pick them up. The other parents talked to each other, knew each other, wanted to get to know each other better. It made him feel like hiding behind a tree. And when he heard a child shout: "Look, Tirza, that's your father," he always felt the urge to look over his shoulder, as though the child was referring to someone else.

The door to classroom nine was closed. He knocked quietly and waited a few seconds. Then he knocked again, harder this time. "Come in," he heard someone call out.

He opened the door.

The desks were empty, the classroom smelled of sweat and chewing gum. It was a smell he didn't remember from his own schooldays. But what *did* he remember of those days, anyway? Very little. His parents' hardware store in Geldermalsen, that was printed more clearly in his mind.

Mrs. Van Delven was at her desk.

Written on the blackboard was something about "than" and "as."

She had already pulled up a chair for him.

Mrs. Van Delven was in her late fifties, well-preserved, sensibly dressed but not too stuffily.

She shook his hand, smiling, not overly friendly but still welcoming, welcoming at least for the purposes of a talk.

They had met a few times at PTA meetings.

Mrs. Van Delven asked about his work and mentioned the titles of a few recent Dutch novels he hadn't read. Apparently she had forgotten that he did translated literature. People often did. As politely as possible he reminded her that he edited literature in translation, and she chimed in right away: "Tirza, let's talk about Tirza."

"Yes," he said. "Is there something wrong? Have there been problems?"

"That's exactly what I wanted to ask you. Have there been problems, Mr. Hofmeester?"

The briefcase, which he'd had on his lap all this time, he put on the floor.

"Problems? No. Not that I know of. Well, she's going into puberty, she's already in puberty, she's fourteen, but problems? No. She goes to cello lessons, she likes that, she swims, she has a couple of close girlfriends. I have the impression that Tirza is a happy child, she's a bit introverted, but . . ."

He didn't finish his sentence. He picked up the briefcase, put it back on his lap, and opened it, without knowing why. He was looking for something, but he couldn't remember what.

"Yes?" Mrs. Van Delven asked. "You were saying?"

"So am I. Introverted."

She smiled, but not wholeheartedly, Hofmeester thought. And why, after all, should she?

"So you're saying that you haven't noticed anything?"

He shook his head and clutched his briefcase a bit tighter. What should he have noticed? Had he missed something? He couldn't imagine what it might have been.

"No."

"Well then I'll tell you," Mrs. Van Delven said. "We have noticed something, and although it is perhaps a bit premature, we've decided, on the basis of past experiences with other pupils, to warn you."

He put his briefcase on the floor again.

"I see."

He was thinking of drugs, or of getting in with the wrong crowd, although he had no idea what wrong crowd that could be. Were there actually wrong crowds on Amsterdam's posh old south side? Could there be anything like a wrong crowd at the Vossius Gymnasium?

Mrs. Van Delven was tapping a ballpoint quietly on her desktop. "We think," she said as she went on tapping, "that Tirza is in the process of developing an eating disorder."

Hofmeester laughed, but only because he was nervous. The mere term. Eating disorder. In a manuscript once, he had underlined it in pencil. And then he wrote in the margin: "Consult with translator."

Hofmeester had ideas of his own about which terms were ugly.

"And on what do you base this suspicion?"

The teacher stopped her tapping. "We've had other experiences," she said. "And, as I said, there are symptoms, there is a behavioral pattern that seems familiar." She raised her hand and let it fall to her lap, as though to say: "I can't do anything about it, that's simply the way it is."

"We?"

"I and few of my colleagues."

He nodded.

"I see," he said after a brief and rather tense silence. "So what now?"

"It's not our immediate responsibility to take action in such cases. That lies with the parents themselves, but we do feel it is our responsibility to inform them. Which is what I've just done."

The parents, that was him. She was referring to him.

She looked at him. Apparently she was finished, because she said nothing else. And she made no attempt to.

"So what now?" Hofmeester aske.

"Have you really not noticed anything?" She seemed to find it hard to believe. But he hadn't noticed anything. Okay, he had noticed all kinds of things, but what mattered were the conclusions you drew from what you noticed.

"Does she eat at home, for example? And what, if I may ask? How much? And when?"

He cleared his throat.

"She's never been much of an eater, not even when she was a baby. She's a light eater. We're almost all light eaters. I am, her sister doesn't eat as much as she used to either, my wife, we're all light eaters. But I'll start to pay more attention."

Mrs. Van Delven leaned back. She looked skeptical. "Doesn't she seem awfully thin to you? For a fourteen-year-old girl?"

"Awfully thin." He had never looked at it that way before. Now he would. Think about it, deal with it, investigate it, thoroughly of course.

"And what about your wife, what does she think?"

"My wife is . . ." He crossed his legs. "My wife is an artist, as I'm sure you know. She spends a lot of time in her studio. A lot of time. Working. Painting, drawing . . ."

Mrs. Van Delven looked at him glumly, he thought. Without a dash of hope, in fact. She stared at him. Without hope. Like at a funeral. Then she glanced at her watch.

"Fine," she said, "I've informed you. Now it's up to you."

He picked up his briefcase, stood up.

"Now it's up to me. Yes, indeed. But what exactly am I supposed to do?" he asked, before shaking her hand. "What do you people expect me to do?" It sounded as though he was waiting for an assignment, and perhaps he was.

"What we expect you to do? Well, what about talk to Tirza? For starters."

"About the eating disorder?" He had a hard time using the term, he found it repellent. Deep inside, he believed Mrs. Van Delven was wrong about this.

"Yes," Mrs. Van Delven said, "about the eating disorder. If that's what she has. And if not, it still can't hurt to talk to her."

"I talk to her a great deal. My youngest daughter and I talk a great deal." Hofmeester felt there was no reason to take this lying down, the way he was being depicted here as a silent, absentee father. He needed to set her straight.

"And about what, if I may ask? What do the two of you talk about?"

"About what? Tolstoy, a lot, lately. His rejection of art, of literature. Perhaps you know that fascinating essay of his, *Was ist das Kunst?* Unfortunately it's only available in German. The one in which he summarizes art as an '*eitle Kurzweil müssiger Menschen*?' An idle pastime for people of leisure?"

Hofmeester had started talking a little more loudly now. He always waxed enthusiastic when he started in about that. *Eitle Kurzweil müssiger Menschen.*

"That's what you talk about with a fourteen-year-old girl?"

He nodded and switched his briefcase to the other hand. He opened the latch, but he wasn't looking for anything. He did it for no good reason. "She is gifted, as you know. Extremely, extremely gifted."

Mrs. Van Delven looked at him penetratingly, and her expression—he couldn't pretend not to notice—was filled with disgust.

He mumbled a goodbye. Perplexed by her disgust, but equally perplexed by her indifference to Tolstoy's dilemma.

Briefcase under his arm, he walked through the empty school building. The echo of his own footsteps sounded unpleasant. He was barely able to talk if it wasn't about things like *Anna Karenina* or *Notes from Underground*, everything outside the world of literature in translation he tried to deal with only in passing. Especially things like eating disorders.

On the stairs the briefcase popped open, spilling his manuscripts, his four pencils, and an apple onto the ground. Someone walked past and Hofmeester didn't dare to bend down and pick up his things. Only when the sound of footsteps had died out did he scrape together his belongings.

That evening he climbed the stairs to Tirza's room. Holding *Anna Karenina*; they had stopped last time at page three hundred and ten.

When he walked into her room she pulled the blankets over her head. "Please," she shouted from beneath the blankets, "no Tolstoy, not tonight. A double helping tomorrow, but not tonight."

He sat down on the foot of her bed, book in hand, but didn't open it. And he didn't pet her to calm her down, as he did on other evenings.

He sat there and asked: "Doesn't Tolstoy have anything to offer you?"

"That's not the point," Tirza shouted, still from under the blankets. "No one my age has their parents read out loud to them anymore. Even Ibi says it's ridiculous. Ibi says you're crazy, Daddy. She says she can prove it."

He felt for her hand beneath the blanket and, after a little searching around, found it. He took his youngest daughter's hand and held it and didn't let go. Somewhere he felt pain, just a twinge, no more than that, a slight twinge, and decided to ignore it. All he said was: "Ibi is going through puberty, Tirza, that's why she acts a little rebellious. It's a difficult age. I'm not crazy. I'm your father."

Then there was silence. She seemed to be waiting for him to go on where they had stopped the night before, at page three hundred and ten of *Anna Karenina*, but he didn't, he needed to say something.

Still holding her hand, he looked at the ceiling, at the posters on the wall. At the books he had given her, which she had arranged in her bookcase in alphabetical order.

"I spoke with Mrs. Van Delven today."

"The old cow," she said from under the blankets.

"You don't think she's nice?"

"Aw, nice, she acts nice, but she's a cow. Everyone at school knows that. When you get to know her better, it's obvious."

Hofmeester waited, he waited for himself, he waited until he knew what he had to say, but it wouldn't come out. A notebook was lying on her desk. He felt the urge to open it and read. Maybe it contained everything he needed to know.

In one corner of her room was the cello. And the music stand.

"Tirza, is there something I don't know about, something I should know? Is there something . . ." He gulped back some spittle, he cleared his throat, but the raspiness in his throat wouldn't go away. "Is there something I should have asked you, but that for some reason or other I didn't?"

She poked her head out from under the blankets.

"No," she said. "Nothing."

In one hand he held her hand and in the other *Anna Karenina*, and he tightened his grip on *Anna Karenina* and thought: I can't do this, if this is what being a father is all about, then I can't do it, then I should just quit, I should find a replacement. Someone who can. Because this isn't going to work out.

"Are you sure about that?"

She nodded. "Yeah, very sure. Why? Did someone tell you something? Why are you asking questions like this? You never do that."

He put the book down on the bed. With his index finger, he tapped softly against his upper lip. "There are people," he said, almost in a whisper, "who think you have an eating disorder."

She sat straight up in bed. "A what?"

"I know it's ridiculous, I know you're simply a light eater, I mean . . ." And Hofmeester kept tapping his upper lip with his index finger. "The only true nourishment is knowledge, that is the one and only nourishment, you know that and I know that, but I felt like I needed to talk to you about it. That . . ."

"What?"

"Well, you know. I started thinking about it. I've thought about it. Of course you are very, how shall I put it, Tirza, you're thin. Aren't you? Can I say that?"

"Do you mean because I don't have breasts?"

"No, no, that's not what I mean. They will come along. They're on their way. They're just a little late. Maybe that's it. You just have to imagine that they're on a train, your breasts, and that they're experiencing a slight delay because someone threw the wrong switch somewhere, but they're on their way, believe me. No, no, I'm talking about your belly, the area around your belly; women, girls, have a belly, a little belly, but you don't, you don't have anything, Tirza, nothing at all."

He had stopped tapping his lip, he had moved to his forehead, gently and rhythmically, and he thought: I can't do this, this is killing me.

She crawled out from under the covers and stood on her mattress.

"Don't you think mine's pretty?" she asked.

She pulled up her nightie. A present from the wife, Tirza refused to wear pajamas anymore, Tirza liked nighties.

The wife had bought one for her. Bright pink, candy-cane pink. A horrible color, Hofmeester thought, the worst kind of pink imaginable, the color of the cathouse. But Tirza thought it was cute. She was too old for pajamas. She said.

"Don't you think it's pretty?" she repeated. Holding up her nightie, presenting her belly to her father, she waited for a reply.

Hofmeester tried not to look. He concentrated on the music stand in the corner. There was a sheet of music on it. Music had been played here not long ago.

"I think you're very pretty," Hofmeester said. "Tirza, you're the prettiest girl I know, but you're too thin. People come to me and complain about how thin you are, we have to do something about it. We have to start eating more, we have to eat better. More regularly."

"Daddy, look at me." She interrupted him in a loud voice, the way she did sometimes when he was reading aloud. Sometimes she enjoyed it. There were parts of *Don Quixote* she'd thought were lovely, Turgenev's hunting sketches had tickled her fancy.

"Look," she said. "Just look here."

And he looked.

She was standing on her bed. On top of the covers. Holding up the ridiculous pink nightie her mother had bought at a ridiculously expensive shop. Hofmeester stared at her navel. Below it she wore a pair of yellow underpants, yellow with dots. White polka dots.

"I'm not a girl," she said. "I'm a woman."

She dropped the hem of her nightie. She laid her hands on the places where her breasts would be.

"I'm a woman with tits," Tirza said.

She placed her hands on her stomach.

"I'm a woman with a belly."

Her hands moved to her thighs.

"I'm a woman with long legs. I'm a woman, Daddy."

Hofmeester got up. "You are gifted, Tirza. Extremely, extremely gifted, but you're not a woman, you still have to become one, and you will. You're a girl, and you have to eat." He walked over to the corner and adjusted the music stand a few inches.

All this time she was still standing on the bed, she just stood there, Tirza, she had pulled up her nightie again. "Say that I'm a woman, Daddy," she said.

He stopped in his tracks. His hand on the music stand. "Tirza," he said.

"Say that I'm a woman," she shouted. "Say it, Daddy."

The book was still lying on the bed. The book he had been planning to read to her. "You're . . ."

He walked back over to the bed, he stood in front of her.

She grabbed him by the hair. That was easy, now that she was standing on the bed. She pulled his hair. "Say it," she shrieked, "Daddy, say it, don't be afraid to say it. Tirza, you're a woman."

He let her pull his hair. It didn't matter to him. He picked the book up from the bed.

"I'm a woman," she shrieked. "Say it, say it, Daddy."

She pulled on his hair even harder, but he didn't feel it, he stood there as though in a trance, as though he were seeing something else, hearing something else.

"Say it," she shrieked, "Tirza, you're my woman. Say it, Daddy, say it."

She was not only shrieking now, the tears were streaming down her face. She fell onto the bed, buried her face in the sheets.

"Tirza," he said, "you're my daughter." He was screaming now as well. "You are my daughter, Tirza, you are my daughter and you will always be my daughter."

Then he ran down the stairs. But he could still hear her shouting: "You don't have a woman, Daddy. I'm the only woman you've got. The only one."

In the living room he sank onto the couch and rocked back and forth. He felt like crying, just like Tirza, but he couldn't, and he couldn't understand why he couldn't.

That next Monday, at lunchtime, he went to Scheltema's bookshop. Between the philosophy and psychology sections, he finally found a saleswoman who had time to help him.

"I'm looking for books about eating disorders," he said as discreetly as possible.

"About what?"

"Eating disorders," he repeated, a little louder now.

"What is it exactly you're looking for? Novels about eating disorders?"

"Information."

She led him to a bookcase.

"This row," she said. "All about eating disorders. This one too. And over there are some more."

Hofmeester bent down. But first he looked to see that no one was watching. No vague acquaintances, no colleagues. The supply of titles was overwhelming. The quantity alone was enough to make you sick.

It took him more than twenty minutes to find two books that seemed slightly cogent.

The girl at the cash register asked: "Is it a present?"

"No," Hofmeester said, "it's for me."

He hurried back to the publishing house. "That was a long lunch break, Jörgen," the receptionist said. Holding the bag with the two books clenched to his chest, he smiled wanly.

That evening he settled down on the couch with the books, his pencils, and a sharpener; he liked to keep his pencils sharp.

Tirza came into the room. She asked: "What are you reading?"

"Nothing," he said, laying his hand on the books. "Nothing interesting. Rubbish, really."

"Daddy," she asked, "doesn't it bother you that Mama's gone so much?"

She was already in her nightie, the color made him nauseous. Someday he'd had to sneak in and steal the thing, burn it on the sly.

"I like being alone," he answered, toying with the pencil sharpener. "I don't like a lot of commotion. Noise. Too many people."

"But don't you think it's weird that she's gone so much?"

"We have good agreements, Tirza. She's busy, I'm busy. Now it's time for you to get some sleep." He caressed her cheek.

"But do you actually have a woman, then?" she asked.

And no matter how much he loved her, the question worried him. The question seemed to him more devious than was fitting for her age, the question was so much more malicious than her character, so much meaner than the sun queen that she was and always would be.

"Mama is my wife, Tirza. You know that just as well as I do. Now get upstairs, I'll read to you tomorrow."

Then she leaned over and nibbled on his nose. The way she did whenever she wanted to be very close to her father. A leftover from her youngest childhood. That was when she had started nibbling on his nose. According to Hofmeester, she did it because she was searching for the breast. That, however, was not particularly logical, for whatever else his nose might have looked like, it wasn't a nipple. And although she was fourteen already, she still climbed onto her father's lap quite regularly and nibbled on his nose.

"You don't have a woman, Daddy," she whispered. "I'm the only woman you have."

Then she bit his nose again and ran upstairs. He remained sitting on the couch, he hesitated about whether he should run after her and tell her how wrong she was. He hesitated so long that he could just as well remain sitting there.

Ibi was at a café with friends, the wife was painting in her studio and receiving her almost exclusively male models, Jörgen Hofmeester sat in the living room and underlined one paragraph after the other in the informative book about his youngest daughter's disorder, and in her bedroom beside the cello Tirza was busy giftedly starving herself to death.

That was how the Hofmeester family lived at the start of the new millennium.

4

From the bedroom balcony, where he has been standing for the last fifteen minutes, Hofmeester sees the light in the shed go on. And off. And on again. And off.

Someone is playing with the light. Only then does he remember that he has left Ester without the "h" in the shed, and that he had promised her a glass of orange juice.

Promises are for keeping. He hurries to the kitchen. He mustn't neglect the guests like this, even if they do hide themselves away in the shed.

Tirza is standing at the sink. For a moment he thinks she is vomiting.

"What are you doing?" he asks.

"Eating a tomato." She's leaning over the sink because of the drips.

"We've got so many nice things to eat. All kinds of things." It sounds desperate and accusatory, both at the same time.

"I just felt like a tomato." She takes another bite, the juice dribbles down her chin. Hofmeester hands her a dishrag.

"Your dress," he says, "is on a bit crooked, I can see your bra straps."

He is about to straighten it for her, but Tirza says: "It's supposed to be that way. What do you think of him?"

He pours himself a glass of white wine, still the Italian Gewürztraminer. Always and above all the Italian Gewürztraminer.

"Who?"

"Choukri. What do you think of him?"

The tomato is finished now.

"Do you want some too?" Hofmeester asks. He holds up the bottle. "It's your favorite wine."

She shakes her head. "Later. So what do you think of him?"

Hofmeester looks at the ceiling. It certainly could use a fresh coat of paint. He counts three big, brown moisture spots. But there's no money left for that anymore. The hedge fund has cut and run. Everything in Hofmeester's surroundings is cutting and running. He invests only in what is absolutely necessary these days, and Hofmeester feels that immaculately white ceilings are not absolutely necessary.

"What can I say? I found him rather withdrawn. Not open, not particularly social, hard to make contact with. But of course that's only a first impression."

"Of course he's shy, Daddy. You'd be shy too, in his situation, and you're shy enough already, which isn't exactly the perfect match."

"I'm not shy."

He refills his glass with Italian Gewürztraminer and knocks it back, then fills it again.

"You *are* shy," she says lovingly, but emphatically. This is one subject on which she is sure of herself. "You're the shyest person I know."

"I'm discreet, Tirza," he says. "Discreet is not the same as shy. It's not my place to force myself on my daughter's boyfriend. I remain in the background."

"Daddy, you're extremely shy, and you know it. When we used to go on vacation you would push us into the restaurant to have us see what it looked like. While you stayed outside. Have you forgotten that? Don't you remember? And when we were in grade school doing a play and all the parents came to the dressing room afterwards because they were so proud, you almost tried to hide behind me. So tell me, what did you think of him?"

He claps his hand together. Without knowing why. He looks at the label on the wine bottle.

"Difficult. If you want to know the truth. Difficult. I found him puzzling. He reminded me of someone. No, he reminds me of someone."

"An actor? He looks like an actor, doesn't he? A French actor? Do you think he's nicer than the ones before?"

"The one before?"

"The ones."

"Were there ones before? I thought that was nothing serious."

Every once in a while he hears a snatch of music from the living room. He thinks he should fry some more sardines. There are so many sardines. What is a person without a task? Nothing. The frying of sardines, that is his task this evening.

"It wasn't. But they did exist. I introduced them to you, Daddy, you saw them all."

"I saw boys, here at the house, that's right, now and then I saw boys, the last few years, some of them spent the night, but no boyfriends. You said it didn't mean anything."

"No, that's right. It was just for fun, but they were boyfriends."

So there, again, was something else he hadn't picked up on. There were so many things he hadn't picked up on, but still, he would never describe himself as naïve. As neither shy nor naïve. As something else perhaps, but what?

"Tirza," he says, holding his hands out to her the way toddlers do when they want to be picked up.

Careful, perhaps that. Jörgen Hofmeester, a careful man.

"Tirza," he repeats, still holding out his arms, "do you mean you really haven't noticed?"

"What?"

"Your boyfriend. That man. Who he looks like. Haven't you noticed?"

She shakes her head. "A French actor, that's what I said, don't you think? An actor?"

He drops his arms.

"No, not a French actor. Not an actor. Not an actor in the usual sense of the word. Mohammed Atta. The same face, the same eyes, the same jaw line. The same hair."

She shakes her head again.

"Daddy," she says.

And the father, leaning against the counter, repeats those two words—Mohammed Atta—as though it has sunk in only now, what he has seen, what he thinks, what he feels.

"Please don't do this," she says.

"What?"

"What you're doing now."

"So what am I doing?" Hofmeester asks. "Tell me, what am I doing?"

Tirza walks over to him. She hugs him. "Please," she whispers, "don't do this. Let me have my happiness."

"But I do let you have your happiness, I wish you all the happiness in the world, the only thing is: he's not your happiness, he's your unhappiness. Mohammed Atta is your unhappiness."

Tirza holds onto her father. "He's my boyfriend. You have to get used to that idea, Daddy. Please. You'll be able to do that, won't you? Don't you think you'll be able to? Won't you be able to do that?"

Her hair tickles his forehead, he feels her breath, which smells vaguely of peppermint. He can't stand here like this, not at her party. Someone could come in at any moment.

"Listen, Tirza, I wish you the best, the handsomest and nicest boyfriend in the world, but Mohammed Atta isn't the best or the handsomest or the nicest. He's pretty much the worst candidate I can think of."

"Stop calling him Mohammed Atta. His name is Choukri and he's my boyfriend."

Hofmeester pulls back from her embrace, he turns around, he looks for the corkscrew to open another bottle of Italian Gewürztraminer.

"Everyone sees things differently," he says as he looks around. "We talk about reality, but what do we mean when we do that? Do you know? You see that man as your boyfriend. I see him as Atta, and I know what Atta wants, I know what he's after, I know what his plans are." At last he finds the corkscrew. He keeps talking, he doesn't care who's listening anymore. It has to be said. It has to come out. The truth, the horrible truth.

"I'm worried," he says. "I don't want my daughter consorting with Mohammed Atta. Even the most unstable, the most progressive father would say: 'My daughter may consort with anyone, an African, a junkie as far as I'm concerned, a Vietcong regular for that matter, but not a terrorist.'"

She slams her hands down on the counter. "You're going too far now," she shouts. "This isn't funny. Stop it, Daddy, stop it!"

He opens the bottle. He has succeeded in initiating an open and honest conversation with his daughter. He treats himself to a glass of wine to calm his nerves.

"Stop it? So what am I supposed to stop?"

"Calling my boyfriend a terrorist. For starters."

"What am I supposed to call him? A freedom fighter? An anti-globalist? An anarchist? An enemy combatant? The victim of false indoctrination? A poor wretch?"

"He's not interested in politics. Choukri makes music, and I love him."

"What do you know about love?"

"What do you know about it, Daddy? What do you know about it, anyway? Who have you ever been able to love?"

He puts down his glass. He wipes his lips. "You," he says after a bit. "I've been able to love you."

They look at each other. He hopes she will say something now, but she remains silent. And he realizes that it is inevitable, that there is nothing more to be done about it, that his life is over, without ever having begun. It's over before it started. A thought that should really make him smile. Because when you think about it, it's insane, and what better reaction to madness than to smile? But the smile won't appear.

"I thought," he says then at last, "in any case I've been told that that's something your generation doesn't go in for anymore, that loving, that it's passé, over and out. Your generation has come up with something else."

"Who told you that?"

"Someone here at the party."

"Oh. Well, I still go in for it, in any case. I love Choukri."

Now he smiles. Now he can.

"He's using you."

"I'm using him too. That's what loving is all about. Mutual use. Respectful use."

It sounds like something she's said before, that she's heard others say, that she read somewhere.

"I have a good eye for people," Hofmeester says. "I've been around longer than you have, and believe me: using is not loving, and loving is not using, and he is Mohammed Atta. If not the Mohammed Atta of September 11, then his successor, his heir, his reincarnation, his second coming, his understudy . . ."

She waves her hand at him to tell him to stop, she interrupts him. "Then I love Mohammed Atta. That's the way it is. You'll just have to get used to that too."

He looks at her in bafflement and wipes his lips again.

She walks over to him. "Daddy, please," she says. "Don't make me cry, not tonight."

He takes both her hands in his. "I'm not making you cry, I'm trying to ward off danger. I never want to make you cry. Not now. Not at all, never."

"But there is no danger. You only think so."

"Oh yes, it's there. I feel it, I smell it, I see it."

He lets go of her hands and she strokes his cheek, his chin.

"Fry some more sardines for us," she says. "I like that. When you fry sardines. It reminds me of the old days."

"I'll do that, Tirza. In a little while I'll get back to my sardines. In a bit. But now . . . Now I have to warn you. Now I have to protect you."

She shakes her head. "Don't protect me, Daddy. Please, don't protect me."

She goes back to the party. Glass in hand, he watches her go. She has changed. There's no denying it. The wife is right. But it didn't happen from one day to the next. It started after her illness. During the illness already. Even though he didn't see it. There are so many things he didn't see. He remembers the books he bought in an attempt to heal his youngest daughter. But when it became obvious that Hofmeester's study of eating disorders and related matters wasn't helping, Tirza began seeing two separate psychologists. The second one asked to talk to her parents and, as was often the case in such instances, Hofmeester went alone.

The psychologist was a stern man, but not unfriendly, Hofmeester thought. Businesslike, which he hadn't expected from a social scientist.

"What's causing it?" Hofmeester had asked him. After all, he had not come here just to answer questions, he had decided, he also wanted to ask a few of his own. He had even tucked a notepad into the inside pocket of his sports jacket, to write down what he heard. And he pulled it out now.

"There's not one cause, there are always a lot of causes. And the causes, at this point, aren't the truly crucial thing. Your daughter is in a pretty bad way."

"But . . ." Hofmeester sat in the easy chair, searching for words, searching for hope. He had come here to hear that everything would turn out well, and he hadn't heard that yet. "What are we doing wrong? What am I doing wrong?"

He had his pencil poised.

"It's not about doing things wrong. Although, within every family, including yours, there are things that could be changed and improved."

Hofmeester looked at his shoes, then at the psychologist's.

"What's she up to?" Hofmeester asked. "You've talked to her, what's going on in her mind? What's bothering her?"

And as he asked that he shook his head, as though trying to make clear that he didn't understand what she was up to. That it was something no one could understand. It was beyond all understanding, and so beyond Hofmeester's ken as well.

"Well," the man said, "that's not so easy to say either. She's busy trying to gain control over her life, regaining control. Her illness, in fact, is a way of doing that. That's probably how one should see it, as a matter of control."

"Control?"

"Yes," the psychologist said. "Control."

"Control," Hofmeester repeated, as though it was a word in a foreign language and he didn't know what it meant, which was also how it felt. He no longer knew what "control" meant. He wrote the word on his notepad, without really knowing why, and underlined it a few times.

"And what am I supposed to do? What can I do?" he asked when he was done writing and underlining.

"Support her."

"But I already do that."

"Perhaps not enough."

Not enough, that was a possibility that hadn't occurred to Hofmeester. He had thought more along the lines of: too much, but it was really: not enough.

They sat there like that across from each other for a bit, without a word, until the psychologist said: "You know, Mr. Hofmeester, eating disorders occur almost exclusively among the white middle-class population, nowhere else. It is a typical white middle-class illness."

It sounded as though that was supposed to explain everything, as though everything should be clear now.

And while the psychologist was getting up from his chair, Hofmeester wondered what the man was trying to say.

"Is it possible," he asked, putting away his notepad and pulling on his coat, "that it has something to do with her being extremely, extremely gifted?"

"Who says that? Who says that she is?"

Hofmeester shook his arms in his sleeves. The question baffled him. "Everyone," he said at last, "everyone has always said that, everyone says that."

"Hmmm," the psychologist said. "Hmmm."

And that was the end of the session.

A peculiar man, Hofmeester thought. Not unfriendly, only rather evasive. As he was unlocking his bike and thinking about their conversation, he was struck by the idea that he was it, he was the white middle-class illness: he, Jörgen Hofmeester, in the flesh.

And later that day he saw his reflection in a shop window and again it struck him. There goes the illness of the white middle class, there goes Jörgen Hofmeester.

That realization was new and overwhelming too, but it could not keep Hofmeester from doing what he had already been doing for weeks. He bought even more books about eating disorders and read them in the evening, the pencil poised, the sharpener within reach. If there was a solution, it could be found in books. Where else?

But no matter how much he underlined and checked off and learned by heart, Tirza continued to grow thinner, her weight dropped, approached a critical limit. There was talk of force feeding. Hospitalization, nursing.

And when the wife came home one evening just before midnight, she found Hofmeester sitting at the dining room table, surrounded by books, all about the same subject. He looked at her, Tirza's mother, and he said: "We are killing our daughter." Without taking off her coat, she sat down at the table. She lit a cigarette. Then she got up and poured herself a drink.

Tirza's illness destroyed not only Tirza herself, but along with her illness began the destruction of the Hofmeester family, and the more the members of that family fought against it, the faster it seemed to take place.

She put her drink on the table. She sat back down. She hadn't taken off her woolen cap either.

"We?" the wife asked. "We? Is that what you said? We? No, not we. You." She pointed her finger at Hofmeester.

He slammed shut the book he was reading.

"Me? And why me, if I may ask? At least I do something. What do you do? What have you done?"

The wife inhaled.

"You," she said, "you are the one who's poisoned that child. Never leaving her alone for a moment. Never giving her a moment's rest. If she didn't have to go to cello lessons, then she had to go to swimming lessons, then she had to be read to aloud from some book or other from the Russian Library, and if she wasn't being read to she had to go along to buy wine. You destroyed her the way you tried to destroy Ibi, but Ibi was too strong for you, thank God. Tirza isn't. To Tirza, everything you say is true, Tirza idolizes you, and you're all too pleased to let her, you love finally being an idol to someone."

Hofmeester picked up a pencil and began sharpening it. "What you're saying," he said when he was done, "is such a far cry from the truth. It's such a nasty lie. It's nastier than nasty. I fretted over her because you neglected her. Someone had to fret over her, someone had to pick her up from swimming lessons. Someone had to take her to cello lessons."

"But no one had to force her to swim, force her to do this, force her to do that, no one had to talk all the time about how extremely, extremely gifted she is. How would you react if that was what you heard all day? Wouldn't it drive you just a little bit crazy? Wouldn't it make you go a wee bit off your rocker? You destroyed that child, you and no one else. You tried to turn her into a colleague, and a friend, and your wife, that's right, your wife too. Everything you couldn't find in the real world you tried to get from her, and the only thing you can blame me for is that I didn't stop it, that I didn't do anything, in any case not enough to make you stop. But I have a life too, I'm only human too, I also have a right to a little happiness. That's right, I'm only human, Jörgen."

He massaged his temples and then said: "If you say that one more time, 'I'm only human,' if I have to hear one more time that you're only human, I'm going to strangle you."

"Do it," she said. "Strangle me."

He kept massaging his temples and finally he said, more calmly than before: "I didn't talk all the time about how gifted she is, I just tried to stimulate her. That's not a crime. Yes, I loved her, I do love her, perhaps I have more of a special tie with her than with Ibi, but that's not a crime either. And I don't need anything in return. What I get in return is enough, more than enough. The way she smiles at me, the things she tells me, her company. If I've done anything wrong, I don't know what it would be."

He broke one of his pencils in two, it cost him a good bit of effort, and that effort distracted him for a moment from his rage.

"Is that your only thought on the matter?" he asked. "That I destroyed her? Is that all that's left of our marriage, the question of who's to blame for Tirza's illness?"

She stubbed out her cigarette. "Yes," she said, "that's all. I'm sorry, but you've never been a father to Tirza. A friend perhaps, a lover, but a father is not a lover, Jörgen."

He stood up. "What are you insinuating?" he asked. "Just because you're too distant and too cold to even touch her doesn't mean that someone who does touch her is a criminal. People need warmth. That's what they live on. That's what they live from. That warmth is not a crime. The lack of it is a crime."

She got up.

"Where are you going?" he asked.

"To my studio."

"To do what?"

"To sleep."

"There's no bed there."

"There's a sofa."

He went after her. In the vestibule he pushed his wife against the wall and squeezed her throat with one hand.

"How dare you say that to me?" he hissed. "How dare you say the things you said? How dare you? You, who haven't the slightest idea what it means to be a mother, who never goes to a single PTA meeting, who doesn't give a damn about anything, how dare you say that I'm not a father? You don't have to love me, I've known for a long time that you don't, but you can at least summon up some respect, some appreciation for what I do."

Her face turned red, but he didn't let go. She kicked him, but he didn't let go.

Only when his hand started hurting did he let her go.

He stayed in the vestibule, she ran to the kitchen. He heard her coughing, heard the water running in the sink. More coughing, he heard her talking on the phone.

Five minutes later she came out of the kitchen.

"What were you doing in there?" he asked.

"I was calling the police."

Then she walked out the door.

At first he remained standing in the vestibule, then he went back to the living room, arranged the books about Tirza's illness on the dinner table into three equal piles, and emptied the ashtray.

Then he sat toying with the two halves of the broken pencil. He hummed.

At a quarter past one he went upstairs to bed. Quietly, he opened the door to Tirza's room, he wanted to see whether she was asleep. Her eyes were open.

Hofmeester sat down on her bed. He couldn't look at her. If he let it sink in, what he saw there, it made him feel like hanging himself. He was furious, because he couldn't shake the feeling that he had failed, and he hated the wife, he hated everyone who reminded him of that failure.

He took Tirza's hand and looked around at the furniture in her room. He sat there like that for a while. At last he said: "Things can't go on like this, Tirza. This has to stop."

"I know," she said, and it occurred to him that her voice had been corroded by the illness too. "I know, Daddy, but I can't stop anymore. It's too late."

He focused on her desk chair, the books on her desk, a geography book that lay open. He concentrated.

"Did I do something I shouldn't have?" he asked, looking at the geography book. "Are there things that bother you? Here around the house? Things I do, or that Mama does? Have we done something wrong, have I?"

He tried to concentrate on something else. The curtains. Red curtains. Tirza had picked them out herself.

"You know, don't you, Tirza," he said, talking now almost as quietly as her, "that we, Mama and I and Ibi, that we love you whether you're gifted or not, don't you? It doesn't matter what you are. You don't have to be the best, you don't have to be anything, we love you the way you are."

He wasn't really expecting a reply. But a reply came. Louder than the last one. Loud and clear.

"No, Daddy," she said, "if I'm not the best, no one loves me."

He remained seated in silence, for a few seconds. Humiliated by the funhouse mirror of his ambition, his well-intentioned and, all in all, reasonable ambition. Defeated by his child, for whom he would have given up everything, because she made him guilty. No matter what she excelled at, she would never excel enough to wipe out his guilt.

Then he could stand being in the room no longer. He fled.

He went back downstairs and stood beside the dinner table. With his forefinger, he tapped quietly on the tabletop. A minute, then another minute, he stood there like that for fifteen minutes, for half an hour. Until the doorbell rang and he jumped. It was almost two o'clock. Maybe it was the wife who had forgotten her keys. Ibi was already home, Tirza too. It could only be the wife.

Standing at the door were two policemen. Mere boys, really.

"Mr. Hofmeester?" one of them inquired, a foreigner from the sound of it.

"Yes," Hofmeester said, "that's me."

"We received a call. Is everything all right?"

"Who called you?"

"Your wife," the other policeman said. "You do have a wife, don't you? You do live here with your wife and children?"

"Oh, that," Hofmeester said. "A little disagreement. It's all over now. Sorry to have bothered you."

He was about to close the door. He had no desire for company.

But the foreign policeman said: "Could we come in for a moment?"

"If you like."

He let them in, showed the gentlemen to the living room. They looked around. The foreigner picked up a book that was lying on the table and flipped through it slowly.

"Your wife wanted to file a complaint," he said, holding the book. "Is she at home?"

Hofmeester shook his head.

"No, she's not. You know how women are. Especially Scorpios."

"Is she a Scorpio?" asked the policeman who was not a foreigner.

"Yes, oh yes," Hofmeester said. He had no idea why he had said that. He realized that sometimes, when he didn't know what he was going to say, things came out that he wasn't always pleased with. Scorpios, where did he come up with that? She *was* a Scorpio, but whose business was it? He had to concentrate. He had to get a grip on himself, a firmer grip.

"November fourteenth," Hofmeester said. "Scorpio. She's gone to her studio. She paints. Men, mostly. Sometimes fruit. Apples, a pineapple, a lonesome strawberry on a plate. But mostly men. The occasional self-portrait, but otherwise only men."

"She said on the phone," the foreigner said, "that you accosted her, assault, that's what she called it. Is that right? Did you accost your wife? Did you assault her? Of course you're not obliged to answer, if you don't feel like it, if you think it will cause you problems. You do have a right to remain silent."

Hofmeester thought about it. He couldn't remember too clearly what it had been about, the discussion with his wife.

"We play games," he said at last, "my wife and I, we play like two little puppies. We don't know our own strength. Sometimes the game gets a little out of hand. Then she calls the police. She's a sore loser. But it's part of the game. She's an artist. As I said, she paints. Apples, oranges, summer fruit, but also men. Unemployed men, I suspect. The long-term unemployed. They don't get paid for it, a cup of tea at most, but then they have to take all their clothes off. I ask you, would you take off all your clothes for a cup of tea?"

The foreigner put the book back in place on the pile. "So assault, that's not your kind of thing? I'll ask one more time, very clearly: Did you or did you not assault your wife?"

"No," Hofmeester said. "No, of course not. As I said, it's a game. I'm the assailant, she's the victim, our house is the city park. I am . . ." He ran his hand over his lips, his forehead, his eyelids.

"Yes," said the agent who was not a foreigner, "go on? You are?"

"I am the beast. And she is . . . she's a beast as well. We're both beasts. That's our game. Two beasts. Two savage and lonesome beasts. Our living room is the steppe, our breath the polar wind. But sometimes it gets a little out of hand. Then she calls the police. It's part of the game. The first one to stop playing loses. She's always the first one to quit. We play . . . We play because . . ."

Hofmeester heard himself talking, but he no longer recognized himself. So, when it came right down to it, he *did* possess social skills. Peculiar social skills, to be sure, but still, you couldn't call it anything but a social skill. He could talk.

The policemen eyed him suspiciously, but he also looked a wee bit perplexed.

They said nothing else, they looked around and perhaps, finally, they did see the steppe, did feel the polar wind, right there in the Hofmeester family's living room.

"Well, good luck then," the foreigner said, "and next time try to keep it a bit under control."

Hofmeester showed them to the door. Before closing it, he thanked them for going to all the trouble, although he himself had no idea what trouble he was referring to. The policemen didn't seem to know either.

In the living room he parted the curtains a few inches and watched them drive away. Then he turned off all the lights.

In the upstairs closet he rummaged through the inside pockets of his sports jackets until he found the notepad he had bought specially for his meeting with the psychologist. There wasn't much written in it. One word: control. Underlined twice.

He looked at what he had written, at that one word by itself, as though that word, as though the two lines benath it, held the key to everything. To his life, his daughter's illness, the illness of the white middle class, the illness that was him and that he no longer wanted to be. He undressed and sat on the bed. But he couldn't sleep. He hummed, he opened the balcony doors and closed them again. He waited, as he so often did, for the wife to come home.

The next morning he drove Tirza to a clinic in Germany that specialized in eating disorders. He didn't ask if she wanted to go, if she felt like, if she herself thought it might help after everything else he had tried, after all those books he'd read: he just drove her there. Without stopping. And without talking. She sat in the backseat, or rather, she lay on the backseat.

The secretary at the publishing house had given him the address.

Late in the afternoon Hofmeester dropped off his daughter at the clinic, like a package. He himself took a room in a nearby boarding house.

That evening he called home, but the wife wasn't there.

Ibi answered the phone. "I've brought Tirza to a clinic in Germany," he said. "Please tell Mama."

The village with the clinic had one restaurant. Hofmeester became one of the regulars. They knew his kind there. Parents who dropped their children at the clinic, parents who were usually at the end of their ropes, more dead than alive. Not speaking a word, not even to each other, when they happened to come as a couple.

After a few evenings he met a sociologist from Frankfurt who had just brought his daughter, three years older than Tirza, to the clinic.

For a few evenings Hofmeester talked to the sociologist about sociology, about Adorno, Expressionism, the Central European highlands, Tolstoy, the little boat in which the sociologist sailed the Baltic each summer. The sociologist's little boat came up again and again, because sailing was so lovely. Everything was talked about, everything but the clinic, the child, the illness. But on the fifth evening the sociologist said: "Do you mind if I don't sit at the table with you this evening?"

"Not at all," Hofmeester said. "No problem."

He had apparently said something the sociologist didn't like, perhaps a rather vehement but, in the sociologist's view, unfounded opinion about an Expressionist poet. Or had he not been enthusiastic enough about the Baltic? Hofmeester didn't know what had caused the rift, but it pained him, this trivial incident. It hurt.

For a little while he had made contact, for a while he had found someone, but it hadn't lasted long. And after the evening when the sociologist said that he wouldn't be sitting at Hofmeester's table, they only nodded to each other, from a distance. Extremely polite nods, almost invisible to outsiders. Failed fathers, keeping each other at a distance.

Weeks went by and what no one had expected, particularly not Hofmeester, took place. Tirza began recovering, slowly, very slowly. There was the occasional relapse, but still, there was no denying it, she was getting better.

All that time Hofmeester stayed at the boarding house. The people at the publishing house understood. And if they didn't, that was their problem. Twice a day he visited his daughter at the clinic. In the morning and at the end of the afternoon. Never for long. Twenty minutes, maybe fifteen. Gradually, he worked up the nerve to start looking at her again.

And in between times, come rain or snow or shine, he walked through the hills. Now and then he ran into the sociologist walking along the same path and they would nod slightly to each other without stopping. At such moments, Hofmeester felt a light and calm sorrow.

It became clearer with each passing day: Tirza was doing what her father would not or could not do, and he knew it, he sensed it. During his walks he sometimes thought: I should ask her how you do that, get better. Where you start and how you know when you're finished. But he didn't want to bother her with difficult questions.

And, after three months in the pleasant, almost innocent countryside of Southern Germany, Tirza was released. She was allowed to go home.

The father took delivery of her and was reminded of her birth, of the cold, rainy day at the hospital in Amsterdam when a nurse had handed her to him. A little package. A bundle. A worm wrapped in blankets. And he and the wife had taken her home in a taxi. He had been proud then, but also fearful.

He had the feeling now that she was just as fragile and vulnerable as an infant.

In the car on the way back to Amsterdam, she didn't say much. Only when they got to the border did she ask: "Do you think I'll have to do this year all over again?"

"I don't think so," he said. "I think you'll be able to catch up. And if not, well, it's no real disaster."

He had not been a father to his youngest daughter, that was what the wife had said to him. A friend, a colleague, a lover, a platonic lover to be sure, but a lover still, just not a father.

Now he had to become a father. In the world of fathers he was a convert, and like all converts: a zealot.

At night he no longer climbed the stairs to read aloud to Tirza, he no longer took her to cello lessons, he no longer encouraged her to take part in swimming matches; he maintained his distance.

Sometimes he would still pause in front of the bookcase, but now that he could no longer read aloud to her, the Russian Library had lost its appeal. There was no one left with whom to share his enthusiasm, and gradually he came to wonder what he himself had ever seen in those books.

It felt as though someone had wrapped them in muslin. As though the contents had grown musty. As though the correctness of Tolstoy's claim dawned on him only now. *Eitle Kurzweil müßiger*

Menschen. No longer a comic and at the same time tragic opinion from an aging writer, an anomaly in other words; no, an ineluctable truth.

He paused before his bookcase more and more rarely, and he never pulled out a book down off the shelf anymore. The only reading he did was for his work.

And so Hofmeester had become a man who was afraid of becoming what he never wanted to be again: the lover of the woman who was his daughter.

He wanted to practice fatherhood as it was meant to be practiced, he never missed a PTA meeting, never ignored a phone call or a letter from school, yet still he was careful not to be too overbearing. When Tirza had a visitor he crept around the house, sometimes he went to the shed so as not to disturb her privacy. He did his best not to ask where she had been or where she was going, he served her and cared for her, he loved her in silence and isolation.

Only now he can no longer maintain that silence. Even the most abject of fathers would say: "No, child: Mohammed Atta, that seems like a bad idea to me."

For a moment he thinks he sees lightning, he expects to hear a thunderclap. But, through the kitchen window he sees that what he thought was lightning is actually the light in the shed. It goes on and off. On and off. Then he remembers what he was doing. Getting Ester a glass of orange juice.

He looks around, no longer sure whether he hasn't already poured her a glass of juice. He can't find it, anyway.

Hofmeester fills a wine glass with orange juice. The light in the shed keeps blinking on and off. Is the child trying to cause a short-circuit out there? Has she gone mad?

With a firm tread, glass in hand, Hofmeester walks to the shed.

He pulls open the door angrily. She is sitting there, on the upturned bucket, the light cord in her hand.

"Would you please stop that?" Hofmeester says curtly.

"Am I doing something wrong?"

She looks at him in sincere amazement. As though she never realized that grownups don't play with the lights, as though she does that all the time at home.

"Yes, you're doing something wrong. You're playing with the light, and you have been for a while. You're going to cause a short-circuit."

"I was thinking. I'm sorry."

She takes the glass of orange juice. She nips at it, as though it contains booze.

"Is this from a package with pulp in it?"

"What?"

She takes another sip.

"I think it's from the bottom of the package, the last little bit. Am I right?"

"It's orange juice, and if you don't like it you don't have to drink it. Listen . . ." He folds his arms. He thinks that pose lends him a certain authority. "I don't know what you're used to doing at home, but as far as I'm concerned you've been in the shed long enough. You can either go home, or go in and join the party."

She sighs. She looks fatigued. "Who's at the party?"

Hofmeester looks down sternly at the girl who has seated herself on a bucket in his shed and doesn't want to get up anymore.

"Your classmates, your teachers, my daughters, my wife, Mohammed Atta. Go look for yourself. Don't hide yourself away like this."

Again, that look of fatigue.

"Who was that again, Mohammed Atta?"

They don't know anything these days, not even about the history they've lived through themselves. They slept right through it. Old people too deaf to hear the doorbell. The youthful elderly, that's what they are. Elderly before they even hit puberty.

"A rapper."

"Oh yeah."

"He rapped like mad," Hofmeester continues, "and he's still rapping. Ester, I'm going to escort you to the living room, where you can continue this conversation with people your own age."

She gets up from the bucket. Slowly, provokingly so.

"There isn't anyone I really like."

"Then learn to like them." Now that he's settled into the role of educator, he can't stop. In fact, he loves this role. The role of educator gives Hofmeester something to hold on to. The mild irony of the patronizing mode is his crutch, his reading glasses, his hearing-aid.

"They don't like me either."

"I think you're wrong about that. Believe me. There are people who appeal to you and people who appeal to you less."

"Do they like you, Mr. Hofmeester?"

She looks at him. Naughtily, provocatively.

"Who?"

"People?"

"Once they get to know me, yes. Usually," Hofmeester says as matter-of-factly as possible. It's true. People like him. A certain inconspicuousness is perhaps conducive to being liked. People look right through him. It's actually too much trouble not to like someone like that.

Unexpectedly, there is a gleam in her eyes. "Are they bobbing for apples?" she asks.

"Where?"

"At the party? Are they bobbing for apples. Did you organize that for them, too?"

She opens her mouth and pretends to be biting at something.

"Chomp," she says, "chomp, chomp." Then she starts laughing uncontrollably.

"There is no bobbing for apples," Hofmeester says. "If you want to play party games, you'll have to organize that yourselves," but he can barely make himself heard above her laughter.

She keeps laughing. Loudly and unrelentingly. Between gales of laughter she chomps wildly at the air. Hofmeester finds it a frightening display. Distasteful. He seizes her by the shoulders, shakes her back and forth. "Stop it," he shouts, "stop this hysterical nonsense."

Only after a minute's shaking does he realize that Ester is no longer laughing, she's weeping. Maybe she was weeping the whole time. Another thing he didn't notice.

He pokes around for his handkerchief. Better a used one than no handkerchief at all.

As tenderly as he can, he puts his moist handkerchief in her hand.

"Easy now," he says, "take it easy, it's not all that bad."

"What?"

The sobbing has stopped. She's not chomping at an imaginary apple in the air anymore either.

"Whatever it is that's bothering you. It's not that bad. Okay, you failed a year at school, you don't eat fish, nobody likes you, but forty years from now, when you get to be my age, you'll think: I was all worked up over nothing. The worst was yet to come."

She wipes her face with his soiled handkerchief, then hands it back.

"Why do you act like you know everything?"

"Not everything." He folds up the handkerchief. "I don't know everything. Just calm down now. Take it easy. It's not that bad. It's . . ."

He doesn't finish his sentence, he can't remember what he was going to say.

Her eyes are red with weeping, it doesn't look bad on her. She had something tragic from the very start already, when she was standing there on the doorstep without a present. Even without the red eyes she had radiated something he couldn't put into words at the time, but which has been spoken aloud now: people don't like her and she, in turn, doesn't like people.

She grabs the sleeve of his sports jacket. "Mr. Hofmeester," she says, "is that true, what you said?"

"What?"

"That you did away with love?"

He can't help smiling at the memory of it. A tender memory, almost.

"Oh," he says, "back then? I was little more than a child. I had to do something. God had already been pronounced dead. Progress too. Civilization. And democracy. When you're young, you need a project. A plan. A belief. I pronounced love to be dead, at fifteen, maybe sixteen. It was in the summer, in any case. And I did away with it."

Again he smiles, even if only because he hasn't thought about himself as a fifteen-year-old for so long, it's almost like thinking about someone else.

"And what was that like, when you did away with it?" She still has a hold of his sleeve.

He thinks about it.

"Like being a law unto myself," he says, "autonomous. The truth, I'm afraid."

"The truth?"

"I'm afraid," Hofmeester says, "I said: I'm afraid." And he feels that calm, light sorrow he remembers from his walks in the foothills when his daughter was lying in the clinic, busy getting better. So calm, so light, yet still sorrow. Curious. There was nothing hysterical about it, not like what you saw so often on TV, women yanking out their hair, men clenching their fists impotently.

"And then?"

"What do you mean, and then?" He wants to pull away from her, but he doesn't dare.

"And then, after that? What else did you do away with?"

"I didn't do away with anything. As I told you. It was a mistake. After God and progress, it was love's turn, but I failed. I betrayed my own principles."

He can't quite help laughing at those words. He can barely talk about himself without laughing. He doesn't know how to go about it, to explain yourself to someone else, clarify your own actions. A person is what he does, but Hofmeester is primarily what he hasn't done. His silence is an act. His career, the authors he has left undiscovered.

"Now," he says, "now I'm old, and I have to get back to the party. It was all so long ago, and hardly worth talking about. Beside, I've forgotten most of it. Lots of big words. I remember that. Big words to make you forget how small you really are. I need to fry some sardines."

She pulls harder on his sleeve.

"But what if you were right?" she asks.

"Then," he says—and now he is the one who can't help sighing, because he doesn't feel like having this conversation, not now, not tonight, it's too much for him, what he feels like is more Italian Gewürztraminer—"then it was a worthless sort of being right, the kind of being right that was no good to anyone, is no good to anyone, something you can't grow old with, a kind of being right that would be better off not existing. I have to get back. Please let go of me."

"I did away with it too," she says, but she's still holding on to him. She tugs on his sleeve.

"That doesn't matter." He tries to sound as light-hearted as possible. "It's something people will keep doing. It's a club, a club of people who have done away with it, sometimes they recognize each other, sometimes they don't. I have to . . ."

Hofmeester doesn't finish his sentence. He takes her face in his hands. His palms are moist, from the heat and the tension. Gewürztraminer makes Hofmeester sweat even more. He presses his lips against hers, he kisses her. It's been a long time since he kissed so deliciously, it's been a very long time.

It does him good. Strange as it may seem, it comes as a release. This kiss. Maybe the wife was right after all. The beast is not dead.

It has only hidden itself away carefully, it's been loping along on Hofmeester's leash. Where was it all this time? In what lair was it hiding?

While he goes on kissing her, while she lays her hands on his head and he feels her tongue moving faster all the time, yes, she is kissing him, she is kissing him back, and he finally experiences something that feels suspiciously like happiness, all he can think is: help me. Screaming inside himself for help, he cradles the face of Tirza's classmate in his hands.

But he keeps on kissing. He no longer knows what he's doing. His hands slip under her blouse, find her bra, his hands with which he has weeded the garden so faithfully, pruned branches that have grown too heavy, sowed the grass, and mowed the lawn. She doesn't resist. She lets him do everything.

He pushes her bra up, runs the fingers of his right hand over her nipples, too roughly perhaps, but what is too rough in this place? This is what you have left, after doing away with love has turned out to be a fiasco. A self-willed and sloppily repressed longing that slithers between all conventions and agreements.

He pushes his hand into her jeans, he twists. Then, with difficulty and really quite clumsily, he unbuttons her jeans and then the rest of the buttons too.

His hands slip off of her. "Ester," he says. A word to which a body is suddenly attached, and what a body, a word of flesh. "Ester," he repeats.

He has become a man without a memory, with no sense of time or place. A man who is nothing but what should have been over long ago, the mutinous remains of stubborn desire. Nothing is left of what he was, of what he thought he was. What lives on inside him is the paltry remains of desire once nipped in the bud.

He squats and, with one mutinous tug, pulls down her jeans and panties. Fanatical, that is the word for it, enthralled.

Forgotten are the sardines, the sushi, the sashimi, even Mohammed Atta. The Third World War, the hedge fund, none of them have a chance.

He stands up, lays his left hand on her shoulder. With his right hand he feels around in her crotch. Roughly, again, but somehow tenderly as well, with the echo of tenderness. And he thinks: She's wet, she's moist, I'm exciting her. She wants me. They wrote me off, but too quickly, the world wrote me off too soon. I may have lost everything, but Jörgen Hofmeester still exists.

And while he is reflecting on the fact that he still exists, while he is realizing that he is alive and that he seems, for the moment, to have caught view of the substance of that life—this, this is life, nothing but this, this vanquished despair—he fingers her. Not very adroitly, not very precisely, not gently, overpowered as he is by his own desire, but still not too badly for a man his age, at this hour of the night, standing in the shed.

After a bit of fumbling and feeling he locates her clitoris, and now there's no stopping him.

Like with a typo in a manuscript, he doesn't quit until he's found it. That's how he searches for Ester's clitoris, as though it were a wayward quotation mark, a missing comma. His old fingers kneading her the way they do when he works the soil in the garden.

"Do you think I'm nice, Mr. Hofmeester?" she asks.

"Very nice," he says. He is short of breath. He talks like someone who has been running too fast. "Very nice, more than nice, much more than nice, not just nice. Sweet, sweet, terribly sweet."

And he rubs her clitoris as though it's what he does all the time, on a daily basis. As though it were his vocation. Like gardening. Raking, sowing, pruning. Manual labor which he has never tried to avoid, especially not after his youngest daughter's illness. It distracted him from that calm, light sorrow that had never gone away again, in fact, after those walks in the foothills. He had figured that that was life, that light and calm sorrow. But no.

Then he gets down, he kneels, in his good trousers, in the dirty shed, and starts licking the cunt of Tirza's classmate. He licks and licks and forgets all about the party, the sushi and the sashimi, the time, the partygoers' parched lips, their growling stomachs. He seems to have erased the party from his mind now, once and for all. The only thing that exists for him still is Ester.

So this is how you went about forgetting: kneeling in the shed, licking like a dog, your hands on the buttocks of your youngest daughter's classmate. And isn't forgetting the same as getting better? Isn't he getting better now, at last? Isn't it his turn?

He presses his face harder against her cunt, he presses his nose against the clitoris of Tirza's classmate who no one thinks is nice, he rubs it with his old, flaky nose, and he smells, he smells, he sniffs. Like someone who has been underwater for too long, and who now rises to the surface at last and gasps for air. The smell, the smell alone, that is life, the more he smells it, the more he covers himself with it, the more he knows that he is alive. Only that smell is real: the rest, reflections on death, detours, distractions.

"Do you think I'm pretty?" Ester asks.

He rises to his feet. Out of breath, spittle on his lips, on his chin, covering part of his cheeks, his nose. His whole face is wet with his own spittle and Ester's moisture. He looks like a savage.

"Pretty," Hofmeester says, "more than pretty. Much more than pretty."

He unzips his trousers, his hands shaking in haste and excitement. But he still exists. That is all he feels, all he sees, all he perceives, the sensation of an existence of his own that is overpowering, that cuts through everything, that leaves no convention intact. The personal lust that watches over no one and nothing, that finally claims its rightful place in this God-forsaken universe. And then, as he pulls down his pants and his underpants, he has this insane idea: my lust, that is God. That is the only true and living God.

He turns Ester around, she staggers, she holds on to the bar of the lawnmower and a wooden shelf. "How pretty do you think I am, on a scale of one to ten?" she asks and he rubs his member over her pubic hair, searching for the opening. He can't find the opening.

"How pretty do you think I am, Mr. Hofmeester, how pretty do you think I am now?"

She's whining. She's nagging. His Ester without the "h." She's asking him questions at a moment when he has lost all ability to speak. No more words, no more words at last. Deeds.

She has to help him. His deed calls for assistance.

She shoves him inside her.

She helps him, because she wants him, he thinks.

As fanatically as he pulled down her jeans, that's how he fucks her too. Snorting, gasping for air. And everywhere is the smell of her. The sharp odor of her sex, and vaguely too the odor of feces. Fresh feces.

Then, far away, he hears someone shouting "Daddy." And then again: "Daddy, where are you?"

Within a second, a fraction of a second, his memory comes back. Or at least a part of it.

"Daddy," he hears again.

He lets go of Ester, abruptly, startled. Something dawns on him. Where he is, who he is, what he is doing.

He stumbles out of the shed, his pants still around his knees, and finds himself standing in front of Tirza.

She was already closer than he had thought.

"Daddy," she says, "Miss Veldkamp is getting ready to leave."

Tirza looks at him, her gaze slides down him. Her eyes are like two instruments of torture. He can feel them.

He is still breathing heavily. Now he sees Miss Veldkamp as well. There she stands, and she looks at him, laughingly at first, now a bit more seriously.

The teacher and the father. Immobile. Two people in a garden, on a warm night in early summer. Both of them equally powerless to speak a word. In the living room, the graduation party thunders on.

Then Miss Veldkamp recoups. She once again becomes the teacher who maintains order in the classroom, even in the face of the unexpected. She continues to maintain order. Even here. Even now.

"Mr. Hofmeester," she says, "when I arrived you were half-naked, and now here you are again."

He bends over, pulls up his trousers, fumbles with his belt, he can't find the holes. Where are the holes? What was he thinking? What has he been up to? Where are the holes in his belt?

He pants and everywhere he can smell Ester without the "h," everything smells of her, the whole garden, even Miss Veldkamp smells of Ester without the "h."

But Hofmeester recoups too. Now that his crotch is hidden from view, he once again becomes who he should have remained, the host, the man with the sushi and the sashimi, Tirza's father.

"I'll show you out," he says.

"Don't bother," Miss Veldkamp announces, "you seem to have enough to do here in the garden."

Then she turns and walks away. Peevishly. That's the way she walks.

She looks back one last time and in her look he sees that she is absolutely not amused. She looks back as though at a hideous road accident. He wonders where Tirza has gone to.

"Tirza!" he shouts.

She has gone into the shed. He hears her talking to Ester, but he can't hear what they're saying. And he still cannot find the holes in his belt.

He comes closer. With uncertain tread. Staggering, actually. Dizzy from the pleasure that he so narrowly missed. Always so narrowly.

Ester is standing there. Still with her jeans around her ankles. She stands there like a statue. And he would almost be willing to swear that she looks triumphant. Perhaps even happy. He would be willing to swear.

"Daddy, what has been going on here?"

He shakes his head. "Nothing," he mumbles, "nothing." He pulls Tirza out of the shed, leads her to the back of the garden, to the dark part where he thinks no one can see them.

"Tirza," he says, "my Tirza."

"What happened?" She's being insistent. She isn't satisfied with the word "nothing," even though it covers so much ground.

He takes her face in his hands, the same way he held Ester's face a bit ago. She pushes his hands away.

"What happened?" she shouts.

"Sshh," he says, "sshh."

But she is not about to be hushed up. Tirza has no desire for silence. Not anymore.

"I know what happened. I know exactly what happened. I'm not stupid. Do you think I'm stupid or something? She's in my class, Daddy. Ester is in my class."

She answers on his behalf, she speaks on behalf of the father who, with the best will in the world, is unable to speak.

He tries to grab her, to calm her down, but she pushes him away.

She is crying.

With Ester, at least, it had started with laughter, with chomping at an imaginary apple.

He hates it when Tirza cries. And now he hates it even more, on this evening more horribly than ever.

"How could you?" she shouts. "At my party, how could you do this?" And she keeps repeating: "Why, at my party? Why, at my party? Why, at my party?"

As though it would have been better if he had let Ester come back some other time, on a Thursday evening after the Ghanese housekeeper had straightened the place up. As though it wouldn't have mattered then. As though it would have been all right then.

Despite her resistance, he takes her head in his hands, he holds it tight. He has to say something now, now he has to remember something.

"She seduced me," he says slowly.

"She seduced you? She's my age, no, she's younger. She couldn't have seduced you. Someone like that couldn't seduce you, Daddy."

She twists away from him. Tirza rubs her eyes. Which are now as red as Ester's were just then.

"And even if that were true, what kind of excuse would it be? What kind of lame excuse? You know what you are? You're a dirty man. A dirty man."

She's crying more loudly now.

He has to seek support against the trunk of a tree, he's afraid he'll fall over.

"She seduced me," he says again, and he remembers how wet she was, she was so wet, so moist. She was dripping wet. He wants to tell Tirza, he wants to say: "Tirza, my Tirza, Ester was dripping wet," but he restrains himself, he says: "She was . . ." He lets go of the tree. He takes a few steps towards his youngest daughter.

"Don't touch me," she shrieks. "Go away."

He stands there. A glass of Italian Gewürztraminer would do him a world of good.

"I'm not going to touch you, Tirza," he says. "I'm . . . I'm . . . I'm a man too. I can't help it, I'm a man too."

She covers her eyes with her hands.

"You're not a man," she says, "you're dirty. That's what you are. How can I look at you anymore? How can I touch you? How can I still think of you as my father?" And she screams: "Go away! Go away!"

Why must Tirza behave so crassly and unpleasantly? Ibi is the one he's used to having act like this.

He holds his hands out to her. "But that's what men are," he says quietly. "Tirza, that's what they are. I can't do anything about it. I don't know any men who aren't dirty. A man is his own dirtiness."

"Go away," she whispers, "go away, Daddy. Please go away. I know it will turn out all right, it will be okay. But you have to leave me alone now."

He stands, wavering, a few inches away from his youngest daughter. He wishes he could throw himself at her feet.

"Come with me inside, to the party," he says quietly. "We'll go inside together, Tirza. It's so lovely, your graduation party. I'm going to fry some more sardines, as though nothing has happened. Nothing has happened."

"Go away," she whispers.

For a moment he stands in front of her, then he turns and walks slowly towards the shed. The light, calm sorrow that had for a few minutes changed, thanks to Ester, to a contagious happiness has now become something that is neither light nor calm, but burning like a venereal disease, fierce like a hurricane, fatal as an earthquake.

The light is on in the shed.

Ester still has her pants around her ankles. But she's sitting now. On the bucket.

Hofmeester stands in the doorway. He looks at the girl on the bucket.

"Are you all right?" he asks.

"I'm peeing," she says.

Only then does he notice that the bucket is no longer upside-down. He smells the urine now as well. He can smell everything again.

He walks away, quickly. As quickly as he can without falling over. He has no desire to go back into that shed for the time being.

In the kitchen he pours himself a glass of wine. For a moment he thinks about nothing, there is only the taste of the wine.

Then, more out of habit than from necessity, he takes the last tray of sashimi out of the fridge.

When he enters the room, he sees that the wife has climbed up on the table. The lights have been turned down even lower. The children are standing around her. She's miming to someone else's voice. Dolly Parton. Of course, who else. Her heroine.

One of the wife's breasts is clearly visible.

As she mimes the words to the song, she is busy peeling off the clothes she borrowed from her eldest daughter.

Mohammed Atta is standing in one corner of the room. Ibi is keeping him company.

"Jolene, Jolene, Jolene," Dolly Parton sings, and Hofmeester can't stand this howling.

He wants no Dolly Parton, no sentimental outbursts from the mother of his children.

"Get down from there," he shouts. But she doesn't hear him. No one hears him. The music is too loud. The lights are too dim and the wife is lip-synching the words as though her life depended on it. "But I can easily understand how you could easily take my man, but you don't know what he means to me, Jolene."

They're lapping it up, the young people. Hofmeester's wife up on the table. They think it's lovelier and tastier than his sushi, his sashimi, and his sardines. They egg her on. They scream at her to dance faster, to take off more of her clothes, and she's taken off a lot already. Too much. Ibi's denim skirt.

They've never seen anything like this at home. Hofmeester's wife is the hit of the evening.

Still holding the tray, he goes to the bedroom. He puts the sashimi on the floor and sits on the bed. He holds his face in his hands and once again he smells Ester. Very clearly, in fact. He smells her as though she were in the room.

The way Tolstoy saw art at the end of his life, that's how Hofmeester sees sexuality: "*Eitle Kurzweil müßiger Menschen.*"

The light, calm sorrow had smelled of the conifer woods of Southern Germany.

The shame is the only light and calm thing now.

But this, for which Hofmeester knows no words, this pain, if there has to be a word for it at all then let that word be "pain," this smells of the genitalia of Tirza's classmate.

No, it smells of Tirza herself.

5

Hofmeester remains sitting motionless on the bed. A prisoner in his own home. He hears the music, hears the front door open and shut, Tirza's voice, the voices of people he doesn't recognize. Guests are being shown out. The party is slowly drawing to a close.

He would pay a king's ransom for a glass of Gewürztraminer right now, but he doesn't dare to go downstairs. He has to stay here until everyone has left.

Upstairs, he hears someone moving around. The tenant is awake too.

There are thoughts, countless thoughts, but Hofmeester can't make them line up. All he knows for sure is that there is no hope. He has lost Tirza, he has wagered her away. Like a player out of control, he has gambled away the best, the loveliest thing he had, and for what? What was he expecting? To double the ante?

It feels to him like he has been sitting on this bed for days. Half a lifetime, sitting on a bed, across from a closet. A man who doesn't dare to leave his own bedroom.

Then the door opens. He raises his head, he's expecting the wife. It's Tirza. His Tirza. The sun queen. She stands there. She looks at her father.

"What are you doing?" she asks.

He regards his daughter, he observes, in as far as he is still capable of that. "I'm waiting," he says.

"For what?"

He shrugs. "Has everyone left?" he asks after a few moments' silence. A tense, unpleasant silence.

"Most of them. There are still a few people down there. The last ones."

"And? Did they finish everything?"

"What?"

"The hors d'oeuvres. The sushi."

"I don't know, Daddy, I really don't know."

She looks around the room. Hofmeester does the same. He sees that the wife's things are covering her half of the bed again, as though she's never left. His shirt hanging over the back of a chair. Ties. The wife's shoes. Sandals.

"Daddy," Tirza says.

"Yes." He speaks without looking at her.

"What are we going to do?"

"About what?"

"About you."

"About me?" Now he does look at her. "Tirza, what kind of question is that?"

"What are we going to do about you?" she repeats.

He shakes his head. "That's not something you have to worry about. What to do about me. Your own future is what you should be thinking about." And he remembers how, when she was ill, he had said to her: "You have your whole life in front of you, your entire future." As though that future were the decisive argument against starving yourself to death.

Hofmeester is sweating. He notices the wet spot under his arms. The moisture of a night that has lasted too long.

"What got into you?" His daughter doesn't sound accusatory, more like inquisitive. Curious, almost.

"When? What do you mean, what got into me?"

"With Ester. Just now. What . . . what were you thinking?"

He runs his hand over his cheeks, his mouth, his forehead. He wishes he could say something, but nothing occurs to him. The beast in him had spoken, and the beast speaks without words. The language of the beast is wordless. It bites and licks, it spits and rends. But speak, the way people speak, no, not that.

"Thinking about it is bad enough, but then actually doing it. At my party."

He looks at the balcony. The doors are still standing open.

"It was a nice party," he says slowly. "A good time was had by all, I took care of all the guests. No one lacked a thing. There was enough sushi. And the sashimi isn't finished yet either."

"Daddy, answer me."

"What was the question?"

"What got into you? What were you thinking? What came over you? Did something come over you?"

He shrugs, a typical gesture for him, and while he shrugs again, as though that should be answer enough, she sits down on the bed. Beside him, but not too close, they aren't touching.

"I don't want," she says, "to be unable to think of you as Daddy. Mama doesn't exist anymore, at least not for me. But I don't want to be an orphan. I want you to keep being Daddy. I'm too young to be an orphan."

He wishes he could scream, like a wounded soldier whose only hope is for someone to put him out of his misery, but whose comrades can't find him. Hofmeester is unfindable. And, to be frank: no one is looking for him.

"I'm still who I was," he says hoarsely. "Everything's the way it was. Nothing has changed."

"But I already think of you as dirty, you know. To me, you've become dirty." Despite these words, she lays her hand on the back of his neck and for a moment he thinks that he is dying, for a moment he thinks he knows what that is: dying.

"Come on," he says, "let's go downstairs. We'll go downstairs together. It's all right. Ester and I were playing. And it got out of hand. That can happen. Especially at a party."

He tries to get up, but he has to muster strength, courage. And while he is doing that, he tries to come to grips with the word "dirty." It seems to him that he has always been dirty, in his own eyes and in those of others, and that his attempts at getting closer to others were nothing but attempts to be less dirty. In that one, casually spoken word, it seems, lies the core of his existence. The unbroken thread.

"So what were you playing?"

"A game," he whispers. "A game, Tirza. Sometimes you need to play that you're someone else. That's only normal. One must deal flexibly with one's identity. Only the insane remain the same person all the time. I am your father, and you are my daughter, my dearest and my youngest daughter, my most beloved daughter. But sometimes we play that we're someone else: that you, for example, are the sun queen and that I am the high priest. We have to play, in order not to go completely crazy. In order not to lose our senses. We have no choice. The more intelligent you are, the better you are at playing. You're very intelligent, that's why you're able to play so well."

Whenever he thinks of the word "dirty," he thinks of the fear of contagion, he thinks of himself: as a man with an abnormal fear of contagion, a man who sees his own body as a filthy public toilet. And as that body goes further and further into decline, the fear, which is really nothing but disapproval, grows.

"I don't understand you," she says. "But that doesn't matter. I think. It doesn't matter that I don't understand you. If only you didn't deny everything. You could also say: 'I'm sorry.' "

"Oh, yes," he says, "you do understand me. You understand me very well."

She still has her hand on the back of his neck and now, more so than just a minute ago, he feels the need for a glass of Italian Gewürztraminer, the pouring of it alone would bring relief, the opening of the bottle, the bouquet.

"I need you as my Daddy," she says, "can't you understand that? I need you as my Daddy."

"I need you too," he whispers. "Tirza, I need you too." And he puts his fist in his mouth and bites. He bites like the beast he thought he had defeated, the wordless beast that lives inside him.

He can still hear music coming from downstairs.

"Were you drunk?" she asks.

"Yes," he says, relieved. "It was the alcohol, it had to be. The alcohol."

Now he feels able to stand up. Now he has the strength. A simple yet effective answer.

But she still has her hand on his neck.

"So I don't have to worry about you when I'm in Africa?"

"Of course not," he says, "why would you worry? About whom? About me? Why would you?"

"Everything will be okay, even if I'm not here? Even if Mama goes away again? That won't matter? You'll stay here and take care of yourself?"

"Of course," he says, "I will go on living. I'll take care of myself, even when you're in Africa. The same way I have always cared for you. I don't need anyone's help. I live from one day to the next, you know that."

"But Daddy," she says, "that's exactly what you can't do. Live. You're completely incapable of that."

The way her hand feels on the back of his neck tells him she is crying.

His fist is still clenched in his mouth. That calms him. His teeth in his own flesh admonish his thoughts to remain calm.

"Why did you make the two of us, anyway?"

He has bitten hard enough. He can see the tooth marks on the back of his hand. "It was your mother's idea," he says, "but as soon as I saw the two of you I was sold. I was sold—completely sold."

"Oh."

He stands up, straightens his shirt, tucks it more neatly into his trousers. For a moment he has the feeling that everything is back under control. That he has once again become the father he tried to be during the last few years, the man who sees fatherhood as a vocation into which all his ambitions come flowing down. Who is distant, but charming. In the wordplay lies the tenderness, in the silly remarks and jokes with which he welcomes his daughter and her friends lies the love, which needs to remain lawful.

"And what will happen," he asks, "when you're in Africa with that Mohammed Atta and come across a seven-foot Negro who you think is very nice? What then?"

"Then I'll send you a postcard," she says. "Then I'll write: 'Hi Daddy, I just met a seven-foot Negro who I think is very nice.'"

Through the floor he hears the strains of "*Bei mir bist du schön.*"

They've started in with the music again. Everything starts all over again

He walks to the door. "Come on," he says, "come along." The tray of sashimi is still on the floor, but he leaves it there.

Gingerly as a gray-haired old man, he descends the stairs.

There are still five or six people in the living room. Mrs. Van Delven is standing in a corner, talking to one of her students. There are glasses everywhere, napkins with the remains of raw fish, a great deal of rice on the floor, even more glasses, beer bottles, remnants of the garnishing with which he had decorated the trays. Against the wall, close to the dinner table, the wife is pressed up against a boy whose face remains hidden to Hofmeester. They are in the midst of a kiss. He doesn't see Mohammed Atta anywhere.

Everything in the room smells of party. Old party.

He turns to Tirza. "Where's Mohammed Atta?" he asks.

"Choukri," she says emphatically. "Choukri has gone home. I told him to go ahead. I didn't want him to have to watch this anymore."

She points at her mother. And in that one, casual gesture lies the explanation for a great deal. The mother who cannot contain herself. The mother has never tried to contain herself.

On a little table beside the couch is half a glass of wine. Hofmeester picks it up and drinks it down.

"I'll take you," he says. "I'll take you there. You two are flying out of Frankfurt, aren't you? I'll take you to the airport." It is an impulse, but one that gives him renewed energy. Suddenly he has hope again.

"You don't have to. We can take the train."

"No, no," Hofmeester says, "please, allow me. And then we'll spend a night in the Betuwe, at Grandma and Grandpa's old house. That way we can spend a weekend together. Before the two of you take off. I don't mean anything bad with that Mohammed Atta. He does look like him, but there isn't much he can do about that. Don't take it so hard, it's nothing to feel so bad about."

"We'll see," Tirza says. "We'll see."

Father and daughter stand staring at Hofmeester's wife. She is in another world. The world of the lust that goes along with mild intoxication.

"Do you know that boy?" Hofmeester asks.

His daughter nods.

"Daddy," she says then, "the party's over, don't you think? Enough is enough. We need to send the people home."

"Yes, send them home. You're right."

The graduation party for Hofmeester's youngest daughter has reached its conclusion. Somehow that comes as a relief.

He turns all the lights back on, turns down the music and starts gathering up a few glasses. His clothes are sticking to his body, his hands stick to the glasses.

"Hey, Jörgen," the wife shouts, "do we really need the bright lights?"

A stack of three empty beer glasses in his hand, he walks over to her. She's not really undressed, not like when she was up on the table pretending to be Dolly Parton, but you can still see that she was recently half-undressed.

"The party's over," he says pointedly. "It's finished. Over." He looks at the boy, it's the boy who has eaten dinner with them a few times. The boy with the short name. He's already forgotten it. One syllable.

One of the boys of whom Tirza had said: "He's staying for dinner tonight." But maybe he had misunderstood. What, after all, is "staying for dinner?" In Tirza's world, "staying for dinner" might mean more than just a hot meal. What, for God's sake, does "staying for dinner" really mean?

"Young man," he says, "please say goodbye to my wife. It was a lovely party. But now it's over."

"So formal, Jörgen, please. You're so old-fashioned. If he wants to stay a little longer, then he can stay a little longer. This is my house too."

He shakes his head slowly. "No, not anymore. Your house is a houseboat. And if you're no longer welcome on that houseboat, there's nothing I can do about that, but this house is no longer your house. Here, you are a guest."

As he says this, he recalls the long evenings he spent waiting for the wife, he remembers that he even thought she was sweet, sweet he thought she was, back in the beginning, and those memories tear him apart. They make him soft, fluid. More fluid than all the Italian

Gewürztraminer in the world. He stares at her and for a moment he feels the urge, just for a moment, to touch her. Wreck that she is. The problem is that he recognizes it. Hofmeester's wife is the most recognizable wreck he has ever seen. And in that recognizable wreck he sees his own life.

The boy says nothing. He is too drunk to even look contemptuous or fearful. The hangover that usually starts the morning after seems to already have him in its grip. He walks off in a daze, without saying goodbye. He doesn't even look back at the wife. As though he has already forgotten what he was doing only two minutes earlier.

Hofmeester hears the front door open. Tirza must be letting out the last few guests.

"Couldn't you leave well enough alone?" he asks. "Do you have to draw other people into this game we play?"

The wife wipes her mouth with the back of her hand. Her mascara is running a bit, but not enough to make much difference. Even under these bright lights it doesn't look all that bad.

If you didn't know her it would hardly be a problem, if you didn't share a past with her, there were other things you would see.

"What game?" she asks. "What game, Jörgen? What are you talking about? If a game is all there is and everything's a game, then it's not playing anymore. We stopped playing our game years ago. You're behind the times again."

He feels a draft. In another part of the house, a door slams.

"Let's . . ." he says, "let's do like we used to do. The living room is Vondelpark, it's nighttime, dark everywhere, and I'm the beast. The beast that comes to tear you limb from limb, the beast that pounces on you, let me be the beast."

"No," she shouts. "Don't you get it? Don't you understand anything?" She grabs him by the front of his sports jacket and shakes him, in as far as she still has the strength to do that. He almost drops the beer glasses.

"We're not playing at being ruined, Jörgen, it's what we are. How often do I have to tell you that before it sinks in? I only came back because I don't have anywhere else to go. No one wanted me. Do you understand? Has it sunk in now?"

She lets go of him and he mumbles: "I'm sorry, I don't understand." As though he's just received a strange message on the phone.

Then he walks to the kitchen. There are two young people still sitting forlorn on the couch, they seem to be asleep; the front door is open, and he hears Tirza's voice coming from the street.

He quickly pours himself a glass of wine. Then he goes into the garden. The torches have gone out. He'll put them away tomorrow. The only light is the one from the shed.

He goes to turn it off, but then he sees Ester sitting there, still on the bucket, although her jeans are no longer around her ankles.

Hofmeester stares at her, no longer as a lover, but as a host. As the graduate's father. A friendly father.

"The party is over," he says. "Everyone has gone home. It would probably be better for you to go too."

She looks him over with a smile. Haughty, that's how she looks. As though she stands above him, far above this old man who still can't come to terms with his own body, who hasn't come to terms with anything, you might say.

He doesn't know how to explain his deeds to her, but he wishes he could. Even at this hour of the night he remains in search of explanations, explanations that culminate in apologies and compliments. A man who explains himself is a man who compliments himself on his own shortcomings.

"So could you call me a taxi?"

"Where do you have to go?"

"Amstelveen."

"Amstelveen." He repeats the word, as though she had said "Mars."

Then he goes back to the kitchen and calls her a taxi.

The front door is still open. Tirza is out on the sidewalk, talking to someone. Just like the old days. Whenever she showed her friends out after dinner she always stood on the stoop for hours, even when it was cold or drizzling.

"Jörgen," he hears. "Jörgen."

The sharp and at the same time throaty sound of the wife's voice.

She's carrying glasses, plates and empty bottles to the kitchen. When she was young, truly young, she had worked in restaurants.

She flips open the trash can. He sees the remains of sashimi, whole sardines, and cigarette butts disappear into it.

"I'm going to take them," he says, "Tirza and her . . . her boyfriend."

"Where are you going to take them?"

"To Frankfurt Airport. That will be nice. We can spend the weekend in the Betuwe. I really need to go there again anyway."

She nods, but he doesn't have the impression that she's listening to him.

"We can do the rest tomorrow," he says. "Tomorrow the cleaning lady is coming too. We'll just ask her to stay a little longer. She's done that before, stayed a little longer. She doesn't mind."

He opens the last bottle of Italian Gewürztraminer.

"How long are you planning to stay?" he asks.

"You mean here? In the kitchen? Or in this house?"

"Here. In this house, yes. I'd like you to tell me that now."

She shrugs. "I don't know," she says. "Like I said already: I have nowhere else to go. Where am I supposed to go? As far as that's concerned, we're a lot alike. There's nowhere for us to go."

She takes his hand, his warm and slightly moist hand. He knows that they're not playing at being ruined. That's what they are, but exactly what he's supposed to imagine by that, he has no idea. Has he ever been anything but?

"That's the way it is," she says. But he doesn't know how it is, he still doesn't know how it is.

"If you like," she continues, "if there is no other woman in your life, I could undress slowly for you. Then you can look at me, if you like. In return for room and board."

And there is the wreck again, as recognizable as it had been a few minutes earlier. He wonders when she started that, started becoming a wreck. And whether that's why she has nowhere else to go.

And if she is a wreck, then what is he? Why hasn't he been able to grow old the way other people do? Dignified and rather gradually. With the kind of naturalness common to all animals. The naturalness of the decay, both of one's own body and those of others.

"Daddy."

Tirza's voice is so lovely, he thinks.

She's calling him, the way she used to when she was on the potty. Or in her room, when she wanted to ask about her homework.

"Coming," he shouts back, and he thinks: that must be the taxi. That's why she called him: the taxi is waiting.

He walks to the shed.

"Your taxi's arrived," he says to Ester, who is still sitting on the bucket.

She doesn't get up, she doesn't even look at him.

"Do you have money for the taxi?" he asks. "How much does it cost anyway, to Amstelveen?"

She says nothing.

He searches for his wallet. He pulls out a hundred euro note. He tries to give it to her, but she doesn't take it.

"That's too much," she says.

"I don't have anything else. Come by sometime and bring me the change. Come to dinner. Or just come by when you have the time. Come by sometime."

He hoists her up off the bucket. And for a moment she is standing close to him, in his arms. For a moment he smells her, an intoxicating smell. A smell that, more than anything else, is young, healthy, and feminine. Everything he isn't and never will be again, that's why he loves it so much.

"Doesn't that hurt your rear end?" he ask. "Sitting on a bucket like that all night?"

"My rear doesn't hurt. No more than usual."

As though she were injured, as though she can no longer walk on her own, he helps her through the kitchen to the street. During the last stretch he holds on only to her upper arm. The way you might hold a child who tends to dawdle as it crosses the street. The father, concerned about oncoming traffic. His grip a little too firm, holding the child's arm a bit too high up for comfort.

Tirza is standing on the curb, talking to a boy. She ignores her father.

The taxi hasn't arrived yet. He has no idea why Tirza called him. But he doesn't dare to ask her. She's talking. He needs to leave her alone.

Mrs. Van Delven comes out of the house. She unlocks her bike. She gives Tirza a little wave, but pretends not to see Hofmeester and Ester. It feels like a slap in the face. The invisibility, the forced invisibility.

"Goodbye, Mrs. Van Delven," he shouts.

There is no reply. She hangs her lock on the handlebars.

"Goodbye, Mrs. Van Delven," Hofmeester shouts again. "Thanks for coming!"

Again, no reaction. She bikes away as though she's been visiting the neighbors and not the Hofmeesters.

This is no calm and light sorrow, this is sharp pain. The pain of dismissal, rejection, of failure.

"A very amiable woman," he says to the girl once Mrs. Van Delven has turned the corner. "And very well-preserved."

They stand there like that at the curb, waiting, Ester and Hofmeester. His street, Van Eeghenstraat, the best street in all of Amsterdam, and therefore the best in all of Holland. He has lived here. He lives here. But it hasn't helped.

By the time the taxi finally arrives, Tirza is inside.

He hustles Ester into the cab.

"Where do you live?" he asks.

Again, no reply.

A haughty look. But not—how must he put it?—not unfeeling. In the girl's look he recognizes something of his own desire, and as soon as he recognizes the desire he can't help thinking about her genitals, about his hand groping around those genitals and how wet she was. Wet for him, and because of him.

And it seems as though all the dignity and humanity he still possesses is located in that girl's moist genitals, as though it were there, in that moisture, in that love juice, that he had regained his dignity, as though with that he has left Mrs. Van Delven and all the others far behind, even if only for a moment.

"Where do you live?" he repeats. He squeezes her arm.

"Somewhere in Amstelveen," says Ester with the "h."

"She's going to Amstelveen," he tells the driver. The man looks at him suspiciously. Disdainfully, Hofmeester thinks.

"Amstelveen," Tirza's father repeats then, smiling like a man for whom no one need be afraid.

Then the taxi takes off.

Hofmeester waves after the vanishing cab without knowing why, and without supposing for a moment that Ester will look back at him. He waves to her the same way he has waved goodbye to imaginary passengers at Schiphol, in order to remain inconspicuous.

When he tries to go back in, he sees that the front door is closed and realizes that he has no keys in his pocket. He has to ring the bell. Briefly at first, but then, when no one answers after thirty seconds, louder and more persistently. Impatiently. Even though he doesn't want to be that.

He shivers.

Tirza opens the door.

"Ibi's already asleep," she says. Admonishingly, but not coldly.

"Is everyone gone?"

"Everyone is gone."

She doesn't step aside. She leans her head against the tile wall of the vestibule.

"Did you think it was a nice party, Tirza? Was it, despite everything, a nice party?"

She doesn't answer.

All she says is: "Despite everything," but she says it as though she's asking: "What do you mean, despite everything?" That's the way it sounds.

"Daddy."

He wants to go inside, he's cold.

"Daddy," she says again, "if I don't live here anymore, how's that supposed to go? I need to know."

"Let me in," he says.

"How's that supposed to go?"

Hofmeester thinks about the weeks he spent at a boarding house in Southern Germany, while she was busy getting better at a clinic. He thinks about her cello. About the music stand. About the recitals at the music school. He always sat in the front row. And he always stared at his daughter as though he had to hypnotize her, as though he thought she might play the wrong note if he stopped looking.

"Play something for me," he says.

"What?"

"On your cello. Play something for me."

"Right now?"

"Right now."

She laughs. "You're insane." As though he had told a joke, like at the table, when a couple of her girlfriends were over for dinner. A not particularly funny joke.

Whenever her friends came over to eat or to play, he would tell jokes. A father, in Hofmeester's view, is given to pretentious display.

"It's important."

She has to play for him, the way she used to, on her cello. That's all he can think about now, that is all that can save him. His youngest daughter and her cello.

"I haven't played for years."

"It doesn't matter. You haven't forgotten. You don't forget something like that."

"Everyone's asleep. Mama has already gone upstairs."

"They'll sleep through it. They're used to it, like they were in the old days."

"Daddy," she says, still leaning her head against the tiles, "you're insane. Ibi told me that years ago, and she was right. You really are insane."

Amid all the other thoughts, he wonders what it would be like to have a father who is insane, but because he doesn't know the answer he says: "I am perfectly sane, Tirza, as sane as you are. All I'm asking is for you to play something for me. A sentimental request, perhaps, a strange request in the middle of the night. But not insane."

She looks at him. Her lips curl. He has no idea whether this is a smile. "Daddy," she whispers. She looks at him sweetly, understandingly. "I'm perfectly willing to play something for you again, but not now."

"No, now, Tirza. Right now. Tonight."

She says nothing.

He can't figure out why this should be so important to him, a matter of life and death, now that all other matters of life and death have vanished, disappeared. What else could possibly be important in his life?

He pulls out his wallet. "I'll pay you for it," he says. "I'll give you some extra pocket money, for Namibia."

He counts out all the bills in his wallet. "Here," he says. "A little more than five hundred euros. That could come in handy in Africa."

"Daddy."

She caresses his cheek with the back of her hand.

"Daddy, why do you want me to play so badly?"

He stands there with the banknotes in his hand. It's all he has. Maybe it's all he's ever had. Banknotes, meant to hide the fact that he had nothing else to offer. He pays. Payment is freedom. "Because it makes me happy," he says. "Because it makes me so happy." He tries to press the money into her hand, but she waves it away.

He is more than willing to pay for happiness. Hidden away inside happiness is an unbearable guilt. A faux pas. Something he has to buy off.

Now that he's no longer cold, he feels flushed. He can feel the sweat running down his back again. It's as though he has a fever, as though he's caught a cold.

Tirza looks at him, but no longer as the daughter looking at the father, not even as the caring daughter who looks at the man who has cared for her, she looks at him quite differently. In her eyes he sees the stranger. The tenant who looks at the landlord as he thinks about the offer he has just been made.

She turns around, she walks away from him, he hears her running up the stairs. Like a fawn, Hofmeester thinks.

In the kitchen he pours himself a glass of Gewürztraminer. There isn't much left. The wine isn't very cold either. It doesn't matter. He's still shivering. From fatigue, from the emotion, the shame.

Then he hears Tirza coming down the stairs. He goes to look. She has the cello with her. She's dragging it along. As though it were an animal, a stubborn cow being led to the slaughter. She walks past her father without looking at him. She puts the cello in the living room.

He stands in the doorway, the empty glass in his hand, watching how she does this.

Once again she goes upstairs. She comes back with the music stand and sheet music. She sets up everything in front of the window. She picks up the cello, the bow.

"Are you sure you want me to do this?" she asks.

He nods.

"Is this what makes you happy?"

He nods again.

"Sit down then," she says. The bow held at the ready.

And he whispers: "Elgar, you were always so good at that, you played that at the music school too. Elgar. It was Elgar, wasn't it?"

He can't remember anymore. He sits on the floor. Amid the party's remains, amid the sticky grains of rice and bits of pickle that have flown out of someone's mouth.

Standing is too much for him. There's not a whole lot that isn't too much for him. He lays the money on the coffee table.

She tunes the cello.

"Daddy," she says. "You're insane. Is that hereditary?"

"Hereditary?"

"Am I that way too? Should I worry about becoming like you? Should I be afraid of going crazy?"

Then she starts to play.

Her shoulders and upper arms are bare, he can see one of her bra straps.

He looks at her and remembers everything. A shivering body that hears the music, that sees his daughter and remembers everything. And while Hofmeester listens to the music and watches his youngest daughter play for him, for him and him alone, for the first time he begins to wonder why life is so painful.

Why, in fact, it always hurt so badly.

Not everyone's, not life in general. There are people who aren't bothered by it. A lot of people aren't bothered by it. *His* life. He has thought about everything before, some things perhaps not as thoroughly as others, but never about pain. That was for sissies, that's what he'd always figured. And now that he thinks about it for the first time, he still notes a slight distaste. Disgust.

He had everything, now he has nothing. Even when he had everything, it still hurt.

Of living he remembers an uneasy silence, a stiffness of the muscles, a tic, a narrowly repressed lust. The everlasting need to act civilized under all circumstances.

Then Tirza stops playing.

She lays the cello down carefully. The way you put a baby to bed who has fallen asleep on your arm. In the hope that he will stay asleep.

She gets up, she steps over her father, who is sitting on the floor, like a child not yet able to sit in a chair or on a couch.

"Take it," he says.

"What?"

She stops. She looks down. There she sees her father, her old father, who perhaps shouldn't have started in on having children at all, if fate hadn't forced him into it, as he himself liked to say: fate in the form of a woman.

He did it for others. His children, the house, renting out of the top floor, his job, keeping his parents' house even after they were dead. And never writing that reference work about Expressionist poets, that was something he did for others as well. A life lived for others. In the assumption that only then did you truly live, when you did it for others, that a self-sufficient individual amounted to nothing. To be content with just yourself, with just your work, content enough with Schiphol, that is the true sin unto death.

"The money. Take it."

She looks at the banknotes on the coffee table.

"Take it," he repeats. "Tirza, you played for it. Please, take it. I promised."

He sees her hesitate.

He himself doesn't dare to touch it. It's already hers. It's on the coffee table. All she has to do is pick it up. That's all. Just pick it up.

"Take it, Tirza," he says. "Just take it. For you and Mohammed Atta, when you two are in Africa."

"Choukri."

"Okay, Choukri. For you and Choukri, for if the two of you want to go out to a nice restaurant."

She shakes her head.

"We're not going to Africa to go to a nice restaurant, Daddy."

"You can have a nice meal anywhere these days, even in Africa." He recalls how he stood in the kitchen about twelve hours ago, cutting the raw fish.

"Please," he whispers, "please, my sun queen."

She bends down.

She takes the money. Then she walks away.

He wants to shout after her, he wants to say something, but all that occurs to him is "Good night."

He hears her footsteps.

"Good night, Tirza," he calls out. "Good night. It was a lovely party."

He rubs his face. He's still shivering. Like a sick man.

"You played so beautifully," he whispers.

From the hallway she calls out quietly: "Sleep well, Daddy."

He hears her climb the stairs.

Hofmeester stays sitting on the floor where he was. Then he crawls over to the cello. He tries to pull himself up on the music stand.

It doesn't work.

The music stand is lying on top of him now, or rather: he is lying under the music stand. With not enough strength to stand up, or even to move.

He remains lying there like that, for who knows how long. After a while he realizes that he is looking at his daughter's feet. Tirza's feet. After a few minutes, maybe longer.

She reaches out to him, she pulls him to his feet. With difficulty. With distaste, it seems.

He holds onto her. Or she holds onto him.

Because he's almost unable to stand.

Finally he is back on two feet again, like a human. Like a host, supported by his youngest daughter.

"You're so dirty, Daddy," she says. "So incredibly dirty."

She kisses him on the nose, the cheek, the forehead.

They're almost the same height, father and daughter.

He whispers something, but she doesn't seem to understand. Five, six times, until he sees that she gets it.

"Sun queen," he says. "Sun queen. Sun queen."

She doesn't let go of him, she seems afraid that he will fall down again, that he won't get up again after that, not even with her help.

And now Hofmeester whispers something else. He has a question, a question at last for the sun queen. Not a word of advice, not a silly joke, not a practical request for her to let him know what time she'll be coming home; no, a real question.

"Sun queen, why does everything hurt so much? Why does everything hurt so badly?" he whispers in her ear.

She doesn't say anything. She shakes her head gently. The only reply she gives is to hold on to Hofmeester, in the living room, beside the cello and the fallen music stand, as it slowly grows light.

She can't do it either. Let go.

It runs in the family.

III

The Desert

1

In the third week of July, on a Sunday evening, Tirza and her boyfriend are going to fly from Frankfurt to Windhoek. Air Namibia was the cheapest ticket she could find. She had originally planned to take the train to Frankfurt, but Hofmeester convinced her that it would be faster and more fun if they went by car. And if they spend a weekend together at the house in the Betuwe, then everything will be fine. A weekend in the Betuwe, that's what you might call a respectable start to a trip around the world. And a fine farewell. All of them together, one last time. Well, not quite all of them, the wife won't be going along of course. She wasn't invited, and Ibi went back to France a long time ago, to the B&B with her swarthy husband.

After a bit of protest, Tirza agreed. Hofmeester had to promise, though, that he wouldn't call Choukri "Mohammed Atta." And not

"Atta," either. She took him at his word. When you're off on a trip around the world, you're willing to humor your father a bit.

On Friday morning they are going to leave Amsterdam.

Hofmeester gets up early. Since he's going to be there all weekend anyway, he wants to do some work in the garden of what has served as the Hofmeesters' country house for more than a decade.

It's been months since the last time he was there. In the spring he hadn't had time to prune some of the fruit trees. He will this time. The lawn will need mowing, and he'll sow a little grass seed here and there.

In the shed, Hofmeester gathers the tools he wants to take along, either because he doesn't have them at the country house or because the ones that are there are in need of repair. Or because they've actually become too decrepit to use. Jörgen Hofmeester's parents were collectors out of miserliness. Throwing things away was a fundamental sin.

He drags the hoe, the chainsaw, a bag of seed, and a shovel out of the shed where he spent an evening with Ester, three weeks ago now, and carries them to the kitchen. An evening is a bit of an exaggeration perhaps, probably more like half an hour. When he thinks about Ester it isn't with nostalgia or regret, more like a slight discomfort and at the same time a vague desire to smell her again, that sharp odor of happiness.

Ester had never come by to bring him the change. Hofmeester didn't care much about the money itself, but he would have liked to talk to her before Tirza left. He wanted to see her so that he could explain himself again, but better this time, more accurately, more convincingly. Explain why he had once wanted to do away with love and why doing away with it was no longer such a high-level priority for him. But that he wished her all the luck in the world with the things she hoped to do away with. She would make it. She knew a thing or two.

He probably wanted to see her one more time in order to convince himself of something, although he didn't know exactly what.

Until at some point he realized that she wouldn't be coming by at all, not for the change, not for dinner. At first he resigned himself to it, to the inevitable. They would have to make do without explanations. Without a conclusive conversation. The role he would continue to play in her life would be that of a father who had been unable to control himself. A man who, for a moment, had no longer known what control was and who, remarkably enough, had felt happy at that very same moment. Or, at least, had felt alive. For the first time in a long time: truly alive.

He didn't dare to ask Tirza: "So how are things with that Ester, the one without the 'h'?"

The incident in the shed was never brought up, the whole party was never brought up. Two days later it was as though it had never happened.

Only a few days after deciding to resign himself to the inevitable, however, he went into Tirza's room—she was off visiting Atta—and searched through her things for Ester's phone number. In a drawer he found a list of students from the Vossius Gymnasium, class 6A. Ester's name was on it, along with her address and phone number.

That same evening, while the wife was taking a bath, he called her from the kitchen. First he got a man on the line, probably the father. "This is Hofmeester," he said, "I'm trying to reach Ester."

No questions were asked, no comments made. All he heard was: "Just a moment." A few seconds later he had Ester on the line. I really am insane, he thought.

"Ester," he said, "this is Jörgen Hofmeester, Tirza's father. Maybe you still remember me?"

"Yeah."

"I'm sorry to bother you, but I've been waiting for you to bring back my change."

"Change?"

"From the taxi. I gave you a hundred euros. You were going to Amstelveen. That doesn't cost a hundred euros, not even for a taxi."

He rubbed his index finger over the counter.

"Oh yeah, it was something like forty. So you get sixty euros back from me. Do you want me to do a bank transfer?"

For a moment he thought he heard Tirza coming home, but it was the wind. She was probably sleeping over at Atta's. She did that all the time now.

"You can also give it to me in cash. In fact, I'd prefer that. Shall we meet up for coffee tomorrow? Maybe somewhere around here? There's a nice café across from the Stedelijk."

Silence.

"Hello? Ester?"

"Yeah, okay," she said. "Tomorrow afternoon?"

"Four o'clock?"

The next day at five to four he was sitting in the café across from the old Stedelijk Museum, he had come back especially from Schiphol to be there. Lying on the chair beside him was his briefcase, he was reading yesterday's newspaper. Even old newspapers didn't bore him.

At ten past four she showed up, wearing jeans this time too, and a slightly faded shirt.

The chair beside him was empty. But she sat down across from him.

He could have picked a different café, he realized now, further from home, but oh well, this was innocent enough. It would remain innocent. A conclusive and enlightening conversation, what could be more innocent than that?

They sat across from each other, his daughter's friend who wasn't really his daughter's friend, and Hofmeester.

"This used to belong to my grandfather." She rubbed the tail of her shirt between her fingers.

"Oh. Do you wear your grandfather's clothes often?"

"Sometimes I wear my father's clothes too."

She looked at him boldly, but not provocatively. Haughty, but in a natural kind of way, almost as though she regretted that the world did not meet with her approval.

"How's it going?"

"With what?"

"With you," Hofmeester said. "With you, of course, Ester."

"Good."

"What would you like to drink?"

"Oh, red wine for me."

He ordered red wine for Ester, and although he had told himself he would stick to coffee, he ordered a glass of wine for himself anyway. It was late enough in the afternoon. He folded the newspaper neatly. The war against terrorism was rolling on.

To his own amazement, after they had both sipped at their wine, he felt peaceful. Calm. And just a wee bit alive again too.

The occurrence in the shed wasn't mentioned, which was perhaps all for the better. There isn't a whole lot one can say about occurrences, once they've occurred.

"How are your plans coming along?" he asked. "To do away with love, I mean, how is that coming along?"

"This is my summer vacation. I'm not doing anything right now. My pocket calendar is one big blank." She took a sturdy slug of her wine, licked her lips, and asked: "And how's Tirza doing?"

He nodded. "Very well. Excellently. She's at her boyfriend's now. They're going on a trip together soon. To Africa."

The conversation was not going quite the way he had hoped, the way he had imagined.

"Perhaps you recall," he said, talking more quietly all the time now, as though he were about to tell her a secret, "that I too once planned to do away with love, to pronounce it dead and buried. It was a project, it was supposed to be a treatise, a hefty treatise, with footnotes. Scientific. Substantiated. Evidence-based."

"Really?"

"I still have some of the background material in my archives, if it's of any use to you, if you'd like to take a look at it."

She shook her head slowly, again a bit haughtily. "No, Mr. Hofmeester," she said, "I don't want to write a treatise. I just know how it works, and that's enough."

She looked at the people passing by. The trams. A taxi.

To his own annoyance, he said: "I enjoy your company." He corrected himself immediately. "I find your ideas refreshing, interesting."

She shook her head again. "I don't have any ideas. I just know how it works."

From the breast pocket of her grandfather's shirt she pulled out sixty euros and laid the money on the table. "Your change," she said.

"Yes. It was . . . it's not important."

"But that's what I came for." She looked at him a bit accusingly.

"I wanted to explain myself further. I am, of course, Tirza's father, I'm almost exclusively Tirza's father, that's the main thing, but there are also matters of secondary importance. Little, unimportant matters. I am also someone who enjoys your company."

He could have expressed it better, but he could also have done much worse. This was the version with which she would have to make do.

"I have to get going," she said. "I like being alone a lot. When I get up in the morning the first thing I do is sit on the floor for half an hour and pet myself." Just as she had in the shed that evening, she caressed her own arms, with concentration and care. "I hope I'm not disappointing you."

"Not at all. What I said, well, I wanted to say that. That's all."

She got up.

"I brought something for you. A little something." He opened his briefcase and took out a little, black paperback. "Unfortunately, I could only get it in German. It's called *Was ist Kunst?* It's a treatise by Tolstoy, all you have to do is replace the word "art" with "love," it's actually his farewell to it."

"I can't read German."

"Maybe you'll be able to later."

She took the book, kissed him once on the cheek, and walked out of the café. He watched her go, in the direction of the Concertgebouw. Her grandfather's shirt was really too big for her, he saw only then.

He paid the tab, went by Pasteuning's delicatessen for three bottles of Chilean wine, and walked home.

"Did they give you the afternoon off?" the wife asks, lying on the bed, as Hofmeester noses around in the closet for a sports jacket to wear on the trip.

"I took the afternoon off," he says. "They don't have to give me anything." For a few seconds he can't help thinking about the managing editor, who had said that soon men without much education would find their way to the book as well, albeit not necessarily by way of the bookshop. It amazes him to realize that he has never once missed his office, with its view of a tree and a garden that could also be called a courtyard, never missed his colleagues, the routine, the Monday-morning production meetings.

For mid-July, it's cold and rainy out.

He puts on a blue sports jacket that is slightly worn, but which he likes to wear.

Hofmeester goes to the kitchen and looks contentedly at the tools with which he will attack his parents' garden. From the fridge he removes the ingredients he's bought, for the purpose of giving Tirza one final good meal before she leaves for the Third World.

Hofmeester loads everything into the back of his Volvo. It's a car that fits his address, he thinks. The way he himself fits that address, or perhaps he should say: fit that address.

Then he knocks on the door of Tirza's room. She's busy packing her backpack, the one she bought specially for this trip.

Hofmeester had suggested that she buy a sturdy suitcase, a good brand, but she laughed at him.

"I'm going to Africa, Daddy," she'd said, "not the Cote d'Azur."

Hofmeester detests youth hostels and backpackers. The backpacker's characteristic lack of privacy gives him the shivers. It's not snobbism. It is a deep, almost animal fear of the dormitory and the bunk bed.

From his student days, and then particularly those few months when he lived in a fraternity house, he remembers how the other students would come by to "fluff up" his bed after a night on the town. They flipped you over, mattress and all. Then they walked all over you for a while, as though it were some special form of Thai massage. The other fraternity members didn't seem to mind too much, but he did. He tried to defend himself, tooth and nail, which only made things worse.

"Are you almost ready?" he asks. Without waiting for a reply, he pushes open the door.

Tirza's room is one huge mess. Clothes everywhere, articles of toiletry, a passport with her inoculation card, her iPod, her notebook, underwear, a bathing cap, a pair of goggles.

"I can't decide," she says, "and there isn't enough room for all of it. Somewhere in Africa it's bound to be really cold, don't you think, Daddy?"

"I'm sure," he says, "somewhere in Africa it must be very cold. Antarctica isn't that far away."

"But a warm sweater takes up so much room."

"I told you not to buy a backpack."

"Oh stop it," she says. "You don't know how people travel. When was the last time you took a trip? I don't mean a few days at the Frankfurter Buchmesse, I mean to really travel?"

She pulls something out of her pack and stuffs a sweater in its place.

"Or would a turtleneck be better?"she asks.

"A turtleneck itches."

He goes downstairs to the kitchen. The coffee he put on fifteen minutes ago is ready now. Hofmeester pours himself a cup and shouts up the stairs: "Tirza, would you like some coffee?"

There is no reply.

He has the feeling that Africa starts right here in his kitchen, that Tirza is already there, in the middle of Africa, and that puts him in Africa too, a bit.

At the greengrocer's, an older woman who had worked there for years said to him one day: "You're daughter's going off traveling, isn't she? My son left for Asia a year ago, but he sends me a long email every week. That way I know exactly where he is and what he's doing. That way I can enjoy the trip along with him."

Hofmeester said "Yes" and, after a pause: "Yes, yes of course." Then he paid for his vegetables with a friendly smile. Enjoy the trip along with him. The phrase seemed to follow him around for the rest of the day.

Even though she hadn't answered him, he pours a cup of coffee for Tirza too, just to be sure. She likes the coffee Hofmeester makes for her in the morning. They always had breakfast together in the kitchen before she biked to school. Or rather: he sat and watched her eat breakfast. That, for him, was the essence of fatherhood: to look on in encouragement. And if she had girlfriends over, to go out of your way a bit, to put your best foot forward. Looking on in encouragement, that was what it finally boiled down to, and he could have learned to live with that.

Hofmeester leans his elbows on the counter. It has started drizzling. Africa, he thinks. He hopes she'll give up on her foolish plan to travel from south to north by public transport, but he's not so sure.

Tirza comes downstairs with the backpack and a little shoulder bag.

He looks at her luggage and smiles. The wise old man. The role he enjoys so much. Too old and too wise to join in with anything. But he was already like that when he was fifteen.

"Just because you're taking a trip around the world," she says, "doesn't mean you have to be inelegant."

"I didn't say anything," Hofmeester says, "I was only looking." He wonders what it will be like to miss someone horribly. It's a question he's been asking himself for the last few days. He has never missed the wife; he has waited for her. The more she hurt him the more urgently he waited for her, but really miss her, no. He never missed his parents either. He's never missed anyone.

He hands his daughter her coffee. She drinks it quickly and heedlessly.

"Do you want some breakfast? Shall I make some toast?"

She shakes her head.

"I'm not taking any jewelry along, just these two rings. That's okay, isn't it? Don't you think? So if I lose them or they get stolen, it's no big deal." She holds out her left hand.

One of the rings is the one he gave her when she turned seventeen, the other one she'd bought for herself. Or maybe she got it from a boyfriend, but didn't want to tell him that. An older boyfriend, someone with money.

Hofmeester has trouble imagining that, though, in light of her latest choice. Tirza likes men with no money. Poverty attracts her. She devours books about poverty in Africa; the natural surroundings are of only secondary importance. Malaria she finds more important than a decent sunset. Other people's misery gives her something to live for.

Hofmeester stares at the rain. "You're right," he says, "it's no big deal. What are rings, anyway?"

He had offered to swing by and pick up Tirza's boyfriend, but she said: "No, he'll come here. That's easier."

In fifteen minutes, maybe even less, he will no longer be alone with his daughter. In fifteen minutes the rest of his life will start, the epilogue. The epilogue to an inconsequential life, because if he'd ever had any doubts in the last couple of decades about whether or not it was inconsequential, those doubts are gone now. A man who interferes with one of his daughter's classmates in the shed at that same daughter's graduation party is, first and foremost, inconsequential. Superfluous and redundant, and unable to shove the blame onto anyone else. Somewhere in his life he must have crossed the divide between promising and inconsequential, but he can't remember any divide. The divide must have risen up unnoticed.

She puts a hand on his shoulder. Together they look at the garden, in which he sees Africa, and he doesn't even find that strange. The only thing he finds strange is that he had never noticed before that Africa started in his own garden.

"We've got to leave in fifteen minutes," he says. "I hope he's punctual, this . . ."

He was going to say Mohammed Atta. He gulps it back.

"Yes, Daddy," she says, "very *pünktlich*, for a Moroccan extremely *pünktlich*."

She runs upstairs, as though she's forgotten something. Hofmeester pours himself another cup of coffee.

He has put underwear in a leather valise, along with some socks, two shirts, and a pair of trousers he wears to work in the garden.

He's nervous, as though he were leaving on a long trip himself.

For the umpteenth time that morning he counts the money in his wallet, runs through his daughter's flight schedule, and examines the list of chores he's planning to do in the garden that once belonged to his parents.

Just as he finishes doing that, the wife comes into the kitchen. She's wearing her bathrobe. A new one. She shops a lot. Still. She holds out her arm.

"Goose bumps," she says, "you see that? That's how cold I am. Can't we turn up the heating?"

He lays his hand on her arm, absently, then puts his wallet back in his pocket.

"When are you coming back?" she asks.

"Sunday evening. I'm coming straight back from Frankfurt. Their plane leaves at eight, so by seven I will be done waving them goodbye."

"By seven you will be done waving them goodbye," she says. "How long does it take to wave goodbye, anyway? Then we'll be on our own, Jörgen. Then we'll have to get by with just the two of us."

"What do you mean?"

"Just what I said: Then we'll be on our own. We'll be *à deux* again. Just like in the old days."

He goes into the hall. Tirza comes down the stairs, takes her luggage from the kitchen, and puts it outside, in front of the door.

"Your boyfriend isn't here yet," he says. "Why do you have to wait outside already? On the street, in the rain?"

"I'm not standing in the rain."

He picks up Tirza's backpack and carries it to the Volvo. "Jesus, this thing's heavy," he shouts. "What have you got in here? A corpse?"

He opens the hatchback, and after he's wormed the backpack in as well as he can, he remains standing there like that, bent over. As though he were arranging something, the saw that was in the way, a plastic bag of grass seed. But what he doesn't want is for his daughter to see him break down. That's what he's doing, like a machine: breaking down.

After he has recovered he goes back to the kitchen, picks up his leather valise—an old, worn valise that used to belong to his father—and takes it out to the car.

The wife has come outside too.

The three of them stand there in the portico. Like a unit, like—there's no other word for it—a family. The family standing there one last time in the portico.

"I'm cold," the wife says. "This isn't summer. You call this summer? This is more like winter."

And Tirza replies: "Go on back inside, I'll say goodbye to you now." She kisses her mother, once on each cheek.

Then she steps back, as though to get a better look at the woman she crawled out of eighteen years ago. The woman she has hated for years.

"Drop a line now and then," the mother says, "or call. Collect is okay too. I'm sure your father won't object."

She goes back into the house, and Hofmeester watches her go. She's not inelegant, not for her age. Through all the decay she still has something of the woman she was long, long ago: the woman who thought, not entirely without reason, that the world lay at her feet. When Hofmeester first met her, the world had put her on a pedestal. And now? They had run out of pedestals. That's how fickle the world is.

Now the two of them are standing in the portico, father and daughter. The father more nervous than the daughter, toying with his car keys, plucking at his sports jacket, rummaging through his pockets. Amid all this he takes his daughter's hand and squeezes it.

"Can't you call him?" he asks.

"He'll be here in a minute."

They remain standing there like that, for two minutes, three minutes, ten minutes. Not saying a word. The man who is in the process of breaking down, the daughter who is leaving on a long trip.

Until she cries: "There he is!" She's looking to the right, up towards Jacob Obrechtstraat, and Hofmeester looks with her.

He sees a man in a jogging suit, walking in the rain, a gym bag slung casually over one shoulder. Mohammed Atta, he thinks. There he is. He's back. He has returned. That she can't see that.

Tirza runs to meet him. Hofmeester stays in the portico and sees how she hugs him. He follows her movements, studies Atta's hands that clasp his daughter's back. He shivers.

Then the two of them walk up to Hofmeester, close together.

Atta shakes the father's hand.

"I hope I didn't keep you waiting too long?" he asks.

"Fifteen minutes," Hofmeester says. "That's all."

He opens the back of the car and stuffs Atta's gym bag in beside the shovel.

"You don't have much with you for someone who's taking such a long trip. Not even a backpack."

"Anything I need I can buy along the way, and clothes dry quickly in Africa," Atta explains, as though he knows the continent like the back of his hand.

"That's true." Hofmeester nods. "Everything dries quickly in Africa." He remembers washing clothes by hand in Italy, during holidays. He remembers the vacations they took when they were still a family, a family that was more or less intact. More or less.

Hofmeester climbs in behind the wheel, he turns on the windshield wipers. Tirza takes the front seat, beside him. Atta remains alone in the back.

Conversation falters. By the time they get to Utrecht, they've exchanged two sentences. Tirza is listening to her iPod. In the rearview mirror, Hofmeester sees Atta nod off now and again.

The last stretch goes more smoothly. They actually carry on a civilized discussion about the pros and cons of development aid.

After they arrive, Tirza installs herself in what was used as the guestroom even when Hofmeester's parents were alive. Atta walks around the garden and sniffs at a flower here and there. After fifteen minutes or so he comes in and sits in the living room. He and Tirza play a game of Scrabble in front of the fireplace.

Mohammed Atta plays Scrabble. Interesting. Who would have thought?

Hofmeester himself goes to work in the garden. He needs to shake off the tension of the drive, the tension of what he feels to be a superfluous and ignoble remainder: the last part of his life.

Occasionally he peeks in through the window and sees his daughter and her boyfriend playing a board game. It does not ease his mind.

Now that his children have left home, he needs to learn to die. But he doesn't know where or from whom he can take lessons.

At around one-thirty he goes inside and asks: "Are you two feeling hungry?"

"Not really hungry, not yet," Tirza says. "But we're pretty cold."

"I'll light the fire," Hofmeester says. "Actually, I was hoping we'd have dinner in the garden this evening. But it's going to be more of a winter meal."

He struggles a bit, but finally gets the fire lit. Crouching hurts his back. "Hurts" may be putting it too strongly, it makes him aware of his back. An awareness he never had before.

When the fire is finally lit, after a good bit of fanning and poking on his part, he remains looking at it for a few minutes, poker in hand. It's nice. He forgets where he is. He is a man who, in the process of breaking down, looks at a fire and that fire summons up memories, vague and unsentimental memories of his parents, his youth, his college days.

Only when he hears his daughter say "Daddy" does he succeed in withdrawing from his thoughts.

"Daddy," she says, "I'm going to make a toasted cheese sandwich, do you want one too?"

"I'll do it," he answers. "You just stay where you are."

He hangs the poker back in its rack, wipes off his hands on the old trousers he uses in the garden, and looks for a few seconds at the word his daughter is spelling out on the Scrabble board.

"Only cheese on mine, please," says Atta.

"Oh, would you like one too?"

"Please, but then only cheese."

"No problem whatsoever," says Hofmeester, looking at the game. She's good at it, Tirza is, at Scrabble. "In our family we always make toasted sandwiches with cheese and tomato, we're not fond of ham, we don't like sticky meat."

He fries the three cheese-and-tomato sandwiches in a pan. Hofmeester's parents never owned a toaster.

He eats his at the table in the living room, while Tirza and Atta go on with their game of Scrabble. Every three or four seconds he wipes his mouth with a paper napkin, afraid as he is that crumbs will remain sticking to his lips.

"Do you like Scrabble too?" Atta asks.

"No," Hofmeester replies. "And I'm not very good at it."

"But Daddy, you used to play Scrabble with me all the time."

His daughter looks at him, amazed. As though he's been caught lying.

"I don't really hate it, but I liked it more when we played Risk, for example, or Monopoly or gin rummy."

"Shall we play Monopoly then this evening, Mr. Hofmeester?" Atta suggest.

Hofmeester looks at him, at this man who's doing his very best, who even sniffs at flowers in the garden in order to please his girlfriend's father. But Hofmeester couldn't care less. He'd like to tell him: "Don't bother trying so hard. It won't help."

"Fine," he says, "if I can find it, we'll play Monopoly tonight, after dinner."

Then he goes back to the garden and focuses on his work, to keep from thinking.

Around five, while he's busy sawing the dead branches from an apple tree, Atta comes up to him.

Hofmeester turns off the saw. He climbs down from the ladder.

"I'd like to ask you something," Atta says.

"Be my guest."

"You don't mind, do you, if your daughter and I sleep in the same room?"

Now the father can't help laughing, for the first time he really has to laugh at this man.

"What were you two planning to do in Africa?" he asks. "Sleep in separate bunk beds? Make reservations at two different youth hostels? What do you take me for?"

"Not that. Of course not. But here, in your house, it's a little different. Maybe."

"This is just as much Tirza's house as it is mine. If she has no problem with sleeping in the same room with you, then it's fine with me too."

Atta looks at the apple tree.

"You're good at it," he says. "I mean: the way you trim the branches."

"My parents had a hardware store." Hofmeester still can't say it without feeling slightly embarrassed. A hardware store. But it explains a lot. He learned to use a saw at an early age.

"Right, Tirza said something like that. Anyway, I just needed to ask, my parents are also . . ."

"Oh? What are they also?"

Hofmeester stares at him, at Tirza's boyfriend. The man he thinks is not only too old for his daughter, but also just plain unpleasant. Unpleasant in his politeness, unpleasant in his being here, unpleasant at first sight.

"You would never think any man was good enough for Tirza," the wife had said. But that's not it. It's intuition.

"My parents are quite conservative too."

"I'm not conservative," Hofmeester says, "I'm realistic and practical. Are they religious?"

"My parents? Yes, that too."

"That too," Hofmeester repeats.

The young man lingers in the garden, Hofmeester climbs the ladder again and goes on sawing. Five minutes later, when he sees that Atta is still there, he climbs down again and asks: "Would you like to try it?"

"What?"

"Sawing branches. Pruning. Working in the garden."

Atta laughs. "I've never done it before."

"Don't your parents have a garden?"

"They have a balcony."

With the back of his hand, Hofmeester wipes his mouth, his chin, his cheeks. "Oh, but an apartment with a balcony can be very nice too. Do you want to try it out?"

Atta hesitates.

"You're going to Africa, aren't you? You're going to the jungle, right? So a little fruit tree in the Betuwe shouldn't be much of a problem. Start with that small branch over there."

Hofmeester points up, at a branch he could just as well leave on the tree. Not exactly what you'd call a dead branch.

Atta hesitates, then takes the chainsaw.

The weight comes as a surprise to him. That much is clear. But anyone who picks up a chainsaw for the first time has a little trouble getting used to the weight. With tools, as with people, you need to establish intimacy gradually. The better you get to know them, the sooner they do what you want.

Hofmeester shows him how to start the saw. How to turn it off. The safety catch. The proper way to hold it.

"It's a Stihl MS 170," Hofmeester says, "the best in its class."

The young man climbs the ladder. Once he's at the top, he shouts: "Do you think this is really a good idea, Mr. Hofmeester?"

"It's an excellent idea. Once you've mastered it, you'll benefit for the rest of your life. The MS 170 is very safe."

Tirza's father points again at the branch in need of sawing. "Don't be afraid," he shouts. "Just stay calm."

Safe, that's what they'd told him in the shop where he bought the chainsaw. Safer than the electric ones with a cord, easier to use too.

Tirza's boyfriend stands on the ladder and saws. Before long, the branch falls to the ground. It's a little one.

Atta climbs down. He looks pale.

"Were you afraid?" Hofmeester asks hopefully. "Did it scare you badly?"

"A little," says the man, who now looks more than ever like a boy. A friendly boy, all things considered. If you didn't know better. "I don't think I'm feeling too well. Kind of tired."

"It's a matter of getting used to it." Hofmeester takes back his saw. He looks at the tree contentedly. His life has arrived at the epilogue, but he still knows how to handle a fruit tree. He knows how to deal with a garden. No one can take that away from him.

"My parents," Hofmeester says, "loved fruit trees. They loved the trees more than they did each other."

"And they ran a hardware store together?"

"Yes, sort of," he says, gruffly now. "The shop was my father's. My mother sang in a choir." He regrets having let the conversation run on. What does this boy care about his parents? He bends down to pull some weeds under the tree. The last thing he needs is for this man to get any closer. No proximity. Anything but proximity.

"And they didn't want you to take over the store?"

"They wanted me to go to college," Hofmeester says, still holding the clump of weeds. "They thought that was important. That their only son go to college. They worked for that. And I did go to college."

"Yes, that's right," Atta says. "I know about that. German and criminology, right?"

"I never finished my study of criminology. Due to circumstances. I was offered a job as editor at a very prestigious publishing house. I couldn't turn down that offer. All expectations were that I would become a publisher."

He walks over to the trash can and throws away the weeds.

When he comes back, Atta is still standing beside the apple tree.

"Is this actually the right time to prune trees?" the young man asks.

"Not really," Hofmeester says, "but I'm here now, so I prune them. I have to make use of the opportunity. I saw when I'm here. Where's Tirza?"

"She's asleep. She's tired too."

Atta goes back inside, but just before he gets to the house, he turns around. "Mr. Hofmeester, can I help you in the kitchen later on? Fixing dinner?"

Hofmeester shakes his head. "I always do that myself. Most of it is already done. All you have to do is eat it. You're my guest. Don't forget that."

He remains standing, watches as the young man goes inside. Through the curtains he sees that Atta has seated himself in the living room, in front of the fire. The slight sense of euphoria Hofmeester felt a few minutes earlier is gone now. He has not won, he has lost. And winning is the only thing that counts. Everything that is not winning is an excuse, a deftly camouflaged excuse, but an excuse nonetheless. Yes, almost everything that enjoys prestige in this world, art, politics, is an excuse for losing.

Hofmeester has slid the dinner table around in front of the fireplace and made three steaks—rare for Tirza and for himself, well-done for Atta—which he serves with bread, salad, and fresh fruit.

The fire crackles, Hofmeester opens the day's second bottle of red Bordeaux. "What do your parents think, actually," he asks Atta, "about you going to Africa with my daughter?"

"Do you mean my going to Africa, or my going with Tirza?"

"Both." Hofmeester cuts a slice of bread and dips it carefully in the gravy left on his plate. It's not the polite thing to do, in fact, but at his country home other rules apply.

"I don't really have much contact with my parents anymore. I don't see them much."

Hofmeester chews his bread. It tastes good.

"Choukri is estranged from his parents," Tirza says, squeezing her boyfriend's shoulder.

Estranged, the word reminds him of Ibi, but she didn't become estranged from her parents, she just went away. That's easier than estrangement.

"And why, if I may ask?"

"They had different ideas," the boy says. "Ideas that were different from mine."

"Different ideas?" Hofmeester has finished his bread. He cuts off another piece and offers it to Atta, who declines politely.

"Different ideas?" Hofmeester repeats

"Different ideas. The way that goes. Other ways of thinking. About life. I'm sure there must have been moments when you and Tirza didn't exactly see eye-to-eye. About life. About what's good. About how you should live. About what you have to do to be a good person."

Hofmeester looks at his daughter. He wonders what she might have told Atta. About him, the wife, the tenants he's run through, the way the wife ran through lovers.

"I have no idea," he says. "Do I look like a man with ideas?"

Atta plucks a last leaf of lettuce from his plate. "Well, okay, ideas, I mean that maybe you had thoughts about your daughter's life. What it would be like. Later on."

"Thoughts? Later? When I'm dead? Do I look like a person who knows how you're supposed to live?"

Atta laughs nervously.

Hofmeester senses that he is backing the boy into a corner. He likes backing people into corners. Because he's afraid of them. Because he doesn't know how else to deal with them. He used to back his children into corners too. Verbally, only verbally, to make them strong. To expand their vocabulary, to teach them the art of rhetoric. For him, language is mostly a means to besiege people, to back them into a corner, to cut off their final escape route. Language, one huge attempt at humiliation. Maybe that's also why he has grown more silent lately. Out of respect. By way of surrender. Silence is his white flag.

"So you think I had thoughts about my daughter's life? That I know what you should do to be a good person?"

"I mean . . . what I was trying to say is that all parents have expectations. Sometimes a bit too many. Sometimes the wrong expectations too."

All this time, Tirza says nothing. She is still chewing on her steak.

"Wrong expectations? How do you know if an expectation is wrong?"

Atta shrugs. "Anyway," he says.

So Hofmeester pushes on alone. "I *have* had expectations. I have withdrawn them. The way you might withdraw troops, because I saw in time that those expectations weren't good for Tirza. A father can learn things too. I have no expectations, not for Tirza, and not on her behalf. I expect nothing."

"I guess I would like a little bread." Atta's voice sounds more timid now.

Hofmeester cuts off a slice. "You're a good eater," he says, and Atta begins chewing on the bread without dipping it in the gravy first.

"And now?" Atta asks.

"Now? Now I share in Tirza's expectations. To the extent that she has them. And I probably have the occasional opinion of my own. But often I don't. Why should I? I trust her judgment. I have no idea at all about what one has to do to become a good person. In fact, I even wonder whether you should aim for that. Isn't it more important to remain a living person, rather than become a good one? And what about you? What do you expect from Tirza, actually? Leaving aside the sexual part."

"Daddy," Tirza says, "shall we skip this subject tonight and just play Monopoly?"

The father fills everyone's wine glass. "It is a fairly important subject," he pronounces, "particularly when one is traveling to the magical nexus of the AIDS epidemic."

Hofmeester used to talk quite often about people's sex lives. The less sex he had, the more he talked about it. Not in the vulgar way most men did. In an enlightening, almost scientific manner. He unraveled the sex life of the human being. Particularly when Tirza's girlfriends would stay for dinner, he would begin his unraveling.

"I don't know what I expect from Tirza," Atta says quietly. "When you love someone, does that mean you expect something from them?"

"Are you finished eating?" Hofmeester asks.

Tirza nods.

He piles the dishes and, standing beside the table, asks: "So you love Tirza?"

The sarcasm in his voice is impossible to miss. There he is again, the man who was going to do away with love, the man who was so sure he would succeed at that.

Atta nods and Hofmeester can't help thinking about Ester, about the party he had looked forward to, that he had lived for, more than Tirza herself.

"That's wonderful, that you love her. That's wonderful."

"Daddy," Tirza says.

He clears the rest of the table without a word.

At the back of the closet he finds the Monopoly board.

He counts out the money, gives everyone a token.

They concentrate on the game. Conversation remains at a minimum.

Only when Hofmeester gains the upper hand and Choukri has to mortgage his properties, does Hofmeester ask: "Have you actually ever read the Koran?"

Atta tosses the dice. "Most of it," he says. "Out of curiosity as well."

He has thrown a pair of fours.

"Curiosity?" The father leans towards the boy, across the board.

"Interest."

Hofmeester looks at the boy's hand, in which he is holding a blue token.

"Eight," Hofmeester says. "You threw an eight. That puts you on my hotel."

Even in the olden days he had played Monopoly the same way he collected the rent, with misgivings but greedily, in the end always out for blood. As though he suddenly remembered that everything that wasn't winning was an excuse.

"I have it with me."

"Oh, do you?"

"Tirza was curious."

"About what?" Hofmeester asks. He doesn't remember exactly what they were talking about. His answers come automatically, his thoughts are elsewhere.

"About the Koran."

"Oh yes. I'm curious too," the father says. "Always have been. Not just about the Koran. About everything about other people. About the other. The other has always fascinated me. Because the other determines who I am."

The boy shakes his head. "I determine who I am," says Atta. "I'm Choukri. I play guitar. I love your daughter. That's who I am. The other has nothing to do with it."

They play on for another twenty minutes or so. The suspense has gone out of it. It's already obvious who's going to win.

Tirza and her boyfriend are the first to go upstairs.

Hofmeester stays downstairs to put out the fire in the hearth and bring the last glasses and plates to the kitchen. He starts picking up the game slowly, as though the movements cause him pain. Finally, he decides to leave it on the table. Maybe they'll want to play again tomorrow. It's a way to pass the evening.

In the bedroom where his parents used to sleep, he opens the cupboard. A few of his father's suits are still hanging there. A forgotten shirt.

He sniffs at the suits before lying down on the bed. Now he knows for sure that he is nothing, a black hole that livens up for a moment when someone else looks at him. The way a game show host who has been in the business too long only comes to life when the camera's red light blinks on.

He falls asleep, wakes again at two-thirty in the morning, undresses carefully, pulls on an old pair of pajamas, and goes back to sleep.

The next morning the weather is still gray and drizzly. Still wearing his pajamas, Hofmeester fries three eggs, but because Tirza and her boyfriend are sleeping in and he doesn't want to disturb them, he eats the eggs himself, standing at the kitchen counter.

Then he goes to the garden and begins mowing the lawn, but when eleven o'clock arrives and Tirza and her boyfriend are still asleep, he loses patience. He knocks on the door of the guestroom. "Tirza," he calls out. "Sun queen."

He opens the door carefully.

His daughter is still asleep, only half covered by the blanket. She is, as far as he can tell, completely naked. On the other side of the bed lies Atta. Completely naked as well.

Hofmeester remains standing in the doorway, looking at his daughter. Tomorrow she will fly to Africa. In a little more than twenty-four hours he will be at Frankfurt Airport.

"Tirza," he says, "it's eleven o'clock already."

Her only reaction is to roll over. Lying on the nightstand is the iPod, which she is so happy with, a little black book in which she makes notes about her life and in which she sometimes pastes things too, theater and train tickets, sometimes the bill from a restaurant, a recipe for honey cake, the label she has soaked off a bottle of wine.

He backs out of the room and closes the door quietly. In the kitchen he washes his hands. Then he goes and sits in the Volvo. He leans his head against the steering wheel, and had anyone seen him like that they would surely have thought Hofmeester was sleeping. After five minutes he starts the car and drives to the village. Although he has brought almost everything he needs from Amsterdam, he goes shopping anyway. The people at the bakery recognize him. They try to strike up a conversation about his parents, but Hofmeester fends it off. Then he drinks two quick glasses of white wine at the café before driving back to the house.

When he gets there, Tirza and her boyfriend are awake. They are sitting at the dining table downstairs. Tirza is wearing a long T-shirt, nothing else. Atta has on a pair of jeans and a shirt Hofmeester can only describe as old.

He offers to boil or fry an egg for them, but all they want is fruit and a little coffee or tea.

"Besides what I brought along from Amsterdam," he says, "we also have grapes. I just bought them in the village."

He washes the grapes and brings them into the living room on a plate.

Uninvited, he pulls up a chair and sits down with them. Occasionally he puts a grape in his mouth. He swallows the seeds.

When the bunch is almost finished, he says: "So show it to me."

"What?" Atta asks.

Not without a certain satisfaction, Hofmeester notices the slight alarm in the boy's voice. The discomfort. It's the discomfort that makes the other person human.

"Your Koran," Hofmeester says, "show it to us. You brought it with you, didn't you?"

"Upstairs, in my bag."

Hofmeester searches the bunch for a grape that's still whole. "I raised my children as agnostics, but I did read to them from the Bible sometimes, just like from Tolstoy and Turgenev. Do you know that lovely sentence at the end of *Anna Karenina*? 'My reason will still not understand why I pray, but I shall still pray.' Do you know what I mean?"

"I've never read *Anna Karenina*."

"That doesn't surprise me," says Hofmeester. "But get it. Your Koran."

The boy goes upstairs.

There they sit at the table. Father and daughter. "You're acting a little hostile," she says quietly.

"Me? I'm keeping up my end of the conversation. I'm showing interest. I'm doing my best."

She shakes her head.

"Daddy, do you think you'll ever have a girlfriend, a real one? I mean: Do you think you'll ever fall in love again for real?"

He thinks about the wife, and about the cleaning lady from Ghana with whom he maintained sexual relations for a time, on a modest scale. No one else knows about that. You don't go around broadcasting things like that. For all those years, however, the cleaning lady was girlfriend enough for him. But he was not in love with her. In love. Typical of Tirza, really, to demand that he fall in love again. As though it weren't hard enough already, now he's supposed to go and fall in love. With whom? And besides: he has *her*, doesn't he? He has the sun queen. A real father, one deserving of the name, is in love with his children. For life. Till death. And even afterwards.

"Should I place a want ad?" he asks. "Is that what you're getting at?"

"I don't know. But I think you should look for someone. This business with Mama can't go on forever. You just need to fall in love again, like me."

Atta has come back down. He is holding a green book. Hofmeester gulps back what he was about to say.

"The bilingual edition," Atta says. "Bought it specially for Tirza. In fact, I'm an agnostic too."

The father flips through it some, reads a bit. "Nice," he says, "quite nice. But it's not Tolstoy."

And in an attempt to be less hostile, he asks: "So what can I do for the two of you?"

"Nothing," Tirza says. "Right now there's nothing you can do for us."

He shrugs, goes to the garden, and resumes his work. At least it's not raining. He rakes up some leaves, pulls some weeds, gets out the saw again to prune a few branches he must have overlooked. Time goes quickly when you concentrate on gardening.

Occasionally he thinks about the epilogue that is his life, about the cleaning lady from Ghana, who of course doesn't count as a girlfriend. A girlfriend is someone with whom you have more than just a little physical contact at set times. But still.

It had come about gradually, unexpectedly and to their mutual satisfaction. From one day to the next she was not only Hofmeester's cleaning lady, but also his lover. Obviously, from that day on, her wages went up. The woman from Ghana not only cleaned Hofmeester's house, she also took care of his body, she regulated the juices.

What's more, he had put her in contact with a lawyer he knew from his college days. The lawyer would be able to help her. Like all women from Ghana, she was in the Netherlands illegally, but she was a good housekeeper. Hofmeester knew there was a connection between her obliging him and her not-entirely-legal immigration status, but he didn't mind. It is the illegality that makes people obliging. Perhaps he himself was illegal, without knowing it. There was certainly no denying that he was rather obliging.

Around six, it starts to rain again. He brings all the tools into the kitchen. Tomorrow he will have to re-pack it all and take it with him. First to Frankfurt, then back to Amsterdam. The garden there needs caring for too. The grass, the trees, the bushes.

He opens a bottle of wine and drinks a glass. "Tirza," he shouts.

Hofmeester is now on his second glass. "Tirza," he shouts again, "where are you?"

He goes into the living room. His daughter is lying on the table.

It takes a fraction of a second before it sinks in, what he's seeing. They have neither heard nor seen him.

In the doorway he stands staring at the beastly, at the horrific, at the inconceivable. The Koran is still on the table, and a plate bearing the remains of a bunch of grapes. The Monopoly game. He knows he should turn and leave, but he can't tear himself away, it's as though he's mesmerized. He doesn't understand either why they don't see or hear him, why they don't realize that there's someone else in the room. He has difficulty seeing in his daughter the daughter who is now lying there like that, being used, being torn open. She murmurs something.

He has to hold on to something. He feels nauseous, as though he's eaten something that doesn't agree with him, a bad oyster, an acute case of food poisoning. He feels dizzy, he takes a step back, reaches out with one hand for support, touches with one hand the poker hanging in its stand beside the fireplace.

Jörgen Hofmeester snorts like a rheumy old dog.

The room spins before his eyes, but they don't hear him. They don't see him. They remain caught up in their play. That's what they call it, don't they? Love-play?

Finally he slinks back into the kitchen, drinks three glasses of wine, and washes his face and hands.

Then he goes to the garden and, ignoring the rain, begins pulling weeds. There are a lot of them, especially beneath the trees and along the edges. He works like a madman, as though he were twenty again. Without taking a break, without wiping his hands. This is how he worked when his parents were still alive, when he still lived at home, he worked like a dog because his parents had taught him: work is the only thing that makes a man happy. After half an hour he is soaked from the rain and the sweat, there is dirt everywhere. Even in his ears.

He goes back into the kitchen and wipes his hands on a dish-towel, filthying it immediately. It doesn't matter.

He can't hear them anymore now. The playing is over. Is sex really a game? Isn't that a misconstruction, doesn't sex start, in fact, where the game ends? Yes, that's right. It stops at sex, something else starts there. Reality, that which can no longer be called a game. Death. There is sand in his ears.

"Tirza," he shouts. "Tirza."

He goes into the living room.

Lying on the table is the iPod, the Koran, a die he apparently forgotten to put away last night. The Monopoly game. He picks up the book, leafs through it. He puts the volume back down on the table, noting that it is made with India paper, typical of sacred texts, as well as some early editions of the Russian Library.

His shoes leave huge, muddy tracks on the floor. He should really take them off. But he doesn't. Water is dripping from his hair. His shirt is sticking to his back.

"Tirza," he shouts again.

He starts to climb the stairs, but stops halfway. He hears the shower running in the bathroom, but it could also be the sound of rain. They must be taking a shower. The shower comes after the love-play. The wife used to jump into the shower right away too, after he had made love to her, as though Hofmeester were some sort of pigpen. Tirza is even more beautiful than the wife was in her younger years.

He goes back downstairs. In his hand he has the die from the Monopoly game. They always get lost. Especially back when Ibi still played. She was a sore loser. Whenever she lost she would throw away the dice, and months later you'd find them under the radiator.

In the kitchen he opens another bottle of wine. This is the one he likes most. Italian Gewürztraminer. He drinks two glasses, cleans his shoes. He drinks standing up and thinks for a moment, without knowing why, about Ester, who wants to do away with love.

Hofmeester decides to go into the village for takeaway; he doesn't feel like cooking on this last evening. He wants to be with her, with Tirza, alone with her, to enjoy the little time they have together. He can still hear the sound of the shower, they never stop showering, they want to warm up. That's what you get from fucking on the dining room table.

"No," Hofmeester says quietly to himself, "it's not the shower, it's the rain. They're taking a little nap."

He washes himself in the kitchen, his face and hands, he feels so dirty. Upstairs he changes quickly. He puts on one of his father's shirts.

Holding a plastic bag above his head, he runs for the car. He drives into the village quickly. He drives through puddles. The water splashes up on all sides.

Although it doesn't get dark till ten at this time of year, he drives with his brights on. The roads are empty. In some of the gardens along the way he sees little inflatable swimming pools. People had been counting on different weather.

At the Indonesian restaurant, the woman behind the counter recognizes him.

"Aren't you Mr. Hofmeester?" she asks. "I remember you from a long time ago."

He nods.

"You look pretty terrible."

"I've been working in the garden."

"In this downpour?"

He ignores her remark.

"I need dinner for three, make it something special, a bit of this and that, and an extra order of shrimp crackers. My daughter loves shrimp crackers. And she's going to Africa tomorrow. Namibia, Botswana, Zaire; she wants to see everything."

"Oh yes, Africa." The woman's look tells him it's a place she'd never dream of going, and rightly so. There are so many lovely things to see close to home. As long as you keep your eyes open for the little things. The ants, the beachside restaurants, the roads. The houses. The birds, the dunes.

"I'll make a little rice table out of it. That's always nice."

"She's only going to be gone for a couple of months. She's coming back for college in the fall."

Fifteen minutes later, the woman hands him the two plastic bags with dinner for three and an extra helping of shrimp crackers.

He drives to the house, the car radio on. A musician he's never heard of is singing something in Dutch.

On the dining room table he arranges the rice, meat, and fish dishes. The little plastic tubs aren't exactly what you'd call festive, but to compensate for that he lights a couple of candles. There's also some plastic cutlery in the bags. He decides to use that, since they gave it to him anyway.

"Tirza," he calls out. "Dinner's ready."

He carries the bottle of wine to the table and opens another one, just to be sure.

They're still upstairs, they'll be coming in a minute. They're back in bed again, he knows how that is, he remembers that. Sex, excellent. But why lollygag around so long afterwards? Or even worse: fall asleep. If you're going to have sex in the middle of the day, then do something afterwards, something useful. Ibi wasn't any better. How often had he opened her bedroom door late in the afternoon and seen her lying with some man in her arms? Having sex and sleeping, and if he said anything about it, she would answer: "You're insane."

But he wasn't insane, he was concerned. Hofmeester knew the future the way you know a holiday campground you've gone back to too often.

Tirza's iPod is lying on the table. Absent-mindedly, Hofmeester begins toying with it. Just as absent-mindedly, he puts the buds in his ears. He listens to music that is unfamiliar to him. Then he gets up and starts to dance.

This is how Tirza dances in front of him sometimes, in the kitchen or the living room. The silent disco, she calls it.

Normally speaking, Hofmeester doesn't dance, but he is not afraid of being seen now. He loses himself in it.

The rain hasn't stopped. The patch of lawn he sowed yesterday has become a pool of mud. He puts the iPod back on the table and goes into the garden. Pity, he thinks. Everything washed away, all the seed. Gone. Vanished.

He sticks his hand in the earth. He needs to learn to die. He's working on it. When it comes to dying, Hofmeester is a self-taught man.

And as he squats there in his garden, he tries to imagine what tomorrow will be like. The last day, the day of Tirza's departure. The last day before the epilogue to his life begins.

He will get up early, as always. He'll start the day by making a nice breakfast for three. He himself will eat breakfast standing in the kitchen, he won't be very hungry anyway. On days like that, he never feels much like eating.

He will bring his daughter and her boyfriend breakfast in bed. They will sit up in bed, without saying anything. As though they too find it strange and uncomfortable, this last day in old Europe. A final day like this one with Hofmeester, and Tirza will take his hand, before he turns around to go downstairs again. "You need to fall in love again for real, Daddy," she'll whisper. "Really in love for real, just like me."

They will leave the house at eleven. Just to be sure. There may be traffic jams, construction work. You never know. And you don't want to be stressed while you're driving, you don't want to arrive at the airport with your nerves frazzled. They'll get to Frankfurt much too early.

They'll drink a cup of coffee in the departure hall, hastily, but without saying much. His palms will be sweaty.

When they go to the check-in counter he will leave them alone, the couple that isn't a couple but a mistake. He'll wait for them close to the sign that says "meeting point."

Before they go through customs, they'll come back to him one last time. Timidly.

There's so much he has been intending to say, but when the moment arrives, all he'll be able to come up with is: "Take care. Take good care of each other. Be careful."

Atta will shake his hand.

Then Hofmeester will press Tirza to his breast.

Atta will step back, politely.

Hofmeester will fight back the tears, and he'll win, he has always won out over the tears.

"Will your cell phone work down there, do you think?" he'll ask.

"Daddy," she'll say, "I'm not going to turn it on while we're there, that would be way too expensive. If I had coverage at all."

He will squeeze her arms. He'll squeeze and squeeze, he'll squeeze the despair right out of her, like the last bit of toothpaste from the tube.

"Call me when you get there. It doesn't matter what time it is. Call me. Call collect," he'll say.

She will let go of him. "We have to get to the gate," she'll say.

He will walk with them to customs.

There will be a long line.

Once the customs official has checked her passport, she will turn around one last time to wave to her father. And he will wave back and keep waving, even when he can't see them anymore, wave and wave and wave again. He's seen it countless times at Schiphol. He knows how it goes.

As the last light of day is fading, he realizes that Tirza and her boyfriend have fallen into a deep sleep. He walks to the foot of the stairs and calls up to them again, but they don't react. It looks like he'll have to eat the rice table all by himself. That's how rude Mohammed Atta is: taking everything that comes his way, making use of everything, but not contributing a whit to the social interaction. A complete lack of social-mindedness. Hofmeester remembers exactly the same thing with Ibi and her boyfriend. In the end, they stopped showing up for dinner too. That is the colored influence. Asocial behavior.

Before eating, he pours himself another glass of wine. Sitting at the table he stares out at the garden that belonged to his parents, the garden where Ibi and Tirza once played, and once again he runs through the day to come. In that way, prepared and all, he can better fight against the tears, the tears he won't allow himself to shed, that are superfluous. Disgusting.

At two in the morning, he gets out of bed. He can't sleep. Carefully, in order not to wake anyone, he tiptoes down the stairs. Hofmeester opens a bottle of wine, Italian Gewürztraminer, and drinks a glass quickly, as though someone might catch him at it.

He is afraid he is losing his mind, he has to do something in order to calm down. He goes into the garden in his underpants. It has stopped raining. The fluorescent lamp in the kitchen sheds enough light. And he starts tidying up the garden. He arranges everything. The grass, the flowers, the bushes. He smoothes the soil, sows more grass seed. Yes, this is good for him. He works so hard that, despite being scantily clad, he doesn't notice the cold.

After an hour he goes back into the kitchen and opens another bottle of wine, even though the first one is still three-quarters full. There's no need for him to worry, Tirza will come back from Africa. The Tirza-less episode will be brief. It is an episode he will survive.

By the time he stops work in the garden, as he is cleaning his tools and laying them on the kitchen floor to dry, it is already becoming light.

Meticulous as he is, he also tidies up the landing and the living room, as though important visitors might arrive any moment. He leafs through the Koran. A peculiar book for peculiar people.

Then he lies down on the bed. She wants me to fall in love, he thinks, she wants me to fall in love again for real, but I already am in love for real, I already am.

He manages to catch a little more than two hours' sleep.

That Sunday everything goes exactly as he'd imagined. For once the future holds no disappointments for him. At Frankfurt Flughafen he stands and waves, the way he thought he would the day before.

And just as Hofmeester promised himself he would, he keeps waving, first only with his right hand, then with both hands. He rises up on tiptoe, so that Tirza can still see his hands, above all the other waving hands.

Until he has the nagging feeling that, just like at Schiphol, he is waving to no one.

Slowly, almost at a saunter, he walks to the parking garage. He has to search around a bit before he finds his car.

Once he's found it, he sits down behind the wheel and notices that he still has dirt under his nails. He has spent a weekend digging in the mud. Living in the mud, you could almost say.

Just as he is about to start the car, he sees Tirza's iPod on the dashboard. He feels like hopping out of the car, running to the departure hall, but realizes then that they won't let him past customs.

For a moment he sits there with the little thing in his hands, hesitantly. The charger is on the dashboard too. He tries to call her.

Maybe he can mail it to her youth hostel. In any case, he wants to let her know that she doesn't have to worry about her iPod. She's so fond of it. But she doesn't answer. He gets her voicemail, he hears her voice. "Hi, this is Tirza. I can't answer the phone right now. But be sure to leave a nice message."

He puts the buds in his ears and listens to Tirza's music. Occasionally a song comes by that he recognizes. The Andrews Sisters, she put it on there too. For him. He hums along.

At a cruising speed of almost one hundred and eighty kilometers an hour, he takes the autobahn in the direction of Amsterdam.

Close to Oberhausen he stops at a gas station. He can't hold out anymore.

He walks to the restroom, as though in a trance. All the toilets are occupied. He waits at least five minutes for someone to come out. Then he goes in and vomits. Shrimp crackers, wine, more shrimp crackers.

Standing between a couple of truck drivers in front of the mirror, he washes up embarrassedly. It doesn't really help. As he walks back to the car, he is feeling shaky.

He sits down at the wheel. Again he picks up the iPod. He looks at it and thinks about Africa. They've been in the air now for almost two hours. Where would that put them? Somewhere over southern Italy.

Without thinking about it, he toys with the iPod, he wonders whether he remembered to lock up the country house properly, he turns the iPod over and only then does he see that there is something engraved on the back.

He has to squint to read it in this light.

"Sun Queen" it says. Two words, two lines, one under the other. Sun Queen.

He puts the player on the seat beside him and gets out of the car.

Again, he walks to the toilet. No, he runs.

He vomits again. This time, everything comes out.

Hanging over the pot, still unable to move, he mumbles: "Sun queen. Sun queen." The words comfort him. As long as the words exist, his world still exists.

Back in the car, he puts the iPod and the charger in his briefcase.

For minutes, he sits there like that. Maybe longer. Until someone knocks loudly on the car. He sits up straight. No, he can't sleep here, he's not allowed to sleep here. He knows that.

Hofmeester looks at his watch.

Italy is behind them now too. Libya, that's where they must be now. They're already over Africa.

"I beat the tears," Hofmeester says to the steering wheel.

2

By twelve-thirty in the morning he's back at the house on Van Eeghenstraat. His bag of clothes is the only thing he brings inside. The tools can go into the shed tomorrow. He opens the front door cautiously, assuming that the wife is already asleep.

But she's sitting in the living room, at the table, with a newspaper and a bottle of wine. He looks at her.

She ignores him, or doesn't hear him come in. He stands there like that for a minute, bag in hand.

"What are you doing?" he asks at last.

Now she looks up from the paper.

"A crossword," she says. "I've been working on it on and off all day. It's a tough one."

She taps the pen against her forearm.

"What happened?" she asks. She doesn't sound worried. More like a bit peeved.

He puts down the bag, he comes closer. The taste of vomit is still in his mouth.

"What do you mean? What could have happened?"

"The way you look. You look so . . . so . . . how should I put it, you look so messed up."

He sits down at the table, rubs his hands together. "It's this weather. I worked in the garden. There was a lot to do. I should really go there more often. The place is going to seed. Dead branches, weeds, more dead branches, more weeds."

"You stink," she says.

"Of what?"

He starts to reach for the wine bottle, but sees then that it is empty. He wouldn't mind having a glass, but to open a new bottle at this hour of the night . . .

"Stench. Nothing in particular. Just stench. How did it go? Did you wave goodbye?"

He nods, almost relieved, as though it occurs to him only now that he has just taken his child to the airport. That he waved goodbye to her there, the way parents do when their child leaves home for a while. As though he realizes only now what he's doing here. Coming home, that's what he's come to do. Homecoming.

"Good," he says, "fast and good. You know how it goes. At an airport. Everyone's always in a rush."

He gets up from the table and feels her eyes on him as he walks away. He knows she's examining him, wondering why he looks so disheveled. But not for long. Not really. The crossword puzzle is calling. How much interest can you summon up for someone else anyway, especially when you know that other person so well? And especially when you've know them for so long. So terribly long. Half a lifetime almost.

In the bedroom he undresses. He takes a shower. After he has dried off, he takes a pair of clippers and cleans the dirt from under his nails. He can't get them completely clean. He puts on clean underpants, sprays deodorant under his arms.

He goes downstairs in his underpants. With no real purpose in mind. Water the plants, that's a possibility. The performance of everyday activities, that should be purpose enough. The comfort that brings. It's all he needs for the moment, all he's looking for right now.

The wife is still sitting at the table with her puzzle.

He sits down on the couch, across the room from her. What he really feels like doing is putting on some music, but he can't move a muscle.

"Have you been inside the house all day?" he asks.

"I was in the garden for fifteen minutes or so," she says without looking up from her newspaper. "Why would I go outside? In weather like this?"

Hofmeester looks at his feet. His toenails could stand clipping.

"I just took a shower," he says.

"Great."

Now he musters up the strength to stand. He walks over to her.

"I'm fresh and clean again. I don't stink anymore."

"That's good," she says. Decisively.

Hofmeester stands there at the table, in his underpants. He doesn't like crossword puzzles. He's too impatient for that. Crossword puzzles are for people who don't take language seriously.

He feels an urge coming on, but doesn't know what kind of urge. All he knows is that it's proof that you're alive, when you feel an urge. Not desire, that sounds too romantic, not lust, because that reeks of meat. An urge. To talk to the wife, for example. To hear her voice. The voice of his children's mother.

"Did you know that I . . . the cleaning lady and I?" he asks.

"You and the cleaning lady? The old one?"

"The new one, from Ghana. Did you know that she and I . . . That we had something going? Did I tell you that?"

She shakes her head. "No," she says, "I didn't know that. You didn't tell me. Is it important? Is there something you want to say about it?" There is a touch of irony in her voice.

"No, not important. I just thought I'd tell you."

She puts down the pen. "That woman from Ghana?" She looks at him disbelievingly. In amazement now as well. She considers it, he sees, a rather remarkable story.

He sits down. "Yes, from Ghana. That's what I said. On Thursdays. At lunch time I would bike back from the office, and then . . . then I would take her. That's what they say, isn't it?"

"Yes, you can put it that way. If that's what you did, I have no idea, but if that's what you did, then that's what you should call it."

"On Thursdays. At noon. I usually made sure I was on time. It started when I stayed home sick one time. A bad flu. By accident, really. Coincidence. You had already left by then. You were already on the houseboat. After that it became a ritual. It isn't that we didn't talk to each other. You shouldn't think that. But she barely speaks Dutch, and her English isn't so fantastic either. That's why I took her. Here on the couch. We didn't go upstairs. A bedroom is so . . . so intimate. So personal. Besides, the bed was always covered in books and newspapers. It seemed convenient. And I thought: if she comes upstairs, I'll have to put them all away. When it was over, I would get dressed again. Sometimes I took a shower. If I'd been sweating a lot. There are days when you sweat so much, when it takes so long, that it takes a lot of effort. On days like that, you know. She would go back to cleaning the house and I would bike back to work. It's not that I was in love with her, although of course that might have been possible. She's not ugly. It was . . . it was sex between friends."

"Between friends. I see. But why are you telling me this now?"

He touches her. Her hand, her arm. Only his fingertips. Like a blind man.

"I figured it was good that you knew. All these secrets. Why keep that up? Why should we hide anything? From each other? We're strangers, right? Strangers, but acquaintances. Exes. Maybe we'll become friends, maybe."

"Maybe." She smiles. "Maybe," she says. "But in the last month you haven't done anything with her, right? At least, not that I've noticed."

"No, no, we haven't for a while. She understands. She doesn't ask about it. She can do without it. But I still give her her little tip."

There is a cork on the table. The shower didn't wash the taste out of his mouth. Vomit. Shrimp crackers. Old, wet shrimp crackers.

"Do you think I'm normal, really?" he asks.

"Normal?" She looks at him, amazed again, baffled. "Why? Why do you ask that?"

"No reason, really. Just asking."

He picks up the cork, bobbles it in his hand.

"Am I normal?"

"Christ, Jörgen, why do you care? I mean: Isn't it a bit late for that? You're almost retired. You've gotten by so far, so why worry? It doesn't matter anymore. What you are. I mean: it's over. Your life is finished. Who cares?"

The cork falls to the floor. He picks it up.

"But when," he goes on, "can a person say: 'I have a normal sex life'? When you don't have sex at all? Or twice a week, in an otherwise monogamous relationship, in the bedroom, and once every three months in the kitchen, after a party at a friend's? When can you truthfully say, 'I have a healthy sex life'?"

He is still running his fingertips over her arm, her shoulder, her neck, and now her face as well.

She closes the newspaper demonstratively. "I don't know. I don't think I'm the person to ask whether you're normal or not. Do you mean: What's the norm? The average. How often do they do it?

Other people? I've known you too long, too well, I can't say that about you. Why don't you ask your friends at work? Maybe ask your daughters. Ask someone else."

His head is pounding like an infected wound, but still, it isn't what you'd call a headache.

"What positions are normal?" he wants to know. He no longer cares what he says or doesn't say. What he gives away, what he keeps to himself, what secrets he will drag with him to his grave. "Which ones aren't normal? When the anus starts bleeding, is that still normal? Where does the abnormal start? Where's the borderline? What's the moment when you realize: Damn, I just crossed over something, I just stepped across a line and I can't go back, not if I wanted to, I can't go back. I've ended up on the other side, but what's the other side? What is it?" His index finger is resting on her nose.

"Is the anus bleeding? Whose anus? That woman's from Ghana?"

Coming from her, it sounds like a joke. A punch line. But he missed the beginning of it, and now he doesn't know what he's supposed to laugh at.

Hofmeester falls silent, he no longer has any idea what to say. He half expects the wife to get up and go upstairs, but she remains seated.

"Maybe," he says after a time, "the most normal thing is not to have sex at all. Or only with yourself, in the bathroom. You, early in the morning, lying in bed, while I'm downstairs making coffee. Alone with your thoughts and vague fantasies. Indeterminate, unfulfilled fantasies that no one can punish you for."

She picks up her glass, which still has a little wine in it. She finishes it.

"I was your fantasy," she says. "Remember? Your fantasy, that was me."

He nods. He's tired, his thoughts are blurred. "My fantasy," he mumbles. "Yes, that was you."

She gets up. "I'm going to bed." She folds the paper, takes the glass. "You just shouldn't think about it too much," she says. "The things you do with that woman. She's only the cleaning lady. Don't get worked up about it. I mean: hey, that woman's from Ghana, I bet she's been through worse. And she's our cleaning lady. Your cleaning lady."

She goes to the kitchen. He follows her. He stops and looks at the clock above the counter. "They're over Mali now," he says. "Or Cameroon. What's that place called?"

"Who?"

"Tirza and Mohammed Atta."

She stands beside him for a few seconds, looking at the clock too.

"Or maybe they're over Ghana. Maybe they're flying right now over the family of that cleaning lady of yours."

She laughs and throws an arm around the shoulders of the man she's made children with.

"Am I sick?" he whispers in her ear. "Is that what I am? Is that what people don't know?"

She lets go of him. "Oh, but they do know. They just don't care, that's all. As long as it doesn't cause them any problems."

She goes upstairs. She walks quietly, as though afraid to wake someone.

"Then what are *they*?" he shouts after her. "If I'm sick, then what are they?"

He opens a bottle of wine anyway, to rinse the taste out of his mouth.

He drinks a glass and a half. And he shouts up the stairs again: "Then what are *they*?"

No answer comes.

Seven days after Tirza's departure, the wife asks Hofmeester: "Have you talked to her already?"

"Who?"

"Who? Tirza, what do you think?"

He shakes his head.

"But she was going to call when she got there, right?"

"She was, but she didn't."

They are sitting in the garden. The weather has improved.

The wife is sunning topless, to avoid the stripes that come with sunbathing in a bikini.

"Should we be worried?" Hofmeester asks.

"Of course not." She takes a tube of suntan lotion and rubs lotion over herself. "I was just wondering whether she'd called. Ibi never called either, when she went traveling. But Tirza. I don't know. I was just wondering. It seems like she'd call. Have you checked your email?" She rubs herself in as though it were her job.

"I called her twice," he says. "On her cell phone. She hasn't sent an email either. At least not to me. Not to you either?"

"She has never sent me an email, Jörgen. So what happened? When you called her?"

"I got her voicemail."

The wife takes off her sunglasses.

"Of course, there's no coverage there. What did you expect?"

He has put on a straw hat against the sun. Ever since he has started going bald, his scalp burns easily, even in the shade. It turns red and starts to itch.

"Do you think I should alert someone?" he suggests.

"Who would you alert?"

"The youth hostel, for example. The youth hostel where they were going to stay for the first few days."

"Jörgen, Tirza is with her boyfriend, they're in Africa, it's warm there. She's on vacation. Stay out of the picture a little. Do you know what those two are doing the whole time? They're screwing."

"You don't have to go to Africa to do that, do you? She wanted to see things, figure things out. Gain some experience. And you're the one who starts asking: 'Did she call already?' You're the one who's stirring things up around here. Don't blame me for it."

"I'm not stirring things up. I asked a normal question. Has she called already? That's a normal question."

"No, that was not a normal question. Not the way you asked it."

"Listen, your favorite daughter is a fuck bunny, so get used to it. It's not that bad." Her voice is derisive, taunting.

"Knock it off," he shouts, "with that foul mouth of yours. Knock it off. The only fuck bunny in this family is you."

He goes to the kitchen and opens a cold bottle of wine. He holds the bottle against his forehead. A fuck bunny. How can you call your daughter a fuck bunny? What kind of person would you have to be to do that?

That evening he calls the youth hostel in Windhoek where Tirza planned to go for the first few days. He had copied all the information she had about her trip into his pocket diary, as befits a good father.

The woman who answers the phone speaks very proper English. They have never heard of a Tirza Hofmeester. They can't find a reservation either. Not even that. No, it can't be some mistake. They keep track of everything. She hasn't been there. Not in the past few weeks. Maybe last year. Maybe a long time ago. That's possible.

"One moment," he says.

"What's that Choukri's last name?" he calls out to the wife.

She looks at him in amazement from where she's sitting on the couch. "No idea, I thought you knew. You said his name was Atta. Atta was his name, wasn't it? How am I supposed to know his name?"

"Thank you. Thank you for going to all the trouble," he says into the phone, and hangs up.

He sits down on the couch. There is a zooming in his ears. He's hearing sounds again that aren't there.

"Listen, Jörgen, Tirza is no fool. Stop acting like a mooning teenager. She'll show up. She just wants a break from us. She's gone to another youth hostel. A better one, with cleaner showers and beds that aren't as filthy. Or something."

"Why would she want a break from us? I've left her alone, and God knows you did, you never worried about her at all. A break? What are you talking about?"

She lights a cigarette.

"Besides, you're worried too," he goes on. "I can tell. For the first time in your life you're starting to get worried. Awfully late, but then better late than never."

"I'm not worried. Not yet. Things aren't at that point yet. I'm just curious. I wondered whether she was having a good time. That's all. Aren't I allowed to express interest in my own daughter anymore? Do you really want her all for yourself? Okay, I've said nasty things about her now and then, but mothers do that. I just happened to be prettier when I was her age. Feistier. And you know it, Jörgen, you know I'm speaking the truth."

"Oh," he says, "well, Tirza's no slouch either."

While the wife is asleep, he goes to Tirza's room and pokes around. He has no idea what he's looking for. A bit of comfort, probably. But there's nothing to be found. Nothing that resembles comfort. Diaries he's already read. A pocket diary with her email address and password, appointments she crossed out after they were kept or canceled. Photos. Letters from girlfriends and boyfriends. A notebook with short messages, which he realizes only after a time are text messages she's written down. Texts from friends, he supposes. "I miss you. Where are you?" That kind of thing. Neatly written down in a booklet, with the date and time beside them. Only no names.

He sits down on her bed, he looks around. On the desk is a little bag of makeup, for which there was no room in the backpack.

Hofmeester gets up, opens her closet—the clothes are arranged by color—he picks up a pair of shoes, stares at the soles as though he were a shoemaker. Then he sits down on her bed again. It's neatly made. She left it spick-and-span. Her toy donkey is tucked beneath the blanket. She could come in the door any moment now. That's how it seems when he's in here. She could come home any moment, like after a party, tired and hoarse, enveloped in the smell of cigarettes and alcohol. Downstairs, in the kitchen, her girlfriends are still having a drink of one thing or the next.

He lies down on the bed, presses his face against her pillow, wraps his arms around her blue donkey and tries to sleep. He finds four of Tirza's hairs on her pillow. He can't fall asleep.

Early in the morning he goes to his own bedroom. But he can't sleep there either. He sits straight up in bed. He watches as dawn comes through the lace curtains.

Until the wife wakes up. "What is it?" she murmurs. "Jörgen, why aren't you asleep?"

"I'm looking at the sun."

She takes her watch from the nightstand.

"It's still early. Go to sleep. You're keeping me awake."

"I can't."

"Can't what?"

"Sleep."

"Lie down, you'll see, you'll fall asleep."

She rolls onto her side, pulls the blanket over her.

He remains sitting up straight.

"Did you know that I don't work anymore? That I don't have a job anymore?"

First there is no reaction. Then she asks: "So where do you go every morning?"

"To Schiphol."

"What do you do there?"

"Walk around. Keep an eye on things."

"You keep an eye on things? You walk around?"

"First through the departure hall. Then to arrivals. I wave to people."

Now she sits up straight too. The wife is wide awake.

"Who do you wave to?"

"People. People no one else waves to. I wave goodbye to them."

She runs her hands over her face, her fingers through her hair.

"Why aren't you working anymore?"

"They didn't need me. They were going to win the war with fresh troops."

"What war?"

"No idea. The war for readership, I suspect. The book war."

"And couldn't you find some other job? At another publishing house? In a bookstore? A library?"

"They're going to keep paying me until I reach retirement age. I'm too old to fire. But I don't have to come into the office. I'm not much use anymore. I only get in their way. The fresh troops."

She gets out of bed and walks to the bathroom. He hears her peeing.

When she comes back, she lies down beside him again and asks: "And what now?"

"I go to Schiphol, like I said. It's interesting, an airport like that. You see all kinds of things, but actually it's always the same thing. It's a kind of industrial process. A slaughterhouse. Something goes away, and something else comes in its place."

He has to sneeze.

"Why doesn't she call?" he asks.

"Who? Tirza? Jörgen, stop it. This is harassment. Your restlessness is harassment. Your worrying is harassment. It's contageous."

"I'm going there," he says after a few seconds of silence. "I have to go there."

"Where?"

"To Africa."

"What are you going to do there? Look for a job? Do you think you'll suddenly be of use to someone there?"

"Not for work. I'm going for Tirza. It's not normal, not hearing anything like this for so long. I'd blame myself for the rest of my life."

"Don't get hysterical, Jörgen."

"I'm not getting hysterical. I know myself. I don't want to have to blame myself. Later on."

She piles the pillows up more comfortably behind her.

"Where are you going to look? At the youth hostel they've never even heard of her. Where would you start? Are you going to stand on the street corner with a sign around your neck? Go from bar to bar with a photograph?"

"Windhoek isn't a big place, or so I've heard. People will have seen her. She's a striking figure. Maybe it's not necessary. So then maybe I've wasted a couple of thousand euros. No real disaster."

She takes him by the arm. "It won't help."

"What?"

"She's eighteen. She's there with a man. Jörgen, she's not a child anymore."

"Don't start in again with that fuck bunny business. If you start in about the fuck bunny, I'll hit you."

He holds his head in his hands. He has more memories than is good for him. They get all jumbled together, his memories. His thoughts confuse him.

"She has other things on her mind besides calling us," the wife says calmly. "And it won't help. She's taking a trip around the world or whatever you want to call it. And then she's going to college. Or else she'll keep traveling around the world forever. Or she'll start a B&B, like Ibi, but she's not coming back here, Jörgen. If it's too quiet around here for you now, go out and buy a pet. Go to work at an old people's home, if you need someone to talk to and want to seem attentive, but going to Africa is ridiculous. You'd make a fool of yourself. And even if you did find her, she'd laugh in your face.

She's gone. I mean: she's left home. She's starting a life of her own, without you. You probably don't want to believe it. But she can do it. People can live without you. I could. Ibi did. Tirza can do it too. And besides: I'm back. So why would you need Tirza anymore?"

"And what if something really did happen?"

"If something really did happen, then you're too late, Jörgen. If she's been raped by ten black Africans and murdered, then it doesn't matter whether you catch a plane now or next week."

She squeezes his arm, as though that might press home her arguments.

Hofmeester says nothing. What she says is convincing, but it still doesn't reassure him. He also has a strong suspicion that she is not entirely reassured by her own arguments. He needs to go there. Peace of mind, isn't that the thing, once the epilogue to your life has begun? He needs to go there for his own peace of mind. And for the wife's.

"Let's play," he says quietly.

"What's this, what do you want to play now?"

"The way we used to."

"What did we use to play?"

He takes a deep breath. He has to concentrate. A man who wants peace of mind must, first and foremost, impose order within his own head.

"The living room was the park."

"Yeah, yeah," she says, "I remember that."

"You were the girl on the bike. It was nighttime. Dark everywhere."

"I remember that too."

"And I was the rapist with a knife."

"But Jörgen . . ." She runs her hand through his hair. "We played that when we were in love. Then it was a nice game. Now it's not a nice game anymore. It's a sad game. We shouldn't play it. It wouldn't be good."

He grabs her wrist. "Let's play it one more time," he says, "just one more time. Let's pretend this is back then."

"That's impossible."

"Why?"

"Because this isn't back then. This is now. It's summertime. You've been fired, or at least, not really fired, you've been removed, that's more like it, put out to pasture. You're useless, you told me that yourself, and if you ask me you always were useless. You should be happy they didn't figure that out a long time ago. And Tirza is in Africa, and we're not hearing anything from her, and I'm . . . I'm someone who has nowhere else to go. That's why I'm here. What are we supposed to play? For whose benefit?"

He tightens his grip on her wrist. "One more time," he says, "before I go to Africa. Like then. Please."

Put out to pasture. The words stick in his head. So that's it, that's what they did with him. It feels like it's sinking in only now.

"But why don't you call before you make such a long trip?"

"Who am I supposed to call?"

"The Dutch embassy in Namibia, for example. Maybe they'll know something."

He lets go of her, she climbs out of bed, opens the curtains.

"If anything has happened, they'll know," she whispers, "but I'm almost sure she's just somewhere in the desert or the jungle. That she's having a good time. It's Africa, you don't have telephone booths all over the place."

She turns around. "Okay," she says, "all right. We'll play one more time."

He goes to her. She grabs him by the neck. He puts his hands on her shoulders. "But only because we're ruined, Jörgen," she says, "that's the only reason. Don't forget that."

Late in the afternoon he gets the Dutch embassy in Windhoek on the line. They haven't heard anything about an accident or an assault, so everything must be all right. The man on the phone tells him, above all, not to worry. The public phones in Namibia use cards, and you can't buy those everywhere. Especially not out in the desert.

Hofmeester passes this along, almost word-for-word, to the wife.

They live as though nothing had ever happened, no houseboat, no departure, no return, no graduation party. They live as though they were on a ship bobbing about without a rudder. Waiting for the wind to drive them in a given direction.

Each morning Hofmeester leaves for Schiphol, and although the wife has said something about it a few times, she doesn't insist that he stop the nonsense. He has explained to her that he really has to get out of the house, that otherwise he'll go crazy. That is why he leaves with his briefcase in the morning and walks through departures and arrivals, occasionally leafing through the manuscript by the author from Azerbaijan. In order not to go crazy.

In the garden one evening, more than two weeks after he took Tirza away, the wife says: "Maybe we should call again?"

"Call who?"

"The embassy in Windhoek. Maybe there's a public transport strike going on and they're stuck somewhere. Or a sandstorm. You never read about Namibia in the paper. Have you ever read anything about it?"

He gets up from his garden chair and begins pacing. "What am I supposed to ask them? Excuse me, but are you having a public transport strike down there? Or a sandstorm? Who says the embassy keeps written track of every little sandstorm? They'd think I was crazy. Besides, the only way she can get around down there is to hitchhike, I know enough about colored people by now. We're talking about Africa. Not the Alsace or the Austrian Alps. And I already called the embassy once. I'm sure they haven't forgotten."

"Sit down. There's no use getting riled. It doesn't help."

Accidentally, he steps into the bowl of nuts the wife has put down beside her chair. It's a lovely evening. Warm, but not too sticky.

"You call," he says. "You call. Or else I'm going down there. Maybe I should just do that. This is ridiculous. Waiting here like this. This sniping at each other. This waiting. This panicking about what's probably nothing at all."

She is quiet for a bit, she bends down to pick up the nuts that have fallen from the bowl.

"Yes," she says when she's done doing that, "maybe you should go there."

"What do you mean?"

The question catches him off balance.

"Just what I said." She eats the nuts that have fallen on the ground. "Maybe you should go there. What can we do here?"

The garden chairs are old. When they first moved in, Hofmeester had thought it was a waste to invest in garden furniture. He likes to make a good impression, and he likes to maintain a certain degree of style, particularly for those around him, but garden furniture does not have high priority.

"And then," he says, "once I'm there?"

"Well, you're the one who started in about it. It was your idea. Then you find her. Then our minds are at rest. That's how it will go. And then . . . Yeah, then I don't know."

He leans back. "You," he says, "you haven't worried about her, the last few years you didn't even call. You were too busy doing God knows what. And now you're playing the concerned mother, the woman who can't sleep because she doesn't know where her daughter is hanging out in Namibia, if she's still there at all. Maybe they're in Botswana by now. Or Zaire."

"I had a life of my own, alongside that of my children, that's right. That's not a crime. That's my right."

"Alongside? You call that alongside? It wasn't alongside. It was right over them, straight through them. Not alongside."

"Whatever I did or didn't do all those years, and whatever else I've said about her and what she's said to me, I'm still her mother.

I'm not your woman anymore, but I'm still her mother."

He gets up. In the kitchen he holds his wrists under the cold tap. He shivers.

Slowly, he dries his hands.

He sees her folding the garden chairs and carrying them to the shed. She seems to think it's getting too cold. She arranges the wine glasses and nuts on a tray. She walks towards him. She looks at him.

"All right," he says, "I'll go. You're right. I have to do it. It would be better. The useless one goes to Africa."

She puts the tray on the counter and takes his hand with a tenderness he finds provocative. At this point in his life, tenderness comes as a shock.

"She'll probably think it's fun, too, if you suddenly pop up in Africa. You know how crazy Tirza is about you, right? She is so crazy about you."

"Probably," he says, "yes, she'd probably think that was fun. It wouldn't surprise me. She *is* crazy about me."

He pulls his hand away, holds his wrists under the cold tap again.

The next morning he buys a ticket to Windhoek, by way of Zurich and Johannesburg, aboard South African Airways. He has to wait three days before he can leave. The flights for the next three days are all full. Cheap tickets are no longer available.

During those final days, he no longer goes to Schiphol. He works a little in the garden, does some shopping, walks around Vondelpark.

The evening before he is to leave, he packs his suitcase, a little blue suitcase that he took on business trips a couple of times. New York. Turin. He never really took that many business trips.

He doesn't pack a lot, a suit, a couple of shirts, two pairs of light trousers. He won't be staying long. Ten days should be enough. In ten days you can do a lot.

That next Saturday afternoon in August, at around one-thirty, he is ready to leave the house on Van Eeghenstraat. The wife is in the garden, reading a women's magazine.

"I'm going to wait outside," he shouts from the kitchen. "I've already called a cab."

"Wait," she says, "I have something for you."

She goes to the bedroom and comes back with a package.

"What is that?" he asks.

"Open it."

He opens the package. It contains a dress, a blue summer dress.

"For Tirza. It was on sale, and it's exactly her size. I thought: a little something, it could come in handy down there."

He laughs. "How thoughtful of you. How sweet." He looks at the dress. "It will look good on her," he says. "It's her style. She likes simple things."

He repacks the dress carefully.

Snapping open his suitcase, he sees that there is room for the wife's present, under his overnight bag.

"I'll call you," he says, "when I get there."

He gives her a little peck on the right cheek.

But she doesn't go back to the garden, she walks with him to the front door.

"It will turn out fine," she says, "it will be all right. It's because we've gotten old, that's why we worry about our child. Because we're old and bored."

"Yes," he says, "that must be it. Because we've gotten old. Go back to the garden now. It will start raining again before long. Enjoy the sun while you can."

"Here," she says, "you need to take this too." She hands him a little envelope.

Hesitantly, he takes it.

"What's in here?"

"A photo. I thought: it could be useful to have a photo with you."

He takes the photo out of the envelope. Tirza, not longer before her graduation party, a couple of days before, two weeks maybe.

"Thanks," he says. "Thank you. Where did you find it?"

"In her room. You never know. It could come in handy."

"You never know," he says, tucking the envelope into his inside pocket.

"Have you said anything to Ibi, actually?" she asks.

"Not me," he says. "Not me. I haven't spoken to her for a while."

She goes back to the garden and he stands waiting in the portico. He's carrying his suitcase and his briefcase containing the iPod, the charger, Tirza's pocket diary and notebook, the manuscript by the Azerbaijani author and four pencils.

The taxi takes at least ten minutes to arrive. A neighbor greets him as he walks past. He paces up and down in front of his house like a caged animal. His luggage is still in the portico. That luggage seems to want to tell him something, but he doesn't know what.

The seat next to him remains vacant all the way to Zurich, and he is able to sleep, but between Zurich and Johannesburg he sits beside a French couple. During dinner they start up a conversation. They are going to explore South Africa. What about him, they want to know.

"I'm going to visit my daughter," he says in barely passable French.

"In Johannesburg?"

"In Windhoek." He cuts off a slice of chicken. The conversation stifles and dies.

After the meal he pulls out the manuscript and his pencils and begins reading, as usual.

At Johannesburg he has to wait almost four hours. The exhaustion makes his head hurt. He buys a cup of coffee, sits down at the window with a view of the planes, but is too restless to stay seated for long.

Briefcase in hand, he walks around the airport, which isn't very big, certainly not compared to Schiphol or Frankfurt.

A few times he takes the envelope out of his pocket and looks at the picture of the sun queen. In a shop he buys an adapter for South Africa and Namibia, and a hat to protect him against the sun. The sun is bound to be blazing there. He puts on the hat, looks in a mirror, and decides to keep it on. It doesn't look bad on Hofmeester, it gives him an added something.

Now he is a man with a hat.

With plenty of time left, he walks to the gate.

A ground hostess tells him: "We haven't started boarding yet, sir. Another fifteen minutes."

He takes a couple of steps back and stands there, waiting.

She glances at him, then asks: "Are you going on vacation to Namibia?"

He takes the envelope out of his pocket. "I'm going to visit my daughter," he says in reasonable English. He shows her the picture.

"A lovely girl," she says. "Congratulations. And such lively eyes."

He takes another good look at the photo, perhaps to check on the liveliness of Tirza's eyes.

In the shuttle bus that takes them to the plane, he notices that the people have changed. They are still white, but white in a different way from him. Different clothes, different faces, even a different way of moving. He hears German, Afrikaans, Italian, a bit of English.

In the plane to Windhoek he sits beside an Italian who is traveling with a group. The Italian is reading a guidebook. He occasionally underlines things with a pen.

To Hofmeester's surprise, even on this short flight they are served a meal. Meat with beans. He eats a few beans, he's not particularly hungry.

"First time?" asks the Italian in almost unintelligible English, once the trays have been collected.

"First time what?"

"Africa? First time?"

"First time," Hofmeester says. "My first time."

"For me," says the Italian, "second time. I love Africa."

Hofmeester nods.

He falls asleep, he wants to sleep, long and deeply. A winter sleep that gradually fades into total absence from all that lives, from life itself.

The landing is quite turbulent. Hofmeester is not afraid, but the shaking makes him nauseous. Afraid as he is of having to vomit, he holds on tightly to his seat.

As they near the runway, he looks out the window, expecting to see a town, or at least a few houses. But all he sees is desert. Various shades of desert. A bit of red, a bit of gray.

The airport at Windhoek is small, almost endearingly so, Hofmeester thinks.

He takes his hat from the overhead locker. He lets the others go first. He's not in a hurry. The others are.

There is only one other plane on the tarmac, a big gray one with "Luftwaffe" written on it. Once Hofmeester has descended the stairs, he stops for a moment. He breathes in the hot air. Here is where Tirza landed, here is where she walked. This is Windhoek. Here close by is where she must be, this is where she wanted to go.

He looks at the sky. Fluffy clouds, lots of fluffy little clouds. The heat doesn't seem too bad. It's a dry heat.

After about ten minutes in line, he gets to a stocky female customs official and hands her the form he had filled out on the plane.

"What's the reason for your stay?" she asks.

"Tourist" was what he'd written on the form, wasn't it? So doesn't she believe him?

He pulls the envelope from his inside pocket. He shows her the photo. "My daughter," he says, "I'm paying her a surprise visit."

She doesn't look at the photograph. She stamps his passport.

Beside the baggage carousel in a little, rather stuffy hall, he really notices for the first time how different he looks from the other travelers, with his neat Dutch trousers, his somewhat worn but still smart sports jacket, his hat. He is the foreigner. There is no denying it. It's a status he doesn't mind having. The temporariness that clings to the foreigner suits him. The foreigner's actions never reach very far, the consequences of his actions are limited, the foreigner will be gone again before long. He is, by nature, light. As a leaf. As a plastic bag.

Once he has his suitcase, he walks resolutely to the arrivals hall. At moments like this a determined tread is what it's all about. In fact, he's always been temporary. A temporary man, that's why it was so easy for them to put him out to pasture.

The arrivals hall looks charming to him too. A dollhouse. In one corner he sees an automatic teller machine. He tries to withdraw some cash, but it doesn't work.

The exchange office is closed.

Pulling a handkerchief out of his pocket, he wipes his face. He takes a deep breath. Looks around fruitlessly for something that might resemble a tourist information counter.

Then, with a determined tread, he walks outside. His shoes, which he polished before leaving Amsterdam, still shine.

A young man calls out: "Taxi?" He has a hold of Hofmeester's suitcase, and before Hofmeester quite realizes what is going on, he finds himself in the back of a blue Mercedes from the 1970s.

"Windhoek?" asks the dark young driver.

"Windhoek," Hofmeester says.

"It's more than forty kilometers from here, you do know that, boss?" The cabbie speaks English with an Afrikaans accent.

"I didn't know that. But it doesn't matter. I have to get to Windhoek."

The car starts. Hofmeester rolls down the window.

"Where to in Windhoek, boss?" the driver ask.

"I don't know yet. I'm looking for a hotel, a good hotel. Can you recommend something? And please don't call me boss."

He takes the handkerchief out of his pocket again, but it's impossible to get his face dry.

"I won't call you boss. My name's Jefried. Aren't you with a group?"

"No, I'm not with a group. I'm traveling alone."

Jefried drives fast. But there's no traffic, so that helps. Still, Hofmeester searches around on the back seat for a safety belt. Just because he has to learn to die doesn't mean it has to happen right this minute.

There is no belt. Or rather: there is a belt, but it's broken.

"Come to see the country?"

"I've come for my daughter."

Hofmeester produces the photo and shows it to Jefried, who pulls it out of his hand right away.

Jefried hits the brakes. They have pulled over to the side of the road, in the sand. The cabbie opens the glove compartment, pulls out a dingy booklet, fishes a crumpled photograph from it and presses it into Hofmeester's hand.

Hofmeester stares at five little black children.

"My family," Jefried says. "My children."

Hofmeester opens the car door. "I need to get out for a minute," he says, "for a breath of fresh air." He climbs out of the car, holding his hat and briefcase.

He puts on the hat, clenches the briefcase under his arm. No traffic on the road. No houses. Sand and withered grass. Here and there a tree almost bare of leaves. Gently rolling hills. The sand seems to change color every kilometer. Where am I? Hofmeester asks himself, what am I doing here? What is this?

Now Jefried has climbed out as well. He stands beside Hofmeester.

"Don't be frightened, boss," Jefried says. "I believe in Jesus."

"I'm not frightened, I just needed some fresh air. And don't call me boss."

A blast of wind knocks off Hofmeester's hat. Jefried goes running after it. Like a dog. He gives the hat back to Hofmeester, who doesn't put it on, but holds it in his hand.

"Jefried, where are the animals?"

"What animals, boss?"

"Don't call me boss."

"What animals, sir?"

Hofmeester points at the half-scorched and empty plain.

"The wild animals. Where are they? I don't see anything."

"They're hiding, sir, this is the middle of the day. It's too hot for them. They're there, but we don't see them. They see us though, sir. They see us and they smell us."

They stand there like that. Two men along the side of the road. The first one waiting for the second, the second man waiting for something he can't put his finger on. For a cue. A memory. The memory of what it was he actually came here to do.

"Sir," Jefried says after five minutes, "would you mind if we drove on to Windhoek?"

Hofmeester shakes his head. "No, not at all. Which hotel were you going to take me to? I looked for a tourist information counter at the airport, but everything was closed. What's a good hotel? Are you familiar with the hotels in Windhoek?"

"In Windhoek. There are lots of good hotels there. What are you looking for exactly? Big hotel, little hotel?"

"The best hotel."

The best one, why not? On his first night in a strange land, Hofmeester doesn't feel like taking any chances. And it probably won't be so expensive here. Now that financial independence has gone by the board, a bit of money wasted should be no problem.

Jefried starts thinking out loud, and Hofmeester notices how dry his mouth is. He climbs back into the car. The picture of Jefried's children is still lying on the back seat. He hands it to the driver, and in return gets back the photo of his youngest daughter. He glances at it again. Lively eyes. Yes, perhaps that is the first thing that strikes you when you look at Tirza, in this picture at least. Lively eyes. Comforting eyes, in a strange way. As though the world has put her mind at ease, and now she must do the same thing for the world.

"Heinintzburg," Jefried says.

"What?"

"Heinintzburg."

"What about Heinintzburg?"

"That's a good hotel. Just the thing for you, sir."

Heinintzburg. It sounds like the name of a village somewhere in the Teutoburger Wald.

"Heinintzburg," Hofmeester repeats.

"Are you German?"

Jefried starts the car.

"Me? No, Dutch."

"But they speak German there, right? Where you come from? Don't they?"

"They speak Dutch."

"But you speak German?"

"I studied German at school. And criminology. Never finished that. I was offered a job at a publishing house, an offer I couldn't refuse. All expectations were that I would become a publisher."

Jefried seems to have stopped listening. He's driving fast again. He turns on the radio.

When Hofmeester sees the first houses of Windhoek, he asks: "Do you take euros?"

Jefried looks at him in the mirror. "Rather not, sir, but there are banks, we can stop."

"Cash machines?"

Jefried nods. "This is a modern country, sir. We have everything. Except jobs. There aren't enough jobs. Otherwise we have everything."

In a street that looks like the main street of a ghost town, they stop at a gas station. Klein Windhoek, Little Windhoek, is the name of this place, Hofmeester saw that on a sign. Little is about right.

Jefried points him to a cash machine.

Tirza's father walks over to it.

The only other people on the street are black. Maybe it's the neighborhood, maybe the time of day. The few whites he sees are passing in cars. While he's putting his Dutch bank card in the machine, he looks back at Jefried's blue Mercedes.

Jefried could drive away now. With Hofmeester's things. It's not a lot, but it would be troublesome.

Despite the fact that his luggage contains little of value, he is distressed by the thought that Jefried could take off with his suitcase. A colored man remains a colored man. As he stands at the cash machine he tries to keep an inconspicuous eye on the car, and notices at the same time that three attendants from the service station are staring at him.

He pushes the hat down more firmly on his head.

Here he is able to withdraw money, but he has no idea of the exchange rate for the Namibian dollar. Atypically, he has not prepared well for this trip. That is: not at all. He decides to withdraw one thousand Namibian dollars. That should be enough for Jefried.

From the service station it's only five minutes to the Heinitzburg Hotel, which turns out to be a little castle on a hill.

Once Jefried has parked the cab, two young man walk up to the Mercedes. They take care of Hofmeester's luggage. They try to pull the briefcase out of his hand as well, but he doesn't let them.

"How much do I owe you?" Hofmeester asks Jefried.

"Four hundred, sir."

He gives Jefried four hundred and fifty. And Jefried says: "If you need me, sir. I drive safely. You've seen that already. Wherever you want to go. Walvis Bay, Swakopmund. Or further. To the north. I know this country. If you need me. Call me." Jefried hands Hofmeester a business card.

The business card belongs to someone else. Jefried has written his name and phone number on the back.

Hofmeester walks up the hill, he follows the signs for the reception. He has put the card in his inside pocket.

For a moment he thinks: What if they don't have a room for me? But if that's the case they'll just call a taxi for him, if he has to go somewhere else. It doesn't matter. He's here, that's what matters.

The lobby looks neat and clean. A tray with apples, a rack full of postcards. A man in a white shirt bids him welcome and asks Hofmeester what name the reservation is under.

"I didn't make a reservation," he says, "I'm sorry, I ran out of time. It all happened rather unexpectedly. Do you have a room for two or three nights?"

"How long exactly? Two or three?"

"Three nights. It depends."

The man doesn't ask what it depends on. He starts flipping through a big book.

Twenty yards away, the two boys are still standing beside Hofmeester's suitcase. They look at him. They wait.

"You're in luck," the desk clerk says. "We have a room for you. A large, lovely room."

"Excellent," Hofmeester says. And then: "Thank you." As though someone has done him a favor.

Hofmeester takes an apple and bites into it. He's feeling dehydrated.

"Could I ask you to fill in your information here?"

The clerk turns the hotel register around to face him. He fills it out neatly, where he lives, his passport number, the only thing he doesn't know is where he's going from here. He leaves that blank.

"I'll show you to your room," the man says.

The room is, indeed, lovely. Even by European standards, and those are the only standards Hofmeester knows. A four-poster bed, a bathtub, a rose beside the sink. Africa is not bad. At least not for Hofmeester. So far.

The two boys carry in his suitcase together. He gives them both a tip.

Then he is alone. He sits down in a chair. This is Windhoek, Namibia. This is where she wanted to go, his daughter, this was where her trip around the world was always going to start, from the word go. Well, trip around the world, her trip through Africa. She has read a lot about it, she has seen photos. She is socially involved, Ibi is involved too. That's the way young people are. But they grow out of it.

He puts his briefcase and hat on the bed. His sports jacket he hangs in the closet. Trousers and shirt over the back of a chair. In the bathroom he takes off his underpants and socks.

He looks at himself in the mirror. Not too bad for a man his age. The belly, the sag. The decay.

Then he steps into the shower.

The water feels good, it gives him energy. He lets it run over him for minutes, without moving. Without thinking.

Then he pulls on a pair of light slacks and a short-sleeved shirt. From inside his sports jacket he takes out his cell phone and the envelope with the photo. He is about to leave the room, then remembers and takes the briefcase and hat from the bed.

He walks downstairs to the reception desk.

"Can I get a bite to eat here somewhere?" he asks.

The desk clerk nods and leads him to the other side of the building, where there is a patio with a view of the town.

There's no one else there.

He settles in. Puts the envelope and his phone on the table. The briefcase and hat on a chair.

A girl asks him, in not particularly friendly fashion, what he would like to drink.

"I'd like to eat something too," he says.

He turns on his phone and slides the picture out of the envelope.

Lively eyes, that's right. That's it. They are so incredibly lively, those eyes. Still, strange that no one notices that she has such lovely lips and cheekbones, beautiful cheekbones.

After a quick glance at the luncheon menu, he decides to take the chicken kebab. They can't do much to ruin that, chicken kebab.

"And to drink?"

He looks at the menu again.

"Mango juice."

"Mango juice and chicken kebab." She doesn't write it down.

"Oh, and a glass of white wine."

"Instead of mango juice?"

"No, both. Along with the mango juice. At the same time."

He has coverage here, he sees. After a moment's hesitation he calls the wife, but she doesn't answer. "I've arrived," he speaks into her voicemail, "I'm in Windhoek. It looks fine here. I'll talk to you later."

Reaching into his briefcase, he pulls out the manuscript and his pencils. He rummages around in the case and sees that he has forgotten his pencil sharpener. One of these days he'll have to buy one here in town.

When the girl brings over the beverages, he sees her looking at the photo on the table.

"My daughter," Hofmeester says with a friendly smile, "my youngest daughter, Tirza."

"What?"

"Tirza."

He has to spell it for her. It seems to be an unfamiliar name in this part of the world.

"She's here in Windhoek," he says, "she's here on vacation. Maybe you've seen her around."

It's not a question, and therefore it receives no reply.

He drinks the mango juice thirstily, then the wine.

In the distance he can see a building. The tallest one in town, he suspects. The sign on it says "Kalahari Sands." He stares at it for a while. Kalahari Sands.

Now that he's here, he needs to come up with a plan. But the longer he looks at the city down below, the more empty and bare his thoughts become. Whatever he thinks of, it seems pointless to him before he even begins.

He eats the chicken quickly and greedily, like a dog, without drinking anything along with it.

From his briefcase he takes out Tirza's notebook and reads the text messages she received the last few months. Funny that she didn't write down the name of the sender. Or might they all have been from the same person?

Maybe these are her own sent messages? No, that doesn't seem likely. These are messages she received. She has something of the bookkeeper about her, the way she's noted all these texts so assiduously. Some of them are incomprehensible to an outsider, like "I m here," or just one word: "Kiss."

On a blank page he writes in pencil: "Windhoek, Kalahari Sands. Daddy calls the sun queen." And below that, the date: August 10, 2005.

When the girl comes to clear the table, he asks: "Where do young people go, here in Windhoek? Tourists from Europe, where do they go?"

She looks quite blankly at this man at her table.

"Where do they go?" he asks again. "The tourists?"

"To the coast," she replies. "Or the desert."

He puts on his hat, gathers his things, goes to the reception desk and asks for a city map, which they say they don't have. In the end he gets a photocopy of an old map of Windhoek.

"How far is it to the center of town?"

"By car?"

"On foot."

"Fifteen minutes," says the desk clerk. He finds a green felt pen and draws on the map the route Hofmeester should take.

After five minutes, the sidewalk ends. Hofmeester finds himself walking on the sandy shoulder of a road. The heat has made his feet swell. It hurts to walk. His leather shoes were not designed for this.

Occasionally Hofmeester stops and wipes his face. He can feel the sweat running down his neck. There are huge wet spots under his arms. Later, when he gets back to the hotel, he will take a bath. He enjoys the thought of that.

After about twenty minutes he reaches Independence Avenue, which, the desk clerk told him, is Windhoek's main street.

He looks to the right, then to the left. Someone bumps into him.

At least there are people here. And shops.

He decides to go left. Maybe he should ask someone for directions, but he doesn't quite know what to ask. How does one do something like that? Ibi and the wife would have had done it immediately. Shamelessly, with no qualms. Without thinking twice.

Hofmeester goes into a shopping center, but he doesn't buy anything. He does withdraw another thousand Namibian dollars. He looks at the clothing and souvenirs in the shop windows.

The air conditioning perks him up. Without much interest, he examines a few more display windows.

After walking down Independence Avenue for ten minutes, his feet hurt too badly to go on. To his relief he sees, just up ahead, a gelateria-annex-pizzeria called "Sardinia." Here too. Italians are everywhere. Even in Windhoek.

He limps into the restaurant, where most of the tables are vacant. The waitress is sitting in a corner. He picks a spot close to the counter.

It is pleasantly cool inside. Taking a paper napkin, he wipes his forehead and the back of his neck. Then he crumples the napkin into a little ball and stuffs it in his pocket.

A tomboyish young waitress, who could pass for Italian, asks what he would like.

He orders an espresso and a glass of white wine. Maybe she actually is Italian. It would be a good way to strike up a conversation: "Are you Italian?" And then to pull out the photo and ask: "Do you know this girl, have you seen her around?" How do you search for children when you've never done that before? Grownup children, in a foreign country?

Long after his drinks are finished, he remains seated. He realizes he is going to have to ask her. He has to start somewhere, so why not here? Especially here, in pizzeria-annex-gelateria "Sardinia."

From the table next to his he takes another paper napkin and wipes his neck, his forehead, his throat.

He rummages through the briefcase.

Then he gets up and walks as casually as possible to the counter.

"The bill, please," he says. And right after that he pulls the envelope out of his inside pocket and lays the photo on the counter. "Are you Italian?"

"I was born here." She answers without looking at him.

"Oh, I see. Have you ever seen her?" he asks.

"Who?"

He points at the photograph.

The girl who looks so much like a boy tosses a quick glance at the picture. She hands Hofmeester the receipt.

"No," she says, "who is it?"

He counts out the money, clears his throat. "My daughter," he says. "My youngest daughter, Tirza."

And as he says it, while he's still speaking, he senses that she is not going to believe him.

"Mom," she calls out.

He feels like putting away the picture. But he waits. Maybe the mother will know something.

A woman with bleached blonde hair comes up to him.

"How can I help you?"she asks.

Again he points to the photograph.

"My daughter," he says. "You haven't happened to see her?"

She shakes her head. She looks Tirza's father up and down, from head to toe.

"Tourist or businessman?"

"I'm here for my daughter," Hofmeester says emphatically.

The realization that he doesn't look like a father forces him to accentuate the father in him a little more. He puts away the photograph. First in the envelope, then in his pocket. He needs to ask something that will put the people at ease. For example: "Is there a large Italian community in Windhoek?"

"Are you looking for entertainment?" The mother's voice sounds pointed, but not uninviting.

He shakes his head, walks slowly towards the door.

The mother follows him.

"Are you looking for entertainment? A special kind of entertainment?"

He is standing outside on the sidewalk now, the mother too.

Hofmeester needs to explain himself. He understands that. You can't just show people a picture of your child and say: "I'm looking for my daughter." They need an explanation. Otherwise they become suspicious. Background information.

"I'm here for my daughter. She has never been to Africa before. Three weeks ago she left for Windhoek. Three weeks ago to the day. And since then we haven't heard a thing."

The woman looks at him now as though she understands everything. He feels relieved.

"No phone call, no email. My wife says: 'It's because we're so old.' But what sense does it make to stay home and wrack your nerves when you can go to Namibia? What's a fourteen- or eighteen-hour flight these days? And how much could it cost? How do things go here? With the tourists? Are there a lot of tourists?"

He speaks a bit excitedly, but she smiles. Yes, mothers understand things like that. She'll help him. She'll tell him where he needs to go.

"You're looking for a special kind of entertainment," she says, "am I right? I can help you."

He starts to walk away. After five steps he turns again. She is still standing in front of her pizza parlor, watching him go.

Hofmeester dofs his hat. "Thank you," he calls out. "Thanks for your trouble. I'll come back sometime for sure, but I'm here for my daughter."

Then he starts walking up the hill, towards the Heinitzburg Hotel. Every step is an effort. His shoes feel four sizes too small. His underpants grate uncomfortably. He needs to rub some oil on his anus. Everything is raw.

From the moment he leaves Independence Avenue, the street is deserted. Every once in a while he hears footsteps behind him. He has the feeling someone is following him, maybe more than one person, but he doesn't dare to look back.

He concentrates on each step he takes, in order to feel less pain. He tightens his grip on the briefcase. He has the feeling that Tirza is in that briefcase, that he has brought her along in it. That all he has to do is open the case and she will appear.

3

By the time he gets to the hotel, he seems to be on the verge of a heart attack. At the desk, his face red and wet and his chest hurting, he asks for the key.

"What time would you like to have dinner, Mr. Hofmeester?" the clerk asks.

"Eight, eight-thirty."

"One person?"

"One person."

As soon as he is in his room, he drops onto the bed. He takes off his shoes, closes his eyes, rubs his feet gently.

He lies there like that for at least twenty minutes. Half asleep, half awake.

The sound of the wind rouses him and he looks at his watch. A shutter or a door is slamming somewhere. Almost seven already.

Soon it will be time to go to dinner.

He undresses quickly, fills the tub, and lies down in it.

In the hot water he is able to relax. For a few moments this seems like a normal trip, the kind he used to take sometimes. Visiting an author in his native country, a book fair, a conference now and then. Especially at the start of his career, sometimes, he went to conferences.

Only when he hears his cell phone ringing in the bedroom does the purpose of this trip come back to him. Without drying off first, he steps out of the tub and goes for the phone as quickly as he can. He almost slips and falls, but he's able to keep his balance.

It's the wife.

"And?" she asks.

"And? I'm here. That's all I can say right now. Tomorrow I'll make plans. Go by the embassy. The youth hostels. But Windhoek doesn't seem dangerous. Small, mostly, just small. I don't think they would have stayed here long. Tourists always go to the coast or into the desert, or so they tell me."

She listens without saying much back.

"Call me if you hear anything," she says. "And check your email every once in a while, maybe she'll send you an email."

"I'll do that."

"And Jörgen."

"Yes?"

"No, nothing. Forget it. I'll wait here for you. I'll take care of the garden for you."

He climbs back into the tub. He still has a while before dinner.

In the room beside his, he hears people talking. He tries to hear which language they're speaking, but the sound is coming from too far away.

The talking changes to weeping. But when he listens carefully, he hears that it isn't weeping, it's panting.

Before leaving the tub he rinses the foam off his body under the shower and hums his favorite song. "*Bei mir bist du schön*, please let me explain. *Bei mir bist du schön*, means you are grand."

He dries himself thoroughly with a big white towel and, in passing, thinks about the cleaning lady in Amsterdam.

For the first time now, he opens his suitcase.

He puts the present for Tirza in a drawer. His own clothes he leaves in the suitcase.

He decides to put on a suit, some aftershave. You never know who you'll run into.

Only when he goes to put on his shoes does he notice what a problem that is. His feet are worn to a tatter. The shoes weren't made for heat like this, not for swollen feet. He worms into them with difficulty.

Although he had hoped that dinner would be served on the patio, he has to sit inside.

The waiter shows him to a corner table. Hofmeester is one of the only diners wearing a suit. The other guests are dressed more casually. Like tourists in Africa. But he just isn't the casual kind.

During the appetizer he tries to read a bit in the manuscript. But he stops soon enough. The wine and the fatigue of the journey numb him a bit, but pleasantly so. His mind wanders.

He puts the photo of Tirza on the table, in the hope that someone will ask him about it. But no one asks a thing. The service here is quite adequate. To be sure. No comment is made about the photo. The wine is refilled regularly, and he had ordered a bottle as soon as he sat down. It's not your Italian Gewürztraminer, but it tastes good anyway. He toys with the photo, holds it up at arm's length. Still, no one asks about Tirza. No one wants to know who she is, no one is interested in what Hofmeester might have to say about her.

After the main course, the pain in his feet becomes so acute that he takes off his shoes and socks. The tablecloths here are long. No one will notice.

Relieved, he orders a lime parfait. It's hard to eat when your skin is being pinched.

As he spoons at the lime parfait, he tries to draw up the balance of his life, the way it has gone until now. He can't. Looking back, he finds nothing of which to be proud. What he sees lying there, in the ground fog of his own history, are little, relatively insignificant defeats. No big ones, except a few. Day-to-day defeats, indistinguishable from the daily shame.

He is proud of Tirza. That's true. Of Tirza. Proud. Without really knowing why. What was his contribution there? Seed. The preparation of a few hot meals. The disciplined regularity with which he took her to swimming and cello lessons, although as it turned out later he had been a bit too disciplined in that. No, it is pride without a reason. Senseless pride.

He decides to order coffee and cognac at the bar. The dining room is empty now, except for a few tables. Apparently everyone here goes to bed early. Through the window you can see the lights of Windhoek below. After dark it looks like a fairly big city.

He hobbles over to the bar. A waiter comes after him.

"Sir," the waiter says, "you forget these."

He holds up Hofmeester's shoes and socks.

Hofmeester looks at his feet. They are bare.

Shame is something so overwhelming, so much more powerful than affection.

The waiter hands Hofmeester his shoes and socks.

"Thank you," he says. "Thank you very much. I forgot all about that. How kind of you." And he sits down at the bar.

He doesn't dare to pull on his socks and shoes. The shame disappears, but only slowly, the shame never disappears completely. He stirs his coffee earnestly, as though nothing has happened.

The photo is now on the bar. As evidence. A statement.

The barkeeper does take a look. He has no choice. There's no one else at the bar. Who else would he look at or listen to?

"My daughter," Hofmeester says. "Tirza. She's eighteen."

"What does she do?" the barkeeper asks.

Hofmeester shrugs. "She's going to go to college," he says. "But she still doesn't know what her major will be. One week it's musicology, the next it's psychology. And the week after that it's classical literature. She has no idea. She has plenty of time."

He takes a toothpick and discreetly removes something from his mouth. His speech—he notices it himself now—is slurred.

"And where is she now?"

Tirza's father looks at the photograph as though the answer can be found there.

"Here," he says. He looks around. "Here. She's here somewhere. In Namibia."

He says it as though it is a secret.

The barman pours him another glass of cognac. The last guests are leaving the dining room. Only the staff is there now. Smiling, the barman looks at Hofmeester.

"Are you here on your own?" he asks.

Tirza's father nods. Slowly and deliberately. "I'm here alone," he says, "but not really alone, I'm here to surprise my daughter. So actually, we're together. I wanted to leave my children money. Lots of money. A substantial sum. So that doors would be opened to them that remained closed to me. But it's gone. The money. It's been gobbled up. And you know who gobbled it up?"

He gestures to him, he waggles his fingers. He wants the barkeeper to come closer.

"The international economy," he whispers. "After September 11, 2001, when the markets collapsed—they had already collapsed, actually, but then they collapsed even further—my hedge fund vanished. It ceased to exist. From one day to the next. Bye-bye, hedge fund. As though it had never been there at all. Mohammed Atta gobbled it up. Do you remember Mohammed Atta?"

The barman shakes his head.

“Doesn’t matter,” Hofmeester says. “What matters is that people think: Mohammed Atta is dead. Mohammed Atta is no longer around. That’s what they say. But there are thousands of Mohammed Attas, tens of thousands, millions of Mohammed Attas. Millions of them. The international economy can’t handle that many Mohammed Attas. He was at my house too. Mohammed Atta.”

Hofmeester slips his daughter’s picture into his inside pocket, straightens the hem of his sports jacket. Slowly, he bends down to pick up his shoes and socks. His back cracks.

“Will we be seeing you tomorrow?” the barman asks.

Hofmeester nods. He walks to his room, barefooted. He hears the sound of insects. The night produces buzzing noises, just like in his head. Yes, Mohammed Atta had been to his home, that’s something that will make them sit up and take notice. Something they’ll ask him about someday.

He has to circle around the outside of the hotel in order to get to his room. With every step he takes, he has the feeling that he’s stepping on something, but he doesn’t know what. Little animals, probably. Ants. Leaves. Moss.

In his room he kneels before the minibar. He takes out a can of Coca-Cola and a little bottle of white wine. He presses the can against his forehead, opens the wine. Tomorrow, he decides, tomorrow he will buy new shoes. Tomorrow he will get going.

Before undressing, he stands in front of the mirror. He raises his arms. Then lowers them. And raises them again. There is nothing peculiar about the way he looks.

He places the photo on the nightstand, next to his watch. There are spots on the photo now, greasy fingerprints.

He wakes up four times that night. Once he gets up to drink some water. In the bathroom he realizes that the water here might not be drinkable, that it might make him sick, and he goes back to bed. A realization comes to him. He realizes that maybe something terrible has happened, something irrevocable. That the moment when you see each other again might not come. But he realizes it in his dreams.

In the next few days Hofmeester buys a pair of sandals, goes by the Dutch embassy, walks calmly and systematically around the city, and enters a few cheap hotels. Here and there he shows people Tirza's photo. Occasionally he starts a conversation. No one is able to help him.

Twice he goes to an Internet café, but there is no email from Tirza, only from the wife.

At one of the hotels they actually think they did see Tirza, but they are sure that she was a Swiss girl who was traveling with a group.

"That can't be her," Hofmeester replies. "That's someone else."

At the Heinitzburg Hotel, meanwhile, everyone knows that Hofmeester is searching for his daughter. At breakfast and dinner, people speak to him reassuringly. The staff says that she has probably gone to the north of the country, another time someone says that Tirza has most definitely gone to the Sossus Valley, in the desert. The next morning someone else says that perhaps she has hitched a ride towards Cape Town. Hitchhiking to Cape Town is popular among the tourists these days.

Hofmeester makes notes in the little book that belonged to Tirza, but his conscientious note-taking can't cover up the fact that his own doubts are growing all the time. He doesn't know what else to do, he doesn't know where to go, he has no idea where else he could look. He spends hours walking around a hot city with a photo in his inside pocket, a hat on his head, a briefcase under his arm A lady at the embassy tells him: "This is a hopeless task. You can't do anything here. Go back to Holland. Wait there and see."

The hopeless task, hasn't that been his specialty from the start?

The people at the Internet café know him by now too. The man with the hat who is waiting for a message from his daughter. They sympathize with him, as one does with the character in a movie, but it doesn't help. And his feet still hurt, even with the sandals.

Each morning he extends his stay at the hotel by one day. Where is he supposed to go? Back to Holland? Out of the question. He talks to the wife on the phone on two occasions, receives and responds to her friendly but often rather peremptory emails. She sounds troubled. She says: "I decided to tell Ibi anyway. I mean, what sense does it make not to tell her?"

All Hofmeester says is: "That wasn't necessary. She'll show up in a few days. There's no need to upset people."

One day, late in the afternoon—he has spent a few hours walking around town again, the envelope with the photo in his inside pocket, the briefcase under his arm—he climbs the hill towards the Heinitzburg Hotel. In a little while it will be getting dark.

Hofmeester's mouth is dry. For the first time, he thinks he is able to distinguish between pain and despair. Despair is dull and a bit crippling, also numbing. Despair is not a feeling, it's the opposite; the awareness that you are no longer feeling, that feelings are in the process of slipping away, of leaving you behind on your own.

On a quiet street not far from the Hertz rental agency, he notices that someone is walking right behind him. He clenches his briefcase even more tightly. Although the fear of the first few days has faded, he's still prepared for anything. This is Africa.

He quickens his pace.

"Do you want company, sir?" he hears someone say.

Without stopping, he turns and sees a little girl of—how old could she be, nine or ten?—in a slovenly dress.

He picks up the pace. The voice echoes inside his head: "Do you want company, sir?" Is it, in fact, a question at all? Isn't it more like the confirmation of a condition? "Do you want company, sir?" Why hasn't anyone ever asked him that before? It's so obvious, it would have been so little trouble. "Do you want company, sir?" Five words, that's all. Five simple words.

There is no one else on the street. Even the guard who usually stands in front of the Hertz agency is nowhere in sight. He has probably gone to the toilet. Even guards have to urinate sometimes.

The girls walks along with him, or rather: she jogs along with him. He turns into a street that is not on his route at all. This is not the street that leads to the hotel. He never goes down it normally. He has to go back. He has blisters on his feet, they hurt, the corns too.

"Do you want company, sir?" she asks again.

"No, no," he hisses without stopping. "Go away! Go away!"

At an intersection he stops and waits for the light to change. He wipes his face with a handkerchief. She's still there. Behind him at first, now beside him.

Once he has put away his handkerchief, the child takes his left hand.

She doesn't let go. She holds onto that hand.

The light turns green. He stands there for a moment, holding the child's hand. She's supposed to let go now, but she doesn't. She holds on to him. Then he crosses. With the little girl.

They walk in silence towards the Heinitzburg Hotel. Man and child, white and black, a person with a hat and one without.

At the next crossing he glances over at her. Fleetingly and in embarrassment, as though at forbidden fruit.

Only then does she notice that she is wearing no shoes.

He sees her feet. He thinks: There could be trash on the street, glass, garbage, scraps of food. Softly, he squeezes her hand.

She doesn't squeeze back. She just holds on tightly.

At the desk, when he asks for his key, she is still holding his left hand.

The desk people look at him and at the child, but no one says anything. As on every other day, they hand him the key, and as on every other day, they ask: "Will you be eating with us in the restaurant this evening?"

Hofmeester nods.

Back in his room, he sets the child down in a chair and sits down on the bed. His hand is clammy with sweat.

He takes off his hat, wipes his face with the handkerchief.

The child looks at him, it follows his movements. Alert, but not alarmed.

Hofmeester puts his head in his hands, he ask himself what he has gotten into. He came here to look for Tirza. Now he has a child in his room, a black child in a frumpy dress and no shoes.

He opens the minibar. "Water?" he asks. The child nods. He pours water into a glass and hands it to her. She drinks thirstily.

He sits down on the bed again and watches her. Then he takes off his sandals. His right foot is bleeding in two places. He rummages through his overnight bag for bandages.

They are his last bandages.

When he is done treating his wounds, he asks: "What's your name?"

"Kaisa."

"Ka-isa?"

She nods.

"I'm Jörgen," he says. "Jörgen Hofmeester." He speaks English with her, slowly and clearly, as though he were back at the Frankfurter Buchmesse, talking about books that, to be frank, don't really interest him at all. They are disappointing, but then what isn't disappointing compared to Tolstoy?

They sit across from each other like that. He on the bed, she in the chair.

Somewhere in the distance he feels a headache coming on. The start of an illness. Flu.

After fifteen minutes, she asks the question she has already asked him twice.

"Do you want company, sir?"

He shakes his head, opens his briefcase, and remembers that he still hasn't bought a sharpener. He was looking for something in his briefcase, but what?

Her glass is empty.

"Water, Kaisa? More water?"

She nods.

He opens the minibar and hands her a bottle.

This time she drinks less thirstily. He starts to analyze the situation, to the extent that that is possible, to the extent that his life still allows for anything like analysis, reflection, perusal, conclusions.

There is a child in his room. That child is making no move to leave. He will have to give her something to eat, for starters.

"Are you hungry?" he asks.

She nods.

He looks at his watch; another hour, then they can go to the dining room.

"In an hour," he says. "In one hour we will eat something." He wonders whether she knows what that is, an hour.

They sit across from each other in silence again. She looks at him, but it never becomes an impolite stare. The child looks at him as though he were on TV, a puppeteer who might open the curtains and start the show any moment.

He pulls the envelope out of his inside pocket. He shows the photo to Kaisa.

The child takes the photo, glances at it. Then she looks at him.

Hofmeester sits back down on the bed, the same way he'd been sitting there all this time.

"Tirza," he says to Kaisa. "That's her name. When she was your age, I used to read out loud to her. From Dostoyevsky too. *Notes from Underground.* One can't begin too early with a certain dose of nihilism. Because you have to go through it. Like a train through a tunnel. And she understood that. She was . . ." He almost can't get the word out of his mouth, but still he succeeds. "Gifted," he says in a tinny voice. "She's gifted."

Again he feels that he is about to break down, like a machine. His lip trembles. But he braces himself, everything is under control.

There is a knock at the door. The chambermaid. She wants to make the bed for the night. He lets her in. They know each other, the chambermaid and the guest. They have seen each other a number of times before. Still, it remains uncomfortable. And now, with Kaisa in the room, it is more uncomfortable than ever.

The chambermaid acts as though she doesn't see the child. Hofmeester withdraws to the bathroom while the bed is being made. He brushes his teeth.

Once she has left and he has come out of the bathroom, he finds the curtains closed. Unlike other evenings there is not one little chocolate on the pillow, but two.

He chuckles, he can't help it.

Hofmeester takes them, the chocolates, and hands them to Kaisa.

She puts them both in her mouth, at once. Without taking her eyes off him. She is alert.

"Tirza," he says, "has lively eyes. Like yours." He takes the chocolate wrappers from her and tosses them in the wastebasket.

Another forty-five minutes. Then he will have to take this child with him to the dining room. He doesn't know how he's going to do that. He and this black child in her frumpy dress.

He opens the minibar and takes out the little bottle of vodka, raises it to his lips.

"Would you like to wash your hands?" he asks.

He doesn't wait for a reply. Hofmeester holds out his hand. He leads her into the bathroom, opens the faucet, gives her a bar of soap. She is barely able to reach the sink.

The child washes her hands. When she's done, she looks at him questioningly.

"Would you like to wash your feet, too?"

She shakes her head.

"It might be nice."

She wears her hair in a little ponytail, Hofmeester notices now. He hadn't looked carefully at her before, he hadn't dared.

"Are you sure? I'm going to wash my feet too. You can join me if you like."

He fills the tub halfway, fetches the bottle of water from the room for her, and for himself the little bottle of white wine that is replenished in the minibar each day.

He sets her down on the edge of the tub with her legs in the water.

"Not too hot?" he asks. "Is it okay like that?"

She nods.

Hofmeester hitches up his trouser legs and sits beside her. They take a footbath, the man and the child. Compared to the child's skin, his looks not only pale, but actually unhealthy, sickly. Corroded.

It does him good, a footbath. Even though he knows that his problems will be none the less for it. For the first time since he has arrived here, his problems have actually become acute.

In a little while he will have to take her to the dining room. How is he going to do that?

The wine is finished.

He pulls his feet out of the water and takes another bottle of vodka from the minibar. Hurriedly, and with a grimace, he knocks it back. It is a medicine.

"Come," he says, "let's get something to eat."

On the bathroom floor he spreads out a big white towel. He picks her up, puts her feet down on the towel.

Hofmeester kneels and dries them thoroughly.

"Between the toes as well," he says, "otherwise you'll get athlete's foot. You know, I have two daughters. Older than you. Actually, I didn't want to have children. I didn't want to get married either. My wife talked me into it. I had plans. Different plans."

Her left foot is dry. Now her right foot.

"I wanted," he says, "to prove that neither God nor progress was dead, only love." He laughs as though he's just told a good joke. He holds onto her ankles and laughs.

"All done," he says. "Now it's my turn, then we can go eat."

Behind a closet door—he remains discreet—he changes his clothes, puts on his suit. Because he has a guest with him this evening, he wears a tie.

He puts on his hat. Quickly, he drinks a minibar bottle of gin. The vodka is finished.

The child watches.

"It's medicine," he says. "Against shame." He takes out another tiny bottle of gin and drinks half of it. "And you know what shame is? It's civilization." Standing up, feeling a slight shudder, he empties the second bottle as well. Still holding it in his hand, he sits down on the bed. "Ah, civilization," he mumbles. "That's it. Civilization. Civilization. Civilization."

He gets up, picks up his briefcase, then takes her hand. Like her, he is barefooted.

They walk to the dining room.

When he comes in, the other diners stop and look at him. And at the child. People look from him to the child and then back again.

The girl who has waited on him countless times says: "Well, Mr. Hofmeester, I see you have a guest this evening."

He nods. He helps Kaisa up onto her chair, takes off his hat. He feels like dying, but he pushes on. The conversations around him have fallen still.

This evening, by way of exception, he orders a bottle of flat mineral water. He leans over to the waitress as though he wishes to confide in her. "Please do excuse the bare feet," he says. "It's the heat. Swollen feet. The fluid can't get out. The fluid collects in the feet. Why in the feet? I have no idea. But it collects there, the fluid. Please present our apologies. To the other guests as well."

"Of course," she says, "Mr. Hofmeester, of course. No problem."

In the bread basket she puts on the table there are, as always, a few long breadsticks.

He breaks one of them in half, hands it to Kaisa. "Eat," he says.

She eats, staring at him the whole time.

He taps his index finger softly on the tabletop. The conversations around him pick up only haltingly.

"Well," he says, not knowing what to do, "Kaisa, I come from Holland. Do you know where that is? It's in northern Europe. A long way from here. A fourteen-hour flight. Eighteen, if you have to change planes. I'm . . ."

He hands her another long breadstick. This time he doesn't break it in half.

"Or would you rather have normal bread?"

She shakes her head.

"I've almost reached retirement age. In fact you could say I'm already retired, because I'm no longer actively employed. They wanted to fire me, but the man from the legal department said that was impossible, because of my age." He wipes some crumbs off the table.

This restaurant plays the same music every evening, he realizes only now. It strikes him that he has had to listen to the same songs a hundred times. Every evening the same songs, three or four times over.

"I am," he says, calmed by the medicine, but still a little ashamed, "an unhappy person, in the final account." Again he laughs as though he has just told a joke. He has done a lot of laughing this evening. "But," he goes on, "no one ever noticed. Why would they? What reason would they have had to notice that? And when it comes to unhappiness, you have to ask yourself . . ."

The waitress hands him the wine list, and without giving it much thought he orders a South African Chardonnay. "And for the young lady," he says, "a soft drink? Coca-Cola?"

She nods.

"Coca-Cola?"

She nods again. This time with more conviction. Even with a certain enthusiasm.

"Coca-Cola," he says, "for the young lady." As though they've been traveling together for days. As though this is all they do. Eat, sleep, get up, eat. They seem to be completely in tune.

He gives her another breadstick.

She eats with relish.

"Unhappiness," he says, "that's what we were talking about. Everyone's unhappy. And once you've figured that out, it doesn't matter anymore. Happiness is a pose, a myth, a form of courtesy, at parties and dinners. I'm unhappy, but no unhappier than anyone else, that's what I've always told myself when the going got hard. My unhappiness was average. I have two children. A nice house. A very nice house."

Suddenly he stops talking.

"Now it's your turn to tell me something."

She stops eating. She still has a piece of the breadstick in her hand. In her little fist, that was more like it. And Hofmeester thinks about the qualification "little fist," as though thinking about himself before he became this way, before he became defined, when he was still barely shaped or not at all. A story still unspun, one that could head in any direction.

"All right," he says, "so now you tell me something. How old are you?"

The Chardonnay arrives. He tastes it without tasting. Hurriedly, almost rudely. Even though that is precisely what he does not want to be. But he has no patience anymore.

He waits, for a minute, for the child's Coca-Cola to be served.

"Would you like a slice of lemon in it?" he asks. "Do you like that? Tirza, my daughter, always drank her Coca-Cola with a slice of lemon. Even when she was little. But she wasn't allowed to drink it very often. We didn't approve of Coca-Cola. I didn't approve of Coca-Cola."

She shakes her head. No, no lemon.

"Fine. Then let us drink to . . . To this evening, to our having met. To you, Kaisa, to you."

He ticks his glass against hers.

She drinks like him. With abandon.

When the menus arrive, he notices that she can't read, or at least not well enough for this. She stares at the menu the way she stares at him. Her mouth half-open. As though something is on its way. As though the menu is going to start talking.

He orders chicken soup for her. Chicken soup, they say, is also a medicine.

"And after that," he asks, "fish or meat?"

She looks at him, the last piece of breadstick still clenched in her little fist.

"Fish or meat?" he repeats. "Kaisa, what will it be?"

"Meat," she says.

Lamb, he decides. Always a winner.

For himself he orders the springbok carpaccio for starters, and then fish.

The waitress writes down their orders, then walks away. He sees her whispering to her colleagues and he suspects, no, he knows, that they are talking about him. For the first time since his arrival in Namibia, there is someone else at his table. A black child. "And he claimed he was looking for his daughter," they're probably saying. "But what he was really looking for was entertainment. Special entertainment."

He leans back.

"Eat," he says.

She eats the last piece of breadstick, which she's been holding all this time.

"So where were we?" he ask. "Oh yes, how old are you?"

At moments like this, it is precisely the art of conversation that matters. All the cocktails parties he's attended, book launches, book fairs, they've been good for something, he has learned something from them.

"Nine," she says.

He leans his head in his hands.

"Then I'm more than fifty years older than you," he replies, "half a century, let's say, more or less. Half a century."

Again there is that look of hers. Neutral, but inquisitive.

"Fifty years is half a century. You know that, don't you? How old is your mother?"

The conversation is one-sided, but Hofmeester isn't about to give up. His life depends on it, at least that's how it feels. He takes a few more gulps of wine. It is the only effective medicine against shame.

"How old is your mother, Kaisa? Do you know that, how old she is?"

"Mama is at home."

She says it quietly and almost questioningly, but not entirely that either. In fact, in exactly the same way she said: "Do you want company, sir?" Almost questioningly, but not quite. As though she already knew that's what he wanted. As though she had seen that.

"Aha," Hofmeester says. "At home. Yes, as she should be. My parents are no longer alive. They died, one soon after the other. My own children were still little then. But they were never very enthusiastic as grandparents. Towards the end, they wouldn't open the door anymore. Not even when we came by to visit. We would have to turn around and go back to Amsterdam. Unpleasant for the children, because they thought they were going to see Grandma and Grandpa."

He pours her a little more cola.

He waits for her to say something, but what follows is silence.

Even more silence. So he resumes his monologue. He has to talk, as long as he's talking everything is fine, and besides, this time at least it doesn't matter what he says.

"My parents weren't sick. But they weren't completely healthy, either. Or actually, they were, extremely healthy, too healthy. They were converts, and they were afraid the village would find out. That they were converts, that in fact they had been raised as . . ." he lowers his voice, as though about to tell a terrible secret, "as nothing. No one was supposed to know that. And no one knew it. They were afraid of being different, of standing out. At first only outside their home, but later at home as well. It became second nature to them. They hated everything that deviated from the norm. Do you understand? Everything that wasn't white. Everything that was different, everything that was sick. Because everything that didn't fit the norm was sick. For my parents, there was no different between psychiatric patients, Jews, Negroes, homos; all incurably sick. They themselves had been cured of a sickness, but they were still afraid that something had been left behind, a scar, a residue, a stubborn hearth of infection that might flare up again. Which is why my father once beat a Jewish man to within an inch of his life. Right in front of his hardware store. With a shovel. So that no one in the village would doubt that he had been cured. They took that seriously, being cured. But, anyway, towards the end they stopped opening the door. Even when we showed up."

He looks at the child. She sees me as a puppeteer, he thinks. I'm the puppet show.

"Do you know what I really like about you?" Hofmeester says. "You're someone I can talk to."

The first course arrives, and Hofmeester tells her to be careful, that she must blow on the soup before putting the spoon in her mouth. He takes the spoon, shows her how. And she blows.

That is how they work their way through the meal. The people at the other tables pay less and less attention to the pair at their table.

Are they actually a pair? Hofmeester asks himself. A temporary one perhaps, but still, anything more than that? A pair. Pairs are temporary by definition, even more fleeting than youth itself.

After the main course, of which she eats very little, he talks her into taking a dessert, a sherbet, and he orders his usual cognac. This trip is turning out to be more expensive than he'd expected. But what does it matter? Once you've lost almost everything, you might as well lose the rest.

Before the cognac arrives, he gets up and goes to the men's room. In front of the urinal he steps in something wet, and remembers that he has to die. That there is only one way out, that all other exits have been blocked. Standing with his bare foot in someone else's urine, he tries to imagine his own death.

As he pees, he supports himself against the wall with one hand. He feels a slight dizziness. Nothing serious.

Back at the table—the sherbet and cognac have arrived—he says again: "I really like the fact that we can talk to each other, Kaisa. Really talk. What does your mother do, anyway? And your father?"

She shrugs.

"Is she a housewife?"

Again the child shrugs.

And as though it only occurs to him then, he asks: "Won't she be worried? Shouldn't you call her?"

She shakes her head. "No," she says with a mouth full of sherbet.

"She won't be worried? Won't she want you to come home? Of course, you're a big girl already."

And as he empties his glass of cognac, he realizes that it's actually something you have to learn, that you might even have to have a certain flair for it, for dying.

He gets up, helps the child off her chair. She takes his hand.

As he does every evening, he walks to the door.

As they do every evening, the staff says: "Good night, Mr. Hofmeester."

But despite all the medicine he's taken, he sees that they look at him differently than on all those other evenings. In their eyes, he has become someone else. He is no longer the man who is looking for his daughter, he is the man who is looking for special entertainment. Looked for it, and found it.

Still, that's not the way it is. He wishes he could explain himself further. He wishes he could say: "It's not what you people think."

Across from hotel desk, he stops. "All right," he says, "it's been a lovely evening. I don't know where you have to go, where you live, but I can call a taxi for you."

In Africa, the night makes noises. He hears insects everywhere. Unfortunately, he knows very little about insects.

Above the desk is a machine to electrocute small flying pests. Every time a fly is electrocuted, the machine crackles good-humoredly.

"Where is your house?" he asks. "Is it far away, Kaisa?"

She doesn't let go of his hand. Even though the moment has arrived to do so. He needs to go to bed. To sleep. Sleep for the dying.

"Do you live in Windhoek?"

She doesn't seem to hear him. Like him, she is now staring at the machine for electrocuting small flying pests. "Do you want company, sir?" she asks, more timidly than at first, with less conviction.

His gaze remains fixed on the machine above the door to the reception area. Then he looks at the child. "No, no," he says. "But if you want, you can sleep here. If it's too late for you to go home."

He takes off his hat, wipes his forehead. Windhoek is at a high altitude, almost six thousand feet above sea level. It cools off pleasantly here at night, but still he feels hot.

"It's fine," he says, "if you want to sleep here. It's a double room. I don't know what they're going to think of us. But what they think of us doesn't matter to you, I suppose, and not to me either, really. I'm a stranger in these parts. For a long time it did matter to me, what people thought of me, because you are what people think of you. But here, now, in this country? I'm a tourist. What can they expect?"

They walk to the room, hand in hand.

He turns on the lights, hangs up his hat.

She sits down in the same chair where she sat earlier.

"Well," he says, "here we are again." He turns on the lights in the bathroom too.

"I don't suppose you have a toothbrush with you?" he asks. "No, you don't have anything with you. That's young people for you. Go out to sleep over, don't take anything with you. Footloose and fancy free. But wisdom comes with the years. I always had to bring all kinds of things to Tirza when she slept over at a friend's. You can borrow my toothbrush, I'll clean it off for you first."

He holds his toothbrush under the tap and, as he cleans it, looks at the child.

She is sitting there, motionless.

"Come on," he says.

He gestures to her.

She approaches hesitantly. He puts toothpaste on the brush. He kneels and brushes her teeth. Even though his toothbrush is actually too big for her mouth.

It has been a long time since he last did that, but he hasn't forgotten how.

She opens her mouth without question or protest.

He brushes her teeth thoroughly.

"All right," he says, "that's all. It's important. Your teeth."

He leads her to the bed, throws back the covers. On the side where no one sleeps, usually.

She needs a pair of pajamas. Sleeping naked is a possibility, but it doesn't seem like a good idea to him.

"Wait," he says.

He goes to the closet and takes out the dress that the wife bought for Tirza. He removes it carefully from its wrapping paper, which he puts back in the drawer.

"Take off your dress," he says.

Within a second, she is out of her clothes. He hands Tirza's dress to her.

"They're not real pajamas," he says, "but it will have to do. You have to wear something at night. It cools off around here. This belongs to Tirza."

With a bit of difficulty—it's been a long time since he put clothes on a child—he helps her into Tirza's dress.

She looks as though she's playing dress-up for a party. He shakes his head and can't helping laughing a little.

A game of dress-up, that's what it has all boiled down to. This trip. His life. Everything.

He tucks her in.

He undresses in the bathroom, keeps his underpants on. He didn't bring pajamas either.

Then he lies down on his side of the bed.

"All right," he says, "sleep tight."

Her head on the big, white pillow. Comical, that's the word that occurs to him when he looks at her.

"All right," he says again, "it's time to go to sleep. It's been a long day."

She sits up. "Do you want company, sir?" she asks.

He shakes his head slowly.

"Stop it," he whispers. "Stop that nonsense, Kaisa. Not today. It's too late. Is that what I look like to you? Like someone who wants company? No, really not." He reaches over her to turn off her reading light.

"I'm not used to sleeping in the same bed with strangers anymore," he tells her, "so please excuse me if I sleep rather restlessly.

For the last few years, I've always slept alone. Until my wife came back. I like using one side of the bed as a table to put papers on, newspapers and books and so on. But after she came back, I couldn't do that anymore. Good night."

Now he turns off his own light. He lies awake for at least twenty minutes. Now and then he holds his breath to hear whether Kaisa is asleep.

In the middle of the night he wakes up. He has been dreaming about Tirza. They were cycling in the Betuwe. His parents were still alive. He gets up, turns on the light in the bathroom and sits on the edge of the tub. His thoughts are still a bit muddled. Vaguely he recalls that there is a child lying in his bed. He has been in Windhoek for more than a week now. He tries to remember the last time he heard Tirza's voice. It was when he called her and got her voicemail. Quietly, he starts talking to her.

"Tirza," he says, "I'm in Windhoek. A strange city, not a city really, more like a village. I have to talk rather quietly, because I'm not alone."

At eight-thirty he wakes up. Kaisa is already awake. She is sitting up in bed, looking at him.

"Good morning," he says.

He rubs his face. Reaches out to the nightstand and grabs his watch.

"So late already," he says.

Without showering, he puts on his clothes.

"Do you sleep over often?" he asks.

More silence.

"I asked whether you sleep over at other people's places very often?"

"Yes," she says.

"You can stay for breakfast, of course, but after that I really must get going. I'm here for my daughter. We've lost her. Do you know what I call her? The sun queen."

He lifts her out of bed. The dumpy dress is all she has to wear. Carefully, so as not to damage it, he helps her out of Tirza's dress.

He repacks it, puts it in the drawer and hands her her own dress. She doesn't put it on. He squats down in front of her.

"We're going to breakfast," he says. "You need to get dressed."

She seems like she's planning to rub noses with him, but finally presses her lips against his. He jumps back.

"No, no," he says, "there's no need for that. That's not necessary."

He feels how warm it has become already, and notices that the clothes he is wearing now stink a little. What difference does it make? Body odor in Africa is not like body odor on Van Eeghenstraat.

"I need to get you dressed," he says. "We're going to breakfast."

Hofmeester helps her put on her dress.

For a moment he remains sitting there, as though he has forgotten something. "After breakfast," he says, "we can brush our teeth."

The photo of Tirza is on top of the minibar. He puts it in the envelope and tucks the envelope into his inside pocket. This morning he actually puts on his sandals.

Slowly, he and Kaisa walk to the breakfast buffet on the patio.

Two of the tables are occupied. He recognizes people from last night.

Again, conversation stops when he appears with the child.

They sit down. The guests are supposed to serve themselves from the buffet, but Hofmeester doesn't get up yet. Walking is difficult.

The girl who waited on them yesterday asks: "Coffee, Mr. Hofmeester?"

He nods. "And for the young lady," he says, "hot chocolate, does that sound good? Hot chocolate."

He didn't put on his hat this morning, but he has his briefcase with him. It contains everything he needs.

Just when he is about to get up and show the child to the buffet, the phone in his pocket starts to buzz. It's the wife.

"Why haven't you called me?" she asks.

"Were you worried?" he whispers, even though no one can understand him. "Don't be, I'm fine."

"Not about you. About Tirza."

"I don't think she's in Windhoek anymore. I think she's gone to the coast, or the desert. I'm going to go and look there."

"Go and look? Jörgen, this isn't a scavenger hunt. Isn't it about time you went to the police and reported her missing?"

"I know it's not a scavenger hunt. Do you think I would make an eighteen-hour flight for a scavenger hunt? What do you expect?"

"What I expect is for you to do something."

"Are you worried?"

"Ibi is worried. She calls me twice a day. She's getting me worried. She's making me nervous. I know it's ridiculous, but still. Have you already gone to the police?"

"The police? This is Namibia."

"Okay, but you'll have to go to the police at some point. Or would you rather do that in Amsterdam?"

"I'll call you later. Everything's under control. She'll show up. You said so yourself. She's just forgotten about us for a bit."

He closes the cover on his cell phone, puts it away.

The child is looking at him, noncommittal as always.

"My wife is worried, she thinks it would be a good idea for us to go to the police."

Hofmeester stands up, walks with the girl to the buffet. In front of the buffet, the child takes his hand. She points to a croissant. He puts the croissant on a plate.

"Yogurt?" he asks. "Yogurt with fruit?"

When they are back at the table and the child's hot chocolate has arrived, he says: "I have to tell you something, Kaisa. Actually, it's sort of funny."

He picks up his teaspoon and tastes a bit of her yogurt.

He leans over to her, still holding the spoon. "My life is drawing to a close," he says, "and there's nowhere for me to go."

There is something triumphant in his voice, he hears it too. As though, somehow, it is an achievement to have nowhere to go. To no longer be able to escape.

She nods. It must be his tone of voice that brings a smile to her lips. The sound of someone broadly telling a joke, the sound of a man about to start tickling a child.

"People," he says, "make stories out of their lives. That's how they impose order. That's what stories are about. Imposing order. The story that I made of it is . . ." He takes a gulp of coffee. "Has gotten out of hand."

For a moment he feels the calm sorrow he knew in the hills of Southern Germany, when his daughter was lying in the clinic.

"When there's nowhere for you to go," he says, "then the game stops, then you've finally arrived at reality. My wife and I used to play quite often. Back then. I was the rapist with a knife, she was the girl on the bike. In Vondelpark. In Amsterdam. At night. We played, my wife and I, what we did with each other was a game."

He shrugs. He doesn't know what else to say.

When the girl comes by to freshen up his coffee, he sees on her face that he can no longer stay at this hotel. He sees a disapproval that is hardly different from rage. They are not fond of travelers in search of special entertainment, and although he wishes he could explain that he is not looking for special entertainment, not even for normal entertainment, he knows there is no use.

He gets up, helps the child off her chair, and walks to his room. As they walk, the child grabs his hand. It doesn't surprise him anymore when she does that. It seems like the way it's supposed to be.

At the door, he stops. He bends down. "You have to go home now," he says. "Where do you live, Kaisa?"

She doesn't reply, she looks right past him.

Again he repeats the question. Still no reply.

"I need to look for my daughter, Kaisa," he says. "She's lost. People are getting worried. People are getting terribly worried. Where do you live?"

He takes both her hands in his, squeezes them gently. "Where do you live?" he asks.

Her reply is no surprise, still it sickens him. "Do you want company, sir?"

He has always considered it nonsense, when people say they are sick with fear. He never believed it. Now it's happening to him. He is sick with fear and he doesn't know what he is afraid of, or even whether there is anything to be afraid of.

Hofmeester opens the door, the little girl slips past him, sits in the chair which she now seems to consider hers.

"All right then," he says, standing in front of the minibar, "you can stay one more day. I like it, because we can talk to each other so well. We understand each other, Kaisa. And do you know why? Because we don't disapprove of each other."

He pushes his hat down firmly on his head, picks up his briefcase again, and takes the child's hand. In front of the mirror, he stops for a moment.

"All expectations were that I would become a publisher," he says to Kaisa, looking at her in the mirror, "but do you know what happened? I didn't become a publisher. I lost my ambition, I fell from faith. My ambition was my faith. A person without faith isn't much. Impervious, perhaps, steel-plated. A tank. Look at us, Kaisa? What are we? People without faith. But still, we do have each other. I float in space, unattached to anyone. Until you took my hand, there at the traffic light. Then I became attached to you. That's how it is. You could have taken someone else's hand, but you took mine. What were you thinking, Kaisa? What did you see when I came by? Was it my hat? Had you approached a lot of people that day?"

He walks with her into town. She on bare feet, he in sandals. Every once in a while he stops at an intersection and asks: "Where are we going, Kaisa?" They eat lunch at a service station, and at four in the afternoon they stop for a soft drink at a billiard parlor. Occasionally Hofmeester says something, about his daughter, his job, Africa. Kaisa listens without replying. Sometimes she whispers: "Money, sir. Money." Then he hands her a few Namibian dollars, but she has nothing to put them in. All she has is her dress. From a street vendor, he buys her a brightly-colored shoulder bag. He shows her that she can put the Namibian dollars in it. "Look," he says, "this is how you open it, and this is how it closes."

It looks good on her, the bag, it perks her up a bit. She totes it in one hand like a doll.

At a park in the center of town he sits down on a bench, close to a playground. There are swings and two slides, a big one and a little one. Hofmeester is the only white person there. First Kaisa climbs the low slide, but after a few times she dares to climb the big one too. Hofmeester walks over to her, through the sand, it itches between his toes, it pricks at his wounds.

"Come on," he says at the bottom of the slide. "It's not scary." He catches her as she comes off the slide, and remembers how he once caught his own children in this same way.

At five o'clock he arrives at the door of the Internet café just off of Independence Avenue. He hesitates for a moment. Then he goes down the stairs to the café. He sits down at his usual terminal, lifts the child onto his lap.

"I come here almost every day," he tells her quietly, "to see whether she's sent me an email."

He opens his inbox, but the only messages are from the wife, and some spam. He doesn't read the emails that have come in, not even those from the wife, he sits at the computer and does nothing. Softly, he strokes the girl's hair.

His surroundings are something he takes less and less into account. He forgets what people around him might think. He withdraws. What they think about him is unimportant. Here in Namibia, they can think whatever they like.

Then he opens the briefcase and takes out Tirza's notebook. He flips past her transcripts of the text messages, only here and there does his gaze fall on a message, a doodled drawing. Probably something she drew while talking on the phone. Some people draw while they're on the phone, but he doesn't.

He takes out her pocket diary, flips through to the page with her email address and password.

Hofmeester looks at it as though it were a letter. A letter not intended for him, true, but still a letter.

Then he types in www.yahoo.com, then Tirza's user name, and then her password: ibi83.

He sees the emails he sent her himself, which were never read, he sees emails from boys and girls she knows, emails from people he has never heard of.

He doesn't read any of those, instead he clicks on "Compose."

The computer here is slow. He waits nervously for the next window to open.

He types in his own email address, and as subject: "Finally."

That's the right word: finally.

With the child on his lap, he starts writing an email.

"Dear Daddy," he types, "sorry that it took so long to get in contact. But I'm in the desert and there aren't a lot of phones around here. The landscape is beautiful."

He stops typing, glances at the child on his lap. "That's right, isn't it? That the landscape here is beautiful?"

He wipes his face with a hankie, then the child's as well. Despite the air-conditioning in the Internet café, they are both sweating.

Then he goes on: "We're going to stay here for a while. As soon as we reach civilization again, I'll call. Don't worry. I'm happy. It's okay. I feel just like a princess. Lots of kisses, hello to Mama. Tirza the sun queen."

That's the way she always signed her cards and letters: Tirza the sun queen.

And that bit about the princess was something she had once said to him when he took her to Paris for a long weekend. The bathroom in their hotel room was huge and fancy. That evening she had taken a bath and shouted to her father, who was lying on the bed watching TV: "Dad, I feel just like a princess."

He got up to look at his daughter in the bath. "That's exactly as it should be," he'd said. "Exactly as it should be." For a moment he had felt light, light and untroubled.

He re-reads the email he has just written, then hits "Send."

The child has remained on his lap all this time. She's sitting comfortably. She has been following everything Hofmeester says and does, and at the same time it seems to have all gone right past her. Kaisa draws no conclusions about what she sees and hears.

Now he opens his own email. He reads the email Tirza just sent to him.

"Tirza the sun queen," he says. More to himself than to the little girl on his lap. As though surprised at what he himself has written. As though he hadn't really expected it.

Pulling the phone from his inside pocket and staring at the email Tirza sent him, he calls the wife.

She answers quickly. She was probably sitting in the garden, or on the couch in the living room. Working on an old crossword puzzle.

"It's me," he says.

"And? Any news?"

The child on his lap reaches for the keyboard. Gently, he pushes her hands away.

"Yes, there's news. I've received an email from Tirza."

Hofmeester keeps his eyes on the message he typed himself. It seems to him that he doesn't know it very well, not well enough. He should read the message over again. He should learn it by heart.

"She's in the desert," he says.

"Okay. Is she all right? What happened? Why didn't she call or mail us before this?"

The wife's voice sounds very different from what he's used to.

"Everything's fine. Nothing has happened."

The wife doesn't sound relieved. Her relationship with Tirza has always been complex. There is apparently no relief at the news that her child is still alive. Being alive isn't exactly what you would call a relief. Death, perhaps. Hofmeester should think about this. When he has time. He himself doesn't understand what it is that's keeping him so preoccupied.

"So what does she write?"

Hofmeester reads the entire message aloud. He is satisfied. The choice of words, the short sentences. The message isn't too long, yet still it contains pretty much everything it should. That bit about the princess, he likes that. It touches him.

"So what now?" the wife asks. "Are you coming home?"

Hofmeester wipes his lips with the back of his hand. It was a question he hadn't counted on. Any other question, but not that one. "I'm going to go to the desert first," he says. "Now that I'm here anyway, I'm going to pay her a visit. It must be lovely there. Empty, lots of sand, apparently it's the way life looked when it just began, when life began."

For a moment she says nothing. It sounds as though the wife has to think about that. "And the dress," she says, "the dress I gave you, will you take that along for her?"

"Of course, of course I'll take it. It's in my closet here. It's going with. She'll be pleased with it. It's a real desert dress."

"Keep in touch," she says, "get in touch soon. I'm pleased. And Ibi will be pleased too." In her voice he hears a strange sort of doubt.

Doubt, he thinks, about whether she will ever hear from him again. The doubt in the way you talk about someone who has vanished forever.

"I'll do that," he says, "I'll call. As soon as I get back from the desert, I'll call you."

"I miss you."

He switches the receiver from one ear to the other.

"What do you mean?"

"Just what I said."

"That's not necessary," he says, "there's no need to miss me. I'll be back. And besides, it's too late, I mean: to miss me, to miss anyone, actually."

"It's so empty around here. Do you blame me for anything?"

He looks at the child on his lap.

"No, nothing. I mean, well. Things go the way they go. I don't blame you for anything. I mean that. Not for anything."

"Tell Tirza I love her, if you see her." Again he thinks he hears that doubt in her voice, but he must be imagining it.

"I'll do that."

"And Jörgen . . ."

"Yes?"

"Everything's going to be all right, isn't it?"

He leaves the question unanswered. He says bye and hangs up.

He lowers the child to the floor and pays at the counter.

"And?" the girl from the Internet café asks. "Any news? Have you heard anything?"

"She's been found," he says, "my daughter, she's been found. She's in the desert."

"Didn't I tell you?"

He nods.

"Children," the girl says, "don't realize how they make their parents worry. I have a two-year-old of my own, and only now am I starting to understand my own mother."

“Oh yes, that’s right, you only start understanding your parents once you have children of your own.” Hofmeester is talking off the top of his head. He never understood his parents, and they never understood him.

He leaves the Internet café. At the corner of the next street, in front of the offices of South African Airways, he tells the child: “You have to reassure people. It’s not always decent, but it has to be done. A reassured person is a happy person. I can’t stand sorrow, panic. I want people to be calm. I hate hysteria. Emotions, they’re the scourge of our times, emotions.” He pronounces the word like a curse. “The way they’re bandied about, the pride people take in them, the faith they have in them,” he whispers, “madness, all madness. Feelings are a religion that ought to be disbanded.”

Then he opens his briefcase to check whether he took Tirza’s notebook and pocket diary with him when he left the Internet café. Everything that should be in the briefcase is in it. But he still hasn’t bought a pencil sharpener. He keeps forgetting.

“I’m going to say goodbye to you now,” he says. “This is the parting of the ways. It was enjoyable, but I must be moving on. I’m going to my daughter, and you are going to your family. Thank you for everything.” He hesitates, doesn’t know what else to say. People are bumping into him with their shopping bags. “Now you really have to tell me where you live.”

He takes her face in his hands, squats down, and says again in a harsh, despairing voice, as though he is afraid he will never get rid of her: “Where do you live, Kaisa? Won’t your mother we expecting you to come home pretty soon now?”

She shakes her head. “I have to work,” she whispers.

He takes the child by the shoulders and shakes her. “Where do you live?” he shouts, there on Windhoek’s main thoroughfare. “Kaisa, where do you live?” People turn and look.

She says a name. Of a street, a family, a neighborhood, maybe even a café. He has no idea.

She says a name that he forgets right away and that he barely understood to start with, but it is something, it is enough.

"I'm going to take you there," he says.

On Independence Avenue he hails a taxi. Once they're in the taxi, he has the child repeat the name she told him. He has no idea where they're going, but they are going to Kaisa's house. That much is certain.

The taxi is one of those that you share with other people. Passengers climb in and climb out. Hofmeester has to hold the child on his lap. Sitting beside him is a fat black woman with two shopping bags, and beside her a man. After a while, sitting in the little car makes him claustrophobic.

"Does your mother worry too, sometimes," he asks the child quietly, "when you don't come home for a few days? Does she get worried then?"

The child seems to shake her head, but it could also be Hofmeester's imagination, it could be the rocking of the car. The driver is going fast. The road is bumpy.

"I do," he says. "From the moment Tirza was born I saw calamity lurking everywhere, everywhere I looked I saw disaster. One little moment of inattention, that was all it would take. In order to be punished forever. Through Tirza I saw the world as it is, dangerous, dangerous through and through. Hostile and irrational. A heating pipe, an elevator door, a bathtub, danger everywhere. Pain everywhere. Little children have no fear. You have to teach them to fear, you have to drill it into them, you have to teach them to tremble. 'Ow,' you have to say, 'that's ow. And that's ow. And that's ow too.' You have to scare little children, otherwise they'll die."

They are driving through parts of Windhoek he's never seen before.

The child looks out the window with a bored expression, Hofmeester thinks. As though she's been here so often. As though she's seen it all so many times.

"And joy?" he says. "That's what people ask you then. Joy, life is a joy, isn't it? Sure, I experienced joy. When Tirza was little, for example. Sometimes I walked with her to cello lessons. I would tell her stories, or she would explain to me how everything worked. That was a joy."

He pronounces the word "joy" the same way he pronounced "emotion." A word he can hardly get past his lips, a hostile word.

"You've also brought joy into my life, but what's it amounted to besides that? Not a whole lot, let's be honest. Joyless, that's what it was. For days at a time, for weeks at a time. I'm not complaining. There are probably other people with more joy in their lives, but not a lot. When I had to edit manuscripts, I used to put four pencils on the table, four pencils all of exactly the same length. There was joy in that for me. I looked for joy in the details."

They both stare out the window now. There aren't a lot of people on the street.

"It was nice," he says quietly, "the time we had together, it was very nice, I won't forget you. But I have to move on."

The fat woman with the shopping bags gets out, along with the man. Now Hofmeester is alone in the taxi, with the girl. She climbs off his lap.

They drive past the airport for domestic flights, it's called Eros, which is a peculiar name for an airport. Eros Airport, the name of an airport where you go looking for special entertainment.

It looks to him like they are leaving the city.

"Where are we going?" he asks. "We're going to your mother, to your family, aren't we?"

She nods.

It will turn out all right, he thinks. The child knows what she's doing. She came up and talked to him, she must know how to get home as well. She's not stupid.

Then they stop. Abruptly. Along the side of the road. Not a house in sight. A highway. But people are cycling here too. And walking.

"Is this where it is?" he asks the child. "Are we there?"

There is no reply.

"What happened?" he asks the driver. "Are you having car trouble?"

The driver mumbles something Hofmeester doesn't understand. He grabs the child by the shoulders. "Are we there?" he asks. "Say something."

He shakes her hard again.

She nods. "Yes, sir," she says, quietly but audibly.

He pays, too much, but he can't wait for the change, his patience has run out. He climbs out of the taxi. Now they are standing on the side of what they call a highway in Namibia.

Hofmeester sees shacks on the other side of the guardrail, little shacks with something like corrugated iron on the roofs.

Three men are roasting meat above a couple of upturned oil barrels

The sun jabs at his eyes. He pushes his hat down on his head.

The child takes his hand and pulls him along, past the men roasting meat.

There are no white people here, and he senses that no white people come here either. This is not the neighborhood for him, this is no place for him. They walk past identical structures that you might call houses. He's not sure about that. People live in them. That justifies calling them houses. But "structure" is better, closer to the truth. A house is like beauty, it's in the eye of the beholder. The child pulls him along, going faster all the time. "Wait," he calls out, "not so fast. Don't pull on my briefcase like that."

Every time they pass someone he lowers his eyes, knowing that he doesn't belong here, knowing that he is hated. He doesn't care. When there's nowhere for you to go, hatred doesn't make much difference.

Still, he is afraid. Afraid of being stoned or pulled apart by the limbs. Afraid of death, even though he doesn't know why. Death can't be much more joyless than life. But it could be quieter, calmer. More peaceful, that above all. In death he sees what he hasn't been able to find in life: healing.

"Where are you taking me?" he whispers. "Tirza, we can't do this."

Only after a few seconds does he realize that he has called her Tirza.

He doesn't bother correcting himself. She probably didn't hear him anyway.

The child walks faster all the time. Now he is the one holding on to her hand. If he lets go, he thinks, she'll slip away into one of these shacks and I'll be lost. I don't even know how to get back to the highway. They'll pull me apart at the seams, slowly and noiselessly. They'll punish me for crimes I never committed.

"Not so fast," he says. "My feet hurt."

Ten minutes later they are standing in front of a shack. The door is a shower curtain.

The vestibule consists of three empty pans on the ground. After that comes a real door, or at least a realer door. Everything is relative here.

It is dark inside. Hofmeester can't see a thing. He smells a great deal though. He smells garbage.

The stench makes him wobbly. The stench irritates him.

He closes his eyes tightly, opens them again, but still sees nothing.

The floor is sand, he can feel that through his sandals. He feels like crying for help, just to hear a human voice. He feels the strange urge to scream that he wants God to appear. Not that he is religious or on the point of becoming religious. But the thought that no one is looking down on him from on high, that only the child sees him, that no one else is looking, is unbearable.

"Kaisa," he says, "say something. Where are we?"

Slowly he grows accustomed to the dark. In one corner of the room, a person is lying on a kind of bed. Under a cloth.

A woman.

The child pulls him over to the woman.

"Is that your mother?" he asks. "Kaisa, is this your mother?"

He fiddles with his sport jacket.

He clears his throat. "My name is Jörgen Hofmeester," he says, hat in hand. "I have been keeping your daughter company for a few days. Or rather: she has been keeping me company for a few days. They were very special days. We talked to each other, and that was very pleasant. Your daughter is a warm person, a kind person."

The mother is not dead, because she opens her eyes. She blinks her eyes. The stench is making Hofmeester nauseous. In any case, he has the unpleasant feeling that he is about to become nauseous, that he will have to throw up. That he will start vomiting in this shack, like a dog, that he will have to crawl across the floor through his own vomit.

"Can you understand me?" he asks. "Do you perhaps speak Afrikaans?"

She moves her lips, she seems to be saying something, but no sound comes from her mouth.

"I can't understand your mother," he says to Kaisa. "I can't understand her."

But Kaisa remains silent as well.

"I can't understand you," he says.

He kneels down beside the bed. His trousers are stained anyway. In Africa, it doesn't matter much. This is not Van Eeghenstraat. Not a lot does make a difference in Africa. Different country, different rules.

There are flies on the woman's face.

He shoos them away.

"I can't understand you," he says, "but I'm a friend of your daughter Kaisa's, a friend from Holland."

Now she moves her hands.

He looks at it, he looks at the moving hands as though this were a kind of exotic puppet theater, and it takes a few seconds before he realizes that this is sign language. That she is speaking to him in sign language.

He stands up. Fiddles with his jacket again. He searches for something in the pockets, in the lining. "I don't understand sign language," he says, exaggeratedly loud and clear.

But he thinks: she's deaf and dumb, that's what it is. She is deaf and dumb.

"What is your mother saying?" he asks. "I can't understand her."

He screams: "I don't understand sign language!"

Hofmeester kneels down in front of Kaisa. "I have to get going," he says. "I have to go back to town. I'm going to give you a little kiss, Kaisa, I can't stay here. I'll give you a little kiss. Do you know what your mother is saying?"

Silence. The sound of insects. Flies land by the dozen on Kaisa's mother's head and body. A landing strip for flies, that's what this body is, no more than that. An airstrip.

"Do you want company, sir?" Kaisa whispers. "Sir?"

"No, no," he says. "No, I don't. She speaks sign language. Can't you see that? She speaks sign language. Your mother. She's saying something, but we don't know what it is."

He looks in his briefcase, but there's nothing in there. At least nothing that will help him any further.

From his pants pockets he pulls out all the Namibian dollars he has with him, finds some money in his inside pocket too, and sprinkles that money over the body of the woman on the bed. Her hands are still moving, manically. Maybe she's cursing him in sign language.

"Here," he says, "here. I can't understand you, because I don't speak sign language. Here's some money. For groceries. Or for . . . for whatever."

Then he leaves the shack like a fugitive. He runs, but his feet hurt too badly to keep that up for long. He passes identical structures. The stench of rotting matter follows him. Just like Kaisa. She comes after him. She's fast. Fast as lightning. She grabs his hand. And he grabs back. He squeezes Kaisa's hand.

They walk past the men who are roasting meat. They shout something to him, the men do, but Hofmeester doesn't stop. And he doesn't have any idea what they're shouting.

"A taxi," he says. "We need to get a taxi. Where can we find a taxi?"

He climbs over the guardrail, he waves his briefcase.

There are no cars.

He can still smell the stench. In Africa, death stinks.

"You don't mind our leaving your mother behind like that, do you?" he asks. "I gave her some money. She needs to see a doctor. I don't know what it is she's got, but she needs to see a doctor. A doctor who understands sign language."

He leans down to speak to the child.

"You need to go home now. You need to let go, you have to let people go, I have to let people go. But you're still too young to let them go, you have to hold onto them. That's why you need to go back to your mother."

A car passes. He waves his briefcase.

The car doesn't stop.

The wind comes up. It blows fine sand in his eyes.

"Kaisa," he says, "you can't go along with me. I'm going to the desert. I have nowhere left to go. I'm going to disappear. You can't go. Disappearing is something you have to do alone. In the end, you have to do everything alone, true enough, but disappearing you really have to do alone. You can't have other people around then, especially not children, Kaisa. No children."

He takes a few steps along the guardrail. A truck roars past. The light is starting to fade.

Kaisa follows him. She takes his hand. "Go away," he shouts. He takes off his hat and waves it like a fly-swatter. "Go away."

He squats down. He kneels on the hot asphalt. Hat in hand, briefcase under his arm.

"Kaisa, can't you see who I am?" he whispers. "Can't you see? Don't you understand? I am what made Tirza ill, I am the illness of the white middle-class. I am the eating disorder."

She remains standing where she is. His words don't impress her.

"What do you want from me?" he shouts, rising to his feet again. "What is it that you want from me?"

She comes closer. She tugs on his hand, he has to lean down. He leans, further, even further.

She raises her lips close to his ear and she whispers: "Do you want company, sir?"

4

At Hertz that same evening he asks for a jeep, but they don't have one. Not even a little one. All they have is a pale blue Toyota.

"Can I go to the desert in that?" he inquires.

"If you're careful," says the girl from the rental agency, "you can go a long away. But don't try to drive on in a sandstorm. If a sandstorm comes up, stop right away. Don't even drive slowly. There's no use. You'll only ruin the car."

"Stop right away," Hofmeester repeats.

Later that evening he leaves the Heinitzburg Hotel. Because he didn't check out on time, he has to pay for an additional night. He doesn't care. At some point, if you've lost enough, you also lose your thriftiness. You lay aside the thriftiness like a warm coat in summer.

The people at the hotel bid him a polite farewell, but clearly with a certain reserve. No one asks about his daughter. Whether she's been found. Whether that is where he's going now. The tip for the chambermaids that he left on the nightstand is brought to him by the girls' supervisor, an older white woman. "You forgot this, Mr. Hofmeester."

He doesn't dare to say that he didn't forget the money, he accepts it embarrassedly.

A young man who works during the day as the hotel gardener helps him with his luggage. Once the suitcase has been loaded into the back of the Toyota, the young man points to his own shoes. Gym shoes.

"They are too big for me, sir," he says. "At least four or five sizes."

The child holds Hofmeester's hand, she looks at the man, whose skin is even darker than hers.

"Someone gave them to me, but they are much too big," the gardener says. "I can't walk on them."

The car door is already open. They are ready to leave, Tirza's father and his traveling companion.

"Do you have any money for some good shoes?" The gardener's voice sounds as though the question is one he should not have asked. A forbidden question.

Hofmeester looks at the child's bare feet, at the man's shoes. For a moment he wonders what the problem is, having shoes that are too big. Better than no shoes at all, right?

Although Hofmeester has already given the man twenty Namibian dollars, he hands him another hundred. He puts the child in the passenger seat, shows her how to fasten the safety belt.

His briefcase and hat he lays on the backseat. As he pulls away, he waves to the gardener, the only member of the staff who has come out to wave goodbye to the Dutchman who stayed so much longer than planned.

Hofmeester drives in the direction of Okahandja. Night has already fallen. The radio is playing, tuned to the Namibian German channel. With schmaltzy popular songs. Music you don't hear anywhere else these days, or not often. "*Theo wir fahr'n nach Lodz. Steh auf, du altes Murmeltier, bevor ich die Geduld verlier. Theo, wir fahr'n nach Lodz.*" Hofmeester hums along. "*Du altes Murmeltier,*" he murmurs. Occasionally he looks over at the little girl beside him, but she doesn't seem to react to the music, or to his humming.

Thirty kilometers north of Windhoek he sees a sign: "Okapuka Ranch." He's going too fast to stop. I'll just drive on, he thinks. But after about three kilometers he decides to turn around. He has a feeling that there won't be anything else out there. That the Okapuka Ranch is the last chance to stop between Windhoek and Okahandja.

And he is tired, too tired to drive much further.

Standing at the gate of the Okapuka Ranch is a watchman. The man walks over to the car slowly, tormentingly slow, Hofmeester thinks.

Tirza's father eyes the child beside him the way a kidnapper eyes his hostage. He should really buy something for her, shoes, a new dress. If he can give the gardener a pair of shoes, he could buy shoes for her too, couldn't he? He has kept putting it off. He thought it might look suspicious, might summon up the wrong associations. He wasn't looking for special entertainment. At most, you could say he was looking for Tirza. That, at most.

"Can I help you?" the watchman asks.

"I'm looking for a room for the night. Are you open? Is the ranch open?"

The watchman looks at the child sitting next to Hofmeester. He's carrying a flashlight, which he shines into the car.

Then he asks: "Do you have a reservation?"

Hofmeester shakes his head.

The watchman doesn't do a thing. He just stands there. Again he shines the flashlight into the Toyota. On the backseat too, where Hofmeester's hat and briefcase are.

Then he slowly opens the gate. There is a sign warning that one enters the grounds at one's own risk. There are wild animals about.

The ranch office is far away, and the sandy road is full of potholes. Hofmeester hears the sound of rocks bouncing against the bottom. He says: "We're ruining the car." The child doesn't respond.

A dark, stocky woman is sitting behind the desk.

Hofmeester explains why he has come. He apologizes for not having made a reservation. She flips through a book, without showing much interest. There is no one else here, as far as he can tell. A little shop with souvenirs, but no one is in there either.

"Will you be wanting to eat dinner?" she asks.

"If that's possible."

She glances at her watch. "Well then, you'll have to be quick." She points at the child. "Do you want a separate bed for her? A child's bed?"

"She's my niece," Hofmeester says, "a double bed will be fine." And as he says that, he realizes that it sounds like a man who is looking for special entertainment and has found it as well. A man who has come to Africa to get what he can't get with impunity in his own country.

"Cabin Eleven," she says. She hands him the key. "The kitchen closes in thirty minutes."

He has to drive to Cabin Eleven. It's too far to walk with the luggage. The route follows a dry river bed. Again he hears the sound of rocks bouncing against the car.

The other cabins look deserted. The Okapuka Ranch doesn't seem to have a lot of guests. Either it's not the right season, or else the Okapuka Ranch isn't very popular. In Windhoek he had heard the owner of a bar complain: "Namibia has grown too expensive for tourists." At that, polite as Hofmeester is, he had ordered an extra helping of apple strudel. The country's German past, at a first glance, seemed to live on mostly in culinary curiosities and a few street names that people had forgotten to change: Bahnhofstrasse, for example. Hofmeester had stood staring at that street sign for a while.

He lugs his own suitcase into the hut. The child follows him. There is a fan on the ceiling. The bed is large, the room clean. There is a slight but not unpleasant smell of wood and disinfectant. This is the Africa of the tourists. The world can be divided into tourists and personnel. Those who can go away again, everywhere and always, and those who serve the tourists. Entertain them. Keep them busy. Those who cannot go away again.

Hofmeester washes his hands and puts on another shirt, one he wore in Windhoek a few times but that is a little less wrinkled than the one he's been wearing all day. The child walks around the room and stops beside a chair. While Hofmeester is buttoning his shirt, he looks at her and thinks about her mother. A woman on a bed. A woman who reminded him of a cow, mostly because of the flies on her face. He associates flies with cows. Especially when they land on the body and don't fly away again. Were they actually flies? Little insects, in any case. Scores of little insects. The animal kingdom is a mystery to him. He should read a book about it sometime.

"Has your mother always been deaf and dumb?" he asks, his fingers working at the buttons. "Was she born that way?"

The child smiles knowingly, or is Hofmeester only imagining it? She shakes her head. Aha, so the mother became deaf and dumb only later on in life.

"Your mother must have been a very pretty woman when she was younger," he says.

Then he takes her hand. "Come, let's get something to eat. Don't worry about your mother. I left her some money. I put some money on her bed, enough for some shopping. For a week. For a month. She needs to get out a bit. Too much sleep isn't good for a body. It can make you depressive. Physical activity, even if you're not feeling well, has a salubrious effect. Oh, your mother's bound to be okay."

He sounds like an old man jabbering away during the daily coffee hour, but he can't help himself: he needs reassurance. He needs to reassure.

They walk through the sharp grass in the direction of the restaurant. The child is holding his hand. She stops. "Sir," she says.

She points at an animal.

He hadn't noticed it. His thoughts were somewhere else. On Van Eeghenstraat. With the wife, the dress she bought for Tirza. For years she failed to get in touch, and suddenly she shows up with a dress for Tirza's big trip. Typical thing the wife would do. Unpredictable. Impulsive.

The animal is about twenty yards away from them. Hofmeester has seen them before only in pictures, in books. This is where Tirza wanted to go. Namibia. For the wild animals, but especially for something else, for the culture. Culture. He laughs.

The animal runs away, vanishes into the darkness, with barely a sound.

Hofmeester doesn't believe in culture, in as far as anyone could possibly believe in something like that. What is culture? His own survival strategy is one of adaptation, the ability to render yourself invisible. Or could that be culture too? The more invisible, the better. The invisible one is invulnerable.

But he tried to raise his children differently, as critical individuals who didn't view society as a safety net, but as a cage. Who excelled, in the swimming pool, at music school, in Latin and Greek, in mathematics and physics. When you excel, the money comes of its own accord. All true freedom is money, and if money can't buy freedom, then it's simply a matter of there not being enough money. But where he sees freedom, Tirza and Ibi perceive a capitalist conspiracy. That's back in fashion again. And no matter how Hofmeester insists that it is not a conspiracy, that it is freedom, they refuse to believe him.

As a child, Tirza had every reason to be happy. She was extremely, extremely gifted, she took part in swim meets and won them, she played the cello better than other children her age. And at the zenith of her extreme, extreme-giftedness, she decided to starve herself to death. A transgression, an outrage.

"Nice, isn't it?" Hofmeester says to the child. "Nice, isn't it?" He doesn't know whether he is talking about the animal they saw running away, about the sharp grass, the cabin, or simply the world in and of itself.

The dining room has no less than eighteen tables, but only three of them are occupied. By older people. South Africans from the sound of it, and two Germans just past middle age.

People look over at them. Even by Namibian standards they're unusual, the old white man and the young, the extremely young black girl. And as always there is that moment when one stands face to face with the shame, the moment when Hofmeester wishes he could set everything aright, wishes he could explain himself. But that moment grows briefer with each passing day. Every day he becomes a little more the man who people here have started seeing him as: a Westerner with an unmistakable bent towards special entertainment.

Isn't that, in the final account, the one true end of man? To become what others would like to see in you?

He and the child are given a table at edge of the dining room, with a view of what reminds Hofmeester of a steppe. There are no windows, windows aren't necessary here. The whole thing is open. Only a roof. In case it should start to rain.

The menu is simple. Salad, a cut of springbok filet, dessert.

"Eat," he tells the child.

The child looks out at the steppe, although the darkness makes it hard to see anything out there. She eats slowly and with a certain reluctance.

It tastes good to Hofmeester, though, and the South African red tastes even better. He gives the child a taste. She takes a few sips, but she doesn't like wine. Cola, that's what she likes.

"So here we are again," Hofmeester says once the springbok filet is finished. "Here we are again, Kaisa. We don't seem to be able to say farewell."

He leans back, plays with a toothpick, then orders a second bottle of red wine. And another cola for the child.

He acts as though he is on vacation. And maybe he is. On vacation at last.

"They took everything from me," he says quietly, "first my wife, then my money. Mohammed Atta did it, do you know Atta? Have you ever met him?"

She shakes her head.

"Yes," he says, "Atta. Many have forgotten him already. Foolishly. He took all my money. More than a million. He did other things, too. He took away some people's children. But it was my money he took. My freedom."

He looks under the table for his briefcase, but realizes then that he left it in Cabin Eleven. Along with his hat.

"They took my job away from me as well," he says. "And, in a certain sense, my children. My family. But I accepted it the way people accept changes in the weather. Rain, snow, wind, you can't do anything about it, Kaisa. Invulnerability is a virtue, people have forgotten that. He who believes in nothing is invulnerable. He stands above the masses, he stands above himself. He knows no doubt, because he accepts everything. He who is grieved, doubts. You're invulnerable too, Kaisa. No one can take anything away from you, because you have nothing. Whatever people call you, it doesn't matter, because you are nothing. Even if they would put an end to your life, that wouldn't grieve you. In fact, you're already dead."

He takes her hand, but lets go of it when the second bottle of wine and Kaisa's cola arrive.

Then he takes her hand again. He caresses her hand. Soft, little, yet not without strength.

Hofmeester sees a beetle crossing the floor, a big African beetle, brightly colored. He points to it and together they look at the beetle. As though it were an attraction, brought in specially for them.

"I had," Hofmeester says, "or rather, I *have* a cleaning lady, from Ghana. A friendly woman. An illegal alien, but friendly. When my wife disappeared, I started a sexual relationship with the cleaning lady."

He hold the child's hand tightly. He has the feeling she understands him, that she understands everything he says and can empathize with it. More than the others. She knows him.

She forgives him. At least that's how it seems, how it feels, for the first time really. She forgives him tacitly.

"I can talk to you so well," he says, "I've said it before, but I can't say it often enough. I can talk to you, Kaisa."

There is still a little cola left in the first bottle. He empties it into her glass, before filling the rest of the glass from the second one. Not a thrifty person anymore, but a painstaking person nonetheless.

"It was one of those things between friends. That business with me and the cleaning lady. I found a lawyer for her, slipped her a little something now and then. It was pleasant, extremely pleasant, in fact," he says, deep in thought, searching for words, speaking slower than normal, because of the wine and because of the child who understands him. "I took her on the couch, in the living room. Always from behind. You know, Kaisa . . ." He leans forward a little, and again he takes her hand in his. "The essence of sexuality between adults is the abasement. In itself it's not really much, sex isn't, it doesn't amount to much. Except for the abasement. That's what it's about, that, in fact, is all there is."

He moves his head closer to Kaisa's. He can smell her breath.

"When she licked her shit from my dick, I lost everything that was weighing me down, I had no more consciousness, and therefore no shame, no guilt, I was nothing and everything at the same time, I was the beast. The beast I had always wanted to be, that I've always been. The pleasure lies in the abasement. And the freedom lies in ridding ourselves of our disease, recovering from that disease, from what is our version of AIDS: humanism. And from everything that goes along with it, in the future as in the past, each and every time, again and again. You understand? It's redemption. The redemption lies in the abasement."

He presses his mouth to her forehead, he leans across the table and kisses her on the forehead.

"You people are already redeemed," he says. "You people are dead, even though you go on breathing, here in Africa. Nothing bad can happen to you. You people are the true invulnerable ones, inviolable as a machine, a product, a . . . thing. You people are beyond any future, which means you're also beyond all despair."

Hofmeester drinks his wine. He sees to it that Kaisa drinks too. The other guests have gone to their cabins. The waiters have gone to bed as well, but Hofmeester and the child can stay at the table for as long as they like, someone from the staff told them that. No problem. Into the wee hours, if they like.

And that is what they do. They exercise their privilege. They sit and they remain sitting.

Hand in hand. Occasionally Hofmeester stops talking and kisses her on the top of the head. She lets the kisses roll over her like his words: with great understanding and silence.

Yes, they accept each other, Hofmeester and the child.

"The way we are," he says, "is the way people will become, invulnerable and unapproachable. The others will follow suit. They just don't know that yet, they don't want to know, they cling to faded ideals. They still have hope and faith and don't see that that hope, that faith, will cause them to be defeated. Defeated, Kaisa. Defeated."

He kisses her again, leaning across the table. Not only on the forehead, also on the cheeks. He takes her face in both hands. Carefully, the way one might pick up a precious vase.

"When I was your age," he says, "no, a bit older, I was working on a project. God was already dead. So love was the next thing in line. I did away with love. It got bogged down, my project, sidelined by obligations, a job, a family, a house, a tenant. Children. But I should have given it a different working title: the death of compassion, that's what I should have called it. I, Kaisa, am a man without compassion. I don't know what it is, I don't believe in it, compassion, I've shaken it off like a nasty, stubborn head cold. Not that I think we want to see others suffer, on the contrary. We don't want to see others suffer at all, generally speaking, at least not really. But compassion? What is that? I could rape you, Kaisa, it's possible, and just before I penetrate you, I could think, I could feel—because they say it's something you feel, compassion, those who are supposed to know say so—anyway, I could think: I'm going to stop this. I could feel that. I've torn the clothes from your body, punched you in the face a few times, and now I think, now I feel, suddenly, out of the blue, compassion. I think: This far, but no further. This is enough. Enough of this. Do you understand now why I want to have nothing to do with it? I regard compassion as a personal affront. It insults me. It makes me furious."

He lets go of her face.

For a few minutes he says nothing, just drinks his wine. And then he calls out her name. "Kaisa," he shouts. And again, loud and shrill: "Kaisa!"

She looks at him, startled. But not startled enough to make her want to get up and run away. She doesn't want to run away.

"When I found my wife standing at the door again, I let her in," he says now, but quieter, almost in a whisper. "Compassion? Don't make me laugh. I let her in because I accept everything. Including her return, even her homecoming. Because I'm prepared to adapt, to assimilate. The lack of a wife, the return of the wife. Tirza, that's another story. She was ill, and I was the illness. That's the story. Other people can say: 'I'm sick. I need to get better.' But the sickness itself can't say that. That's the difference between the adjective and the noun. The sickness has to remain the sickness. I'm the noun."

His wine is finished, but her cola isn't. He picks up her glass.

"May I?" he asks. He takes a few sips. The taste doesn't appeal to him. But he is thirsty.

"The story. Yes, the story of the Hofmeester family," he says, "is the destruction of the Hofmeester family. That's the story. That's my story. A world devoid of compassion is harder to imagine than one's own death, that's why people keep coming back to it, that's why people keep picking at it. There were any number of moments in my life when I could have thought: I need to go back. This road is not my road, this road is not the best. But I didn't go back. Oh, you bet not, Kaisa, you bet not . . ."

He rises to his feet, he stands beside her, places his hands on her head, her dress, that part of her back that the dress doesn't cover. "There are choices," he says, "that are right, and there are choices that are wrong, and there are those in between. If the highest form of compassion consists of letting the other person live, I can only concede: I am a person without compassion. I lost control, probably. But only when I lost control did I become who I was. That part of Jörgen Hofmeester that stands outside the law is his solid core. That's why I'm here. That's how I ended up here. Because I no longer need to wonder about who I am."

The child turns her face to look at him. She is not afraid, why should she be? She even seems to be smiling. She smiles at the man who says things she doesn't understand, words she probably isn't even listening to.

There is music coming from the kitchen. Namibia's German-language station. Again.

The two of them listen to the radio in the distance, without being able to make out a word of it. And she smiles.

And because she smiles, because she is finally smiling, he says: "Kaisa, is there a difference between forgiveness and acceptance? I forgive the world by accepting it. I accept everything. There's nothing I don't accept. What about you? You saw me walking, on an afternoon in Windhoek, a hot afternoon. You saw a man who had trouble walking, because he had open blisters on his feet. From the heat. Shoes that pinched. And you came after me. I don't know why. Does it matter? You took my hand, you went along. We can invest that with meaning. Say that it had to be that way. That there was no way it could have been otherwise. That someone had a purpose in it. Maybe it was supposed to be that way, but maybe not. What matters is that you're here. That we both exist outside the law. That's what matters."

He leans down, searches around under the table, but this evening he didn't bring his briefcase with him. He keeps forgetting that. The briefcase is in the cabin. Hofmeester takes the child by the hand. She slides off of her chair. He is "sir" and she is "company." That's their game. It's been going on for days.

In the dark, probably because of the wine as well, he has a hard time finding the path back to Cabin Eleven. They walk through the tall grass. Slowly. Kaisa can't go any faster, Hofmeester can't either. Not at this hour of the night. Not through the tall grass. Not here in Namibia, with his feet that are still slightly swollen.

They walk in circles. Hofmeester notices and says: "We're walking in circles. Where's our cabin, Kaisa?"

He lift the child onto his shoulders. "Where's our cabin?" he asks. "Where do we live?"

He walks even slower now, afraid of falling.

He puts the child back down carefully on the ground.

"Tirza," he says, "Tirza. Yes. The problem with Tirza was that she was . . . is . . . extremely, extremely gifted. Extremely, extremely gifted. For those last few years I lived alone with her."

He sits down in the grass.

"Her sister had already gone to France, my wife had gone to her old flame. I was alone with Tirza and actually, looking back on it, those were the best years of my life. I cooked for her. I stopped interfering too much with her life. I did that. But it was a mistake."

He gets up. Something sharp is poking through the seat of his trousers. Five minutes later, they find Cabin Eleven at last.

Hofmeester turns on the ceiling fan. He pulls Tirza's iPod out of his briefcase. He shows the child the engraving. "Sun queen," he says. "That's what it says. Sun queen."

He connects the iPod to the charger, put the buds in the child's ears.

"This is the music Tirza listened to," he says. "This is her music."

Hofmeester sits down on the bed while the child listens to Tirza's music. The fan sweeps around and around and for a moment Hofmeester no longer knows why he came to Namibia. There's a lot he can't remember. His own past seems like another life. Someone else lived it, someone else was the editor of literature in translation, someone else had gone to all those places, someone else had wanted to do away with love. He had always been in Namibia, with Kaisa.

The next morning they drive straight on to Swakopmund, a coastal town. There are lots of tourists there, more than in other places. Your regular tourists too. Ones who have come on charter flights from Germany, for the sun and the sea and a touch of the exotic. Not the kind of people who feel a special bond with Africa. These people feel a special bond with the sun, they nurture an intimate relationship with their bikinis.

The child and he take a room at a little hotel, the Eberwein, not far from the beach. The staff speaks fluent German, the furnishings seem very German too.

Mrs. Eberwein herself runs the desk. Wrinkled and dried out by the sun, but spry, even a tad aggressive. Mrs. Eberwein is the boss around here. No one would dare question that. She asks whether Hofmeester needs a child's bed. Here too, he states that a large double bed will be fine. "We won't be staying long," he says. "She's my niece."

And because he can't help it, he lays Tirza's photo on the counter. "Have you seen this girl around here, in the last few weeks?"

The woman with the curly white hair, which she probably dyes, looks at the photo. She even picks it up. "No," she says, "never seen her. Who is it?"

"My daughter," Hofmeester says, "my youngest daughter."

Mrs. Eberwein holds the picture up closer, to see it better. "She looks like you," she says. "She has your chin."

Then she looks at the little girl standing beside Hofmeester. As though Mrs. Eberwein wants to check the child's chin as well.

Later, Hofmeester and the child take a walk along the beach, they look at the men fishing from the pier, share a salad at a café called Out of Africa, and while she is riding a carousel, he receives a call from the wife.

He tells the wife almost everything, about his trip, the accommodations, the Toyota, Swakopmund. Everything but the child.

"I'm almost in the desert," he says, "I'm almost with Tirza. It's only a day's drive from here."

"Ibi," the wife says, "thinks it's very strange that she hasn't heard anything from Tirza."

Her voice still contains nothing of the invigorating, hoarse sarcasm he knows so well. The hoarseness that some men find so seductive.

"Ibi shouldn't always think that the world revolves around her."

There is a lull in the conversation. The carousel is slowing down. Kaisa climbs off her horse. Hofmeester waves her over.

"And how are things there?" he asks. "How is it going?"

Van Eeghenstraat seems so far away. A different world. No longer his.

"Fine," she says, "everything here is fine. Jörgen. Oh, before I forget, Choukri's mother called. At first I had no idea who she was. She spoke French."

Kaisa is standing beside him now. He gestures to her that she can take another spin on the carousel. Another one and another one and another. He gives her some money. But she remains standing, her head leaning against his body. As though she's tired. As though she trusts him.

Who knows, maybe she really does trust him. It's a matter of time, and of need. Especially the latter.

He knows no compassion, but he can be trusted.

"Jörgen, are you still there?"

"Yes."

"Choukri's mother called. She wanted to know where her son is. My French isn't too good."

"I thought he was estranged from his family. The boy."

"Oh, well, I don't know, she sounded . . . she sounded friendly, but worried."

"You told her they're in the desert, didn't you? What do those people think, that there's a phone booth every twenty feet in the desert? They come from the desert themselves."

"That's what I told her, that they're in the desert. And that there's no cell coverage there. I promised to ask you to ask Choukri to call his mother. Apparently it's urgent."

The child takes his hand, she seems to want to walk on.

"Jörgen, are you there? You keep fading away."

Atta is supposed to call his mother. It's time for Atta to go home.

"I'm still here. Yes, I'll pass it along."

"I bought a book, with pictures of the Kalahari. And the Namib Desert. What do people do there, with all that space around them? What could Tirza be doing there all day?"

"Looking," Hofmeester says, "looking. You look at it, that's why you go to the desert."

The child is now pulling hard on his hand. She's growing impatient.

Now that she is ruined, the wife is developing maternal feelings. A book with photographs of Namibia. She used to have better things to do.

"I really have to go now," he says. "Tomorrow I'm going to the desert. I'll call you again in a few days, a week or so. Don't worry if it takes a little longer."

"Jörgen, where do we go from here?"

"With what?"

"With us."

"We'll talk about that."

"Maybe we should try again. With each other. Because we have no choice. Because we're old."

"Maybe."

"I told the cleaning lady she doesn't have to come in anymore, I clean the house myself now. I don't have anything else to do anyway."

He hangs up. The child is tired. On the last leg of the route back to the hotel, he has to carry her. In his little room at the Eberwein Hotel he closes the curtains. He lays the child on the bed, and lies down beside her. It is four o'clock in the afternoon in Namibia.

A little past six he awakens. The child is still asleep. Quietly, he gets up and dresses. He takes his briefcase and his hat and leaves the room without a sound.

Darkness is well on its way. At first he wanders aimlessly around Swakopmund. Before the window of a travel agency he stops and looks at a poster for trips to the desert. By jeep or by plane. As you like it.

He looks at the picture of the desert on the poster. He peers at the people in the background, as though one of them might be Tirza.

At a clothing outlet he buys a pair of jogging pants and a T-shirt for Kaisa. And four pairs of underpants he thinks will fit her.

In the check-out line he notices that he is the only white person in the shop. It bothers him less all the time.

Back at the Eberwein Hotel he finds Kaisa weeping on the bed. A sobbing little heap of misery, the sheets and pillows strewn all around her. He takes the child in his arms.

"Don't be afraid," he says. "I'm not going away. I'm really not going away. After all, there's nowhere left for me to go."

He shows her the T-shirt, the jogging pants, and the underpants.

"You need to put on something fresh and clean," he says. "Not that I think you're dirty, but it can't hurt to put on something clean for a change."

He sits down in the only chair in the room. The child has stopped crying.

"How many of you are there, anyway?" he asks as she tries on her new clothes. "How many children are there like you in this country?"

She sits down on the bed and stares at him.

"Do you stay in contact with each other? The children who sell company?"

She continues to stare at him.

He hangs his clothes in the bathroom and turns on the hot water in the shower, in the hope that the steam will remove the wrinkles from his clothing.

That evening they don't go to dinner. They lie on the bed and watch TV. At ten o'clock Hofmeester helps the child into her nightie: the summer dress that the wife bought for Tirza.

Hofmeester awakens in the middle of the night. The little girl is lying crosswise on the bed. She has her feet on his stomach. Carefully, he moves her around so that her feet don't have to lie on his stomach. It takes him at least an hour to fall asleep again.

They get up at six-thirty. When they arrive in the breakfast room, Mrs. Eberwein is still setting up the buffet.

"You're up very bright and early this morning," she says. "Coffee? Tea?"

"Coffee, please, and chocolate milk for her."

Breakfast here is not as sumptuous as it was at the Heinitzburg or at Okapuka Ranch, and for some reason neither of them seem to be very hungry either.

As he is paying the bill, Mrs. Eberwein says: "She's a pretty girl. Your niece. A very pretty girl."

She hands him the receipt, which Hofmeester folds twice and slips into his inside pocket.

He is getting ready to walk away when Mrs. Eberwein says: "There are lots of children here without parents."

Hofmeester has already put on his hat. His suitcase is in the trunk of the Toyota. The only thing he's carrying is his briefcase, clenched under his arm as usual.

He has to reply. But what can he say? What is there to say about children without parents?

"AIDS," Mrs. Eberwein hisses, "because they can't contain themselves. The blacks."

He looks gravely at the woman with the wrinkled face. He knows what she is seeing, or rather, what she thinks she's seeing.

"Be careful," she says. "They seem like children. But they steal. Oh, I can understand it well enough. If I didn't have a thing, I'd steal too. It's in their blood. Always blaming other people for their own misery."

There is a plate with hard candy on the counter. Hofmeester takes a piece of candy and puts it in his mouth. Then, without another word, he walks out to the Toyota, the child following him.

"We're going to Tirza," he says once they are in the car, "we're going to the desert." He unfolds a map of Namibia, the one he got from the rental agency. "Sossusvlei," he says. "That's where she wanted to go. To the dunes." He places his hands on the wheel. No idea what he's supposed to imagine by that. The dunes. He wonders where it is he's heading.

The road is asphalt all the way to Walvis Bay. There it turns to sand. At first Hofmeester doesn't dare to drive faster than forty, fifty kilometers an hour. As time passes, though, he picks it up to eighty, almost ninety.

The sound of pebbles bouncing off the car is something he's grown used to.

The car radio has stopped working. His telephone has no coverage here either. There's nothing out here. He is alone with Kaisa.

Occasionally he glances over at her. She is holding a bottle of water between her knees. When he asks for it, she hands him the bottle. So he can drink without having to stop.

Even though he thinks he's been driving fast, it takes longer than he'd expected. It is afternoon by the time he reaches Solitaire. On the map, it's a dot the size of small town. In fact it's nothing but a motel and a gas station.

He fills the tank and buys two pieces of apple pie. The child eats all of hers. She's hungry.

"Very good," Hofmeester says, as though this were an achievement.

The Toyota is covered in sand and dust. The girl draws lines on the hood with her fingers.

"Let's sit down," he says, "rest for a minute."

A few tables and chairs have been set out beside the pumps. They look old, faded by the sun, time, use. There's also a building that looks more like a real café. But they don't have time for that, Hofmeester thinks. They have to keep moving.

He wipes his forehead with a handkerchief, then he wipes the child's forehead. Even though she's not sweating.

There is a tree and, a bit further along, a water tower. Then nothing. Sand, stones, a few bushes. A fence to separate one plot of land from the other. But what could a plot of land mean around here?

They remain silent.

"Have you figured out what I'm doing?" he asks after a while. "Do you understand already?"

She points to the dusty Toyota.

"No, no," he says. "Not the Toyota. Or well, maybe you're right. I'm busy disappearing. That's what I'm doing." The word "disappearing" comforts him. It's so much kinder and more innocent than dying. It is dying, but then without the violence.

He must have dozed off, because he wakes up from the child tapping him on the cheek. The sun is already lower in the sky. His hat has fallen to the ground.

He rubs his eyes, picks up the hat.

"All right," he says, "let's go."

It takes them two hours to reach the Sossuvlei Lodge. Huts in striking colors, in the middle of the desert, that's the lodge. But there is no room for them.

He hadn't counted on that. On the desert being so popular.

The girl behind the desk says: "Try the Kulala Desert Lodge, maybe they have something for you. Shall I give them a call?"

"Please."

He stands there, holding the child by the hand. Dusty and thirsty.

One of those tourists who hasn't planned his trip well. Careless tourists.

The receptionist makes the call. There is room at the Kulala Desert Lodge. He thanks her kindly for going to the trouble.

Despite the fatigue and thirst, he drives on, fast. Almost a hundred kilometers an hour down a sand road.

By the time they see a sign saying Kulala, it's already dark.

The little road—hardly worthy of the name—that leads to it is almost six kilometers long. It takes them fifteen minutes. The only light is from their own headlights. Hofmeester is finding it increasingly hard to concentrate.

Until at last he sees the Kulala Desert Lodge. A group of tents drawn up in a circle. Only the tents aren't tents, they're cabins in the desert.

He parks the car. Taking the child, his hat, and briefcase with him, he walks to the entrance. He staggers, he is dizzy. He has probably had too little to eat, or too little to drink.

A young woman with a tray is standing at the entrance. She hands him a drink. Her hair is bound up gracefully with a scarf.

Hofmeester drinks thirstily, the drink tastes of both tea and alcohol. The child drinks as well. Today she is wearing her new jogging pants.

She looks good. Less slatternly than in her worn-out dress, in as far at least as a child can look slatternly. The word reminds him of the wife. Slattern, a word like a game that hasn't been played for a long time.

"My name's Jörgen Hofmeester," he says. "Someone just called ahead for me. For one or two nights. Do I need to register somewhere?"

"We'll take care of that later," she says.

A man comes up to him. A white man. A young Frenchman, as it turns out. He welcomes Hofmeester, tells him that the formalities will be dealt with in good time, asks whether they would like something to eat first. The baggage will be brought in from the car later as well. The first thing they need to do is take it easy. Catch their breath.

Hofmeester lets himself be led to a table. He is so tired that he forgets to take off his hat. Too tired as well to notice whether or how people are looking at him and at the child.

When a basket of home-baked bread appears on the table, he and the child devour it within five minutes.

"Kaisa," he says, "we're there. We're almost there."

And at last she says something. For the first time that day. With a smile on her face, a smile that looks almost ironic. "Sir," she says, "more bread, please."

He waves to one of the waitresses. She comes over with more bread. The girl stands at the table for a moment and looks at the child.

"Your daughter?" she asks.

"My niece," Hofmeester says.

Then the little girl starts to sing. She sings in a language he doesn't recognize, and makes clicking noises with her tongue. She has a nice voice, but he's not in the mood for singing. He wants to eat, sleep, disappear.

When the girl is finished singing, Hofmeester pats her arm gently. As she chews on a slice of homemade bread.

"Don't eat all the bread," Hofmeester whispers, "or you won't have any room left for dinner."

She stops chewing for a moment. She smiles at the man she's been traveling with for a few days now.

It doesn't matter to her, he thinks. It doesn't matter to her who I am. Indifference can be forgiveness too.

After dinner he hands the car keys to a boy who will carry the luggage to the cabin. But after a few minutes the boy comes back. He can't open the trunk.

"I think there's too much sand and dust in the lock," he says. "We'll spray it clean tomorrow. But I'm afraid you'll have to spend the night without your bags. Is that a huge problem? Can I get you something?"

"No," Hofmeester says, "it's no problem. We don't need anything."

The Frenchman shows them to their cabin. The cabins are fairly far apart. They have to make their way carefully. The path is marked with stones, but there isn't much light. Sand and dust everywhere.

"Watch your step," the Frenchman says. "The guests usually come earlier. While it's still light."

The hut lives up to Hofmeester's expectations. A bed, a fan, a can of bug spray, a shower.

"If you like," the Frenchman says, "you can sleep on the roof. There are blankets up there. Some people enjoy sleeping out under the stars. It's a unique experience. An attraction."

They go outside and walk around to the back of the cabin, where there is a ladder.

The child stays inside.

Hofmeester nods. "Have you been here for a long time?" he asks.

"About three years," the Frenchman says. "In fact, it's about time I moved on. But I can't say goodbye. The desert is addictive."

They take a look at the cabin roof and the bed that's up there. Can't say goodbye. It sounds familiar to Hofmeester, but at the same time not. What could be so special about this place that would keep you from leaving it?

"And how did you end up here?" Hofmeester asks.

The Frenchman laughs. "I was looking for something out of the ordinary." He is quiet for a moment, as though expecting more questions. Then he says: "Well, I'll leave you alone. Tomorrow we'll clean your car and hopefully get to your baggage. And then you can let us know which excursions you'd like to go on."

Hofmeester goes back into the cabin. He washes his hands. The water is remarkably warm.

"We don't have a toothbrush," he says. "The toothbrush is still in the trunk and they can't open it. You don't mind, do you?"

He undresses, hangs his clothes in a little closet.

"What about just wearing these clothes?" he asks. "We don't have your nightdress either." He points at the jogging pants, the T-shirt.

The child nods. It's all right.

He looks around. There is no phone in the room. It has everything, except for a phone. He opens his own cell phone. There's no coverage here either.

He stands there in his underpants. He pulls back the covers, then thinks of something. "Or would you rather sleep outside?" he asks. "Outside. On the roof? To see the sky? The stars?"

He points at the ceiling, as though afraid that she might not understand.

"On the roof?" he asks again.

"Yes," she says, "on the roof."

A little startled by her reply, Hofmeester leads the child around to the back of the hut. The sand does not feel unpleasant beneath his bare feet. He didn't know she wanted to do this. Sleep on the roof. Well, why not? It's an attraction. Maybe Tirza did it too.

"You go up first," he says. "So I can catch you if you fall."

The child climbs the ladder slowly. Halfway up, she stops. She looks down.

"Go on," Hofmeester says. He pushes against her bottom, afraid that she'll suddenly come down with a fear of heights. Afraid that she'll fall.

Climbing the ladder is harder for him than he'd expected. Stiff joints, flabby muscles, the onset of decay.

Just lying on the sheet, it's fairly cold up on the roof. The desert nights are chilly.

He pulls the blankets over himself and over the child.

The child is shivering.

"Come on," he says, "I'll hold you."

While he holds Kaisa, he looks up at the sky. Stars. As promised. This is beautiful, he thinks, but why is this beautiful? Is it an agreement? Or does everyone think this is beautiful, without knowing anything about an agreement?

Sleep will not come, even though he is tired after driving all day. After a while he notices that the child is not asleep either.

She has her eyes open.

Just like him. But is she looking at something, or does she sleep with her eyes open?

Are you supposed to look at the stars? Is that what this attraction is all about? Specially designed for the Westerner, so that he can finally discover what that is, the open night sky?

"Kaisa," he says, "are you asleep?"

She says nothing.

"Are you cold?" he asks. "Kaisa?"

Again, no answer. He feels something on his cheek. A hand. Kaisa's hand.

She's caressing him, it seems. She has her hand on his face. But she hasn't moved her head.

He doesn't move. The hand remains in place.

Silence. Silence and darkness. That is the desert at night. Every once in a while the sound of the wind.

"Do you know what it was with Tirza?" he says quietly. "Do you know what it was?" There's no need for him to whisper, but he does anyway. It's so quiet, it seems like his voice will carry dozens of meters. "She was like me. That's what it was. She was . . . She was . . ."

The hand moves slowly over his face, like the hand of a blind person. It isn't a caress, it's searching for something. But what could the hand, Kaisa's hand, be searching for?

"I came into the living room," he whispers, "the living room that used to belong to my parents, and she was lying there. On the table. Tirza. She didn't hear me. He didn't either. It makes so much noise, Kaisa, sex. It's so noisy, that's what makes it unpleasant for others. The noise. The noise. Nothing but noise."

The hand on Hofmeester's face doesn't stop moving. His mouth. His ears. His nose. It touches everything.

"I was planning to go away. Into the kitchen. I had been doing something in there, I don't remember what. Drinking wine, I think. Italian Gewürztraminer. But I just stood there. I thought it was strange that they hadn't heard me. That's why I stood there and watched. It was so loveless, Kaisa. Suddenly I saw that. How loveless it was. How . . ."

His lips are parched. He's thirsty, but he didn't bring any water up to the roof and he's too tired to go back down now and to look for a bottle in the hut.

The hand rests on his nose. It's not an unpleasant feeling. It's a pleasant hand. A soft hand.

"Loveless is what sex is," he whispers, "in general, always, under all circumstances, that's what I thought. That's what I saw. It shouldn't have surprised me, but still it did. I mean: the beast knows no love, only rage at best. Hunger, thirst, fatigue. And I thought: What's happening here? My daughter is getting it put to her, that's what's happening, that's what's going on here. And those words, getting it put to her, stayed in my mind, kept circling around, they didn't go away again, like a . . . like a prayer, Kaisa. Getting it put to her, I thought, put to her, that's what my daughter is getting from life. And I looked at his buttocks, Mohammed Atta's buttocks, and I thought: They're so white. He's got such white buttocks for a brown man. How peculiar. White buttocks. I stood there beside the fireplace, I saw them go up and down, those buttocks, like in a movie. I could have gone back the same way I came, quietly and carefully, but I didn't. I didn't move. I just stood there, looking at those white buttocks."

The hand is on his cheek now. The fingers seem to be playing piano on his cheek. And he thinks: She's tickling me. She's tickling.

"Kaisa," he whispers, "you can't imagine it, but I stood there like that. For minutes, it seemed like, it was really only seconds but it seemed like minutes, hours, half a lifetime. And even though I didn't say or do anything, suddenly they saw me, or else they'd heard something. Smelled something. Anyway, Mohammed Atta turned his head. And I thought: I've been through all this before. I'm so old that everything is happening to me twice. And Tirza saw me too and climbed off the table. She wasn't even completely undressed.

She was . . . she was partially dressed, not undressed actually. And I thought: Why on my dining room table? A dining room table is a table you dine on, obviously. You dine at it. I thought: Mohammed Atta, you took my money, and now you're taking my daughter on my dining room table, on the table that belonged to my parents. Okay, the last few years of their lives they didn't open the door anymore, but that's a different story."

The child's hand now begins to move over his forehead.

"Kaisa," he whispers, "your hand is so soft. So soft. That's nice." He thinks. For a few seconds, a minute. "That's right," he says, "she stood there, Tirza, and she said: 'Daddy, what are you doing here?' Not angry, but surprised. Maybe a little annoyed to find me standing there. I could just as easily have asked: 'What are you two doing here? This is a dinner table. Our dinner table. We're going to eat at it later on.' But what I thought above all was: Isn't Tirza lovely, isn't she sweet? What a sweet face she has. And lovely eyes, and a fine character. A thoughtful character. Even as a toddler she was so thoughtful. It wasn't just a matter of our taking care of her, she took care of us too. And I thought about her shoes, her first pair of shoes, the ones I bought for her. They were so little that three or four of them would have fit in the palm of my hand. I have them tucked away somewhere, Tirza's first shoes, in a cupboard on Van Eeghenstraat. And I thought: She is the sun queen, that's what I thought, my sun queen is who she is, my dearest sun queen. And then I picked up the poker and hit her on the head. She fell right away and I hit her again, while she was already on the floor, and again, and while I was doing that I thought: She's my sun queen, my dearest sun queen. She is the sun queen. And I thought about her little shoes, her very first pair of shoes. They were blue, without laces, with Velcro straps."

He feels a hand lying on his face, the child's warmth, he still feels that too, and not much more than that.

"Kaisa," Hofmeester whispers, "your hand is so nice. Your hand

. . . Now you know who I am. I didn't know it myself either. You don't know who you are, not until you lose control. It only strikes you then. And then that Atta, do you know what he did? He ran. The big, brave man. He took off. I found him in the kitchen. He was trembling, he was shaking. He was . . . he wasn't anything anymore. A wreck. Nothing. Not a person. Nothing at all."

Hofmeester's mouth is dry. He swallows a few times.

"Kaisa," Hofmeester whispers, "Kaisa. Atta stood there in my kitchen, beside the door, he didn't even have the decency to dress himself. And do you know what he said? 'Please, Mr. Hofmeester, please,' that's what he said. And only at that moment did I realize that I still had the poker in my hand. The poker that belonged to my parents. And he begged and he wailed. Did I wail? When Mohammed Atta took my money, and my daughter? I never wailed. I took a step in his direction and right then he picked up my Stihl, which I'd put there in the kitchen to dry off and clean later. My saw. I had been working in the garden the whole day. I like to work in the garden."

The wind has picked up. The sound of it reassures Hofmeester. It makes him think that no one can hear him, not even Kaisa. "You have to take good care of fruit trees," he whispers. "A garden requires maintenance, the sawing off of dead branches, pulling weeds, sowing grass seed. That's my work. I enjoy it. I don't let anyone take away my Stihl MS 170, especially not Atta. I dropped the poker and grabbed the saw out of his hands. He wasn't even holding it very tightly. He doesn't know how you operate a thing like that, how you have to hold it. He was trembling too badly. He was confused, he was pale as a ghost."

He feels Kaisa's foot against his leg, but more than that her hand on his head. "Kaisa," he whispers. "Kaisa. My Kaisa. He ran to the living room like a scared cat. With his pants still down around his knees. Atta. I went after him. What was I supposed to do? I couldn't let him get away, I had no choice, Kaisa. He just stood there in a complete panic. Close to a nervous collapse. And on the table, on the dinner table, there was still that game of Monopoly and his Koran. A green book with a hard cover. I looked at it, with the saw in my hand. Then it all fell into place. I understood it, the mistake, the fallacy, the irrational thing that races over this earth like a phantom, like a hurricane. I said to him: 'Atta, who do you think is stronger, Allah or the MS 170? Pray to Allah, maybe he'll come and help you. Or to the prophet, maybe the prophet will come and help you, Atta.' But he didn't want to pray. He refused to pray. Can you imagine that? I tore a page out of the Koran and said: 'If you don't want to pray, then you'll have to eat, Atta.' I stuffed the page in his mouth. And he ate. He ate, Kaisa. But no help came. Of course no help came. I was all the help there was. 'Surely you shall behold hell,' that was what was written on that page, and more of that kind of thing. I came closer, Kaisa, closer to Atta, closer all the time. I could smell him, fear stinks, the smell of fear cuts through everything, and lying on the floor was my daughter, my sun queen. She had been cured of her illness, but apparently not entirely, not of me, she wasn't cured of me, you can't be cured of me.

"What was I supposed to do? He had a page from the Koran in his mouth, Mohammed Atta, like a circus animal. He didn't even dare to swallow it. He wasn't chewing. He stared at me. Like a monkey. 'Where's Allah?' I asked. 'Where is the prophet? Why didn't they come to help you? Could it be that you didn't yell loud enough, that you didn't pray with enough conviction? Call him again. Yell for Allah, yell for him the way you do for a dog that's run away in the park. Let's call him together, Atta, maybe he'll come if we both call him. Maybe he's a little hard of hearing.' And do you know what he said, do you know how he answered me with that page from the Koran still in his mouth? 'I'm not Mohammed Atta. I'm not Mohammed Atta.' 'Of course,' I said, 'you wouldn't admit to being Mohammed Atta, of course you go by an assumed name. Who would dare to admit that he's Mohammed Atta, to admit that these days?' Then I started up the MS 170, and once you've turned that on you don't hear much of anything anymore, no prayers, no voices, not even any howling, all you hear then is the MS 170, and that's a kind of music. Above that music I shouted: 'Call him again, Atta. Yell real loud again for Allah. Maybe he didn't understand you the first time because of your accent. Maybe Allah's off on a short vacation.' But Atta didn't say anything anymore. And then I pruned him, like a fruit tree. Like a sick fruit tree with all kinds of dead branches. First the left side, then the right, then the bottom and all the way at the end the top. The MS 170 is a compact saw, but it will cut through anything. That's why gardening hobbyists like it so much. It also uses very little fuel."

He turns onto his side. The hand is now resting on the back of his head.

"Kaisa," he whispers, "Kaisa. My Kaisa. I washed myself, in the kitchen, as best I could, and scrubbed my clothes and put on a shirt that used to be my father's. My own shirt couldn't be cleaned. It was too filthy. Then I went into the village for takeout. A rice table. A small rice table for three. With extra shrimp crackers. And I ate that whole rice table on my own. I was so hungry, so incredibly hungry that I even licked clean some of those plastic containers. Kaisa, do you ever get hungry like that? Then I dug a hole in the garden. It took me all night. I didn't have time to dig two holes. And I laid the children in it, I dragged them to it, I should say, with my last ounce of strength. The sun queen in her entirety, the other one in pieces. The way you put the pruned branches out on the street for the garbage man. And then I filled the hole. I tidied up the garden as well as I could, it used to belong to my parents. And then I showered and cleaned the MS 170 and then the house, because the sap from the fruit tree was everywhere. Everywhere twigs and leaves I had forgotten to put in the hole. You don't know who Atta was, you don't know what he would have done to us if he'd had the chance. And then everything was clean, everything was put away, only the

Koran was still on the table. And I started reading it. There was only one page torn out. I'm curious by nature, and I couldn't sleep. There are interesting things in it. 'Surely the owners of the garden shall that day have joy in all that they do,' I read. Things like that. And I thought: That's me, I'm the owner of the garden. But the MS 170 is more powerful than Allah, stronger than God, stronger than Jesus. The Stihl MS 170 is the master, Kaisa, our master. And while I was thinking all that, I wasn't feeling a thing. Maybe a little concern about practical matters, but no more than that. Whether the house was really clean. Whether I hadn't forgotten anything. I didn't sleep, only drifted in and out, and in the morning I fixed breakfast for three. I shaved, put on the ointment I use against dry skin, against the flaking. And then I drove to the airport in Frankfurt. And I waved goodbye to the children, until I couldn't see them anymore.

"Now you know who I am, and why I'm here. Because I'm looking for Tirza, even though I know she's never been here. But the crazy thing is, there are moments when I doubt the whole thing. When I'm no longer really sure. When I think: It was all just a game, a game in my own head. When I think that she really did fly to Namibia anyway, with Atta, when I don't remember things clearly anymore. I can't imagine never seeing Tirza again. It's strange, but for years I've had this vague suspicion that I'm a monster, a beast. And when I finally saw that suspicion confirmed, I couldn't believe it. A long time ago, when I was young, I used to play a game with my wife, we played that I was the beast that prowled Vondelpark late at night. It's for all these reasons that I'm here in Namibia, Kaisa, to disappear, to dissolve, because I have nowhere else to go. Maybe that's the definition of a game, that you can always go back to who you were before you started playing it. But I can't go back. I'm cut off from who I was, Kaisa. For you I have no future, no past, I'm as neutral as a dollar bill. A Westerner, one among many, lost in his own life. Those people say they're in search of spirituality, or serenity, or something else, but they all mean the same thing, Kaisa: they want to disappear. I want to . . . I want to tell you how lovely it is for me to talk with you. Your company is . . . it's important to me. People need company before they disappear."

He says nothing more after that, but he cannot sleep. He lies in the desert, feels the child's warmth, digs around in his memory and tastes the taste of old wine in his mouth. There is nothing monstrous about him. Everything that is monstrous about him is buried in his memory. He lies there like a child.

Hofmeester wakes up feeling stiff. He lies there for a while, then wakes Kaisa. It is seven o'clock in the morning.

In the hut he takes a shower, a short one, because he wants there to be enough hot water for Kaisa. Then he gets dressed.

At breakfast the Frenchman asks whether they would like to take part in an excursion. "Yes, please," Hofmeester says, "we'd like to see the desert, the dunes."

"I'll organize a separate excursion for you, then," the Frenchman says, "because you have a child with you. Most people come here without children. Elago will come by and fetch you at two-thirty."

"Thank you," Hofmeester says.

"No need to thank me," says the Frenchman. He seems about to walk away, but stops. "Was she born here?" he asks. He points to the child. Hofmeester nods, and the Frenchman nods as well, as though it's the answer he had expected. As though he already knew. "If there's anything else you need . . . oh, before I forget, we sprayed the lock on your car and your bags will be brought to your cabin in a couple of minutes." The Frenchman walks on to the next table.

Hofmeester watches him go. A friendly man in khaki trousers. Who knows what he was in France. What he did there.

They spend the day at the edge of the little swimming pool. Occasionally the child dips her feet in the water. But she doesn't dare to swim, or doesn't know how to.

Hofmeester lies in a lounge chair, his shirt is unbuttoned, he has no desire to take it off completely.

At two-thirty, a tall black man walks up to Hofmeester. Elago.

The flatbed jeep has been customized to accommodate passengers. The seats are arranged like a grandstand, so that you can enjoy the view over the heads of the people in front of you.

But there are no other people. Only Hofmeester, Kaisa, and Elago.

They drive off, slowly at first, then faster all the time. Elago talks a lot and tells jokes that are rather stupid, but Hofmeester is polite enough to laugh at them.

The desert changes color all the time, the desert turns redder and redder.

There are no stones here, or very few. Only sand and a few bare bushes.

"Are you from around here?" Hofmeester asks, once they've stopped by a dune. The silence weighs heavily on him.

"I'm from the north of the country," Elago says. "That's where my family lives too."

"And do you go back often?"

"We work for three months, then we have three weeks off. In another two weeks I'll go home again."

They drive on a bit. At the foot of two tall dunes, they stop. "This is Big Papa," Elago says, "and that one is Big Mama. Big Mama isn't quite as high as Big Daddy, but the view's the same." He waits for a moment. "If you'd like to go up, if you want to climb Big Mama, I'll wait here with the girl. There are usually more people around here, they usually arrive close to sundown. But it's quiet now. The dune is all yours."

"Yes," Hofmeester says, "I'd like to go up."

"Take some water with you," Elago says.

Hofmeester tucks the briefcase under his arm. He leaves the hat in the jeep.

"Don't you want to leave that here? Your bag?"

"Oh no, I'll take it with me. It's not heavy."

He climbs out of the jeep. Elago hands him a bottle of water and he starts walking.

"Are you sure?" Elago calls out after him. "You can leave the bag here as well. Nothing will happen to it."

Hofmeester pretends not to hear.

At first the sand is hard, but after a while he sinks further into it with each step, up to his knees.

When he turns and looks, he sees that Kaisa is coming after him.

Not another person or animal in sight. Only sand, in all different colors.

They're not even that far up yet, but the jeep already looks tiny and insignificant.

Kaisa climbs faster than him. She'll catch up with him any moment.

"You have to stay with Elago," he shouts. "Stay with Elago. He'll take care of you."

He walks on. His arms hurt, his breathing is labored. The sandals only get in his way. He takes them off.

Twenty minutes later, they are out of Elago's sight.

He sits down. Kaisa remains standing. His body is exhausted, his mouth is dry.

"Go back now, Kaisa," he says. "I'll go on by myself. I'm going to disappear." He has no difficulty saying that. He's thought about it so often, this moment, been through it so many times in his thoughts. He stands up, kisses her on the forehead and hands her the bottle of water, which is still half-filled.

He walks on briskly, the dune goes down a bit, then back up. He is walking along the ridge, where the sand has blown up from both sides. There is no view, only more sand, more dunes.

Hofmeester throws away his sandals. He won't need them any-more. Sometimes he falls, then crawls through the sand on hands and knees for a couple of meters. Yes, this is disappearing. This is how you do it. This is what it looks like.

The sun stings his eyes, but he feels the heat taper off.

When he turns around, he sees that Kaisa is only a few yards away. She has been following him again.

He curses. "Go away," he screams. He waves his arms, he waves his briefcase, to make clear that she should go back to the jeep. Away from here, away from him.

But she only comes closer. She runs through the sand faster and faster, like an animal accustomed to the desert. She doesn't move slowly enough to sink into it. It looks like a dance she's doing, a dance without an audience.

Then he turns and starts walking on, away from Kaisa.

She's faster though, she catches up with him. She grabs his leg.

He tries to pull away from her, and so he falls. "Go away," he shouts. "Kaisa, can't you see what I'm doing? Don't you see?" He's lying on his stomach. There is sand everywhere, in his ears, his nose, in his mouth, in his briefcase.

The child is sitting beside him now. She runs her hand over his hair.

"Kaisa," he whispers. "I told you I need to disappear, right? So let me."

He sits up. He takes the child's hands. "Do you think I'm sick?" he asks. "Is that what you think? But if I'm sick, then what's healthy, what's normal?"

He stands up.

"I'm a product of civilization," he shouts, "I'm what you get when you turn civilization loose on the beast. That's what I am. I've never wanted to be anything but civilized."

The wind drowns out his voice.

He walks on, he staggers, but he walks on. The child won't give up. She grabs his hand. She pulls him in the other direction. They're wrestling, that's what it looks like.

Then, with his last bit of strength, he lifts the child up into the air for a few seconds. He has to leave his briefcase lying in the sand for this final effort.

"Look," he says, "look how lovely it is here. Not a person in sight. Only sand. That is beautiful. A world without people, that's beauty. Darkness is what mankind is, nothing but that, the epicenter of darkness, and the only light he gives off is the light of the beast." He puts the child back on her feet.

"I have to stay here," he tells the girl, "there's no place for me, I've given up my place in the world of people. I've placed myself outside that world. I belong to the world of sand. The sand has to take care of me now."

Hofmeester holds the briefcase to his forehead, to protect his eyes from the light. The sun is sinking lower.

Then he sits down again, he takes the bottle from the child and drinks.

"Years ago," he says, "on Sunday mornings, the Jehovah's Witnesses used to show up at my door all the time. I always opened when they rang. Even though my wife couldn't stand that. But I felt that one should always remain courteous, even if they came to the door to save your soul. They would say things like: 'God is looking for you.' Things like that. But the sand has come looking for me now, can't you feel that, the way the sand is looking for me? Maybe that was what the Jehovah's Witnesses meant after all. I don't know. That the sand was looking for me. And that it always has been. It's possible."

He opens the briefcase. Dust comes out of it.

"Listen," he says, "in a little bit I'm going to just sit down somewhere, it doesn't matter where, one dune's as good as another, and then I'm going to open my briefcase. Everything I need is in here. My four pencils, the manuscript I was reading, Tirza's notebook, her pocket diary, Tirza's iPod, the charger. I'm going to arrange all those things around me, and then wait. I have fond memories of those four pencils. And of Tirza, the sun queen. And of the briefcase. It was a present from my wife. I'll sit there like that with those things, I will be very calm. Sometimes I'll look at the pencils, then at Tirza's notebook, then at the briefcase. That's how I imagine it. The sand will come and have pity on me. And you need to go back now, and take it slowly. Not too quickly, I don't want to be found. 'God is looking for you,' that's what the Jehovah's Witnesses said. I didn't want to be found, not by God, and not by people. Now you know everything. Now you have to go back. This is where our game ends, Kaisa. I'm going to walk on a bit, and you're going to go back."

He rises to his feet. His briefcase under his arm. But Kaisa grabs his hand and won't let go, she seizes that hand and at the moment when Hofmeester starts to win, at the moment when he seems about to shake her off, she bites his hand.

"Ow!" he shouts. "Are you out of your mind?"

Sound doesn't travel far here. Even the animals can't hear him. He can barely hear himself.

Now, in the confusion, she is able to pull him to the ground.

He falls onto the sand, and she climbs on top of him.

She holds him tight, and finally, he holds her tight too.

A gust of wind sprinkles them with grains of sand, the sand gets in his nose. He sniffs, he snorts.

At last Hofmeester shivers, at last he shakes, and at last the tears come. Not because he was planning to disappear, not because he regrets the chances he has missed—if almost everything is a missed chance, there's no longer any need to regret the individual chances missed—not because he misses the sun queen more than he is willing to admit, but because he senses, because somehow he knows for sure, that he cannot tear himself away from this child. That he is once again too weak to tear himself away, and that he will therefore not disappear. Not yet. Not the way he had hoped, not the way he had imagined, not the way he himself had thought.

He gets up, he takes a few steps, but he is not walking in the direction he had chosen. The child is pulling him along. He is walking back, back to the jeep, back to the life he didn't want to go back to.

"Kaisa," he says, "what is this, what is the meaning of this?" But it's a rhetorical question. He doesn't expect an answer, and no answer comes.

Halfway down the dune, they stop. They drink the last of the water. And for a moment, Hofmeester can't help laughing. "Look at us," he says, "do you see the two of us?"

She looks at him, but she doesn't laugh. She holds his hand and pulls him down the dune, as though she were the donkey and he were the cart.

"Where did you two get to?" Elago asks. "I thought you were never coming back. I was worried, because of the child. She insisted on going with you, sir. There was no holding her back."

Then he sees that Hofmeester has nothing on his feet.

"Your shoes, sir."

"I left them up on the dune," Hofmeester says. "No problem. It's too hot for sandals anyway."

Now they are both barefooted, he and the child.

He climbs into the jeep, puts on his hat.

"Would you like something to drink?" Elago asks.

"Water," Hofmeester says.

The child sits next to him and, as though she is still on her guard, as though at any moment Hofmeester might attempt to escape again, she holds on to his hand. The whole time, all the way back to Kulula Desert Lodge.

The next morning, just after daybreak, they drive further south. The desert has nothing more to offer him.

On the map he has seen that there is another town on the coast, Lüderitz. That's where he wants to go. There he'll just have to try again: to disappear.

He thought they could make it in one day, but the roads are bad. Halfway there he stops at a farm that also rents rooms for the night.

The farmer and his wife are the children of German immigrants, well along in years themselves now, who maintain the old German traditions.

At first they don't want to give Hofmeester a room. "Where are your shoes?" the wife asks.

"I lost them in the desert."

"Your German is so excellent," she says, "where did you learn to speak it? I can tell that you're not German, but you do an awfully good job of it."

"I learned it at the university, I almost took my degree in German."

That is an answer that satisfies her. His talent for conversation has done its work again.

Hofmeester realizes that respectable people wear shoes, but his feet really are too swollen. At her age, the farmer's wife is mild and wise enough to understand that some tourists who have lost all sense of where they are might lose their shoes in the sand as well. But that, in spite of that, they may still be civilized.

He is given a room with two single beds against the far walls. The mattress is hard. The room is rather stuffy. In the closet he finds a worn piece of clothing from another guest: a T-shirt.

During dinner, which consists of meatballs and cabbage that has been boiled a little too long, the conversation turns to Heinrich Ernst Göring, Hermann's father, who was the emperor's commissioner here in Namibia and had at least been able to maintain a little law and order.

The farmer and his wife don't eat, they've already had dinner, but they keep a good eye on what their guests work back, and also on what they leave on their plates.

"The native population respected him too," the wife says.

Hofmeester goes no further than to nod now and then. From where he sits he can see a cupboard with glass doors, containing a few pieces of porcelain. And beside the cupboard a large crucifix.

The conversation takes place in German. Proper German, without loan words from other languages.

"In Lüderitz," she says, "you should stop and buy yourself a sturdy pair of shoes, We always go to Keetmanshoop to do our shopping, though."

And at nine she says: "Nine o'clock, that's the farmer's midnight. Time for lights out."

Kaisa has fallen asleep at the table.

Lifting the child in his arms, Hofmeester goes to his room.

He is too tired to undress himself or the child. They lie in bed as they are. Sticky and dirty. Insignificant.

At breakfast the next morning, the farmer and his wife sit at the table again with Hofmeester and Kaisa. The two of them are apparently something of a novelty in these parts. Not a lot of tourists come by here, and those who do drive on quickly.

They talk about drought. The farmer says: "It takes us three or four years to fatten up a cow around here."

He sounds sad, but also resigned.

"Our herds have shrunk," the farmer says. He points at his wife: "And now we're shrinking too."

At that, Hofmeester gets up and pays the bill.

Once they are back in the car, he looks at the child and realizes that no matter how much he zigzags back and forth across this country, a time will come when he will have to stop. You can't move from one place to the other forever. What he said before about the child applies to him, applies to him even more, much more. He is a man without a future but not, as he had expected, without despair. That he still hasn't disappeared, and that in fact he doesn't know how to go about doing that, maddens him. He has no idea how one is supposed to say farewell to one's own life. Still, it can't be all that complicated.

On the sandy road sixty kilometers before the town of Aus, they get a flat. Hofmeester and the child climb out of the car. The sun is blazing hot.

They need help. There is a spare tire in the trunk, but Hofmeester can't change the tire by himself.

The two of them stand beside the road and try to flag down passing cars. Not a lot of cars pass by.

Hofmeester holds his briefcase over the child's head to protect her from the sun.

They don't speak a word.

But she sticks close to him, she keeps an eye on him, even when he walks off into the bushes to pee.

She still doesn't trust him, she's afraid he'll to try to disappear again. And the more Hofmeester allows this fear of hers to sink in, the more he is conscious of it, the clearer it becomes that he is going to have a hard time disappearing. That he has perhaps already missed his chance.

Whatever the roles may have been, now he is the little girl's prisoner.

At last, two South Africans in a white jeep stop and help him change the tire. It takes them twenty minutes. Hofmeester offers to pay them, but they refuse. "Around here, we help each other," they say. "We depend on each other."

Hofmeester thanks them lavishly and at length, then drives on.

At a crossing he stops and stares at his travelling companion for a few seconds.

"I'm not the solution," he says, "I'm the problem. You do understand that, don't you?"

But apparently she doesn't, for she takes his hand. She holds his hand tight, she squeezes it, she gives it a little kiss.

The asphalt resumes just outside Aus. Here he has coverage again; Hofmeester's phone begins to peep. Someone has tried to call him a couple of times. It's the wife, he sees.

In Aus he fills the tank, gets out of the car to stretch his legs and make a call. The child stays in the car, she watches him, she doesn't let him out of her sight.

Standing beneath a tree, he connects with Amsterdam.

It takes a while for the wife to answer.

"You called," he says. "What's so urgent?"

"I'm glad you called." She sounds nervous. Rattled. Her voice makes him uneasy. Just like in the old days, when he could tell from her voice that something was going on. That something was usually the same something: a man.

"She's been found."

"Who?"

"Tirza, Jörgen. Who else? You have to come home."

He is silent for a moment, he looks at the child sitting in the car.

"Yes, of course," he says at last.

"You have to come home right away, Jörgen, do you promise?"

And again he says: "Yes, of course."

"Jörgen, do you promise? We can't run out on each other now. Jörgen . . ."

He hangs up.

Slowly, he walks back to the car. The pump attendant watches him.

Hofmeester gets in behind the wheel, runs his hand over the stubble on his cheek.

"Shall we buy some candy?" he asks the child. "Do you feel like eating candy? Chocolate?"

5

The town of Lüderitz reminds Hofmeester more of Scandinavia than of Africa. The sea is cold. And the wind blows so hard through the streets that the noise is unbearable, even in the hotel room with the windows closed.

The harbor is dilapidated. Boarded-up warehouses. The airport is only a little control tower in the desert. A landing strip in the sand. Otherwise nothing.

Nest Hotel is the name of the place where he and the child are staying. He has been there for three days without leaving the room. He sits on the bed, watches TV, listens to the radio. In the evening he calls room service. Before going to sleep he hangs a note on the door saying what they want for breakfast the next morning. Always the same thing. Toast and marmalade for him, yogurt and fruit for the child. And coffee and chocolate milk.

There's not a lot more to do. There's not a lot more, that's how it feels. The present has been reduced to a hotel room, a bed, and a child. The opposite of the future, that's what a child is, he knows that much by now. For Kaisa, a day is a year. There are moments when that comes as a relief to him. The absence of expectation and hope, the absence of plans big and small.

As soon as they got to town, he had gone to a stationery store and bought colored pencils, a sharpener, and a sketch pad. He didn't buy shoes. He did buy some candy and chocolate.

A Westerner in bare feet, a briefcase under his arm, a hat on his head. People barely notice that in Lüderitz. Some Westerners just happen to go mad in Africa. They founder, they fall apart, they never go home, they take on the hue of their surroundings.

The girl draws. Hofmeester follows her movements. Every once in a while he goes to the window and looks out at the sea. The windows are dirty. A window-washer can't get to them.

There are memories, but he no longer has them under control. They are mostly details, not necessarily connected to other details. A hedge fund, baby shoes, blue, with Velcro straps, the MS 170.

At high tide the waves spray almost all the way up to their window. When the noise of the wind becomes too much for him, he turns on the radio, loud. The German-language Namibian station here, too.

He listens. Music, and conversations with listeners who complain about Namibia's failing postal service, or who sometimes are simply in need of something: a ride to Cape Town, for example.

Hofmeester has turned off his cell phone. People are waiting for him, waiting for him urgently, perhaps more urgently than ever before in his life. But what does that mean?

Twice a day, he takes a bath.

Thoughts come, about Expressionist poets, the reference work that was never finished. The love that was declared dead and done away with, but, all things considered, that doing away with was another resolution that merely petered out. Just like the reference work. Love's warm corpse, that's what he is stuck with.

And with every hour that goes by he realizes more clearly that he will not be able to stay here, that Lüderitz is also not the place where he will disappear. Even though he's sure that the sea would have as much pity on him as the sand. He doesn't doubt that. But he has missed his chance. Now he's here with a child at the Nest Hotel. A child who can no longer be called a stranger. That's how quickly it goes. That's how quickly the other stops being a stranger. In Namibia, too, he has a history already, he is a man with a past. That's why he needs to go back. Back where he came from. He has been summoned. People want to talk to him, even if only because the thought that actions can have no consequences is unbearable to them. People look down on everything that has no consequences. A game has to have consequences too. Even if that means that it stops being a game.

He postpones it. Going back is worse than disappearing. Going back is worse than death.

"You know," he says to Kaisa, on the fourth day of their stay in Lüderitz. The child is sitting on the bed, drawing, her mouth smeared with melted chocolate. "You know," Hofmeester whispers, "when Tirza was three, we took her skiing for the first time. My parents always thought that skiing vacations were nonsense. In the summer we would go to a place in the south, near the Belgian border, for three weeks, and that was it. That was enough. Why waste money? But I thought: Tirza should learn to ski. And the earlier you learn, the better you get. She even did a little racing now and then. She was a good skier, but an even better swimmer."

He is lying on his stomach on the bed. The child keeps drawing. He can't tell what it's going to be. A house perhaps, a tree. The sun. A person.

He talks calmly, as though they've known each other for years and he, one evening over dessert, suddenly comes up with a new yet oh-so-familiar anecdote.

Hofmeester falls silent, he listens to the radio. Schmaltzy music. More schmaltzy music. Always more schmaltz.

He wipes Kaisa's lips. "I never went skiing myself," he says. "I waited for her at the bottom. In the hotel. Or under a tree halfway down the slope. Sometimes I would see her come by, like a flash. In the very beginning, when she was three, I would run after her. Through the snow. She didn't go that fast back then. In case she fell, that's why I ran after her."

She looks at him, the child, differently than she did at first. She looks at him the way she might look at someone she knows.

"You know," he says, "you know, Kaisa . . . it sounds strange, but I think I'm about as old as you are. I'm . . ." He's not sure what he wants to say, or yes he is, he's sure. Of course he is. He wants to say that he, Jörgen Hofmeester, the adult Jörgen Hofmeester, editor of fiction in translation, doesn't really exist and never did. It was a role the child played, to the best of its ability and in the end with mounting precision and refinement. A game.

He takes Kaisa in his arms, he gives her little kisses all over, and while he does that, he listens to the radio.

A woman is singing. "*Lass uns leben,*" she sings, "*jeden Traum. Alles geben, jeden Augenblick.*"

Hofmeester doesn't stop kissing the child. He kisses her without thinking about it, he kisses her as though it were a matter of course. Every part of her, all over her head, her back, her stomach, he kisses as though he has some catching up to do.

He tries to recall why he has never gotten past the age of nine, but he can't come up with anything. He even has trouble remembering what he was like at that age. What did he look like? What did he wear? What did his parents say to him, and he to his parents? His memory is a desert.

All he knows for certain, more certainly than all the rest, is that he has never actually been anything but a nine-year-old. His body has grown, of course, his feet, his head, his nose, all of that has grown, but the rest remained what it was. The growth of the heart, the soul, whatever you want to call it, stopped. As sure as he is that he is beyond all prospects of a future, he is equally sure now that, although he has almost reached retirement age, he is about the same age as Kaisa.

And the woman on the radio sings: "*Bist du bereit, für unsere Zeit?*"

He hums along a bit, the melody pleases him. "Kaisa," he whispers, "I have to go back. They're waiting for me."

He doesn't say who is waiting for him. He isn't exactly sure himself.

The girl picks up her pencils and resumes her drawing. He pats her shoulders. The chocolate and the colored pencils have left spots on the sheets, he notices. That will come out in the wash.

For the first time in the last forty-eight hours, he gets dressed. He even puts on a tie. There has to be something to compensate for the lack of footwear.

Then he dresses the child. The T-shirt, the jogging pants. He has done a little washing by hand.

"Come on," he says, "we're going for a walk."

The wind is staggering, it tugs at their clothes, their hair, at Hofmeester's hat. Only occasionally does the lee of a house or a wall offer a bit of protection. They walk carefully. There could be glass on the street.

The child holds his hand tightly. And he no longer wonders whether he is sick. He knows that he is not. Sick people don't see reality. They hear sounds that aren't there, they see things that don't exist. Everything he hears, everything he sees, exists.

It feels good, walking with Kaisa like this. His presence in her life is natural and inescapable. This is how it should be.

At a sidewalk café, in a shopping center that seems disgustingly modern to him, they drink tea with lots of milk and sugar. He has no hope, but he is not sick. The opposite perhaps: healthy. A figure of health. Jörgen Hofmeester.

"I'll come back," he tells Kaisa. "I'll come back. Maybe I can even adopt you. It couldn't be that difficult. Then I'll take you with me to Europe. You'll get a good education there. I could be mistaken, I don't know you that well yet, but I think you're gifted, extremely, extremely gifted."

Extremely, extremely gifted. He utters it in the same tone others use to speak of the Prophet or God.

They walk through the town, past the church, a train station that no longer serves as a station, walls with drawings and texts like "Combat AIDS, not people with AIDS."

There's isn't a lot more to see.

When it starts getting dark, they go back to the hotel.

"I could also," Hofmeester says, "set up a foundation. A foundation for children like you. For street children in Namibia who sell something. How many of you are there, anyway? A thousand? Ten thousand? Do you know each other?"

As soon as darkness settles in, the people disappear from the streets. Lüderitz in the evening is a ghost town. Even more so than during the day, although during the day it seems like a ghost town too. Abandoned and forgotten, and always that howling wind. It drives Hofmeester to distraction.

"I'm going away for a bit, Kaisa," he says, "but I'm coming back. I have some things I need to do. And when I come back, I'm going to set up a foundation. Maybe I could come and live with you? With the street children? In a house or a tent. We could also sell something together. I can help you set up an organization. I used to be active in the literary translators' union, they weren't organized either. It's the same principle."

For the first time since arriving in Lüderitz, they don't order room service, but go to the dining room. A group has arrived, an organized tour. A busload of men and women in their forties. The mushroom soup is floury and the shrimp are dry. Hofmeester doesn't care.

At dessert, he sings quietly for Kaisa. "Ridi," he sings, "ridi." And when he is finished singing, he whispers. "It's so nice to be sitting here with you. I'm wild about you."

She toys with her spoon and asks: "Do you want company, sir?"

It's no longer a question, it's the confirmation of a state of affairs.

After dinner they don't go back to the room right away, but sit at the bar. He runs up and fetches the colored pencils and paper for Kaisa. He orders wine and cola and watches her draw.

Happiness it is not, he wouldn't call this happiness, never. But for a few seconds he does feel cheerful. An insane and incomprehensible good cheer that comes out of nowhere and will soon enough disappear back into that nowhere.

That night, before they fall asleep, he whispers: "I'll come back and adopt you, I'm still young enough to be a father again. I have a few years in me still."

Early the next morning they drive off in the direction of Keetmanshoop. He had been planning to drive in one day to Windhoek International Airport, but it's already evening by the time they get to Mariental. From there it is still a three or four hour drive to Windhoek. He decides to spend the night in Mariental.

There is a hotel. There are hotels everywhere. A bed, a bathroom, a nightstand, a few hangers for your clothes. He could keep this up for a long time. Moving from hotel room to hotel room, with the child, his hat, and his briefcase. Where the world can't find him. But he has to go back to Holland, back to Van Eeghenstraat. In order to adopt Kaisa, he has to go back, to explain himself further.

For a moment it surprises him to realize that he's never thought about adopting a child. But why would you adopt a child you don't know? He knows Kaisa. And she knows him. They go well together. They complement each other. They see something in each other. The two of them.

In Mariental he buys shoes, for himself and the child. Plain black shoes for him and brown sandals for the girl. The store isn't what you'd call a shoe shop, more like a supermarket, but that doesn't matter. Now they are no longer barefooted.

The shoes hurt. Too bad, but he knows he can't arrive at Schiphol barefooted. They would arrest him right away. Times have changed. Danger is lurking everywhere.

Kaisa is proud of her sandals. In sandals, she walks differently. She walks like a lady.

"I could," he says that evening in the little dining room of the hotel in Mariental, "I could give all of you lessons. If I came to live here. I could teach you German, for example. I could read aloud to you. I could tell you about Tolstoy, about how literature, art, doesn't make people happy. And that that's why he renounced them. But we have to come up with a plan, a plan is important. What do you children need, you children who sell company? You don't have a house and you don't have shoes. You have to establish your priorities first. A person who has no house and no shoes, the first thing they need is shoes."

The child doesn't reply. He is still eating, but she takes his hand, as though she senses that he wants to disappear again, that he wants to escape again. Now she's eating with only one hand. Because she's not letting go of him.

After dinner he calls the wife.

"I'm leaving here tomorrow," he says. "I just wanted to let you know."

"You have to come as quickly as possible," she answers. "I've been trying to call you the whole time, Jörgen. They've been here. And . . . And . . ." The sound of her voice doesn't please him, it pleases him less and less. So nervous, so rattled, so unsure of herself too. "I'll tell you everything when you get here. Everyone's been looking for you, everyone is waiting for you. Reporters have been calling too. Where are you?"

"I told you, I'm flying out tomorrow. That means I'll be home the day after tomorrow, in the afternoon. I'm in Namibia. Where else would I be? Don't be worried. Everything is going to be all right."

"We can't run out on each other now. We should never have run out on each other."

"No, of course not," he says. But he has no idea what she's talking about. No idea. "I've never run out on you, have I?"

"Jörgen, come back as quickly as you can. Please. If you come back now, we can still . . ."

"Chin up," he whispers.

With those words he puts an end to the conversation. He turns off his phone. He doesn't want to be disturbed, not for the last few hours.

He asks the desk clerk to call South African Airways and change his flight to the next day. It takes a lot of doing, because he's neglected to give proper notice, but when he tells the woman from South African Airways half the story, about the missing daughter, she says: "I'll make sure everything is arranged, Mr. Hofmeester. I can imagine that, under the circumstances, you forgot about us for a bit."

"Kaisa," he asks, "what do you want to do? Do you want to take a little stroll?"

They walk around Mariental. Empty streets. The gas stations are the only thing still open.

"I'm in doubt," Hofmeester says as he's buying a package of Gummy Bears at one of the gas stations, "I'm in doubt, more and more all the time. I mean: What did happen, and what didn't? How seriously can you take a game? I used to play with my wife too. It was nighttime, always nighttime, and I was the beast, always the beast. And when my first daughter was born, I played at being a father. At the publishing house I played at being an editor, I've always played. It was all I could do."

He squats down and cups her face in his hands. In the line for the cash register. "Because, actually, I'm the same age as you. I've always played. But not with Tirza. That was different."

That night neither of them is able to sleep. She draws, and he stares at the ceiling. He has a bad feeling that he can't put his finger on. But it's not a bad feeling, it's his own life.

His flight to Johannesburg is scheduled for ten past three in the afternoon. Before noon, he is already at the airport in Windhoek. He drops off his car at Hertz, the damage is inventoried. Hofmeester doesn't protest. He assumes the responsibility for all damages, even the damages he himself hasn't caused. Then he withdraws all the cash that the ATM will give him and puts that in his briefcase. He checks in.

"Would you like to take this as carry-on luggage?" the South African Airways man asks.

Hofmeester looks at the suitcase that he used to take on business trips sometimes.

"No," Hofmeester says, "I'll check it through."

Now the briefcase is all he carries.

He and the child wander aimlessly around the airport. They look at the passengers, eat a chicken sandwich, pluck the pieces of chicken off the bread because chicken is all they want, but finally leave half of that untouched too. They go outside and sit on a bench. In front of the departure hall. There are tourists walking around with wooden giraffes that they're taking home as a souvenir. The two of them laugh about that a little. A wooden giraffe.

Until he can deny it no longer. He has to go through customs, he has to go. This is where it ends. This is the limit.

On the little strip of grass, he squats down in front of Kaisa. "I'm going now," he says, "I have to go. But I'm coming back, I promise I'll come back."

He picks up the briefcase.

"Look," he says, "I'm leaving this here. This is for you."

He opens the briefcase.

"Four pencils," he says, "a pencil sharpener, Tirza's iPod, the charger, Tirza's music, her notebook, maybe you can write things or draw in it. Her pocket diary. A manuscript from an author in Azerbaijan. See what you do with it. And in this pouch here is the money. But I'm coming back. I promise you that I'm coming back. On this piece of paper is my number, my address in Amsterdam. If you want, you can call me. And, oh yeah, two packages of Gummy Bears. But don't eat too many sweets, it's not good for you. You should . . ."

He stands up, looks at his watch. She takes his hand.

Hofmeester squats down again.

"I'm coming back, Kaisa," he whispers, "this briefcase is the collateral. As long as you have this briefcase, you can be sure that I'll come back. My life is in this briefcase. I have to come back then. I can't do anything else. Everything I have is in here. Take good care of it. The way you took good care of me."

He puts his arms around her. "Kaisa," he whispers, "Kaisa, I forgive you, I forgive you for not letting me disappear, I forgive you for enticing me into staying here, I forgive you everything. But now I have to go."

He glances around.

No one seems to be looking at them.

"I don't know," he whispers, "how you're supposed to die, when you realize that you've never played a role in anyone's life, not even your own. How you're supposed to do that, when you realize, when you take the possibility into account, seriously take into account the possibility that no one cared about you, that no one was important enough, that . . . I'll come back to learn how to die, Kaisa, I still can't do it, but you're going to teach me. I'll teach you German and in exchange for that you'll teach me how to die, that's the deal."

He starts singing to her. "*Unerreichbar,*" he sings, "*schweres Herz.*" He's forgotten the rest. "Ridi," he sings, "ridi ridi ridi."

He walks away from her. It feels strange, without the briefcase.

She comes after him, takes his hand.

He pulls his hand away. "I have to go," he whispers without looking at her, "but I'm coming back. Go back to town now. I'm coming back, Kaisa."

She grabs his hand again. From the corner of his eye he sees how big his briefcase is for her. A kind of house. Draped over her shoulder still is the brightly-colored cloth bag that he bought for her in Windhoek, to keep money in. A person who sells company needs to take good care of their money.

He's almost at the customs desk now.

He turns around. Someone from security is holding the child back.

"I'm coming back," he calls out, "Kaisa, I'm coming back." He waves with one hand. And then with his hat. Someone behind him in line is pushing him along. "I'm coming back," he shouts again. Then he can't see her anymore.

The line is not long.

He hands his passport to the customs official.

And although he can't see the child anymore, he suddenly hears her voice. "Do you want company, sir?" she screams through the departure hall. Her voice carries farther than all the rest.

The official stamps his passport and hands it back. And again he hears Kaisa shrieking in the departure hall at Windhoek. "Do you want company, sir? Sir?"

Hofmeester has to hold on to the customs desk. He feels like he's going to vomit. He shivers. But he holds on in order to hold himself back too. Not to lose control, not give in to this urge: to run back to the departure hall. To grab Kaisa. To rent a car. To drive away. To vanish. Along with her.

Now Hofmeester knows the alternative to dying, he understands now what happens to people who don't disappear on time.

Early in the morning he arrives in Zurich; his plane lands at Schiphol that afternoon. It's eighteen degrees in Amsterdam, and partly cloudy. At the customs desk he only has to hold up his passport.

He decides to take the train as far as Amsterdam-Zuid/WTC. From there he can take the number five tram. There are almost no thoughts. What would Kaisa think of riding the number five? What would she make of a tram? He looks at the city through Kaisa's eyes.

At the corner of Willemsparkweg and Van Baerlestraat, he gets out. Everything is familiar, but still strange, because he sees it through the eyes of Kaisa.

His suitcase isn't heavy, and it isn't far. He could walk it easily, but because he sees the number two approaching, he decides to go a couple of more stops on the tram.

Why not? Why do things the hard way?

It all seems strange. Unreal. Absurd. A backdrop.

At Cornelis Schuytstraat he gets out. He is the only one.

In front of the wine shop he stops, he looks at the display window. There are people inside, but no one sees him. They are asking the salesman for advice, the man holds up a bottle for them to see. Hofmeester's nose is almost pressed against the window.

His hat is on his head. Still, he feels naked without his briefcase.

He feels the urge to look back, to see where Kaisa is. He waits for a hand to slip into his.

After a few minutes he walks on.

He turns the corner.

Now he's on Van Eeghenstraat.

There are a lot of people in the street. He notices that they are standing right in front of his house. They are milling around in front of his house. An accident, he thinks, something must have happened.

He comes a little closer. Some of the people look familiar. There are cameras there too, he sees now. Yes, he recognizes some of the people. From TV. Famous faces are standing there in front of his house. And he sees a policeman too, probably there to keep the curious at a safe distance.

You have that at moments like this. Curious people who have to be kept at a distance.

Hofmeester sets his suitcase on the ground. He wipes his face with his handkerchief. It's not a hot day, but he feels hot. Terribly hot.

Out of the crowd in front of his house, a woman emerges. She comes towards him. The wife. He recognizes her. By her movements. And she has seen him too.

Then he remembers. There was something about Tirza. But what was it exactly?

He thinks of the song he always sang for her. When he picked her up from cello lessons, after swimming, when she had won a match, but also just after practice, during their ski vacations, before reading to her aloud.

"Of all the boys I've known and I've known some. Until I first met you I was lonesome. And when you came in sight, dear, my heart grew light. And this old world seemed new to me." Yes, Hofmeester does remember a thing or two. "Ridi," he sings softly, "ridi, ridi," as the wife comes running towards him.

He hears someone say to him: "Do you want company, sir?" But it isn't Kaisa, it is Tirza's voice. He thinks he hears Tirza's voice.

Tirza, the sun queen. The extremely, extremely gifted sun queen. His life. His hope. His future.

He tries harder and harder to remember precisely what happened to it, to that life of his, that future that is now so close, so terribly close by. His sun queen. He has an inkling, except it's so vague. So horribly vague.

Jörgen Hofmeester stands before his own memory as before the gates to the paradise he will never enter.

Another thirty yards or so and the wife will be with him.

Now it comes to him. At last.

She's been found.

Found is she. Tirza. That name alone. That word. Tirza.

He needs to call her, to tell her that she has been found. He pulls the cell phone out of his inside pocket.

He dials her number.

The wife is only ten yards away now. She stops. She looks at him, pleadingly it seems. Bedraggled, that's how she looks. Unkempt. As though she's been mangled by a beast.

She presses her index finger to her lips. She stands there like that. And she looks at him pleadingly, her finger held to her lips.

The people in front of his house are coming towards him too. They're running. Not only do they have cameras, he sees now, but also microphones on boom poles. He will address them, if that's what they want. If it's Hofmeester they want to talk to. If they wish, he will tell them about the foundation he is planning to set up. For children who sell company.

Then finally he hears her voice, the voice of the sun queen, which is beyond compare.

"Hi, this is Tirza," he hears. He presses the phone tightly against his ear. He doesn't want to miss a word, not a letter, not a breath. "I can't answer the phone right now. But be sure to leave a nice message."

Arnon Grunberg was born in Amsterdam in 1971. Starting his own publishing company at nineteen, he wrote his first novel, *Blue Mondays*—a European bestseller—at age twenty-three. Two of his novels, *Phantom Pain* and *The Asylum Seeker*, won the AKO Literature Prize, the Dutch equivalent of the Booker Prize. Living in New York, he writes columns, book reviews, and essays for newspapers and magazines.

Sam Garrett has worked as a literary translator as well as a freelance journalist. His recent translated works include *The Cave* by Tim Krabbé and *Silent Extras* by Arnon Grunberg. In 2009, he won the Vondel Translation Prize for his translation of Frank Westerman's *Ararat*.

Open Letter—the University of Rochester's nonprofit, literary translation press—is one of only a handful of publishing houses dedicated to increasing access to world literature for English readers. Publishing ten titles in translation each year, Open Letter searches for works that are extraordinary and influential, works that we hope will become the classics of tomorrow.

Making world literature available in English is crucial to opening our cultural borders, and its availability plays a vital role in maintaining a healthy and vibrant book culture. Open Letter strives to cultivate an audience for these works by helping readers discover imaginative, stunning works of fiction and poetry, and by creating a constellation of international writing that is engaging, stimulating, and enduring.

Current and forthcoming titles from Open Letter include works from Argentina, Germany, Iceland, Italy, Poland, Russia, South Africa, and many other countries.

www.openletterbooks.org

SUMMIT FREE PUBLIC LIBRARY